PRAISE FOR THE AUTHOR

'Ryan is a freaking good storyteller. What a brain!'
— Ron Davis, author of *Disadvantage Line*

'A ripping good yarn, well told.'
— Capt. Martin Knight-Willis MC Rtd.
Formerly New Zealand SAS and Rhodesian SAS

'Ryan is that rare breed of thriller writer,
a craftsman and an artist.'
— Lee Jackson, author of *Redemption*

The Mark of Halam

ALSO BY THOMAS RYAN

Short Stories
The Field of Blackbirds (Jeff Bradley Book 1)
Short Stories Volume 2

THOMAS RYAN

The Mark of Halam

THOMAS & MERCER

This is a work of fiction. Names, characters, organisations, places, events, and incidents are either products of the author's imagination or are used fictitiously.

Published by Thomas & Mercer, Seattle

www.apub.com

ISBN-13: 9781503946422
ISBN-10: 1503946428

Cover design by bürosüd° München, www.buerosued.de

Printed in the United States of America

To Meg

a true heroine

1.

A roar erupted from the protestors gathered in front of Auckland's Bledisloe Wharf. He was more than a block away but the chants were easily heard. An American nuclear submarine was about to visit and the citizens of New Zealand's largest city were not happy. He shook his head. So what? He didn't get the fuss. They rallied daily, but from his observations for most it was a game and each night turned into a party; barbecues, jugglers, buskers, alcohol and dancing. Where was the passion? Why hadn't they ripped the dockyard gates down?

In the countries where he had lived, fighter planes fired missiles at buildings while residents slept. And car bombs blew up markets and killed whole families. That was something worth protesting.

He checked his watch. It was well after midday. If she had been coming home for lunch she would have been here by now.

The man opened the entry door to her apartment building and stepped into the foyer. The spring-loaded and sound-proofed doors shut with a barely audible click, muffling the din. He wiped his shoes on the welcome mat. Any grit would make a sound on the tiled floor.

As the elevator began its ascent he kept one eye on the floor numbers and visualised his next moves. When the elevator doors opened he would cross the floor, key in the lock, open the door, slip inside, close the door remembering to hold onto the door handle to make sure it doesn't slam shut. Then pause, catch his breath and listen for movement.

During the day the blonde worked in a law office. A lawyer, maybe? A secretary? What did it matter? The previous evening when she walked home he had followed her. She stopped for drinks with friends. Everyone smiled at the sight of her and laughed at her comments; talked over each other to speak with her. People liked her; he liked her, he liked the way she moved. Her blonde hair, tied back, flicked like a horse's tail as she walked. Her gait was athletic, head held high, not arrogance, confidence. He eavesdropped the conversation between her and her friends and learned her roommate would be gone for two nights.

The elevator doors opened. He moved quickly.

Entering her apartment in the day was risky, but checking the environment was a necessity. He didn't need a dog the size of a horse ripping off his arm, or worse, a dog barking and waking her, or a chain on the door. The apartments that shared her floor had security peep-holes in their doors. At night the sound of elevator doors or unfamiliar noises might alert a neighbour. His movements needed to be smooth and assured so as to not draw attention. He would wear soft-soled shoes to muffle his steps across the tiled hallway floor.

It was easy enough to distinguish her room. Framed photos of her with friends and family hung on every wall.

Today, the trial run. Tomorrow he would return for the real thing.

2.

As he turned the corner Jeff Bradley decided he had enough energy left to sprint the last few hundred metres of his morning run. Rising to the challenge, his companion, Mary Sumner, dashed past him, her blonde ponytail bobbing and flicking like a horse's tail. She turned, smiled, waved and then sped away. The perspiration coating her long legs glistened in the sunlight and the sight of her buttocks trapped within tight black thigh-length leggings offered Jeff some compensation for being bested. He had never beaten the Olympic triathlete medallist on any of their runs and she had never shown him mercy.

"Champions don't become winners by training to lose," had been her response when Jeff pleaded with her to let him win.

Mary was stretching when Jeff ran on to the Cheltenham beach sand. Hands on hips, he threw his head back and sucked air. The rising sun failed to bring any warmth to the morning chill. The bay was empty; the onset of autumn had sent sunbathers to cafés and shopping malls. That was fine by Jeff; he liked the sense of remoteness brought on by an uninhabited beach in the heart of the city.

"Ready for a swim?" Jeff asked.

Mary, her leg extended and resting on a block wall, nodded and bent forward, her nose touching her kneecap. "One more."

She changed legs and repeated the exercise then followed Jeff to the water's edge. "It looks cold, Jeff."

He stripped off his T-shirt and ran into the tide. An involuntary cry escaped from his lips as the cool water sprayed over him. "It's not so bad . . . bloody hell it is cold."

"Don't be a coward," she said, as she splashed him.

"I think this will have to be our last sea swim until next summer," Jeff said. "I hate cold water."

The tepid waters of the swimming pool in the city would be the new venue for their twice weekly water sports. They raced each other out to the yacht moored two hundred metres from the shoreline and put in a burst on the return leg. Again Mary finished well ahead. She was drying herself off with Jeff's T-shirt when he made it onto the beach. She tossed the wet garment at him and ran off. When he caught up with her she was waiting in the driveway of his Church Street house. He waved to his neighbour, Larry Connors, who was buckling his two children into their safety seats. They had never talked but Jeff knew that Larry was an accomplished yachtsman with a growing international reputation if media reports were to be believed. He received a smile and a return wave. The young girls, following their father's lead, waved as well. Jeff considered himself a bad neighbour but he wasn't the bake a cake and welcome to the neighbourhood type of guy and he guessed his neighbour wasn't either. No cake had ever been left on his doorstep.

"Are we weight training this morning?" Mary asked.

"Sorry, I have an appointment with your boss and then I need to get out to the vineyard. I'll go to the gym tomorrow. You use the shower first. I'll brew some coffee and after breakfast I'll take you to work."

"We could share the shower," Mary teased.

"Be careful, or one of these days I'm going to take you up on that offer."

"Sure you will. You're all talk, Bradley."

After a hot shower Jeff threw on jeans, a blue polo shirt and his brown Timberland boots. It took a good half hour to drive from Devonport, down the length of the Peninsula and on to the harbour bridge crossing, and another twenty minutes before he drove into the parking area next to his lawyer's office. Jeff had engaged Quentin Douglas's services when he assumed ownership of the West Auckland vineyard from his grandparents, and over the years they had become close friends.

"I have news," Quentin said when he saw Jeff enter.

He pushed a document across the table. Jeff picked it up.

"One of the properties your grandmother left you. The ten hectares near Huapai? I have a buyer."

Jeff looked up. "I thought you advised me to hang on to it?" he said.

"As your lawyer I must advise you when circumstances change. This is one of those circumstances. You've been made an offer that I'm not certain you can walk away from, two and a half million dollars."

Jeff blinked.

"Yes I know. I was shocked as well. Someone has more money than sense."

"That's way above market value."

"Sure is. And it's in cash. When the agent phoned me I told him you weren't interested in selling. Then he came back. Said the buyer wanted the property and price was no object. Apparently he's a successful merchant banker. More money than he knows what to do with and he wants a country estate near the city. With a pond, just like the one on your property." Quentin shrugged. "I told the agent a silly price and the banker accepted. So, what do you say?"

Jeff scratched his dark brown hair. Too long. He needed a haircut.

"It would mean you'd have enough cash for the divorce settlement and to pay out Rebecca."

"Will she accept a deal and not take the vineyard to auction?"

"With cash in your pocket I can talk to her lawyer. Offer a little extra to clinch it. You need to agree to deal on this Huapai property first though. Even if the vineyard did go to auction you'd have more than enough to make your own bid. Then you can send your ex-wife on her way and get on with your life."

"Funny things happen at auctions, Quentin."

"The money, Jeff, do you want it or not?"

"I guess I have no choice."

"Not quite true, you do have a choice. I'm your lawyer so I know your circumstances. You have more than enough money in assets and cash to never work again. The vineyard is only a hobby for you. It keeps you from spending your days on a stool in a bar somewhere. You don't even like wine, you're a beer drinker."

"My vineyard, Boundary Fence," Jeff said, "is very important to me as well you know. I promised my grandmother I would keep it in the family. And remember, it was overgrown with weeds when my grandmother gifted it to me. I've put in the hard graft to get it where it is today. I'm not letting it go, ever."

"All right, all right, I get it," Quentin laughed. "Keep the bloody thing. Now, do you want to sell the Huapai property or not?"

"I guess so."

"Great, because I'd already accepted on your behalf and the cheque is in my trust account."

Jeff grinned then shook his head. Mary entered, carrying two coffees.

"Jeff, Barbara Heywood from Channel Nine has been on the phone again. They want an interview." She raised her eyebrows and gave a hint of a smile. "Seems like everyone wants a piece of you."

Jeff shook his head. "Just tell them no, Mary. I don't know why they keep bothering me."

"Oh, I think bringing down that terrorist group in Kosovo might have had something to do with it. If you want to keep off the front pages of newspapers don't be such a hero."

"Just tell them no, can you do that Mary?"

Mary smiled. "Do you want me to always say no, or might there be a time you might want me to say yes?"

Jeff poked his tongue out at her.

Mary left the room and Quentin eyed Jeff suspiciously. "Have you two been training together again?" he asked.

"We often train together."

Quentin frowned. "Just training, Jeff, nothing else I hope. Go find someone else to play with but stay away from my staff. And anyway, why is everyone phoning here looking for you?"

"Kimie at the vineyard tells everyone to phone my lawyer. I think it's an East European thing."

"Now. I have other news," Quentin said. "I have a dream," he said with a lousy Martin Luther King accent.

Jeff let out an involuntary groan.

"I want to open a nightclub," Quentin said with a broad smile. "With a live band, bar, light snacks, the whole thing. What do you think?"

Quentin had the twinkle in his eye that Jeff had seen whenever he talked of his band days.

"I think you're trying to relive your childhood, which I remind you was some years ago."

"Of course I am. That's the whole point. Who doesn't want to be young again?"

Jeff knew of Quentin's band days, how could he not, whenever they frequented a bar a few beers was enough to send Quentin down memory lane. Jeff had heard all the stories more than once of

Quentin's golden days of rock. If that wasn't enough he had filled his office with rock paraphernalia. A jukebox sat in the corner and his old guitar hung on the wall above it. From time to time he would let his dark brown hair grow longer than it should until a judge's frown sent him scurrying to the hairdresser.

"Does Jeannie know about this?" Jeff asked.

Quentin's sideways glance told him she didn't.

"I'm going to tell her when the time is right. I wanted to run it past you first."

"Quentin, if you want a nightclub I'm behind you all the way, you know that. You don't need my permission. I'm your friend not your mother."

"Here's a thought. I've made you so much money you could buy in with me. Partners. Fifty-fifty."

Jeff shook his head. "I don't want a nightclub and besides, I don't have time."

"You've plenty of time, but don't worry, you can be the silent partner. I'll run it. You don't need to do anything but come when you want a night out. You'll get to meet a lot of women."

"I don't need a nightclub to meet women."

"Then do it to help me out. I'll owe you. Besides, we can stock it with Boundary Fence wine. If you won't do it for me, do it for your business," Quentin pleaded.

"All right, all right I'm in. But if it becomes a hassle I'm selling up."

"Fair enough."

"You'll still have to get it past Jeannie and I can't believe she'll agree," Jeff said.

"Well, that's sort of why I want you to be my partner."

"You're going to blame this on me. Great. Jeannie will never speak to me again. When do you intend starting this venture?"

Quentin grinned, school boyish. "I started three months ago."

3.

He had waited across the street until he had seen her apartment lights switch off. An hour later he was in the building, and in the elevator. The well-maintained machine ran silent and smooth. From his pocket he produced surgical gloves and pulled them on, pushing down on each digit making them tight across his fingers. A squeal, as rubber rubbed against rubber.

The red light flashed six. The elevator stopped, and the doors rattled open.

He leaned forward to check the corridor. It was clear. A sleeve across his brow absorbed beads of sweat into the cloth of his jacket sleeve. He glanced at his hands. No trembling; as always the thrill of the hunt brought calm. Most men closing in on their prey weakened at the knees, lacked the fortitude to make the kill. Not him.

The unlocking devices in his hand, he filled his lungs with air. There would be no breathing until he had completed the manoeuvre. Her door opened, silent, not a click, not a squeak, oiled on his earlier visit. He slipped inside and pulled it shut, remembering to hold on to the handle. He leant against the wall and exhaled. Lungs the size of balloons deflated. A hand across his mouth stifled the sounds of respiratory wheezing until steady breathing returned.

Street lights illuminated the room well enough for him to move without tripping. He pictured the surroundings: an open plan kitchen, two settees, a coffee table and a cabinet the length of the far wall. Pot plants in any empty space or on any empty shelf. He thought the flowers were a nice touch. If ever he had a home he'd fill it with flowers too. Ahead was the small hallway that led to the two bedrooms; her room-mate's on the left and hers at the end of the hallway, a bathroom door to the right.

But first, the note.

He tiptoed to the kitchen. A spicy, cheesy aroma hung in the air. He lifted the lid of the pizza container on the bench. It was empty. Hunger pangs caused his stomach to rumble. Finding a restaurant would be first on his list once he had finished tonight's task. He pulled the folded paper from his pocket and opened it out. The words, written in large black letters but impossible to read in the darkness, brought a smile. He held the paper against the cupboard door over the sink and pressed against the adhesive attached to the four corners. The police would find it easy enough.

He stiffened as something brushed his leg. It was the cat. He bent and stroked it. A tongue as coarse as sandpaper licked at his fingers. Pets did not exist in the camps and roofing-iron shelters of his youth. There was seldom enough money to buy food for the family let alone an animal. He made a mental note to have a cat in the house he built. A cat reflected substance.

He made his way up the hall. The cat followed. There was little chance his movements would wake her; each step was now cushioned by carpet. The bedroom door was wide open. Enough residual light shone through from the lounge for him to make out the contour of her body under the blankets, her back to him. This was too easy. He watched for a moment. Sympathetic. She slept the sleep of the innocent. A child of God. She would not suffer. He might be a killer but he was not a monster.

He sidled across to the bed and selected a pillow from the pile in the space beside her. How many lovers had shared her bed? For a woman who turned heads when she entered a bar, he suspected many.

He held the pillow to his chest, knuckles white beneath the gloves as his grip tightened. His eyes fixed on her unmoving torso then moved up the silhouette to the back of her head. Knees touched the bed. His tongue flicked to moisten his mouth. His Adam's apple bobbed as he swallowed. In a single movement he was astride her, her arms trapped beneath the blankets. His weight on the mattress caused the bed to lurch sideways and bump the bedside table. The lamp wobbled then toppled over the edge and fell to the floor, the light bulb shattered. Beneath him the woman, now awake, struggled against his hold and turned onto her back. He sensed the blonde's face looking up, her eyes wide open. Confused.

He pushed on the pillow and smothered the bewilderment.

"Rest easy, my child. It will not take long," he whispered.

The second bedroom door opened. Light from within splashed along the hallway.

"Ann? Are you okay? What broke?" a sleepy voice called out.

In the glow of the light he could see the blonde woman. Startled, he looked at the pillow. Who the hell was this?

"What's going on? What the fuck . . ." the blonde woman screamed. "What are you doing? Get off her . . . you bastard!"

A glass object flew toward him. He ducked. The projectile missed by centimetres but smashed through the bedroom window. Who was the woman beneath him? The flatmate? She bucked and threw him off balance. He slid from the bed.

"You bastard."

The blonde woman rushed into the room. She reached behind the bedroom door. A baseball bat appeared in her hand. He grasped the bed linen and pulled himself to his knees. The blonde threw herself across the bed swinging the bat. It struck him on the shoulder and he yelped like a kicked puppy. She swung again. Wild.

Directionless. The bat hit the wall and bounced out of her hand. Then she was on him, punching, scratching at him.

A strong bitch.

He remembered her athletic build, an amazon woman. Gasps for breath came from his victim. In no time she would gain enough strength to help her friend. He would have to fight two. A neighbour must have heard the breaking window. The police might not be far away. He needed to get away. With an effort he pushed the blonde off him and swung his fist. It collided with her face.

She cursed, cried out in pain. Her grip now loosened, he crawled backward and away from her assault then scrambled to his feet and ran from the bedroom. At the apartment door he paused to compose himself. Coughing, moaning and crying came from the bedroom, but no footsteps, no one was coming after him.

In the corridor he decided against the elevator and ran into the stairwell. Halfway down he remembered the note on the kitchen door. The woman was not dead. Would the note still have an impact? Too bad, it was too late to retrieve it now.

4.

Jeff Bradley's eyelids flickered open. He reached for the phone.

"Hello," he mumbled, still half asleep.

"Jeff, it's Quentin."

The digital clock on the bedside table read one-thirty in the morning. "Bloody hell, Quentin, do you know what time it is?"

"Late o'clock. I'm sorry. But I had no choice. I have a problem and I need you."

"Okay, but it better be life threatening."

"It is. Someone tried to murder Mary and her flatmate tonight."

Jeff, suddenly awake, flung his legs over the side of the bed.

"Are they all right?"

Quentin said, "Mary got whacked in the head. She has a black eye so I'm told. The attacker tried to suffocate Ann. Stuck a pillow over the poor girl's head. As you can imagine they're both traumatised to hell."

"Give me a second."

Jeff stood, walked to the light switch and flicked it on. He used the few moments to clear his head. Someone had attacked Mary; a reflexive clench of his fist.

The darkness gone, he sat back on the bed. His right hand ruffled the hair at the back of his head. A habit he indulged in when waking himself up.

"Okay, Quentin, carry on."

"The thing is, Jeff, they can't stay where they are. Ann's from Wellington and Mary's parents are away. Nowhere for them to go at short notice, not where they'd feel safe and secure. The police called me and what could I say. Jeannie is happy to have them here but she's worried the attacker might follow. I can't convince her differently. It's the kids. If they got hurt . . ."

"Are the police leaving someone?" Jeff asked, now fully alert.

"No, mate. They insist there's no need to worry. Not tonight at any rate. They've said a patrol car will pass by every so often and I've been given a number to call in an emergency. That's it." Quentin paused. "Look, I hate to ask it. Jeannie said she'd rest easier if you were on the scene. I don't get a pass mark when it comes to hero types. My wife has it in her head a special forces soldier will protect her family better than me."

"Ex-special forces," Jeff smiled. "When will they arrive?"

"Within the hour."

"I'll be there in forty minutes."

5.

Mary Sumner and Ann Lindsay sat, huddled together on the bright red two-seater settee, blankets draped over their shoulders. The policeman introduced himself as Wayne Johnson, "but call me Red, everyone does," took a chair from the kitchen and placed it in front of the coffee table. He faced the back of the chair toward them then climbed aboard as he would a horse.

Mary watched him, but Red said nothing. Loud voices in the corridor distracted her. She turned to see a man and a woman, both in civilian clothes, enter. The man led the way, the woman, smaller in stature, was barely visible behind the male officer's bulk. Red rose from his seat, faster than casual. The man whispered in the woman's ear and she shook her head, then moved ahead of him. Mary studied the woman. She had a dark complexion, either Maori or Pacific Islander. Too hard to tell. She would go with Maori. Red stepped back from the chair.

The woman offered Mary a sympathetic smile and said, "I'm Detective Senior Sergeant Moana Te Kanawa," a tilt of the head toward her companion, "and this is Detective Ross."

Te Kanawa was a Maori name; Mary congratulated herself, right first time. She often played games in her head when nervous or running long distances, it helped pass the time.

"Red. Get some female officers up here. And find out where the doctor is."

Moana turned the chair round the right way and sat. Detective Ross stood behind her.

Mary flicked away a wisp of blonde hair with the back of her hand then gave her full attention to the sergeant. Ann let her head fall onto Mary's shoulder.

Ross tapped his sergeant's arm. "I'll have a quick shifty through the cupboards for a whisky."

"Brandy on the top shelf over the sink," Mary said, her voice a touch above a whisper.

Ross gestured a thanks with his hand.

"Mary, we've spoken to your boss,' Moana said. "He and his wife are waiting for you and Ann. They've a spare room."

Mary nodded.

Ross returned with two glasses, a quarter filled. Mary took the offered drink and gulped half the contents but Ann showed no interest and her glass was placed on the coffee table.

"That must hurt," Moana said, then reached out and gently ran the tips of her fingers over the blue-black swelling developing around Mary's left eye.

"It's not so bad."

Moana took out her notebook and set it on her lap, pen poised. "Are you up to giving details of the assault?"

Mary nodded.

"In your own time, Mary."

"A noise woke me. Breaking glass. The lamp had fallen off the bedside table . . . when he attacked Ann. Anyway, I thought I'd better check. When I went into the corridor the light from my bedroom lit up Ann's room. And I saw a man. On the bed. He had a pillow over Ann's head."

Mary paused. Her eyes watered. But her voice held steady. She had promised herself she wouldn't cry. Her right hand shook. She held it with her left.

Moana prompted, "Lucky for Ann you're a light sleeper."

"That's just it. Normally when I sleep I go into a coma. But not tonight. Tonight I was in Ann's room. She was in mine. Her bed is uncomfortable."

Mary noted the mention of swapped rooms brought an exchange of eye contact between the two officers.

"Why had you changed rooms?" Moana asked.

"Ann has a DVD player in her room. I wanted to watch a movie and Ann wanted to sleep so she went to my room."

"Then what happened?"

"As I said I saw a man on top of Ann. But I was still half asleep. At first my brain didn't register what my eyes were looking at. It was all a bit weird but I couldn't work out why. Then I saw the pillow over Ann's head. I knew that wasn't right. That's when I screamed. My first thought was to find a weapon of some sort. Ann had a snow globe on her dresser. You know the type. It has a Christmas scene in water and when you shake it up it snows."

Moana nodded. "I know what you mean. An auntie gave me one when I was about ten. I still have it."

"Ann's was about the size of a baseball. Easy to throw. Anyway, her dresser is close to the door so I reached out and grabbed it and tossed. If I'd been more accurate it would've split the asshole's head open. But I missed.

"Then I remembered the baseball bat I keep behind my bedroom door." She shrugged. "I ran into the room and grabbed it. He had fallen on the floor by this time and all I could think was, now the prick is on the ground I can beat the shit out of him. Sorry."

Moana waved a hand. "Don't worry, Mary. The guy was definitely a prick."

Mary smiled.

“Anyway,” Mary continued, “I think I got in a few good shots and then he hit me and that’s about all I remember. I must have lost consciousness. When I came round he’d gone.”

“I’m afraid you’ll have a black eye for a few days as a memento. Did you get to see his face? Could you identify him again?”

Mary nodded. “When he looked up, the light caught him full on. I’ll never forget it. And I have a photographic memory.”

“Really?” Moana stood up.

Mary’s eyes followed the sergeant as she strode to the door.

“Red, get a police artist up here right away, I don’t care if you have to drag someone out of bed, but get someone here. And where the hell is that doctor?”

6.

"They're here."

Jeannie stepped back from the curtain and made her way to the front door. Jeff caught up with Quentin's wife as she pulled the door open. He rushed past her, leapt from the top step and ran across the lawn to the police car. A female officer helped Mary from the car, a blanket still draped around her shoulders.

When Mary saw Jeff she managed half a smile and as he took her in his arms she fell against him, her head resting on his chest. A change in her breathing pattern told Jeff she was weeping, softly, almost inaudible. He bent and scooped her off the ground, and held her as if he were cradling a small child. "You're safe now," he whispered and gave a reassuring squeeze as he carried her into the house. Behind him, Jeannie and Quentin were fussing over Ann.

Once Jeff had assured Mary he wasn't going anywhere and he would be right outside the door, he made his way into the kitchen and left it for Jeannie and Quentin make the two women comfortable.

After twenty minutes Quentin joined him. "The sleeping pills from the police doctor seem to have worked. Mary and Ann have crashed. Jeannie has gone to bed."

Quentin put two cups on the bench. The coffee pot bubbled away on its element. Lettering across the front of the coffee packet read 'A Taste of Arabia'. Jeff's nostrils agreed it must have come from that region; it smelt like camels. Jeannie Douglas told anyone who would listen she travelled the world with her coffee. Every few weeks a new blend. But this time he doubted the origin printed on the pack. The last time he had drifted through Saudi he saw no coffee plantations, only desert.

Quentin dumped the two mugs none too carefully on the unprotected mahogany table top. Brown liquid slopped over the rim. He ripped off a paper towel from the roll on the holder above the sink and sponged up the dregs.

"The police sergeant who phoned said they believe Mary was the target. She had been stalked and the attack planned. Ann was supposed to be away for the night only she cancelled at the last minute. They swapped rooms for some reason and so poor Ann copped it."

"Why do they believe Mary was stalked?"

Quentin shook his head.

"No idea. The sergeant didn't say."

"Okay," Jeff said, thoughtful. He lifted his mug to allow Quentin to clean under it. "Jeannie is right to be concerned if that's the case. Mary could still be in danger."

"The police think not immediately. Not for a few nights anyway. Too risky they say. But who knows. The guy is clearly a psycho. He might feel his unfinished business can't wait."

Jeff nodded. "I won't disagree. But working on logic, he would need to find out where she is. That will take time. I think the police are probably right. Tonight is too soon. However, if he has been stalking Mary then he's followed her to the office. He might also have followed you home."

"Jesus, I hadn't thought of that."

"You need to consider it. Even if he hasn't done so already he might now give it thought. You could be placing Jeannie and the kids in danger."

"Tomorrow I'll hire twenty-four-hour security, but tonight, my friend, you're it. I'm going to meet with the police in the morning. I know the detective sergeant in charge. We've run across each other in the courts. I'll ask her how much security I need."

Jeff nodded. "Want me to come with you?"

"Would you? That would be great. Thanks."

Jeff sipped his coffee. Quentin checked his watch.

"Time for bed. Jeannie threw blankets and a pillow on the couch. Thanks for coming."

"No worries."

When Quentin had gone Jeff sat on the couch to remove his running shoes. It crossed his mind that if the killer *had* followed Quentin he might be outside right now. He switched off the lights then slowly pulled back the drape and peered into the darkness. No movements in the shadows that he could see.

Tonight he would sleep on the floor. He needed to stay alert.

7.

Sergeant Moana Te Kanawa leaned against the third-floor window frame and looked down on the city scene. She watched a patrol car cruise along Mayoral Drive until it stopped at the lights where Mayoral crossed Queen Street. When the lights changed to green the patrol car turned left and disappeared from sight. Her attention was drawn to the Sky City Tower; claimed by its owners to be one of the world's tallest constructions but to Moana it looked like a giant syringe reaching into the sky to jab God. A view of the sea was blocked by a concrete forest of commercial and apartment buildings.

Auckland, a two-port city, servicing both the Pacific Ocean and the Tasman Sea, had continued to expand upwards and outwards like an insatiable, gluttonous land hog. And now most of its one and a half million citizens lived across fifty kilometres of highway and on the slopes of more than forty extinct volcanoes stretching from Papakura in the south to the northern beaches town of Orewa.

Somewhere in that impossibly large search area hid the man who had attacked Mary Sumner and Ann Lindsay.

Moana half-turned and cast an eye over her team. It had been a late night. The orders had been to grab some sleep and be in the station before midday. Detectives sitting round the trestle table rested heads on hands, some yawned, others flicked pen tops and stared at the array of notes and photos strewn across the tabletop.

Moana strode to the front of the room and held up the identikit photo. "Lucky for us we have this likeness of the attacker. Can anyone tell me what that means?

"It means we are knocking on doors."

"Right first time, Red. It's all we have. There is no other evidence. Until there is wear soft shoes and get walking."

A few exaggerated groans drew a glare from Moana.

Her team of four men and one woman would be working round the clock until they found the would-be killer. Plans had been made and now the lot of the copper had kicked in. Their lives would be put on hold. No dinners, no kissing the kids good night, no beers with friends, dates and budding romances cancelled.

Sure, there had been no murder, but they would treat it as a murder all the same. That the two women had survived through the efforts of the gutsy Mary Sumner did not lessen the truth that they might both have died. And they needed to assume the assailant might try again. No one fantasised that knowing what the offender looked like would make discovery easier. Identikit sketches were not photographs. The killer would have altered his appearance; shaved off his beard, maybe dyed his hair.

"How about manpower?" Red asked. "There are a lot of doors in the area."

"Sorry, guys, for the moment you're it," Moana said.

Her boss had none-too-politely informed Moana that extra personnel would not be forthcoming. Manning shortages had affected the whole country and other districts were in the same boat, her D. I. had ranted, parroting the words of the area commander. None of them had complained, he had said, stabbing the air with his forefinger as he said it.

Moana didn't believe for one minute that no one else had complained. Of course she had kept these thoughts to herself. She had two boys in university. Education wasn't cheap and her salary barely covered her living expenses as it was. The increase in salary from her promotion to senior sergeant was going to be a big help and she was not about to toss it away.

She pinned the identikit on the crime board next to the Auckland Central City street map.

"I've marked the territories and put you in pairs. Get round as quickly as possible and don't cut corners. Remember our offender is a dangerous man. We need to find him. Any questions?"

There were none. As her team filed from the room Moana eased back into her seat. Forensics had recovered hair and skin samples from the assault on Mary Sumner. She didn't expect a match to be found but they might get lucky. Not surprisingly there were no finger prints. No doubt the offender had worn gloves.

Moana picked up the file of reports close to hand and began scanning through it. Forensics had swept the apartment but turned up very little. If Mary Sumner's flatmate had been away Mary would be dead. Of that she had little doubt, and the piece of paper inside a plastic folder supported her thinking. The note from the killer had left her flabbergasted. The message included a name she knew from the newspapers but someone she had never met. Well, that was about to change.

Mary had not been shown the note. The first police officers on the scene had seen it for what it was, a message from the man who assaulted her and they had removed it before it was seen. Moana was still deciding when Mary should be informed. A few days either way would make little difference.

She had ordered patrol cars and beat police to stop and question any suspicious-looking characters walking alone at night. Moana laughed out loud as she thought of the instruction. Auckland was a twenty-four-hour city. The streets filled with suspicious-looking characters every night.

The words the intruder had left on the note worried her. The attack on Mary Sumner was only the beginning. Did he have a list or was he right now compiling one? Another attempted murder or, God forbid, a successful one and the words 'Serial Killer in Town' might bump the *USS Ulysses* visit off the front page. The killer was out there waiting to pounce. But where the hell was he?

A knock on the door interrupted her reverie.

Recognising the man who entered the room, Moana rose from her chair. At over six feet tall, he walked shoulders back with his head slightly raised in a challenging manner. His charcoal suit was neatly pressed, his shirt gleamed white and his burgundy-red tie was neatly knotted. Light brown hair had been neatly trimmed and his face looked freshly shaved, shoes highly polished. That he carried himself with military aplomb came as no surprise to Moana; Inspector Brian Cunningham had been a Special Forces officer for years before joining the police force.

"Inspector Cunningham, good to see you, sir."

"I hear congratulations are in order, Moana. Well done. You deserve the promotion."

They shook hands. Moana offered an uneasy smile.

"I take it your visit is business, not pleasure?"

"I read the early morning report on the two women who were attacked last night. I have an interest."

Moana arched her eyebrows. "You're kidding me. This is way out of your jurisdiction."

"The attack, yes. The note, no."

Moana cast an eye down at the document left by the attacker. What was in the note that would be of concern to Cunningham?

8.

A client request and a court session delayed Quentin's visit to the Central Police station. He and Jeff walked through the main entrance in the late afternoon and a constable escorted them through to Moana Te Kanawa's office; a box without a window. Moana had managed to squeeze in a desk, a filing cabinet and three chairs, a small leather settee against the wall, and a tiny dark lacquered wood coffee table in front of it. A small stand held a pot plant. Two prints of beach scenes hung on the walls. The result was cramped but Moana's furnishing skills had distinguished it from a drab linen closet.

An unopened copy of the morning *Herald* had been dumped on the coffee table. The headline read: 'Women Attacked in Apartment'.

"Hey, Quentin." Moana rose from her chair to greet her guests.

"Moana. Meet Jeff Bradley," said Quentin.

They shook hands.

Quentin noticed Jeff stiffen at the sight of the man in the charcoal suit who was leaning silently against the wall. He had never seen the heavy-set cop before but obviously Jeff had.

Moana said, "Inspector Brian Cunningham is sitting in on the meeting. He's here as an observer. The Inspector is with the Special Tactics Group."

"Hello, Jeff."

"Brian. It's been a while."

"You two know each other?" Moana asked.

"We've met," Jeff said, not taking his eyes off the police inspector. "Brian and I served in the special forces together. He was my CO."

Quentin noted Cunningham had not held out his hand to Jeff and Jeff had not offered his.

Moana pointed to two chairs. "Take a seat, gentlemen. How are Ann and Mary, Quentin?"

"Much better. Jeannie's been fussing over them. I've hired a security firm to watch over the house."

"I'd like to say it isn't necessary but I'd be misleading you. Sorry I don't have the men to provide police protection. Can I offer either of you tea or coffee?"

Quentin shook his head. Jeff said nothing, just kept his eyes on Cunningham. The policeman had not sat down. The hostility in Jeff's demeanour made Quentin shift in his seat. He crossed his legs and took a pen from his pocket. Began clicking the end. If Moana had noticed she hadn't as yet reacted.

"Right," Moana said, addressing Quentin. "How can I help?"

"My main concern is for Mary. We want your thoughts on whether or not he'll try again. She's intent on moving back into her apartment and if she stays any longer at my house, well . . . I have a family to consider. I hate that I might be putting them in danger," Quentin said. "However you've pretty much answered my question. I guess for the moment keep Mary at my house and beef up security."

Moana was about to respond but Cunningham interrupted.

"Unfortunately, Quentin, I can say for certain that he will try again. He'll know the two women will be protected for the immediate future. If he can't get at Mary he will choose another target."

Jeff raised an eyebrow. "Really? How can you know that?"

"Call it copper instinct," Cunningham said.

"Come on, Brian, you can do better than that."

"What Inspector Cunningham means is that we have reason to believe this man is determined to murder Mary. Let's say he is obsessed," Moana said.

"Bloody hell," Quentin said. "How can you possibly know that?"

Jeff said, "If he has been hanging around Quentin's office do you think either of us might have seen him?"

"Interesting point; and that's a very real possibility. Mary helped us put together an identikit picture." Moana opened a manila folder on her desk and pushed the identikit towards Quentin.

"No I don't know him," Quentin said and passed the picture to Jeff. Jeff studied it for a few moments and then gave it back to Moana.

"I don't recognise him either."

Moana shrugged. "It was worth a shot."

Cunningham kept his eyes on Jeff. The intensity of his stare had Quentin second guessing. He had spent enough time in courtrooms and considered himself a fair student of body language. In Cunningham he saw expectation. He had seen it enough times in the faces of prisoners in the dock about to hear the foreman of the jury read the verdict. What the hell was going on? Moana pushed a second document across the table. A photograph of a piece of paper with scrawled words across it.

"Jeff, this is for you to look at," Moana said.

Jeff quickly scanned the document then stepped back and spun on Cunningham.

Cunningham smiled.

"What the fuck is this?" Jeff said, stabbing his finger onto the document, eyes narrowed, voice ice cold.

"I think you know exactly what it is, Jeff. And what it means."

9.

Senior Sergeant Te Kanawa's mouth opened, but she shut it when Cunningham caught her eye and gave a slight shake of the head. The message from the Inspector was clear; let this play out, see where it takes us. Jeff caught the exchange between the two and ignored it. Cunningham had always played games, so why the hell would he change now.

The bile in Jeff's stomach commenced a series of small eruptions. His shoulders sagged and he reached out to the wall to balance himself, fearful he was about to topple.

Cunningham said, "As you can see, Jeff, the message from the killer is addressed to you. It was taped to the kitchen cupboard in Mary Sumner's apartment. She hasn't been told yet but eventually she will need to know."

Quentin read the words out loud. "'Jeff Bradley, you killed someone close to me and now I will kill those close to you and then I will cut your throat.' Bloody hell," he whispered.

Jeff rubbed the bridge of his nose, quickly recalling his time with the SAS. Had he assassinated anyone? No. Not ever with the squadron. What then? The only conflicts he could recall in recent times were in Kosovo. The Akbar brothers: but Halam was dead and Zahar in the custody of the Americans. They would never have released him. Could he have escaped? No. Not possible. And yet . . . All the troubles he had experienced during his trip to Kosovo came flooding back.

Jeff turned away from the table, now composed, his stomach no longer threatening to throw up. Cunningham started to speak but Jeff held up his hand. He needed time. Cunningham returned to leaning against the wall. Jeff could have as much time as he wanted. Moana remained passive. Puzzled, but experienced enough not to interfere.

"Jesus," Jeff mumbled, but loud enough for all to hear.

"Tell us what's on your mind, Jeff?" Cunningham asked.

"Not yet, Brian, I might be wrong." It was too fantastic, too much a coincidence. Jeff looked at the identikit photo again. "I have never seen this man before but I know someone who has. I'll phone him."

"This is the man in Kosovo, Barry Briggs," Cunningham said.

"You've been checking up on me," Jeff said.

"When I heard of that message left by the killer, I pulled all the data on your little escapade. I also called in a few favours and saw the SAS intel reports. Barry Briggs, Morgan Delaney and an Albanian Kosovan, Sulla Bogdani, helped you bring down a terrorist network. At the top of the list of the terror shitheads were the Akbar brothers. You killed Halam. If this message is from Zahar Akbar then we really do have a puzzle. According to the reports Zahar Akbar was in the hands of the Americans. Was there another brother?"

Jeff shrugged. "Not that I'm aware of."

Cunningham said, "What is even more puzzling is why make it public. Why not just keep his mouth shut?"

Jeff shrugged then pulled out his mobile phone and opened his contacts list. He hit the dial icon.

After three rings, it was answered. "Hello there, Barry speaking."

Jeff held his finger up to Cunningham, a signal to wait. "Barry, it's Jeff Bradley."

"How are you, mate? How's Kiwi land?" Barry said, his usual buoyant self bringing a smile from Jeff.

"Barry, this isn't a social call. Halam Akbar's brother. Would you still remember what he looked like?"

"Bloody oath I would. I'll never forget what that little shit looks like. What do you need to know for? Do the Yanks need him identified?"

"Something like that, what's your email address?"

Jeff made a writing gesture with his spare hand. Moana slid a pad and pen across the table. Jeff jotted down Barry's email details.

"Okay, I'm going to send through an artist's sketch in the next few minutes. I'll call you back in five. Tell me if you know him."

"I'll be waiting."

Jeff turned to Cunningham and held up the identikit. "Can this be scanned and sent through to this email address? He's waiting for it."

Cunningham said, "I'm only an observer here, Jeff. You'll need to ask Senior Sergeant Te Kanawa."

Moana glanced at the piece of paper. Uncertain. Jeff knew what she was thinking. This was way outside the rule book.

"What's this all about, Jeff?" she asked, looking at the sheet of paper and the email address.

"I need confirmation that this is who I think it is. Five minutes."

Moana nodded. "Okay, I'll go send it."

Jeff paced. He hoped he was wrong. The implications did not bear thinking about if he was right.

"Jeff. What the hell is going on?" Quentin had had enough.

Jeff ignored him. He checked his watch then he redialled Barry Briggs's number. He pushed the speaker button and placed his mobile in the centre of the table. It rang twice before Barry answered.

"Tell me, Barry."

"Well if his body is slightly built and he is about 5' 10" in height then that's bloody Zahar Akbar, Jeff."

"The height is right but he's beefed up a bit. This guy isn't slightly built."

"Maybe he's been lifting weights. Eating too much grub. But this face is his, Jeff."

"No doubts at all?" Jeff asked.

"No mate. No doubts at all."

"Thanks, Barry."

Jeff reached for his mobile and closed it. He sat down and began drumming his fingers on the table.

Kosovo.

When he had returned from the Balkans to recover from his injuries, he thought he had put that blasted country behind him. Now it seemed the former Yugoslav province had tracked him down. A tsunami of memories flooded his brain. Right now he could choose to walk away. Fat chance. If he was the cause of the attack on Mary and worse, if others close to him were in danger then he had little choice, he had to protect his friends. Zahar Akbar worked for the man responsible for the death of Arben Shala, Jeff's former vineyard manager. There would be no running away. He would hunt Zahar down and put an end to it.

"Jeff, how well do you know this Akbar?" Moana asked, breaking into his thoughts.

"Zahar Akbar, not a lot. He's a terrorist I came up against in Kosovo. I killed his brother and the man I spoke to on the phone captured Zahar. I never saw Zahar in the flesh. His brother Halam I'd recognise in an instant but he's dead."

Jeff continued to mislead everyone into believing he killed Halam Akbar but he had not. Morgan Delaney, an American woman who would forever hold a place in his heart, had fired the fatal shots and saved his life. To protect her from reprisals from the people the Akbars worked for, he had taken responsibility for the kill. The four or five who knew the truth would never tell. Now it seemed his decision to do so was correct.

"Moana, whatever this guy is up to in New Zealand," Jeff said, "I can guarantee murder is a sideline."

"Care to explain?"

"The brothers are, were, international terrorists but not with a cause. They work on contract. You pay the money, the Akbar brothers do the dirty work and whoever hired them takes the credit. They started life as Palestinian refugees and learnt their particular expertise in killing in a variety of Islamic training camps." Jeff turned to Cunningham. "You know the type."

Cunningham nodded.

"They are very good at what they do. They especially like to blow people up. The more the merrier. In my opinion it's unlikely Zahar Akbar would risk travelling to New Zealand to avenge his brother; I think finding me here is a bonus. And I think it unlikely he came to kill a few innocent people. He could do that anywhere. The question that needs asking is, what is the real objective? I would add it would be safer to assume he's not alone."

"There is the submarine. That would be an obvious target for a terrorist," Moana said.

"These guys aren't suicide bombers. Or at least Halam wasn't. I assume his brother is the same. They're only interested in money. Security round the sub will be tight. There is no way they could get close enough to plant an explosive and live."

"Maybe not the submarine directly then but I think them being here at the time of the visit can't be put down to coincidence."

"I don't disagree," Jeff said. "The two events are definitely related. As I said, the brothers were bombers. They loved to blow up crowded streets. Maximum casualties."

Cunningham butted into the conversation, "Like a crowd of thousands of protestors?"

Jeff nodded. He noted Quentin's eyes flick between himself and Cunningham, confused that he and Cunningham had switched from hostility to civility. Not forced. Quentin had never been in the military. He had no understanding that when on ops personal grievances were put to the side. He wasn't about to try and explain the nuances of soldiering to a man whose most exciting adventure was playing in a rock band and giving autographs to teeny-boppers. He would never get it.

"Okay," Cunningham said. "So where is the explanation of how this Akbar is in New Zealand when supposedly he was captured and in the hands of the Yanks? How is it he is free? The American special forces aren't in the habit of losing people."

"That's a question I can't answer but I assure you I'm going to find out," Jeff said.

"You're not in the squadron anymore, Jeff. You're a civilian. If you have any information, pass it on to the police. There is also an Intelligence Service that would probably want to be informed," Cunningham said, an edge to his voice.

Jeff stood and moved closer to Cunningham. Now the civility was dead and the two rutting stags were locking horns again.

Jeff grinned. Not friendly.

"Maybe we shouldn't get too far ahead of ourselves. This is all conjecture. It might be I'm wrong and Akbar is just hiding out in New Zealand and the attack on Mary is nothing more than attempted murder."

"Maybe," Cunningham said. "But I'm not convinced."

"I'll let you know when I have the information, Brian."

"I'll be waiting. But I won't be waiting long."

Jeff went through to the crime room and spent the next hour briefing Sergeant Te Kanawa and her team on Zahar Akbar and his older brother Halam and the man they worked for, the Kosovan criminal mastermind, Avni Leka.

~

After the meeting at the police station Jeff and Quentin walked back to Quentin's office.

"What is it between you and Brian Cunningham?" Quentin asked. "I'm surprised the two of you didn't come to blows."

"We were in Afghanistan together. Things happened. I can't talk about it."

"Things happened. You can't talk about it. Are you shitting me? I'm your friend, Jeff. We share."

"Not this, Quentin."

Quentin made to protest. When he saw the set of Jeff's jaw he thought better of it.

"Look, Quentin, there is something you need to think about. If Akbar is out to harm anyone close to me he may come after you," Jeff said.

"I'm a lawyer, Jeff. Even the bad guys, well especially the bad guys, need representation. Why go after me?"

Jeff shook his head, mouth open. He closed it before words came out. Getting angry with Quentin would resolve nothing.

"Why don't you leave this to the police, Jeff? Cunningham is right. You're not in the army now. They could provide you with protection."

"When it comes to self-preservation I'm much happier looking out for myself. And, if Akbar is going after my friends then I need to stop him." He put his hand on Quentin's shoulder. "Listen to me, Quentin. You need to take precautions."

"Okay I'll take it seriously. I'll call my security firm. I'll have a 24-hour-watch and double the security on the house and office and my family until this guy is caught."

"That's a good boy," Jeff said, slapping Quentin on the back. "It's only money and you've got plenty of it."

Jeff's attempt at playful humour belied his true feelings. He could never live with himself if anything happened to Quentin and his family because of his actions. It was bad enough facing the Shala family every time he went to the vineyard after what he had done to their father and husband without Quentin added to the list.

Firstly, he needed to find out why Zahar Akbar was walking the streets of Auckland and not burning in hell. He knew who had the answer to that question. It was time to make the phone call and find out.

10.

Arriving home, Jeff dropped his mail on the bench. The dishes he had left in the sink had been washed, and looking through to the sitting room, he saw that magazines had been neatly stacked and clothes tidied off the floor. A note taped to the microwave door reminded him his housekeeper had been, and he hadn't left her fee. He inserted a cheque for two payments into an envelope and placed the envelope in the arranged place on top of the refrigerator. He debated phoning and apologising, but it wasn't the first time and if Sarah needed the money urgently she knew how to reach him. He hated that he had forgotten. She kept his house livable.

He retrieved a can of beer from the chiller and a bag of crisps from the larder and made his way down the hallway to his office. He ripped the crisp bag open and scoffed a handful. A few gulps of beer washed away the saltiness. He pushed the manila folders atop his briefcase onto the floor then searched through the satin pockets of the case until he found the business card.

Caldwell had said if I ever need him, call.

"Okay, Caldwell, I need you so I'm calling."

He sank into the leather office chair and dialled the number.

The answering voice was American and drowsy. "Caldwell."

"Caldwell, it's Jeff Bradley."

"Jeff. Don't you people sleep in New Zealand?"

"It's only early evening here and I'm not sorry to wake you."

"Aha . . . this is not a social call."

"I'm afraid not."

"Give me a minute, Jeff. I need to turn on a light and use the bathroom."

Jeff took another sip of his beer.

He had worked with Caldwell in Kosovo. Caldwell wasn't CIA but whoever it was he worked for had enough clout to allow Caldwell access to any US government department, including Embassy staff when needed. He considered their relationship standoffish with a mutual respect for the other's sense of duty. The reason Caldwell hadn't hung up the phone on him was that the American would know he wouldn't be phoning to gossip and waste his time.

He would take the time to clear his head so he could fully focus.

"All right, Jeff I'm back. What have you got?"

"I have reason to believe Zahar Akbar is here in Auckland."

Silence.

"Why do you believe he's there?" Caldwell asked, his tone weighted with caution.

Jeff gave the details of the attack on Mary Sumner and her flatmate.

"Could be a coincidence, maybe you killed someone else's brother and can't remember?"

Jeff almost smiled at Caldwell's attempt at humour.

"One of the women who survived the attack was able to help with an identikit picture. And guess what? Barry Briggs identified him as Halam's brother."

"I see."

"Bloody hell, Caldwell, I thought you had this guy under wraps."

"We did. Then we let him go."

Jeff slammed his can down onto the desktop. Beer splashed through the ring pull hole and sprayed over his jeans. He flicked away the droplets with the back of his hand.

"Until now I'd been hoping I was wrong. For Christ's sake, what idiot made that decision? Please don't tell me you had anything to do with it. If those two women had not been so lucky a couple of mothers might have been asking me why they were burying their daughters instead of attending their weddings. And one of them was a close friend. I would have been demanding answers myself."

"Okay, Jeff, I get the point. Unofficially, it was a classic fucked-up operation, now classified with a security clearance level no one will ever be ranked high enough to read. The incompetence has been buried under a mountain of red tape. You know the routine. Anyway those involved were hoping like hell Akbar had gone into hiding and been blown up by one of his own bombs. They won't be happy you found him."

"How did he get away?"

"Between you and me, decisions made higher up on the food chain decided Zahar Akbar was no use to us sitting in a cell. He was let go under surveillance. They even implanted a chip. What can I say? The baddies are just as smart as we are these days."

"Everyone's smarter than you guys," Jeff gulped down some more beer. "I was half hoping you'd tell me I was wrong, that Zahar could not possibly be in my city."

Caldwell said, "I'll be there as soon as I can. I'll text my flight details once they're confirmed."

"I'll be waiting."

"Don't do anything stupid before I get there. You got lucky once but luck runs out."

Jeff put the phone down.

Caldwell was on his way. That was bad news for New Zealand. Caldwell only ever made visits to trouble spots. And people always died.

He walked through to the sitting room, picked up the remote from the arm of his leather recliner and switched on the television. The six o'clock news had started. He watched the headlines, the same as they had been for the last few nights; the protestors and the nuclear submarine visit. The government was under siege, vilified by the press, savaged in parliament by opposition parties and battered by an endless stream of expert opinion from academics on the dangers of nuclear energy.

The USA and Australia must have been overwhelmingly forthright – you are either with us or against us. In 1984 the New Zealand government had passed legislation declaring New Zealand nuclear free. There would be no nuclear power stations, no visits by nuclear-powered warships and certainly no visits by nuclear submarines. All that had now changed. Jeff had no doubt the government had had little choice but to accept the visit. Weekly briefings during his years in the SAS had taught him you cannot legislate your country safe.

The argument Australia and the Americans had put to the New Zealand government was that New Zealand was making no commitment to defence. No money had been spent on upgrading their armed forces. The air force had no airstrike capabilities, no combat jets, only a handful of helicopters mostly used for training. The army had a few tanks and some pieces of artillery but no mobility. The navy had a couple of frigates but these were used mostly to seek out illegal fishing boats. If an enemy ship entered the harbour the air force would have to throw mud at it and the navy would need a few days to return home. If New Zealand faced an invading army there would be little resistance.

The debates in parliament had been heated and two parliamentarians had come to blows but in the end the government carried enough votes for their legislation to pass. Nuclear energy, nuclear-powered ships and nuclear weapons could again enter New Zealand waters. New Zealanders were good people and saw only good in others. It was a naivety that made New Zealand the special place it was. But, it also made the country vulnerable. Now, at least with the new alliance any attack on New Zealand would bring an armed response from Australia and the United States of America.

Jeff switched the television off. His thoughts turned to the Shala family. He should have gone out to the vineyard. Kimie would be cooking a tasty dinner and she would have certainly invited him to stay. Anything would be better than the frozen pizza now thawing on the bench. Should he tell them of Zahar Akbar? He would think on it. However, he would need to think about their security.

Zahar Akbar studied his image in the mirror. The clean-shaven face and glasses had the desired effect. Even his own mother, were she still alive, would not recognise him. There was nothing yet in the papers giving his identity.

He had been lucky with the two women. A narrow escape. Bad planning. If Halam were here he would have scolded him. Halam never missed a detail. He certainly would have known the other woman would be home. Would Bradley know about the note? He would give the police another few days. Sometimes they played games and kept details to themselves. He would find where Bradley's blonde lover was and this time he would kill her.

11.

The last bottle of wine was placed on the rack and Jeff stepped back to admire his handiwork. Kimie stopped what she was doing and came to stand beside him. He placed a hand on her shoulder.

"I think it looks like a wine shop. What do you think?" he said.

"I think it looks like a very successful wine shop. Now, many people will come to Boundary Fence Winery and your wine will be known all over."

"I wish. But for now, it will do."

"Arben would have been so proud," Kimie said. "He would have been so grateful for what you have done for his family."

Two sets of eyes were drawn the framed photo of her dead husband hanging on the wall behind the counter. Kimie had chosen this spot so that all who entered would see that her husband, Arben Shala, had been a very important man. Arben had brought his family to New Zealand under a refugee programme after they had become displaced when Serbia invaded Kosovo. He had worked in the wine industry in the former Yugoslavia. At the same time Jeff inherited his Grandmother's vineyard, Quentin was processing the residency papers for the Shalas. Quentin, aware Jeff knew nothing about wine, recommended he hire the new immigrant from

Kosovo. Jeff agreed. Together they had built Boundary Fence into a successful business.

It was moments like this when he most missed his friend and mentor. Whenever he and Kimie talked of Arben, awkwardness followed. Arben had returned to his former country at Jeff's request to find bulk wine for Boundary Fence. The journey had ended in his death. Jeff made a promise to Arben as he stood at his graveside that he would take care of his family; Kimie, Marko his son and his daughter Drita. The three lived in Jeff's grandparents' house on the grounds of the vineyard he had inherited.

Marko was now the winery manager. Drita still went to school.

For Jeff they were his family and he would never think of them in any other way. Kimie, at fifty, was an elegant, attractive woman. She could remarry, but he doubted she would. Sadness had consumed her and he guessed it would continue for many years. Kosovan women draped sorrow round their shoulders like a comforting shawl.

Jeff had difficulty with emotional moments; he'd prefer to drown them with a cold beer. Usually he fobbed it off with silly quips as he had just done. But then Kimie's eyes would water and that would be an end to him. He would start coughing and find a reason to make his way outside.

Kimie touched the hand resting on her shoulder.

Jeff searched for the right words. Found none. Instead he said, "Too soon to thank me, Kimie; after a few days of working this place you might want to strangle me."

"How was the meeting with your lawyer?" Kimie asked.

"It could have gone better."

"Is the vineyard going to be sold? I can find somewhere else for us to live. Please do not worry for us. We are not your responsibility. You have done so much already."

Jeff put his arm round Kimie's shoulder.

"We're not anywhere near leaving, Kimie, and if I get my way it will never get to that point."

Kimie nodded.

"But you will let me know if it does."

"You will know as soon as I do. But stop worrying."

Jeff hoped to hell Quentin knew what he was doing.

"I have put the carton of wine for the competition in Whangarei by the door." Jeff looked, saw it and nodded. "You will not forget to take it with you, will you?"

"No I won't, I promise. I know how important a gold medallion on our wine bottles is."

Kimie kissed Jeff on the cheek and set about picking the empty cartons up from the floor.

His mobile rang.

"Jeff Bradley."

"It's Brian Cunningham, Jeff. Can you come into the station? We need to chat."

"Something wrong?"

"Yes, there is something wrong. There is a terrorist in town and he's after you. It's against the law for me to stake you to a peg in an open field and use you as bait to lure him out but I can keep an eye on you. It would help if you cooperated and allowed us to put you under surveillance."

"You know that's not going to happen. And don't try it. I'll suss out a tail easily enough. You know I will. But it does lead to an interesting question, Brian. What part are you playing in this investigation?"

"I'm the police."

"Don't bullshit me. Te Kanawa is the lead. From her body language she dislikes your presence more than I do. I take it you're stepping on toes. Whose shoes are you wearing?"

"You know I'm with the Special Tactics Group. We're the police anti-terrorist unit."

"Are you? I thought that was still the SAS role, D Company to be precise. I thought all you guys did was act like a SWAT team. Lay siege to the bad guys when the police have them holed up somewhere," Jeff said.

It didn't surprise Jeff that Cunningham, having left the Special Forces, had ended up in charge of the police Special Tactics Group. The STG had been established by Special Forces officers and its members often trained with their Special Forces counterparts. The police would have gratefully accepted a special forces trained officer. Jeff's first thought was that Cunningham had gone rogue. He and his STG team were probably sitting in a room somewhere twiddling their thumbs. Along comes Akbar and leaves the note and Cunningham jumped to the right conclusion. He would have easily convinced his superiors that as Akbar was a known terrorist the STG needed to be kept informed and then insinuated himself into the investigation. The best way to be kept informed would be to tag along after Moana Te Kanawa, who he was following round like a bad smell.

"Have you confirmed from your source that this guy is Zahar Akbar?" Cunningham asked.

"I was about to phone you," Jeff lied. "It's confirmed. Now you know for certain, will you bring in the Squadron?"

"Not yet. At the moment this guy is just a violent offender. Nothing to indicate terrorist activity. My bosses will not willingly hand over the investigation to outsiders. It would be admitting the department failed. Not a good career move."

"And your STG group?"

"On standby. For the moment I'm an observer working alongside Sergeant Te Kanawa, that's all. Let the detectives do the detecting, I'm no Sherlock Holmes. Te Kanawa doesn't like it. I wouldn't either. A big career-building case and an asshole like me stepping on toes."

"And at some stage maybe taking over," Jeff added.

"I'm no fortune teller. I can't predict the future."

"Yeah, right."

"When the battle begins the soldiers need to take over. Even my tactics force, although well trained, haven't fired bullets at real live targets. That's why I need you. We're trained for this. We can work together."

Jeff paused a moment and stared at his phone. There it was, Cunningham had gone rogue. He didn't trust anyone to get the job done other than himself. He hadn't changed one bit from his military days. Not that Jeff didn't disagree with Cunningham's sentiments; the same reasoning was behind his wanting to remain a free agent and find Akbar himself.

"Jesus, Brian, I'm a fucking wine maker now," Jeff said, playing for time.

Kimie looked up.

Jeff held up his hand. "Sorry." He turned his back to her. Lowered his voice. Should he commit himself to Cunningham? After Afghanistan, how could he trust him? "What the hell do you expect me to do?"

"What you do best. Help me track these bastards down."

Jeff snapped his phone shut cutting Cunningham off.

"There is a problem, Jeff?" Kimie asked, looking worried.

"Yes, Kimie, a big problem, but nothing for you to worry about."

12.

Barbara Heywood tapped her pencil on her pad. Scrawled messages, adhesive notes and doodles covered the top sheet. Untidy piles of manila folders sat in plastic trays on the floor against the back wall. A rarely used grey metal filing cabinet sat in one corner and a coat rack in the other. On the wall to Barbara's right hung a whiteboard. The office was small but comfortable and easily accommodated her desk, three chairs and a small stool holding the ceramic pot and rubber plant given to her at the Christmas party. The tips of the leaves had browned and the stems sagged. The note on her pad to water her plant had been ignored.

There was no rhythm to her beating pencil.

Where the hell was her assistant?

She threw her pen on the desk and walked out to reception.

"Jodie, have you seen Lydia? Has she phoned?"

"I'm sorry, Ms Heywood. I haven't seen her. She did ring through earlier and asked to speak with Jason."

"Really?"

Barbara reached over the counter and plucked a protesting Jodie's phone from the cradle. She punched in her producer's number.

"Talk to me." The producer's phone manner always irked her.

"Jason. Did Lydia speak with you this morning?"

"Barbara. And good morning to you as well. Ah, yes, Lydia did phone. She quit."

"How do you mean she quit?"

"Resigned. Left the job. Her exact words were, let me see if I can remember, oh yes: 'I'm not prepared to work for that bitch any more'. Then I think there was a, 'screw you all'."

"Interns are weak these days. Bad parenting. Too much molly-coddling."

"That's three in six months, Barbara. If I was staying I'd have to send you on a management course."

"I know how to manage people."

"Abusing is not managing. Be nice. Don't scream at them."

"I'm the anchor and, I might add, the award-winning journalist who provides the meat for your top-rated current affairs show, Jason. Being sweet doesn't cut it with news broadcasting. You of all people should know that."

"Just try to be a half-decent human being, that's all I ask. We could be sued."

"All right, I'll be nice. And what do you mean, if you were staying?"

"I'm leaving. Today. I'm going to talk back radio. No prima donnas, so I'm told. I need a change."

"What about me? The show?"

"Hank Challis is taking over."

"Hank the Yank? Are you kidding me? The guy is an idiot. Who made that decision?"

"Well it was a vote of attrition really. Hank was the only producer who would work with you."

"You're an asshole, Jason."

Barbara dropped the phone into Jodie's outstretched hand. "Slam that down will you."

Jodie looked over the rim of her glasses but before she could speak Barbara spun on her heel and disappeared, leaving two swinging doors in her wake.

The day was off to a bad start; Lydia leaving, Jason leaving and now Hank the Yank was to be her new boss. By the time Barbara reached the end of the corridor she was contemplating a new career.

The network employed a small group of researchers who shared an office on the second floor. Mostly they were new graduates prepared to accept a token salary to get a foot in the door to kick-start a television career. Five heads, nestled on stooped shoulders and peering into computer screens, did not swing her way when Barbara entered the room. She had never been in the room before but knew the five were wannabe writers who worked on anything from documentaries to the locally produced soaps and games shows. Barbara surveyed the mix of young men and women. She ruled out a male assistant. She didn't have time to deal with young men having fantasies about getting into her pants.

Finally a head looked up. "May I help you, Ms Heywood?"

The speaker was a young woman in her early twenties. Pretty. Short black hair, two studs in her left ear and probably a tattoo hidden somewhere. She was dressed in a T-shirt and jeans and running shoes. Must be the uniform, Barbara thought, as they all seemed to be dressed the same except the guys' jeans were bigger. The girl looked intelligent. Barbara accepted she must capable enough to have been given the job. Even though the station only paid a pittance they seldom hired idiots. Hank the Yank was the exception.

"What is your name?" Barbara asked.

"Amy Monroe."

"How long have you been working here?"

"One year."

"Where were you before that?"

"I finished university, spent a year travelling overseas then came back and worked as a waitress until I came here."

"What are you working on?"

"Making up questions for a new weekly quiz show. A variation of Mastermind."

"Anyone can do that. Amy Monroe, grab your belongings and come with me."

Amy's head fell back, eyebrows raised and mouth open; the bewildered look of a deer looking down the barrel of a hunter's rifle. She shrugged, pushed back her chair and picked up a pad and pen and prepared to follow.

"No, everything, Amy. Your coat and bag. You no longer work here."

"I don't? Have I lost my job?" Amy looked at the others, stunned.

"Just follow me," Barbara commanded.

Amy put on her jacket and grabbed her bag from under the desk. Barbara had already left the room. Amy scurried off after her and followed Barbara downstairs.

"This was the office of my last assistant. It is now your office. You now work for me. Lydia was the best research assistant in the business. You will try to live up to her standards," said Barbara.

"I'm working for you?"

"Yes. Do you have a problem with that?"

"No. Not at all. Thank you."

"Good. Now, your first job is to go down to the canteen and get two coffees. I have mine black with one sugar. Bring them through to my office and bring a notepad. We have work to do."

Barbara returned two phone messages and checked her emails before Amy placed two coffees on her desk. Barbara took a sip. Too much sugar. She remembered Jason's words and resisted throwing a pen. She instead continued her unmelodic tap, tap, tap, on the desk pad. She knew it used to irritate the hell out of Lydia, and wondered how long it would be before Amy started to cast her glances. Barbara dropped the pencil into the 'Support Black Magic' coffee mug, a souvenir she had bought to support New Zealand's America's Cup Campaign.

"All right, Amy. This is your chance to surprise me. I need ideas for this week's programme. What have you got?"

Amy's mouth dropped open.

"You want me to give you a story,"

Barbara nodded, "I take it you keep up with the world at large, local affairs, life in general."

"Yes as a matter fact of I do. Let me see. Each day is the same. Take your pick. Demonstrations, political statements, food poisoning, drink-driving campaign, anti-smoking campaign, anti-everything campaign."

Barbara smiled. "You're far too young to be cynical. Besides those topics are general news items. I need meat. The station pays us to scoop stories. Comprehende?"

"How about the submarine? It's almost here," Amy offered.

"And when it does get here we'll be on it twenty-four hours a day. The public will be submarined to death. Still, now that you've brought it up, in your spare time start gathering background on the bloody thing. How many crew, what makes it run, why it's so dangerous, if it is?"

"I'll try to track down a retired Admiral or Captain or officer of some sort. There is technical stuff on the internet but it's beyond me."

"On the technical stuff maybe you could try one of the protest groups. They usually have all that information. Their intelligence system is better than our secret service."

"Will do."

"And get a comment from a government spokesperson," Barbara said.

"And if they clam up?"

"Talk to the opposition."

Amy nodded.

"There is one thing I heard," Amy started. "Might be something, might be nothing."

"I'm listening," Barbara said.

"Friday night there was an incident which on its own might mean nothing. Two women attacked in their apartment," she said slowly and measuredly.

Barbara had read about it in the *Herald*.

"Attempted murder is general news. Not for my programme," Barbara said, irritable.

Amy grinned. "One of the girls attacked was Mary Sumner." Amy paused for effect.

"The Olympic triathlete?" Barbara asked.

"One and the same."

"Mary Sumner works for a lawyer. I've spoken to her a number of times trying to get an interview with Jeff Bradley. Quentin is Jeff's lawyer. Poor girl. Wow. A feature on violence against women could be a goer. We haven't touched the subject for more than a year."

"There's more."

"For God's sake, Amy, let me lay it out for you, I hate games."

Amy seemed undeterred by the reprimand. "From what I was told the guy who attacked them was suffocating Mary's flatmate when she came to the rescue. Beat the guy up with a baseball bat and sent him on his way. A real heroine."

Barbara played with a strand of her hair. Not long enough to reach her shoulders but long enough to reach her lips. Her mother would have slapped her wrists if she had still been living with her parents.

"Then there is the real juicy part."

Barbara arched her eyebrows.

"There was a note. The killer was after Mary Sumner. It wasn't random."

"How did you come by this information?"

"I have my sources and they will remain my sources," Amy stated, strength to her tone. Then she blushed.

Barbara stiffened, stunned by the bluntness of her new assistant. But liking her attitude.

"I'm sorry, Ms Heywood, I didn't mean it to come out like that what I meant was—"

Barbara held up her hand, "Don't ever apologise for doing a good job."

"There is something else. It might be something it might not."

"Go on."

"There is an Inspector Brian Cunningham attached to the investigating squad."

"From the Special Tactics Group?" Barbara asked.

Amy nodded, surprised.

"I know Brian," Barbara said. "And don't look so surprised. I'm a news reporter. The police supply us with much of our news. It's my job to know the top brass. We only have one swat team." Barbara reached for her tapping pencil. "The question is, why would the Special Tactics Group be interested in an assault on two women?"

13.

Car keys in hand, Jeff was set to leave his home when a flicking red light caught his eye. Two messages on his answer phone. He pushed the button.

"Jeff, it's Quentin. You need to come into the office and sign the land sale documents."

The other message was from the wine festival organisers in Whangarei. The committee was waiting for the selection of Boundary Fence wine. If Jeff wanted his wine in the competition he needed to get it to them as quickly as possible. Right now, with Akbar about, he disliked the idea of an absence from Auckland for any amount of time, but life went on and Boundary Fence needed prize-winning wine. He could courier it but to make sure it got there he preferred to deliver it himself. He would go up on Monday and come back on the same day.

He had expected a message from Brian Cunningham. He toyed with the idea of phoning then dismissed it. They had fought in a war together. Cunningham didn't need to leave any more messages; he knew Jeff well enough to know he would not walk away. But Cunningham could wait a little longer. Business had to come first. Akbar would lie low for a few days. He had time.

~

The meeting with the wholesaler went well. A pallet of wine per month was a good start. He phoned the order through to the vineyard. Marko promised to have the first pallet delivered later in the day.

Next, Jeff made his way to Quentin's office.

"I thought I might see Mary back at work," he said when he saw Quentin sitting at the reception desk.

"She's in good shape. She wanted to come in but Jeannie wouldn't hear of it. Her mother was up for a couple of days but Mary convinced her to go back to Wellington. You know Mary, beautiful and tough as old boots. Ann, poor soul, is really quite out of it. She still hasn't uttered a word other than a few whispers to Mary. Anyway she has gone home with her parents. Means Mary has no flatmate which is why she is still at my place. Jeannie won't hear of her being home alone. A doctor is coming in later today to give her the once over. If he clears her Mary said she'll go back to her apartment anyway."

"Really? Not a good move I wouldn't think. He'll go after her again. I should move her in with me and keep her close." Quentin shrugged. "Forget it. I told you, keep your hands off my staff."

Jeff frowned. "Hire someone to watch over her. I'll pay. She's in danger because of me."

"Already organised, my friend. I'll overcharge you on your next account."

Jeff smiled. "Where are these documents you want me to sign?"

Quentin opened the folder on the desk. "Right here." Jeff signed where Quentin pointed. "That's it. You're now the owner of a fat cheque and a partner in a nightclub"

Jeff shook his head.

"Now you can buy me lunch. Come down to the club first. I'm looking to open on Saturday," Quentin said.

"Really? That quickly."

"I've been planning it for twenty years," Quentin laughed, "so it doesn't seem that quick for me. Anyway, it needs a trial run. Invited guests, that sort of thing. A trial for the staff mostly."

"Got a name for it yet?"

"Not yet. Been tossing a few ideas round and I need to make a decision today if the sign is to be ready in time."

"What does Jeannie think? I'm surprised she agreed."

Quentin shrugged, and then offered a sheepish grin.

"You still haven't told her. Jesus, Quentin, you're digging a bloody big hole for yourself."

"I have a plan. I bring her along on opening night. She has a great time and then I tell her it's ours."

"Quentin, that's a very bad plan," Jeff said shaking his head.

"Too late now, I've sent out the invitations. I've invited my clients and the media. Hopefully they'll all turn up for a freebie night."

Quentin's office was only a short walk away from the club, which was located on Fort Street in the heart of downtown Auckland's night-time play area. Jeff noted new apartment buildings had gone up on the site that once housed a wheat mill. Cafés, restaurants, bars, sauna parlours, strip clubs and backpacker accommodation lined both sides of the street. Jeff had to admit Quentin had chosen the ideal location. Lots of young tourists from the hostels should keep his club full most nights. Not that he needed them especially. There were hordes of people wandering Fort Street and the surrounding streets most nights until the early hours.

Jeff stood next to Quentin in the centre of the dance floor. Confused.

"What do you think?" Quentin asked.

"It looks like the inside of your office."

Quentin grinned. "That's the master stroke. It's a step back into the past. The theme is a history of New Zealand Rock music. Sort of like my very own Hall of Fame and on the walls, the wall of fame."

"If it's a hall or wall of fame as you put it, how is it the biggest photo montage is of you and your band?" Jeff teased.

"Mock us not, my friend. We were ahead of our time. Anyway this club will feature live bands and promote new artists. Live music, a dance floor and a meander down memory lane. Think about it. Everyone loves living in the past, it's when you had the most fun."

"The people from your past are in retirement villages."

"Not funny. This club is about relaxing and having a good time. I've left the area in front of the bar open for mixing and mingling and the dance floor is big enough for thirty to forty at a time."

Jeff shook his head. But he had to admit there was a relaxing ambience to the place. All the cubicle seating down one wall was upholstered in deep burgundy leather. Four seat tables ran along in front of the cubicles and a line of taller stand tables and stools. Quentin was either going to be very right or down-the-tubes wrong.

What the hell, Jeff thought, for the time being a nightclub might be fun and it would be selling Boundary Fence wine.

14.

Barbara Heywood dialled the number written on the back page of her diary. After three rings an automated voice directed her to press two and wait. A real voice answered and she was put on hold. The pencil from her America's Cup mug appeared in her fingers and began battering the desk mat in a more adrenaline-pumped fidgety way than the usual mindless habitual tapping. Barbara sensed a meaty story within her grasp. In a few seconds it might be confirmed.

"Brian Cunningham speaking."

"Brian, thank you for taking my call. It's Barbara Heywood from Channel Nine News."

"Hi, Barbara," Cunningham said. "What can I do for you?"

Barbara heard a hesitation in his voice. Guarded. To be expected. No one liked talking to the press unless they were a politician. She had met Brian on a number of occasions over police business. A cautious but friendly understanding had developed between them. A colleague had once described cops and reporters as two circling wild animals, one looking to steal the meat and the other looking to bite necks.

"Brian, do we have a killer roaming the streets of Auckland?"

She decided to get to the point. Brian had never come across as someone who liked chitchat.

Brian laughed. "No flattery to get a story. I'm disappointed."

"You're thinking of used-car dealers. We journalists are all mouth and no diplomacy."

"But why phone me? Talk to the detective in charge of the investigation."

"I heard that the attack in the apartment the other night was a murder attempt, thwarted by a flatmate. The girl would be dead now if she had been alone. No apparent motive from what I hear. An alarm bell rang in my head. It led me to think that if someone is seeking to randomly kill a member of the public, the public has a right to know."

"Crime happens like that sometimes, Barbara. Unusual, yes, but I think it's a little early to be jumping to the conclusion a killer is on the loose. No one died."

"A lucky break from what I hear. If the girl attacked had been home alone she would be dead. Am I jumping to conclusions?"

Barbara waited for a response. A trick she had learnt from a sales friend. Sometimes you got more from shutting up, forcing the other person to fill the silence.

"I can see how you might get there, Barbara, but you're way off track."

"All right, Brian, sorry to have bothered you, but I had to follow up on my assumptions."

"Of course, you have a job to do. Feel free to phone me at any time. But as I said, this is a police matter. I'm sure you're aware I'm with the Special Tactics Group."

"One last question while I have you on the phone."

"Shoot."

Barbara said, "Was Mary Sumner the Olympian involved?"

"Where did you get that information?"

"You know better than to ask that," Barbara said. "Was there a note left by the killer and why have you suddenly been seconded to the investigation? What possible interest could the Tactics Group have in an assault on two women? Come on, Brian, what's going on?"

"Please hold a moment, Barbara." She knew he had his hand over the speaker. Probably talking to someone. She had rattled him. She loved this part of the game. "Are you there, Barbara?"

"I'm here."

"There is a coffee lounge in the entrance of the Central Library."

"I know it."

"Meet me there at 4pm."

"I'll be there."

"And, Barbara, I'd appreciate you keeping your theories to yourself until we've spoken."

"You can count on it, Brian. Thank you."

Barbara put down the phone. Jesus. It must be true. She wouldn't do anything with the information until she had spoken to Brian Cunningham. She had always played it straight with the police and they had always kept her in the loop but she had been in the business long enough to know Amy's information was right on the button.

~

Zahar pushed down the kettle button and waited until he heard the hiss from the first boiling bubbles. He turned his attention to the cupboards, found a cup and rummaged through the larder until he found a pack of herbal tea bags. Sami Hadani was going to check on the teams. He had wanted to go with him but had in the end decided against it.

His men had begun bickering. He put it down to cabin fever. They had all the comforts supplied by their minders but were under strict orders not to leave the safe houses. In a few days they would move into operational mode and the grumbling would stop. But between now and then they needed to be controlled. He had every confidence Sami would calm them. Sami was a scary man. Zahar had met many scary men but Sami had an edge and a craziness that made him stand out.

"Good morning, Zahar. You slept well, I hope?"

Sami Hadani stood in the doorway, yawned then scratched at the navy blue T-shirt where it covered his expanding belly. He reached across in front of Zahar with a hand the size of a bear paw and flicked the switch on the espresso machine. Zahar stood back and allowed the big man to spoon coffee grains into the filter. He added water then walked back through the door.

"I need a crap," he said, then disappeared.

They didn't talk much but what he had gleaned from the overweight Kosovan was that he had built a successful export business and long ago fallen out with his wife. She and the children lived in a house in West Auckland. He sent them money but never visited. She had a restraining order against him. Sami complained it was because she just didn't like him but Zahar had little doubt he had beaten his wife. Sami reminded him of many of the villagers he'd met in developing countries where the only joy in their miserable lives was making their wives' lives miserable. In the mind of a man like Sami his reasoning would be that at least someone was worse off than he.

During the Kosovan war he had reportedly raped and murdered Serb women, even young girls. Unsubstantiated reports they might be and Zahar had no way of verifying if they were true but from the short time he had spent with the man he didn't doubt it for a second.

Sami had a nice home in one of the better suburbs of Auckland city. It had a gym but dust on the apparatus and Sami's expanding frame was testament to the lack of an exercise regimen; too much food and too much cognac. He was a bitter man, although Zahar could not fathom why. He had money and a good life. He paid for women when he needed fulfilment. Sami had told him women could offer him nothing except sex so why let them invade his home and mind? He had tried it once and once was enough. A man needs to be a man. No one in a skirt would tell him what to do.

Zahar smiled as he thought it through, if Sami had all he needed, why the bitterness? He had formed the opinion that Sami was unstable. As long as Zahar was in Sami's home he would be forever watchful.

He turned on the television to catch the news. There was a mention of two women scaring off an intruder. No names and no mention of the note and no mention of Jeff Bradley. The police were keeping it quiet. To be expected.

The New Zealand police force was proving to be wilier than he had given them credit for. They were not panicking as he had expected. Had they informed Bradley? He would have to strike again. They had left him little choice. Until pressure came from the public the police would not go public and he needed the media and police and security forces focused on him and his team.

This was one aspect of the operation that had confused Zahar and he had argued with his boss. He wanted to know why they should put themselves at risk. Every available cop and security agency in the country would be out looking for them. Auckland was a big enough city for them to stay lost in and the safe houses and modes of transport and escape routes had been established before he and his men arrived. It would have been much easier for him and his men to complete the mission without the eyes of the world on them. But Avni had said it was not for him to ask such questions. Those paying for their services had paid extra. Avni had offered a million dollar bonus to him if he did it this way. And when Avni had told him that Jeff Bradley, the man who had killed his brother, lived in New Zealand, and once he had completed his mission he could take care of the New Zealander, Zahar had accepted. But he was not about to wait to avenge his brother, if something went wrong with the mission he might miss his chance. Avni Leka did not need to know that his attacks on Bradley had begun.

The plan to leave New Zealand was already in place. One of the minders had bought a forty-seat airplane and it sat on the tarmac at Auckland airport. The New Zealand Air Force had no strike aircraft. Once airborne they would not be shot down. The escape route and flight plans were already lodged and everyone had the correct documentation for customs clearance in the countries on the flight path. Failing that, a freighter was standing by in international waters 250 kilometres off the New Zealand coastline. They would not become trapped on the New Zealand islands.

When this was over he would take his money and retire to the village in northern Iran with the two daughters the village headman had promised to him and his brother. Halam was dead but the village elder was still keen on the original deal. The price for his daughters was already set. The headman had said Zahar would be a happy man with two beautiful women to care for his every need. Zahar was not so sure. It was not the life he had wanted but it was now the only life available to him. Terrorism had no future, and as much as he had learned to live knowing each day his life might end, he had no desire to die. He would fulfil his brother's dream. As his brother's image came to mind he clenched his fist. Halam had protected him as a small child then raised him when their parents were killed. He carried him through the rubble of Palestine and sheltered him in the Hezbollah camps in Lebanon. Halam was his mother and father, his life. Bradley had killed his brother's dream. Bradley was going to experience what it was like to lose someone close to him. Then he would die.

Zahar placed the teabag in the cup and poured in the boiled water.

A sip. Too hot. He placed the cup on the breakfast bar and pulled up a stool.

A knock on the front door had Zahar looking for Sami. Halfway down the hall the big man emerged from the bathroom drying his hands on a towel. He tossed it at Zahar who reluctantly caught it.

"Hang that up for me."

Zahar's glared message, I'm not your nursemaid, stopped him in his tracks. Sami half smiled. "Please. And stay in the bathroom until I call."

Zahar closed the door but the aromas Sami had left behind had him holding his breath and opening the window.

After a minute Sami called out to him.

Esat Krasniqi stood in the lounge, face flushed and rubbing the top of his forehead. Nervous eyes flittered round the room, avoiding eye contact. Zahar inwardly smiled at Krasniqi's discomfort. Avni Leka's man was frightened. Good. Frightened men were more easily controlled.

"How are the men in your care, Esat? No problems I hope."

Esat shook his head. "No, Zahar, I have supplied the men with everything they need just as Avni said I should. They are becoming restless, as I have told to Sami. I am wondering how much longer they will stay?"

"As long as it takes," Zahar snapped. "Is this a concern for you?"

"No. Of course not," Krasniqi answered, the flush of redness now fading to pale.

Sami said, "Zahar, leave him be before he shits himself, I don't want it all over the carpet. Come on, Esat. I will be a few hours, Zahar. Make yourself at home. There is a list of hookers above the phone if you need some comforting. And can you turn off my coffee. Esat can buy me a cup before he buys me lunch."

15.

Barbara Heywood arrived early for her meeting with Brian Cunningham. She sat at a table by the window. The space between it and other occupied tables was enough that they would not be overheard.

The University Campus which had started life on Symonds Street now spread from Waterloo Quadrant past the top of Wakefield Street and down the slopes into Queen Street. The Central City Library had been in the path of this ever consuming academic lava flow. The café, once a coffee stop for readers dropping off and borrowing books, was now a haven for students seeking time out from classes and the bustle of campus life. Hunched figures sat glued to laptop screens, sipping from bottles of mineral water and munching blueberry muffins.

Barbara needn't have concerned herself with the self-absorbed students. None had even glanced her way.

She waved when Cunningham entered the café. He mimed drinking a coffee. Barbara held up her cup and waggled her finger. He was as she remembered him: tall, good-looking, a bulky physique, not fat but underneath the dark suit she doubted she would find a toned body. His healthy crop of brown hair had a suspicion of grey sneaking into the sideburns. Overall Brian Cunningham was a commanding presence.

At drinks after media briefings he had paid her scant attention and when he did speak it seemed to Barbara it was more out of professional courtesy than attraction. However more than once she had caught him watching her and she was certain that on those occasions it was her ass that held his attention and not her ability with a pen. She guessed he was very much like herself. Married to the job. No time for romance. She did know he had married, now divorced.

They exchanged friendly smiles as Cunningham sat.

"I guess a lot is happening," Barbara said.

He smiled. "Am I being interrogated already?"

"Friendly banter," Barbara said. "I promise there will be no traps and everything we discuss will be off the record until you say otherwise."

"Fair enough," Cunningham said. "I'm all yours."

"Do we have a potential killer running about the streets of Auckland?"

"Yes, we do."

Barbara nodded thoughtfully. She ticked off the first question on her notepad and scribbled 'I smell a rat' next to it.

"Was one of the intended victims the Olympic medallist Mary Sumner?"

"Yes, she was."

"And was a note left in the apartment by the assailant confirming he was after Mary?"

"Yes a note was left behind."

Barbara's mouth fell open.

The waitress arrived with Cunningham's coffee. Barbara rested her notepad on her lap until she left.

"Okay, Brian, what's going on here? I ask three straightforward questions and get honest answers. This is unnerving."

"You're complaining?"

"No, of course not, but why are you telling me these things? What's the catch?"

"No catch, Barbara. There have been major developments and the police investigating team aren't certain whether to involve the media or not. Lives are at stake so it's not a decision to be taken lightly. Having said that, you have obtained sensitive information, which is upsetting. It means a leak in the department. Well, okay, what's done is done but I need to stop it going any further for now."

Barbara nodded. It had happened before. She had been in the business long enough to know the police used the media to their advantage. This annoyed crime reporters. They made their livings off the scraps of information.

"I already have enough for a story, Brian, even without police confirmation," Barbara said. "The network does pay my wages."

"I understand that, Barbara, but a much bigger story is developing. Work with me and you can have it all, exclusive. For the moment I'm asking you to sit on it. Your choice."

Barbara tapped her pad with her pen, not happy. What choice did she have? Do as she was told or stay out of the loop. Her nose told her Brian was offering her something special. His presence as head of the Special Tactics Group in an investigation of an assault on two women puzzled her. Why on earth would he be interested? If she didn't play ball she would be locked out and never get to the truth. It was also unlikely the station would air her findings without police verification.

"It seems I have little choice. I could be sacked when the station learns I made this deal. If that happens you owe me dinner," Barbara said, switching to a playful tone.

Cunningham raised an eyebrow. A hint of a smile. The type that a man and a woman throw at each other the first time they switch to intimate. Barbara sensed Brian was assessing if she was flirting. The dinner proposal remark had simply fallen out of her mouth. The result of having a big mouth and never keeping it shut. Her mother told her it would get her into trouble one day. How right she had been. But, now it was out there, if he did ask her to dinner, she might say yes.

16.

Wiki Herewini sat in the cab of his Kenworth truck in a queue of HGVs. His wife, Marama, had made a thermos of coffee. He poured a cup and unwrapped his salami sandwich then settled back to listen to talkback radio. As he listened to an endless stream of disgruntled callers he kept an eye on the cranes at work. It didn't matter how many times he came to the wharf he never tired of watching the cranes.

Auckland's port stretched across the front of the central city business district from the Westhaven boating marina to the helipads at Mechanics Bay, encompassing six wharves. The Fergusson container terminal covered more than thirty-two hectares and moved more than 800,000 twenty-foot-equivalent shipping containers per annum.

At 10.30pm the forty-foot container was firmly secured onto his trailer. He estimated that, traffic willing, he could get to the bonded warehouse in Mount Wellington and be home before midnight. There was no customs officer available at this time of night. He would leave his truck and trailer in the compound and take a taxi home.

At the departure gate he showed his documents to port security. They checked the container number and customs tag was still in place. Satisfied all was in order, the barrier was lifted. Wiki paid little attention to the black Range Rover that pulled in behind as he made his way through the series of gear changes needed for his rig to gather speed.

~

Barbara Heywood typed in the final details of her discussion with Brian Cunningham. A quick scan of the five hundred or so words brought the nod of a job well done. She closed her laptop. But before it had time to click into sleep mode she re-lifted the lid, opened a new document and typed in a few book title ideas. An author once told her that writing down a title meant at least the baby had been born. Well okay, the baby still needed a body, flesh and blood. A 60,000-word manuscript. She had tired of the circus that was the media and needed a career change. After speaking with Brian Cunningham the voices that had guided her through journalism were now screaming at her that a big story was developing in the city of Auckland. *And,* she had a ringside seat. She ran the cursor across the lettering of one of her book-title ideas and clicked on a twenty-four font and shaded them in bold black. A smile and a nod and down came the lid.

She had not gone back to the network after meeting with Cunningham. She had ambled down Queen Street window shopping, then along Customs Street to her Quay West Hotel apartment. Now with her notes typed up the work day was done and it was time to wind down. In the kitchen she pulled a half-empty bottle of Chardonnay from the fridge, poured herself a drink and carried the glass to the sofa. The twelfth floor of the hotel afforded her a view of the lower central business area, the ports and the inner harbour. Across the harbour she could make out lights of Takapuna and followed the sparkle along the Peninsular to Stanley point and Devonport. Devonport seemed so close she felt she could reach out and touch it. She loved the scene, it relaxed her, reminded her of a Christmas tree.

The sound of a rap song averted her attention. Lydia must have changed the ring on her mobile. Payback before she resigned. Barbara loathed rap music.

She leaned forward and pushed answer, then speaker.

"Barbara Heywood speaking," she said, leaning back in the sofa, glass still in hand.

"Hey boss, it's Amy. Sorry to bother you at home," said her newly appointed assistant.

"That's okay. I wasn't doing much. I thought you were out for the night?"

"I am. I'm in the toilet of the Chelsea Bar. You know the one. Where all the students and wannabe students hang out."

"I know it but I'm not sure I'm comfortable talking to someone sitting on a toilet."

"Don't worry, I'm not doing anything. I needed some privacy. I have information. If I don't give it to you now I'll drink too much and in the morning it will be a muddle."

Barbara thought that unlikely. Amy wasn't coming across as the type to forget anything. More likely it was so exciting she needed to unload. She took two steps to her desk for a pad and pen then sank back into the sofa.

"Speak to me," Barbara said.

"I've been drinking with a group protesting the arrival of the nuclear sub. They've been stirring the pot, as they put it, for the last few weeks. They're drinking pretty heavily and buying for anyone who comes and sits with them. Not the normal behaviour of cash-strapped students."

"You rang to tell me you've had free drinks all night?"

"No. Of course not."

"Good. Besides, students these days have rich parents and more money in their pockets than I have."

"Now listen," Amy demanded, slurring her words a little. "I asked them how they could afford to protest all the time. Didn't they need to have jobs? I mean they really were spending lots of money."

Barbara was growing impatient.

"Anyway. They said no worries. They were being paid. I said to protest and they said yes. I wanted to learn more. So I told them I thought that was bullshit and if it was true then I wanted on the payroll. They said no problems."

"Okay. That is interesting. But professional protestors are hardly news. They've been around since forever."

"Yes, well I started to get a little closer to the guy next to me. You know. Using my feminine wiles. I can be irresistible when I want to be."

Barbara laughed. "Just how much have you had to drink?"

"Lots. But listen. I'm trying to tell you something. Where was I . . . ? Oh yeah. They've been provided with a free office to organise from, free computers and all the brochures and banners etc, are paid for."

"Really? Okay you have my attention. Who's paying for all this? Did he say?"

"No names," said Amy. "Charlie Agnew the organiser said he was approached by a man to set it up. The man was a foreigner. Had an accent but he couldn't pick which country. And anyway Agnew said he didn't care as long as the money continued to flow. The man told him he supported their cause and wanted to help by providing funds. Brian said he wasn't going to argue and readily accepted the offer. As I said everything is paid for and they get paid weekly. And really good money. Almost as much as I'm getting paid working for you. There is enough money, Agnew was told, to pay for as many people as he can recruit. He also said there are a couple of other offices operating the same way. I'm not sure where they are but one is on the North Shore. This is big money, boss. It might be some multi-national company behind it."

Barbara said, "For the life of me I can't think of what there would be to gain for a business."

"What about solar energy companies? They must all be anti-nuclear."

"Don't be silly."

"Greenpeace then?"

"Worth consideration but unlikely, they would hold their own protest. Besides, they're in the business of raising money not giving it away."

"Now, I really do have to use the toilet. Want to keep talking?"

"No I don't. I'll see you in the morning. Be careful and don't drink too much."

"Too late, boss. Bye." Amy was gone.

Barbara put her mobile on her lap and looked over her notes. Somebody was funding the protesters. Somebody with a foreign accent. That didn't mean it was a foreign organisation behind it. Could be a new immigrant with an anti-nuclear ideology but it did explain how the intensity had been maintained. Normally protesters would gather in force a day or two before the event and carry it through until the submarine left. But this had been different. She wondered just how widespread the funding might be.

Then she turned her thoughts to the conversation she had had with Brian Cunningham. She decided she should mention it to Brian. A little quid pro quo. If the police could bring pressure to bear on the funders it might bring an end to the violence that was becoming a daily occurrence.

Wiki gave the Range Rover a cursory glance as it cruised past. It cut in front of him, forced him to brake then sped forward. He gave thought to yelling assholes but he countered the thought with his self-imposed rule never to talk to himself out loud. The men in the Range Rover would never hear him in any case.

He returned his attention to the conversations taking place on the radio talk show. Should overweight people have to pay for two seats on a plane? Wiki nodded his head. He thought so. The last time he flew he was crushed against the window by a blob of a guy. If the blob had two seats it would have been a more comfortable flight. The minimum they could have done was put him in the aisle seat.

Wiki slowed as he turned his Kenworth into Felton Mathew Avenue, the Range Rover leading the way.

An expert on dieting had called in. Two slick gear shifts and a controlled coast of his big rig down the slope would take him past the sports complex and then into Panmure. Another few minutes and he would be in the holding yards. He was tired. He would be glad when he was home and tucked up in bed.

Marama had phoned. Her parents had arrived for dinner and wanted to know when he would be home. He had been happy to tell her not until late. Her parents hated him. In their eyes he was not good enough for their daughter and they never missed an opportunity to remind her she could have done better.

Like most truckers he had a love hate relationship with car owners. They had no idea how difficult it was driving trucks – especially trucks the size he drove – and they were oblivious to the frustrations of constant gear changes. And, now, when he had a clear run, the Range Rover began to slow.

Wiki swore under his breath.

The Range Rover's brake lights were flicking on and off. Signalling? There was something wrong with the vehicle. He had closed the gap and was now too close to pull out and go round it. Both vehicles slowly ground to a halt. He rolled down his window and put his head out. No one as yet had got out of the Range Rover. Maybe they had stalled. There was no ignition sound. The driver was not trying to restart it. Aggravated, Wiki opened his door and climbed down from the cab. He walked up to the driver's window. The backseat passenger got out. "Got a problem, mate?" Wiki said turning to him.

"It seems to have stalled," the passenger said. Wiki noted he had an accent. Maybe they were tourists. "Sorry to have stopped you like that."

"No problems. Shit happens." Wiki did not display his aggravation. Better to help them get underway. "I'll help push your vehicle to the side of the road." Wiki offered.

"Can't do that, my friend."

"Why not?"

There were now three men standing outside of the car. Wiki stepped back. Wary.

"I have to get to my depot."

They were watching him. Not making any attempt to push their vehicle to the side of the road. Wiki looked about him; nothing but darkness except for a distant street light. He glanced toward the sanctuary of his truck, wishing he had never left it.

"Okay. Please yourselves. I'll back the truck up and be on my way."

"Sorry. We can't let you do that either." The man standing next to Wiki said. Wiki felt cold sweat dribble down his back. "We are taking your truck."

In his younger days Wiki had been in a gang. He wasn't afraid of a fight. He had been in many scrapes because he would never back down. He'd also been on the wrong side of beatings and carried two scars from bullet wounds in his left leg. But now he was older and slower. There were three of them and one more in the car. He might be able to beat one, maybe two, but not all of them. He straightened his back. Let them come. If he was going to be left in a bloody mess on the side of the road he would make them pay. It was dark. He could get lucky.

"I know what you are thinking, my friend." The speaker went on and moved closer to Wiki, "And it would be very silly for you to try."

Even in the limited light Wiki had no trouble making out the shape of the shotgun that one of the men was now resting on the bonnet.

"Search him," the speaker said.

The third man patted Wiki down. He took Wiki's mobile phone and then stepped away. They were hijacking his truck. Were they now going to kill him? He was mentally preparing himself for his death. He turned and faced the man holding the shotgun.

"Okay. Get it over with." Then he thought, "Not in the face. My wife will have to identify the body."

"You are a brave man," the speaker said. "I respect that but do not worry. We are not going to kill you. I want you to turn around and walk back the way you came. Do not turn around and do not do anything stupid. I know you will be insured for your truck and your load, so there is nothing here worth dying for is there?"

"No," Wiki whispered feeling a little weak in the knees. Then he repeated the word a little more clearly.

"Good. It is good we understand each other. Now on your way." Wiki hesitated. Maybe they would shoot him in the back. "Go on." The speaker repeated. "It will be okay."

Wiki began walking slowly at first and then a little quicker but careful not to run. At any moment he expected to be propelled forward by the blast of two barrels. As he passed the end of his trailer he increased his pace. He heard the sound of his truck motor revving. He kept moving forward. He was not going to turn round even though he could now hear the two vehicles moving away. He started to run. He was going to run all the way home. He wanted to water the flowers. Yes, he thought, when he got home he would water his flowers. Marama would think he was mad but who cared. He was still alive. He was even looking forward to talking to her mother.

~

Brian Cunningham walked into Moana Te Kanawa's office, a coffee in each hand. He placed a cup on the table and holding onto the second sat in the chair against the wall.

"Barbara Heywood phoned last night," Cunningham said.

"Looking for a story?"

"No. With information."

"Really?"

"One of her staff was at the Chelsea Bar drinking with a crowd of protesters. The anti-nuclear lot."

"I wondered where most of them disappeared to at night. Now we know," Moana said with a wry smile. "Mind you it does surprise me. It's not cheap drinking in any of the city clubs these days."

"Drinks loosen tongues. Some of them started boasting about how they were being paid to protest."

"Really?" Moana looked interested.

"It seems that less than a month ago our fledgling anarchists hit pay dirt. Someone not only gave them a lot of money to hire and equip an office but for salaries as well. Apparently they are not alone. There are a number of these groups across the city."

"Who's funding them?" Moana asked. "Did this assistant get a name?"

"No, only that the man paying out the money is foreign but they don't know where from."

"Professional protesters are not uncommon, Brian. The nuclear issue is a hot topic. It's not beyond the realms of possibility that someone with a pocket full of money and strong feelings on the subject would be prepared to spend to ensure the message to government was clear. Anyway, it really hasn't much to do with us. Pass it on to someone else. No crime is being committed. Not as far as I can assess."

"Normally I'd agree, but after talking with Barbara my gut is telling me it's all just a little odd. Her assistant found out that the money comes from a guy with an accent. I can't help thinking it's too much of a coincidence that someone is paying for protests at the same time as Zahar Akbar lands in our city. I know it seems a long shot, but after Jeff Bradley confirmed our wannabe killer is an international terrorist it might not be that far-fetched. The protestors blocking the main roads in and out of the city at rush hour is pissing drivers off. Fights are breaking out. It's bound to get uglier and it's tying up police personnel."

Moana frowned and said, "I hear you but that's still a big jump."

"Jeff Bradley knows this terrorist and he's adamant this guy Akbar is up to something. It worries me that he might be right, which is why I'm here getting under your feet. What if the protests are covering up something else? Distracting us from the real goal."

"You know Bradley well enough to accept this theory has merit?"

"Yes. I trust his judgment."

"Fine. But what would be the point of it all?"

"That I can't get my head round as yet. But police resources are stretched. Once the public knows we have terrorists in town it will be impossible. And remember this guy and his brother blew up city squares. Killed lots of people. What if their purpose is to grow larger and larger crowds? That has been pretty much achieved hasn't it?"

Moana paled. That was a scary thought. She had two sons at university. She would make sure they kept well away. "One question, though, why come to New Zealand and blow people up? The rest of the world is a damn sight easier to hide in and escape from."

Cunningham nodded and said, "That's the argument I've been tossing around in my head. It might be I'm way out on the wrong limb and the theory collapses under me. There is an old saying, better to be perceived a fool than do nothing and remove all doubt. Look, exploding a bomb in a public place might not be Akbar's prime objective but that doesn't rule out the possibility he might do it just for the hell of it . . ."

Moana was thoughtful.

"Tonight I'll send Jessica and Red up to the Chelsea to play the happy couple. See if they can make a connection and find the money man."

17.

Jeff gave a wry smile when he saw 'Jeannie's' in large neon lights above the entrance to Quentin's new nightclub. A cunning plan to mollify his wife, but he doubted it would be enough. Jeannie loved her man child but Quentin clubbing the night away was never going to happen long term.

The music was vibrant and bouncy. Not too loud. Jeff couldn't quite work out if the ambience worked or not. But the band was live and in his opinion, pretty good. Not that he considered himself an expert when it came to music but he knew what he liked and the dance floor was full of bobbing heads so he guessed others thought so too. Quentin had managed to gather a sizable crowd to enjoy the free food and booze. Ice buckets sat on tables holding magnums of champagne and extra staff walked between patrons holding plates of neatly displayed finger food in one hand and paper towels in the other. Open bottles of Boundary Fence wines sat on the bar and in the refrigerator behind more wine and more than a dozen varieties of beer and soft drinks.

Mary sat alone in one of the cubicles. She looked cheerful enough. She waved when she saw Jeff and made her way across to him. Her blonde hair was not in her usual ponytail but down across her shoulders. She gave Jeff a hug.

"You look great," Jeff said, and meant it.

"I'm better. I'm getting back into training next week. Starting slow, but I need to get back to normality. Going to join me?"

"Let me know the times. Not too early," Jeff said.

If Mary was running he would be there right beside her. He was not letting her out of his sight in public. The security man he had hired to look out for her stood just inside the door. They exchanged nods.

She had her smile back. The blackness around her eye was barely discernible behind the makeup. The police had offered Mary the sanctuary of a safe house until Zahar was caught but she had refused. She was not going to let some asshole tell her how to live her life. Her reaction was no more than Jeff would have expected.

"Top athletes are a tough bunch," he had said to Cunningham. "And none tougher than Mary."

Jeff had decided that if protecting her meant training with her then he would train with her even if he had to ride a bloody bike. She didn't blame him for the attack even though the note showed otherwise. Her graciousness didn't make the guilt go away.

"Have you heard from Ann?" Jeff asked.

"Yes. She's not coping so well," Mary said.

Jeff nodded. She put her arm through his.

"What do you think of Quentin's club?" Mary asked.

"I think Quentin might just make a go of it. But in the end Jeannie will make him sell."

The band switched to a more sedate tune.

"How about a dance?" Mary asked.

She lifted her chin and her blue eyes signalled she wasn't going to take no for an answer. Jeff had spent a good two years wanting to hold Mary in his arms and for two years he had shown great restraint. But, now he wanted to hold her for different reasons. He wanted to make her safe. Hide her from the world.

He allowed Mary to lead him onto the dance floor.

As they moved to the rhythm of the music she moulded her body into his and Jeff wrapped his arms around her. She rested her head on his shoulder. Her hair brushed his cheek. He inhaled aromas of shampoo and perfume that intruded on his imaginings, heightened anticipation and stirrings of arousal. He fought a full-pitched battle with his feelings. Then the music stopped and the silence impacted the moment. Jeff let his arms fall and stepped back.

The band announced a break. Jeff shrugged. "Sorry, looks like no more dancing."

Mary pouted and feigned disappointed. The spontaneity had passed but they stayed standing close to each other almost touching.

Mary stroked Jeff's arm, "Was that so painful?"

Jeff smiled back. "No pain at all."

"Good, so we can have another dance?"

Quentin and Jeannie joined them. Quentin was all smiles.

"Hey, Jeff. What do you think of our nightclub?"

Jeff leaned forward and kissed Jeannie on the cheek. "What does Jeannie think of 'Jeannie's'?"

"I think I've been conned, Jeff," Jeannie said resignedly. "I have a husband who can't have a normal hobby like model trains or golf. He has to live in the past."

"Anytime you want to leave him I'm always available," Jeff said.

"Can I bring the kids as well?"

"Are they house trained?" Jeff said, with a grin.

"I'm going to sit down," Mary said.

She squeezed Jeff's arm. A gentle reminder she was ready to dance as soon as the band started up again.

"I'll come with you," Jeannie said.

Over Quentin's shoulder Jeff saw Brian Cunningham enter. He recognised the woman with him, dressed in the charcoal trouser suit and navy blue blouse, Barbara Heywood. She was taller than she appeared to be on television. The television presenter had been leaving him messages; another journalist wanting an interview him. Barbara Heywood was a notch above the normal jeans and holey sweater brigade. At some stage through the evening she would no doubt corner him.

"Jeff, come to the bar, there's someone I want you to meet," said Quentin.

Jeff followed.

"Mr Esat Krasniqi," Quentin said, introducing the man he tapped on the shoulder. Jeff shook the offered hand. "Esat is a client of mine. He's from Kosovo. Esat, Jeff was in Kosovo not so long ago."

"Really? Which part may I ask?"

"Prishtina."

"I hope it was not too difficult for you?"

"I coped," Jeff said. "How long have you been in New Zealand, Esat?"

"Some years now. I was fortunate enough to come to New Zealand as a refugee."

"You have a business here?"

"Exporting mostly. Back to the Balkans and also the Middle East. I have many contacts in these parts."

"Exporting is a difficult business. I do a bit myself. Do you work on commission?"

"No. I mostly buy and sell. I have more control that way."

Jeff was thoughtful. Buying product and exporting would require a great deal of capital. Not bad for a refugee who would have arrived in New Zealand with only a few dollars in his pocket.

"How did you achieve refugee status? Did you have family here?"

"No. The New Zealand government said they would take one hundred and fifty Kosovans. I was one of the lucky ones."

"And you like it here?"

Esat placed his hand on his chest, "I love New Zealand. It has been very good for me."

"And now Kosovo has gained independence, will you return?"

"No. I have no desire to return. Not now. Before, maybe. A sense of patriotism and all that but politics in the Balkans will always be unreliable. My future is here so I will stay. I have a good life."

"You have a family?"

"My wife and children were killed by the Serbs. I never remarried."

"I'm sorry. I heard many similar stories during my visit."

"It is in the past and I have come to terms with it. I have women of course." He laughed. "I am not going to become a priest. But another family? No. Not again."

"Well enjoy the evening Esat."

Jeff had put it off long enough. He crossed the floor to where Cunningham and Barbara Heywood were sitting. Cunningham was speaking into his mobile. He whispered something into Barbara's ear. She nodded.

"I've been called back to the office," he said to Jeff. "You and I need to talk."

"When you're ready."

Cunningham disappeared through the doors. Jeff looked down at Barbara Heywood.

"Hi, Brian forgot his manners. I'm Jeff Bradley."

"I know who you are, Jeff. Take a seat. You've been ignoring my phone calls."

"I've been busy. Besides, I've nothing further to add to what you probably already know."

"You destroyed a terrorist cell in Kosovo. Pretty big news, Jeff. You're a hero. The people want to know. Hear your story."

"The people have already moved on and so have I. I'm a wine-maker."

"So I've heard. And yet a close friend of yours was almost murdered a few days ago."

Jeff raised an eyebrow. "Cunningham has been telling tales out of school. Are you and he together?"

She laughed.

"No, we're not an item. Quentin sent an invite to our network's food critic. It landed on my desk. I needed a partner and Brian was the last male I spoke to. I made my own way here and Brian waited for me at the door. The perfect gentleman. So are you going to give me an interview?"

Jeff smiled.

"Did Mary Sumner fight off her attacker?"

"Why don't you ask Mary? She's sitting over there."

"I'm an old-fashioned journo. I have scruples. I'll leave her be until she says it's okay to talk. Brian told me mostly everything. Left out a few small details no doubt but I know enough. My viewers would love to hear how a beautiful Olympic medallist beat up on a killer."

"Brian has been chatty."

"We have a pact. He tells me all and I keep my mouth shut. He said you had identified the killer as a terrorist. Someone from Kosovo."

Jeff scratched the back of his head.

Mention of Mary's attacker had him turning his attention back to Esat Krasniqi. He looked over his shoulder. The Kosovan was still standing at the bar nursing a bottle of beer. He seemed decent enough but he *was* Kosovan. Could the world really be that small?

"You're not being very sociable, Jeff," Barbara said breaking into his thoughts. "You're meant to be talking with me, not looking at other women. A girl could get offended."

"Sorry. Not another woman. I was talking to the man standing at the end of the bar earlier. The one in the grey jacket. Something is not right with him."

"Not right. How not right?"

"I'm not sure. Just a feeling. Can I get you another drink?"

"My glass is still half full," Barbara said.

Jeff reached across and tipped the contents of Barbara's glass into the ice bucket.

Her mouth dropped open.

"While I'm getting you a drink I'm going to talk to him. See if I can get a reaction. If I do and he leaves, follow him into the foyer, see what he does. If he leaves the building don't follow, but I think what he might do is go into the foyer to make a phone call. If so, I need to know what is being said, okay?"

"This is a pretty poor attempt at making an impression. A bit too macho for my liking." She forced a laugh. "But what the hell, I'm a journalist. You've got me hooked. The restaurant you take me to when I interview you better be top class."

"If I agree to an interview you get to choose."

"What if he speaks Kosovan or whatever language they speak?"

"It would be either Serbian or Albanian. But if he is speaking to who I think he might phone then he will speak English; the common language between the two. However I could be wrong and nothing will happen, in which case I apologise for tipping out your wine and acting like an asshole."

Jeff walked off towards Esat Krasniqi. He placed the glass on the bar and waved to the barman.

"Hi, Esat. Standing alone. Would you like to join our table?"

"No. Thank you. I'm fine. I enjoy my own company."

"As long as you're having fun."

"I am enjoying the evening very much but I must go soon. Business to attend to. Exporting is never ending."

"There is something I meant to ask you earlier. When you were back in Kosovo did you ever come across a local prosecutor named Avni Leka?"

There was a flicker of the eyes, quickly hidden but there all the same. Jeff saw it and knew he had hit the mark.

"No, I am sorry. I do not know this name."

"How about Halam Akbar or his brother Zahar? Do these names ring a bell?"

"No, I am sorry, I do not know either of these men." Esat licked his top lip. His eyes flicked left and right. "Kosovo might be a small country but there are many people. If you will excuse me for a moment I need to use the bathroom. It is in the foyer I believe."

"Sure, go ahead. I'll catch you later."

Jeff didn't turn to watch Esat leave. He was confident Barbara was too much the professional to not be on his tail. The barman passed Jeff a fresh glass of wine and he carried it back to the table. He smiled when he saw Barbara's chair was empty. She waved from the door. Jeff put the glass of wine on the table and crossed to her.

"He's meeting somebody in fifteen minutes," she said. "He's gone."

"Damn. I used the ferry to get here tonight. I don't have a car."

"We can use mine."

18.

There he is," Barbara said, pointing toward the swiftly moving Esat Krasniqi. "That's my car opposite. The grey Mercedes sports parked outside the pharmacy." She tossed her keys to Jeff. "You can drive. If you get a ticket for speeding or crashing a red light it's on you."

Jeff smiled. Barbara had spirit.

He fumbled the key into the ignition, pulled out and u-turned. Esat had climbed into his car but as yet had not driven off. Jeff pulled over. Esat's brake lights flashed. He moved forward. Jeff let two cars pass then gave chase.

"A white car should be easy enough to keep sight of," Jeff said.

The white Toyota turned into Queen Street and then right onto Customs Street and was soon making its way up Parnell Rise.

"Luckily, for a Saturday night the traffic is light," Jeff said.

Traffic lights opposite the Anglican Church turned red. The two cars between Jeff and Esat turned left on the green arrow signal. Jeff had little choice but close the distance, almost touching the bumper of Esat's Toyota. He held his hand across his face. An instinctive reaction but he doubted Esat could see anything more than a dark outline in his rear-view mirror.

"He's heading for Newmarket," Barbara said.

Jeff kept to the inside lane. Fifty metres before the century-old Jubilee building, now housing the Parnell library and community centre, the Toyota's right blinker flashed and Esat turned into Maunsell, an entry street into the Domain.

"I don't like the look of this," Jeff said, more to himself.

He glanced across at Barbara; her eyes were fixed on the Toyota. She didn't acknowledge she'd heard his comment. Lucky, he thought. He didn't want to worry her, not yet, anyway, but the Domain was a perfect spot for an ambush. In his military days he'd had to study prominent features of Auckland city. As he remembered it the central city park covered more than seventy-five hectares spread out across the crater of the extinct Pukekawa volcano. Not that you'd ever know it was a volcano. Like all Aucklanders, he had been in the park hundreds of times. As a kid he played football on the many sports fields, even been to a concert. He'd been in the winter garden, the cricket pavilion, duck ponds and small copses of trees, but he had never seen the volcano. The crater walls were now camouflaged by trees and housing and further-out roads and commercial buildings.

The one spot Jeff would rather have steered clear of was the kilometre of forest and bush on the seaward side. This was close to where Esat Krasniqi had driven and was now slowing.

Jeff turned off the Mercedes's lights and pulled over. He left the motor idling. Esat moved forward at walking pace.

"What's he up to?" Barbara asked.

"Looking for someone I'd say."

"I guessed that, Jeff. I'm not an idiot. Surely they would have a rendezvous point?"

"Maybe the contact is being cautious. Looking to see if anyone like you and me is following."

"That makes sense, I suppose, but I'm nervous."

Jeff inched closer. Esat pulled over in front of a palm tree. The only one as far as Jeff could see. It was an easily identifiable landmark to use for a meeting spot. Jeff kept his distance. Lights off.

Esat remained in the car.

"Why don't we just call the police, Jeff?"

"Firstly, he hasn't done anything but go for a drive. What would you say to Brian? That you followed a man in a car and you think he should be arrested? Secondly, if these guys operate the way I think they do, individually they will know bits and pieces but no one will know everything. That's how terrorist cells work, but right now I don't know for certain that Esat belongs to one. Anyway, we can always find Esat later but we might never find the man he is meeting if this encounter goes awry. If the contact doesn't get in the car I'm going after him." Barbara touched Jeff's arm. Concerned.

"It's what I'm trained to do," he said.

Barbara's mobile rang. "Barbara Heywood."

"Barbara, its Brian."

Barbara glanced across at Jeff and mouthed, 'Brian Cunningham'. "How can I help, Brian?"

"My call back to the station came to nothing. I was wondering, if you're still at the nightclub and in the mood I might come back, have a drink. What do you think? If you want we could go somewhere for dinner."

"Someone's coming," Jeff whispered.

"Just a moment, Brian."

A stocky, overweight figure emerged from behind the palm tree. Barbara barely dared to breathe.

"If that's not Akbar, it's an associate of his. I'd stake my life on it," Jeff whispered. "And if that's true then I was right all along. Akbar has a reason for being here and he's brought men with him."

"Barbara. Are you there?"

"Please, Brian," Barbara whispered into the phone. "One moment."

She watched as the man moved to the driver's window.

"He's not getting in," Jeff said. "Esat's car is still running. Fuck it." He turned to Barbara. "Stay with the car."

Jeff pushed the door open and climbed out.

"If anything goes wrong get the hell out of here."

"Barbara. Talk to me," Cunningham said. Voice firmer.

Jeff walked at a steady pace towards the white Toyota. Barbara slid across into the driver's seat.

"Jesus. He's going after him," Barbara said into the phone.

"After who?" Cunningham yelled. "Barbara!"

"Sorry, Brian. Jeff and I followed a hunch and it's paid off. Jeff believes a man working for your potential killer-come-terrorist is not more than a hundred metres away. He's gone after him."

"He's bloody well what? Where the hell are you?"

"Maunsell Street. The last street on the right before the Newmarket library. We're parked at the entrance to the Domain where Maunsell cuts across Titoki. Outside the Parnell tennis club. The man came out from some trees."

"I'm on my way. Do not move!" Cunningham screamed and rang off.

Barbara dropped the phone onto the passenger seat. She held her right hand over her mouth. Holding in her breath. Eyes wide. Fearful that the slightest sound might alert the men Jeff was closing in on.

Fifteen metres from Esat's car Zahar's man looked up. Jeff increased his pace. The man talking to Esat looked about him. Uncertain. He stepped back from the car.

The tyres of Esat's car spun on the loose metal, flinging gravel like shrapnel from a grenade as it accelerated forward.

"Hold it right there," Jeff yelled.

The barrel-shaped man turned and ran into the park. Jeff chased after him.

"Bloody hell." Barbara accelerated to the point where she had seen Jeff disappear and stopped, then turned off the engine.

19.

Red drove fast.

Cunningham had not been able to get Barbara on her mobile. The number he dialled kept switching to message. If what she said was true and Zahar Akbar was about she was in serious danger. It surprised him how much getting to her and protecting her had prompted his reaction. Reinforcements and coordinating roadblocks should have taken precedence. Bad leadership. He slapped the top of the dashboard in relief when Red screeched the car across Titoki Street into the Domain and saw Barbara standing next to her sports car.

Brian ran to her.

"Are you okay?" he asked. She nodded. "Good. Now tell me. What the hell are you doing here and what happened?" He looked in the car as he spoke. "And where the hell is Bradley?"

Barbara quickly related the meeting in Quentin's nightclub.

"As I said on the phone, the guy who met the car saw Jeff and ran off and Jeff chased after him."

"Jesus. Red, ring through to the Tactics Group. I want this bloody park surrounded right now. Every available man. Contact Senior Sergeant Te Kanawa and tell her to take everyone off the switchboards if she needs more personnel."

"You don't have that authority, sir," Red protested.

"No. But she can get it."

Even as he spoke he was already thinking it was an impossible task. How do you surround something the size of the Domain with reduced staff?

"Barbara. I thought we had an agreement. Sharing, remember?" He opened his mouth to say more but thought better of it "Forget it. Which way did they go?"

She pointed. "Down through this park, across the bottom road and into the trees exactly where I'm pointing."

"Okay. Now listen to me. Go back to your apartment. Wait there. No arguments. Just do it."

"Brian, I don't need a nursemaid. I'm a journalist, for Christ's sake. This is a top story. And I'm here on the spot. I'm not going anywhere."

"You're also interfering in police business. Do you want me to have you arrested?"

She glared at him. Stood her ground.

"All right. Stay here. Go no further. Got it?"

She held his eyes.

"All right. Stay here for your own bloody safety. Can you at least do that?"

She nodded.

Cunningham turned and ran to the spot she had pointed to. Barbara watched until Cunningham was lost from sight then spun on her heel and walked back to her car.

~

Jeff cursed himself for the idiot he was as he crashed his way through the trees. Chasing a man who might be an international terrorist and who was probably armed, into the bush, in the dark, had to top them all. If the runner had a knife or another weapon of sorts it would be bad enough but if he had a firearm it would be a one-sided contest. Branches tore at his shirt sleeves and scratched at his face; thousands of wooden hands with unclipped fingernails.

Jeff slowed to stealthy steps. The crashing sound ahead stopped. Any movement Akbar's man made would be heard easy enough unless he had the eyes of a cat and could step over twigs and he hadn't and couldn't. Jeff reached down and felt about for a rock. Anything he could use as a weapon.

Ten minutes passed and neither Jeff nor the man he hunted had moved. Jeff was patient. Time was on his side. He spun at the sound of footsteps behind him. His fists clenched, he struck a boxers pose. Ready. How the hell had the bastard circled him?

"Jeff?" he heard his name whispered.

"Brian?"

"Of course it's me. What do you think you're doing?"

Jeff didn't answer.

"Where is he?"

"In here somewhere. He's stopped moving about."

"You have a plan?"

"We were trained to wait," Jeff said. "So we'll wait. He'll have to make a move sooner or later and we'll hear him. I take it you have men on the way."

Sirens could be heard in the distance. "Here comes the cavalry now," Cunningham said.

Twigs crunched a few metres away. A shadow flitted to the left. Jeff ran after it. Zahar's man was quick but Jeff was quicker. As they came together Jeff wrapped his arms round his opponent and they tumbled down the sloping incline. He almost lost his hold but Jeff clung to kicking legs.

Then everything went black.

"Jeff, Jeff, speak to me," Cunningham yelled.

"Stop shaking me," Jeff groaned. "What the hell happened?"

"You've lost your edge, that's what happened. Too long out of the service. You've gone soft."

Jeff sat up and held his head. Cunningham knelt beside him.

"Are you okay?"

"Except for injured pride, I'm okay." He ran fingers across his forehead. "I have a lump on my head."

"No more than you bloody deserve. You let him get the better of you. I'm disappointed."

"Thanks for the support. And why the hell didn't you go after him?"

"Believe me it was my first thought but I had a man down, namely you, and I couldn't very well leave you dying in the woods. We never leave a man behind, remember?"

Jeff accepted Cunningham's hand and allowed himself to be hauled to his feet. He felt his face; blood was running from his nose. The sound of sirens now came from all directions.

"Sounds like an awful lot of cops arriving. Maybe you'll get lucky?"

"My guess is he's a smart guy. He'll get out somewhere."

~

Barbara smiled when she saw them but, as Jeff drew closer, she frowned.

"Jeff. Are you all right? You look awful."

"I think he broke my nose," Jeff moaned with a nasally sound.

Three police cars had formed a road block.

"Did he get away?" Barbara asked.

Jeff nodded, and then winced.

"I'm afraid so," Cunningham said. "I'll get the dogs in. He's still in there somewhere. Barbara, can you take Jeff to the emergency clinic then drop him down at the ferry terminal? I can't spare anyone. It's more than he deserves. He never was one to follow an order."

"It wasn't obeying the order I had a problem with, it was the order itself."

Cunningham shrugged. "I'll talk to you two later."

Barbara opened the passenger door.

"Let's get you to the hospital," Barbara said.

"I'll be fine. I've suffered far worse. Just get me out of here."

She looked at her watch. "You'll never catch a ferry at this hour. You better come home with me. I'll tend to your wounds, soldier, and I have whisky."

~

Inside her apartment Barbara pointed to the lounge. "Take a seat. I'll get us a drink."

Jeff collapsed on the couch. After a few minutes Barbara came through carrying a tray with a bottle of whisky and two glasses and a small bucket of ice.

"Do you think the police will have him by now?" Barbara asked.

She dropped ice into both glasses and poured whisky over it.

"He'll get away," Jeff stated. Despondent. "He was in survival mode. Makes you stronger, more cunning. I'm rusty, out of my depth, totally inept. So now we're back to square one. Both our leads to Akbar got away."

"I have a spare room."

Jeff managed a smile. Another grimace. "You're asking me to spend the night with you."

"Consider yourself fortunate. It's a rare invitation. I value my privacy."

"When a beautiful woman and a celebrity to boot asks me to spend the night with her, I'm hardly likely to turn her down."

Jeff was suddenly exhausted. The second whisky was working its magic. When his head hit the pillow he drifted into a sleep as deep as a coma.

Sometime later, Jeff awoke to sunlight streaming through the curtains.

The bathroom was across the hall. He checked his face. His eye and nose were tender but not swollen. The lump on the side of his head felt like the size of a goose egg. The asshole must have hit him with a rock. He touched the swelling and winced. It hurt but the nose hadn't broken. He used the shower then threw on his grubby clothes. Freshened, he ventured out into to the lounge. Barbara was cooking. She had dressed in tracksuit bottoms and a T-shirt. Casual but cute. How he imagined a Sunday morning might be if they were in a relationship. Nice, was the word that came to mind.

She smiled when she saw him.

"Good morning. Hope you're in the mood for breakfast."

"I'm starving."

He sat at the breakfast bar. The aroma of freshly brewed coffee tickled his senses. Barbara placed a cup in front of him then poured the coffee.

"How's the head?" Barbara asked.

"Not so bad. Any word from Brian?"

"He phoned earlier. He's on his way to pay me a visit. I don't think we're his favourite people."

The doorbell rang.

"Speak of the devil. I'll bet that's him now."

Barbara pulled the frying pan off the element and went to the door. Cunningham had obviously been up all night. He walked past her. She closed the door and followed him into the lounge. He hesitated when he saw Jeff. He looked back at Barbara. Both knew what he was assuming. He glared at Jeff. Jeff sipped on his coffee. Not intimidated.

"Brian, would you like a coffee? Breakfast?" Barbara asked.

"A coffee. Thank you." He kept his eyes on Jeff.

"How's your head?"

"I'll live. He got away I take it?"

"Yes."

Barbara said, "I'm sorry about last night, Brian. No one meant to go behind your back. It was a spur of the moment thing."

"Is that the way it was, Jeff, a spur of the moment thing? This guy Akbar was one of the men responsible for this friend of yours killed in Kosovo. Are you sure you didn't have a little revenge in mind?"

"It had crossed my mind. But no. Quentin introduced me to a man named Esat Krasniqi. He's a refugee from Kosovo. For a man who had been in New Zealand for only a few years he had gotten rich very quickly. I played a hunch and mentioned a few names and it spooked him. Barbara had a car. I didn't. The decision had to be made there and then. We followed him to the park. The rest you know."

"This Krasniqi. Do you know how to make contact with him?"

"Quentin can help you there."

"I'd better go see him." Brian put his cup on the counter. He looked to leave then hesitated. "Can I drop you somewhere, Jeff?"

"Thanks. But after breakfast I'll amble down to the ferry."

"Thank you for the coffee, Barbara. If I think of anything else I'll call you later."

Barbara showed him to the door. When she returned she eyed Jeff. He held her stare.

"I feel terrible."

"Really? Why?" Jeff asked.

"I think Brian thought that he and I might get together last night. I saw his face when he saw you sitting there. I can imagine the thoughts racing through his head. Not that it's any of his business what I do. But it makes me uncomfortable the way you are with each other, and your being here this morning might have made it worse."

"You can relax, Barbara. Really. What you saw between us had nothing to do with whether you and I slept together. Brian and I go back a few years. Let's just say we aren't the best of friends."

Barbara picked up her coffee and cradled it. "Are you going to enlighten me?"

Jeff smiled. "I can't. Sorry."

"Of course you can."

"No, really I can't. What happened between us is under the Official Secrets Act. Sorry."

"Are you for real?"

Jeff nodded.

"Now I really am intrigued. I'm a journalist. Secrets are what I uncover. I'll be watching you, Jeff Bradley."

20.

Esat Krasniqi pulled down his warehouse roller door for the last time. Before he climbed into his car he took a moment for one last look at the building he had occupied for the last three years. There would be no returning. He had a pang of regret for the staff. They had been loyal to him. Helped build his business. He would miss life in New Zealand. It was a beautiful country. He could not return to Kosovo but Albania was large enough for him to get lost in. For Albanian Kosovans, it was the mother country and he would be welcomed like a lost brother. He regretted that he had been forced to betray his new country but Avni Leka had ensured neither he nor the others had any choice.

Zahar's men had managed to get everything into three vehicles the size of DHL courier vans. It had meant manhandling equipment out of the crates. It would have been much easier to forklift the crates onto small trucks. Two of the items had weighed more than two hundred kilos. But Sami Hadani insisted it was less conspicuous in the vans and everyone knew better than argue with Sami. It was done now and they would move out at five-minute intervals.

Sami had not mentioned his driving away and leaving the big man behind in the Domain the previous night. He had at least stayed in the vicinity, and when called upon had collected Hadani in the hospital grounds that backed onto the Domain. But cold eyes had met his when Sami climbed into the passenger seat and the atmosphere in the car turned to ice. Esat had shivered throughout the drive back to Sami's house. He would have preferred it if Sami had yelled at him. But what the hell, all had turned out to the good in the end and Sami was safe. Maybe that was it for Sami. He had lived that sort of life in Kosovo and Serbia – near misses went with the territory.

The details of his escape route out of New Zealand were only known to Sami and Zahar Akbar. Esat would learn the arrangements when they met up. Until then he would hide out with Akbar's men. The police would be crawling all over the building in the next few hours. It would take time to find it. Neither the factory nor his home was in his name.

As he drove down the lane and onto the street he tried to think if there was anything he might have forgotten that might lead police to the others. There was his customer list on the computers but that was in customs as well. They had been good clients. Never argued over price and always paid on time. He and Avni Leka had communicated from time to time but then he had spoken to hundreds over the years. He doubted his communications would lead anywhere.

Right now all that was important was that the equipment from the stolen container had been extracted. In another ten minutes it would be in a new and secure location. The new warehouse was held in a trust. He had assured Zahar that it was untraceable but of course if the police knew where to look they would eventually find it. However, he was not about to say such a thing to Zahar Akbar. He feared the terrorist leader as much as he feared Sami Hadani and was already worried at Akbar's reaction to his leading the police into the Domain. He assumed the only reason he still lived was because Sami had escaped. Praise to Allah that he had. He wasn't about to give Zahar a reason to change his mind.

~

Zahar Akbar tilted the china pot and poured a fresh cup of lemon tea. A chocolate biscuit buried under shortbread and crackers caught his eye. He dug it out and bit off the end, then leaned back in his seat. Freshened from a few hours shuteye he sifted through the information bouncing about in his head. Sami had evaded capture. A lucky break.

This man Bradley. How did he know to ask Esat Krasniqi such questions? What made him think Esat would have any knowledge of the operation? The good news was that he had mentioned the name of Zahar Akbar. It meant the police had told him of the message left in the blonde's house. Esat said the blonde and Bradley danced together like lovers. He was right to choose her. She wasn't just someone he knew from the lawyer's office. Good. He would find her again and this time she would not be so lucky.

The only answer was that he had known Esat was Kosovan and the approach and questioning in the nightclub was a fishing expedition. That fool Esat had taken the bait. What else had he said? This Bradley had managed to find a way to his men when the entire New Zealand police force had failed. Was it dumb luck?

He decided to phone his boss, Avni Leka. Leka did not like surprises. He set up the satellite phone. Avni would not allow the use of any phone that could be traced.

The call was answered on the second ring. "It's very late. I was sleeping. What do you want?"

Zahar ignored Leka's belligerent tone. What did it matter to him if the man had the manners of a pig? Money in the bank was all Zahar cared about and Leka made certain his account overflowed. He had met Avni Leka for the first time in Kosovo. But he and his brother had worked for Avni a number of years before that. When his brother, Halam, and Leka tried to escape across the Macedonian border, Halam had been killed and Leka managed to evade capture and escape to Italy. When he made his own escape from the Americans he had left a series of messages on long-arranged secret email addresses. Avni, now hiding out in Italy, had talked him into taking over the running of the operation left vacant by the death of Halam. He agreed because he needed the money, and Avni had the resources to keep him hidden, turn him into a ghost. And now the ghost had come out of hiding. But Avni Leka was a banker, no more than that. He did not feel inferior to him and he certainly was not about to be intimidated by him.

"We have a problem."

Zahar quickly related the events of the previous evening. "This man Bradley approached one of your exporters and started asking a lot of questions. He mentioned your name and mine and my brother Halam. He knows I am here. Sami Hadani was led into a trap. It could have been messy if he had been caught. Esat Krasniqi has been compromised. They will be after him. They will know where he lives and his business address by now but everything is moved."

"Bradley is not to be underestimated. Your brother did, and paid the price."

At the mention of his brother's death Zahar sucked air through his teeth. It made a whistling sound. His fists clenched as he rose from his chair and paced the room.

"Again he is making a nuisance of himself," Avni continued. "Normally I would not support a man seeking to avenge his brother if it interfered with my business, but now he has found you . . . This man is not a man who will go away. I think there is no choice. You have my permission to get rid of him. The mission is too far advanced. I can't have it jeopardised by a meddling New Zealander. But be careful."

"Don't worry. I will not make any mistakes."

"Maybe it is better that you do not do it. Send some of your men. How is the rest of the project progressing?"

"Under control."

Avni Leka rang off.

Zahar put the phone back into its container and packed it away under the loose floor board. He returned to pacing the room. Avni Leka was right of course. Disposing of Bradley should be a task for his men. Reluctantly he would give up his desire to see this man's eyes pleading for mercy as he drove a knife into his heart. The operation was too important. Right now it did not matter who killed him as long as he was dead.

He turned his attention to Esat Krasniqi. The fool had outlived his usefulness. His stupidity had endangered them all.

~

Avni Leka was unable to return to sleep. Once again the New Zealander Bradley was entangled in his fortunes. Halam Akbar had told him as they attempted to escape in his car across the Macedonian border that men like Bradley had a habit of getting in your face at inopportune times. They needed to be eliminated. Now the words had come back to haunt him. When Bradley and his friends had destroyed his Kosovo operation he had lost his wife, his mistress, and worse, he was now in hiding. All international organisations knew his identity and were looking for him and any day might be his last.

The loss of funds had hurt his organisation but he had recovered. The heads of the terror groups he worked on behalf of had been unhappy but had responded to his moment of crisis. Avni was much too valuable to them to be lost. They respected his genius in establishing a worldwide network of terrorist bases. His links with the Albanian mafia in Italy had secured him a new home on the outskirts of Rome and his millions ensured discretion and anonymity. The ruthless Albanians were feared by their counterparts from Sicily, and Avni and his men grew more powerful by the day. He had woven them into an efficient criminal and security unit.

The blood of many hundreds on his hands was something he had gotten used to. He had no real hatred of anyone. That had dissipated long ago. The dead were only numbers on a balance sheet to him.

But now he had new clients seeking his unique services.

He was moving on to a newer and bolder initiative, and the success of the New Zealand operation would ensure a demand for greater payments than previously asked for. Bradley now threatened it. Well so be it. He might have been prepared to let him be to protect the mission but the New Zealander had forced his hand. He could not stand aside and allow Bradley to bumble his way across the path of the mission and wreck everything as he had done in Kosovo.

21.

Cunningham dozed on the settee in Moana's office; half his body on the settee, his legs on a chair. He was not exactly comfortable, but some wriggling had made it bearable. Barbara Heywood came to mind. The shape of her mouth. Bradley had stayed the night. Had they slept together? Tension and stress could be emotionally disruptive, affect judgment. It sometimes brought people together who might never cross paths otherwise. The thought of Bradley and Barbara together irritated him. And that was a surprise. He had never been good with women. If he had left his run too late then so be it. However he could not deny he had feelings for her. And in the back of his mind he hoped to hell Bradley would fall down a lift shaft.

The squad re-assembled in the crime room. A few hours of sleep had not helped. Elbows on the table supported heads drooping onto hands. Eyes peered through half-closed lids. Moana sympathised but it couldn't be helped. Catch the bad guys, and then they could go to bed for a week.

"There has been a development and we need to act quickly. One of the men Jeff Bradley chased last night was a Mr Esat Krasniqi.

"Mr Krasniqi is an Auckland businessman. He owns two properties, a home in Glendowie and a warehouse in Mount Wellington. Warrants to search both premises will be available in the next few minutes. We'll split into two teams. Inspector Cunningham will lead one and I will lead the other. Inspector, you take the warehouse if you will, I'll take the house." Cunningham nodded, grateful Moana had included him. "If, for some reason, Mr Krasniqi is still hanging about then there is every reason to believe that he might have company. Armed company."

She paused a moment. All eyes were now wide open.

"You will draw weapons and wear protective vests. Any questions?"

"Isn't this a job for the Inspector's anti-terrorist unit?"

"Yes, it is. Any other questions?"

Everyone looked from one to the other, uncertain. "Okay. I know how it looks but this is our investigation. Do you guys really want someone else to take over?" No response. "We don't know the home and the warehouse are occupied. Let's play it by ear. If we see a bunch of bad guys with guns we'll call in the heavy squad."

Red grinned. "Sergeant, it's not that we aren't willing but we're not soldiers. The Inspector might be used to this stuff but the rest of us have never been to war."

Cunningham smiled.

Moana said, "Point taken, Red. As I said, any sign of armed men and I'm sure the Inspector will call in the cavalry. Okay?"

The squad filed out, unconvinced.

~

Cunningham was in the lead vehicle. A chained gate blocked the entrance into the warehouse.

"What do you think, Red?"

"It looks empty to me."

Cunningham studied the fifty metres of sealed car park his team needed to cross to reach the building's outer wall. The warehouse was a single storey with offices at the far end. Cunningham breathed a sigh of relief. A two-floor administration block would have given a gunman an advantaged field of fire. He wouldn't mention that to his team. Red gave him a quick look. Cunningham ignored him. He was not about to tell Red they could be walking into a trap. At the gate end of the warehouse was a roller door, 'Deliveries Only' painted in red lettering on a white board bolted to the wall above it. To the side of the door was a blue knob that looked like a doorbell. No vehicles in sight and no sign of movement inside. But Cunningham knew appearances could be deceiving. He was trained to be perceptive and right now his gut told him they were too late. The goose had gone.

"Okay, Red. Get the bolt cutters out of the boot and get rid of that chain. Tell the other car to go round the back and block any exits."

"Will do."

Cunningham remained watchful. It took a few seconds and a number of grunts before Red had cut through the chain. He pulled back the gates and waited for the lead car to drive forward. He climbed into it, dropping the bolt cutters onto the floor. The cars sped into the compound, Cunningham's targeting the administration block. He and Red leapt from the car as it slowed. Weapons drawn, they dashed the last few metres and flattened themselves against the wall. Red peered in through the window. Shook his head at Cunningham. No sign of any occupants.

The office doors were secured with deadlocks.

"I'll get the sledgehammer," Red said.

Cunningham stood, gun at arm's length and trained on the windows. Red swung the sledgehammer against the lock. Wood splintered exposing the lock mechanism but brass teeth maintained a tenuous hold. A determined Red raised his size ten police issue boot and smashed the door open.

"Well, if there is someone inside they'll know we're here," Cunningham said. He waited for Red to draw his pistol. "Cover me. But stay back. Any shooting get the hell out." He turned to the men standing back. "You two get behind the car and keep your weapons trained in this direction. If you hear shooting, don't shoot Red."

That brought a smile.

Cunningham entered. They were in a small reception area. There were two doors, one to the offices, the other to the warehouse. Two doors further along had male and female toilet symbols. Cunningham pointed to the office door. Red nodded and moved forward. Cunningham knelt on the floor in front of the door his weapon raised.

Red, against the wall reached out and pushed at the door. It swung open.

No activity. Red dived through the door, rolling over and coming up on one knee. No gunfire. Cunningham flicked on a light switch. The office was empty. They cleared the warehouse next, also deserted.

"Well done, Red."

Red grinned. "Thanks, boss."

"I need to tell you this, Red, and I hope you didn't learn what you did in basic training, but you don't need all that roll along the floor rigmarole. Anyone in the room could have emptied a magazine into you before you were ready to shoot back. That's for the movies. Next time just dive through the door, weapon outstretched and shoot anything that moves. Okay?"

Red pursed his lips then made to say something but didn't. He holstered his handgun and brushed dust off the front of his trousers.

A truck with a trailer holding a shipping container filled 70 percent of the warehouse. Nothing unusual in that, Cunningham ruminated, after all it was an exporting company. He told one of the two constables securing the entrance to call through the truck license plates. "Then the two of you go close the gate and stay there, I don't want anyone entering without my authority."

Cunningham and Red moved along the vehicle and past its trailer. Near the roller door were four mattresses. Unfinished cups of coffee covered an upturned fruit carton acting as a table. A number of chairs surrounded it and in the corner sat a gas cooker.

"I think there have been campers here," Cunningham said.

"Looks like it."

The doors of the container were open and it was empty. There were opened crates spread over the floor.

"If I was a betting man," Red started, "I would say there was something very interesting in the back of this truck."

Cunningham's mobile rang.

"Brian Cunningham speaking."

"Inspector, it's Moana. How is it your end?"

"Signs of activity. Campers in the factory but no bodies."

"You'd better get over to Krasniqi's house. We have him."

"On my way. Red, you take charge. Make sure no one touches anything. I want forensics in here ASAP.

It was a fifteen-minute drive from the warehouse to Esat Krasniqi's home in Riddell Road, Glendowie. Even without knowing the correct address it would have been easy enough to find. There were four police cars outside, two camera crews and almost everyone in the neighbourhood by Cunningham's reckoning. Moana had called in reinforcements for crowd control.

The house was two-storied and set back off the road. Lots of trees. Very nice, Cunningham thought. This was an expensive part of town. He parked then walked up the footpath. Moana stood on terracing which ran the length of the house issuing orders. She waved when she saw him.

"Where is he?" Cunningham asked, stepping onto the terracing.

"Upstairs. Follow me."

Esat was lying on the bed. His arms spread. A human cross. He was very dead.

"Jesus," Cunningham whispered. He moved closer and saw it immediately. A black marker pen lay beside the body. Zahar Akbar had used it to write a message across Esat's chest: 'Another one on your head Bradley.' Barbara Heywood's half-hearted supposition had come true. Now they really did have a killer on the loose.

~

Wiki Herewini was ecstatic when he hung up the phone. He went back into the bedroom and woke Marama.

"Good news," he said. "That was the police. They've found my truck."

"That's wonderful," she said sleepily. Then, as she laid her head back on the pillow, "But I'm not certain I want my husband out alone at night driving the streets of Auckland any more."

~

Leaning against the window frame in the crime room, Cunningham looked out across the city. For the first time in weeks the protesters and the nuclear submarine were not the lead television news story. A killer roamed the streets of Auckland and had claimed his second victim. The headline annoyed the hell out of Cunningham because Esat was really the first murder. Why the police hierarchy had seen fit to issue such a press release was beyond his comprehension. This should have been kept under wraps. At moments like this he missed the military. It also meant he might be moved aside. Classified as a murder, the hunt for Zahar Akbar clearly came under the jurisdiction of Moana and her team. Without the terrorism label attached to it, nor any evidence of it, it was a murder investigation. The Tactics Group had no place unless called upon when Akbar was found.

Cunningham had sympathy for Senior Sergeant Moana Te Kanawa. She wasn't the type to play games with the press and had made herself unavailable for comment. The police had public relations personnel. They could deal with it but public image was all part of the career-building exercise and right now her investigation had become high profile. If she didn't step up someone else would. She had surprised him when she chose to go it alone when they raided Krasniqi's warehouse. The Special Tactics Group should have been called in. If it had gone awry it would have wrecked her career. That it hadn't was a feather in her cap. But the Moana he knew was a by the book copper. He doubted she would take such a risk again.

Pressure from the media would bring pressure from above. Journalists would demand to know why the police had not informed the public of the danger, arguing that the public had a right to protect themselves. What were the police doing to catch the murderer? And why had the identikit not been released earlier? The usual diatribe when journalists went on a rant to have themselves viewed as crusaders for good at the expense of the police. It would blow over when a new headline came along. In the meantime Moana would bear the brunt of it and if it ever came out that it was he who had asked her to withhold the information then his own career might be on the line. But it would never be made public. Moana would not defend herself and point fingers. She was a leader and leaders carried the can for their decisions. He owed the detective senior sergeant.

The identikit picture now splashed across all newspapers and television news programmes generated the response from the public that Cunningham had feared. Calls swamped the police switchboards and flooded the emergency lines. A local employment agency offered temps at a reduced rate. The district commander had little choice but to accept. It seemed every single one of Auckland's million plus citizens had sighted the killer.

Moana had asked her superiors for more manpower to broaden her investigative reach. The reply was as expected. None to spare. Professional criminal gangs, aware for some time police resources could not cope, had stepped up their activities. Burglaries, shoplifting, car thefts and robberies were increasing at an alarming rate. Now, from here on in until the submarine left New Zealand waters, crime might become the perfect storm. Cunningham gave thought to sinking the bloody thing himself.

The detective team would now focus on capturing Akbar as a murderer and this muddied Cunningham's waters. Moana would be forced to follow procedure because when they caught him and it went to court any aspect of the legal process not adhered to might see their case tossed. She had been caught with her panties down for withholding information and she wouldn't let that happen again.

That made his ability to investigate the terrorist cells almost impossible; his tactics team were not detectives. He decided he would hang with Moana for as long as he was permitted. It made him feel like a bird on a perch waiting to swoop on any crumbs of information tossed his way. After searching Krasniqi's warehouse there was little doubt Zahar Akbar had a team. Jeff Bradley had been right. Something else was going on and the something else had to do with a team of terrorists. If so, what? For the moment it was all conjecture. He stabbed his silver-plated letter opener through the forehead of the photo of Zahar Akbar pinned to the corkboard.

22.

Jeff pushed through the doors to Quentin Douglas and Associates offices at 8.30am. It surprised him to see Mary sitting behind her desk. A security guard sat on a leather chair reading a magazine. He glanced up, saw it was Jeff then turned back to the magazine and continued reading.

"Good morning," Jeff said.

He received a glare and then a worried look.

"The bruising looks worse than it really is," Jeff said.

Mary came out from behind her desk and gave him a hug, then she touched the side of his face.

"I'll be fine. In a few days it'll be gone."

"Neither Quentin nor I are very happy with you. Disappearing the way you did on Saturday night. He wants to know what you were up to. So do I, for that matter. You promised me another dance. A girl doesn't like rejection. You'll have me thinking I'm a wilting flower and you don't love me."

Jeff gave Mary a peck on the cheek.

"You never need worry on that score. Next time I promise I'll be back for the next dance," he said.

When Jeff walked into Quentin's office he received a similar reaction.

"Jesus what happened to you?"

Jeff sat down.

"I had a run-in with one of Akbar's men. I came off second best."

"He came looking for you?"

"No, I went after him." Jeff quickly related the events of Saturday night.

"So Esat Krasniqi was associated with the killer?" Jeff nodded. "That might explain this," Quentin said.

Quentin laid the front page of the morning paper across his desk. 'Serial killer on the loose' ran the headline.

Jeff snatched the paper from Quentin.

"Esat Krasniqi was found murdered yesterday," Quentin said.

Jeff sat back in his chair.

"My fault I suppose. Playing amateur detective exposed him. Akbar did the rest. Well, Krasniqi learned the hard way. Sleep with wild dogs and one day they'll rip your throat out," Jeff said, dropping the newspaper on the desk. "How was the opening night? Sorry I missed the main event."

"A roaring success," Quentin grinned.

"And Jeannie?"

"She's coming round."

Jeff nodded but wasn't convinced that Jeannie would ever come round.

"Any news from Rebecca's lawyers this morning? Are they still pushing to sell my vineyard?"

Quentin pursed his lips, "Not a word, I'm afraid. Until I hear otherwise your ex-wife is still going ahead with the auction."

Jeff stood up.

"I'd better get up to the police station. I have to meet with Brian Cunningham and Barbara Heywood. Now Krasniqi is dead, Brian won't be a happy chappy. Then I'm off out to the vineyard. Whatever you do, Quentin, keep your security in place until this is over. I'm sure with Akbar's face plastered everywhere he will stay low. But not for long."

~

Barbara was shown through to Moana's office, now seemingly Cunningham's. The constable informed her Cunningham would be along in a few minutes. She scanned through the pages of a magazine. When Jeff walked in she dumped it on the coffee table.

"You still look like shit," she said.

"Thanks for the compliment. Believe me, it looks worse than it feels." He tried a smile but it hurt and he rubbed his jaw. "Well, getting there anyway."

"When Brian phoned and insisted I come here I said I was worried about you. After what happened to Esat Krasniqi, who knows what Akbar might do next. But Brian said not to worry. You can take care of yourself. I wanted to believe him but by the look of your face I'm not so sure."

"It was dark, I couldn't see much and that gave him an unfair advantage," Jeff laughed, fending off the sarcastic remark.

"Don't be a chump, Jeff. Krasniqi will have told Akbar you set him up. You need to be careful."

Jeff nodded. His mobile beeped to tell him he had received a message. "Excuse me a moment."

Barbara studied Jeff as he checked his messages. For the first time she saw it. Determination. Defiance. He would win no matter what the odds. Protect what was his. No one would stop him. It wasn't bravery as such although he had already proven he had courage. No, it was something else. At the height of a crisis where a normal person would be experiencing fear or at least anxiety, Jeff Bradley became calm and plunged himself into danger with the same ease as a mere mortal such as herself pushed her hand into a bucket of tepid water. She had seen it in Brian that night in the Domain. She wondered if all SAS men were the same.

"Where *is* Brian?" Jeff asked, putting the mobile in his pocket.

"Down the hall."

"How is he?"

"On the phone he sounded pretty good really. I'd prefer it if he yelled at me. My first husband used to give me the silent treatment. I hated it."

"The day is not yet over."

Cunningham entered the office and made his way behind the desk. He seemed indecisive as to whether he should sit or remain standing. He stayed on his feet, eyeing them. Barbara thought her heart missed a beat. Jeff looked as unmoved as ever. Finally Cunningham shook his head and sat. Barbara gave Jeff a quick glance. Here comes the berating was her unspoken message.

"There are many words that come to mind," Cunningham started, then paused for a moment. "Next time you have inklings, contact me. Do you both understand?" Jeff and Barbara nodded. "A man is dead because of the actions of you two. Remember that. Worst of all we've lost the only connection we had to Zahar Akbar."

Cunningham opened his mouth to say more then decided against it.

Jeff shrugged. Indifferent.

Cunningham glared. "You are not the police, Jeff."

"What do you expect from me, Brian? An apology? Forget it. Krasniqi was working with Zahar Akbar. The way I see it he is collateral damage. You know about collateral damage don't you, Brian?"

Barbara watched the interplay, chalking a board in her head to remind her to get her assistant, Amy, to do some research on New Zealand forces in Afghanistan. Whatever happened between these two, she wanted details.

"What now, Brian?" Barbara asked. "Where does that leave you? Will you stay working with Moana or is it back to the Tactics Group?"

"Given that the killer and the terrorist are one and the same I have been left in a complicated situation. In the warehouse there were signs Krasniqi was helping others; a stolen truck, an emptied container. But still nothing definitive that screams 'I'm a terrorist'. I have free rein to follow up on any information that comes my way that might lead to Akbar and his men. That's my position until I can prove we have a national security problem. Anyway, forensics and the team are going over Krasniqi's warehouse and home. They wanted to remove Krasniqi's computers, to check for evidence relating to his murder, not the terrorist cells. I convinced Moana to have them leave all the equipment there for the moment. She said it can stay for a couple of days. I know it's a risk. If the computers went missing any evidence that might lead me to Akbar might be lost forever. We wouldn't want that to happen, would we, Jeff? Unfortunately I'm in no position to check over the computers myself. Everything is sealed until forensics give the all clear."

Barbara saw Jeff's eyes squint. A quizzical look. Then he rubbed the back of his head.

"I hear what you're saying. It is a risk. We wouldn't want to lose a potential trail," Jeff said. "If you are saying that from the evidence found in the warehouse there are more terrorists then that seals it for me, Avni Leka is behind it. Zahar is not an organiser, nor was his brother. They are contractors. If Zahar has a team he will have needed funding. Lots of funding. Leka has the money. If I'm right and this is one of his operations then bad shit is about to happen."

"This Leka is the man from Kosovo?" Barbara asked.

"That's the one." Jeff looked Cunningham in the eye. "A lot of people are going to die, Brian. Leka's operations are about maximum casualties. I'm getting more up to date intel on Akbar. I'll let you know when it arrives."

"And where might this be coming from?"

Jeff rubbed his jaw. Should he mention Lee Caldwell? Not at this stage. He would leave it to Caldwell to make himself known if he wished to.

"You both must have watched movies where the little guy is asking someone in the military a question and is told the information he seeks is on a need to know basis. Well this is one of those times."

"You're shitting me, right?" Cunningham blurted out, incredulous. "We're not in the army now. Whether you like it or not it is a police matter. And don't pull that 'I'm a civilian' shit on me. A killer is on the loose, who also happens to be a terrorist who, according to you, might just kill a truckload of Auckland's citizens. So don't go telling me I'm on a need to know fucking basis. Sorry, Barbara."

"No need to apologise. It's a good swearword. I use it all the time."

"You're going to have to trust me on this," Jeff said.

Cunningham looked as if he was about to explode. He snapped his pencil instead. Barbara held her tongue and watched the battle of wills. These two men fascinated her and were involving her in the biggest story of her career. As a woman and a journalist it didn't get much better.

Cunningham's mobile rang. He glanced at it. "I have to go."

He stormed out and slammed his office door behind him.

"Does that mean we stay?" Barbara asked.

"My advice? Time to go."

"I still want an interview, Jeff. At least some background into what happened when you were in Kosovo. Will you at least talk to me about it?"

"I'll tell you what. Do you have to work this afternoon? How about your news programme?"

"It's weekly. I have time today if that's what you're about to ask?"

"I need to drive north this afternoon and drop a carton of Boundary Fence wine off in Whangarei. Up and back tonight. Be at my house in Devonport at 5pm. We can talk on the way. That's the only offer you'll get."

Barbara smiled. "Okay. I'll come for a drive. Don't leave anything out. One thing, though: I'm a television presenter. I need a live interview."

"I'll give you the story and then we can agree on the questions and what goes on television. Then you can come out to Boundary Fence and do the shoot."

⁂

Barbara returned to the Channel Nine studios and locked herself in her office. The stack of documents in her in tray threatened to topple onto the floor. A few dedicated hours should see it reduced before she left to meet up with Jeff Bradley. She went over the details for her next show. The murder was hogging the headlines. Brian had spoken to Moana and she had given permission to use some information unknown to other media companies. Jeff Bradley chasing the killer through the Domain would be the lead story. She loved this angle. 'Hero' human interest stories attracted viewers and Jeff Bradley had a growing hero reputation. She had promised to leave out the connection between Esat Krasniqi and the terrorists. Nothing would be said about the raid on the warehouse.

Amy came into the office. "I need a couple of days off, boss."

Barbara was slightly taken aback. "You can't take holidays in your first week, Amy."

"Undercover work," Amy said, grinning ear to ear. "I've been hired by the protest group I was telling you about. To get to see who brings the cash I need to be with them full time."

"Amy, this is not a game."

"Come on, Barbara. This is what we do. We're investigative journalists, remember."

"I'm an investigative reporter, you're an assistant."

"Semantics."

"Go away and give me a few minutes to think about it," Barbara said.

"What's to think about? I'm in there."

"Amy. There are things going on that I cannot tell you about. I need to think. Now go away and leave me alone." Amy went to protest. "Five minutes. Go." Amy walked slowly through the door. "And don't sulk." Barbara yelled after her.

Barbara picked up the phone. She needed to speak with Hank Challis. They'd exchanged pleasantries when he'd been appointed her producer and little else. Now she needed a face-to-face discussion, but the thought of being alone with him in his office made her skin crawl.

~

Hank Challis stood when he saw Barbara standing in the doorway. As always she was surprised at the size of the man. Large in all directions. Then at the shock of thick white hair swished back Elvis Presley style and plastered in place with hair cream. Beady eyes surveyed her from beneath charcoal black eyebrows sprouting in all directions like blackberry bushes.

He pointed to one of the two chairs in front of his desk.

"Nice to see you, Barbara. How can I help you?"

Barbara rolled out the story. It only took her five minutes, but all the while Challis continuously checked his watch and rifled through sheets of paper. More than once she had to bite back her irritation. But she was determined to keep her cool in front of this man, even if it killed her. When she'd finished he didn't appear to notice at first. Then there was a sudden rise of the blackberry bushes.

"Ah. I see. Well, little lady. I hate to be a source of disappointment for you, but I'm not certain I can give approval to allowing a young member of staff being placed in such a dangerous position. Apart from the legal ramifications – and I'm sure there must be many – if something went wrong I'd be held accountable."

"Come on, Hank. Our job is news gathering. Going undercover for research is the job we all signed on for, for Christ's sake."

"Be that as it may, if there is danger I can't allow it. Fights between protestors and citizens pissed off at being inconvenienced are happening all the time. Hell, yesterday two men were taken to hospital. You want me to give permission to plonk Amy in the middle of that? No. Not likely. Besides, this is hardly earth shattering, Barbara. Professional protestors have been around for eons. In fact I would guess the general public probably believes that all the protestors are professional. Does anyone really care who's paying them?"

Barbara said, "The police have an interest in this other than civil disorder."

"Really?" Challis said, feigning interest but running his finger down the page of his diary.

"They have reason to believe that whoever is funding the protestors may be connected in some way to the man killed over the weekend and the attack on two women a week ago."

Challis's mouth dropped open.

"That seals it. It isn't going to happen."

Barbara shook her head. How on earth this tub of lard ever worked for CNN as he said he did defied belief. The guy did not deserve to sit at the desk as producer of the most successful news show in the country. She must have really pissed someone off on the top floor.

"Is this not something the police could do?"

Barbara said, "Yes. But it would take time and we don't have time. Amy has got herself into this group. Someone out there is murdering people. This could lead to the break they need to find him. The police would credit Channel Nine with the capture."

Challis nodded. "When you put it like that it certainly raises the stakes, and of course I'd agree to help if I could, but I can't, so there it is. A closed book."

"What do you mean 'a closed book'? Who the fuck do you think you are?"

Challis eyed Barbara with mild amusement. She suspected from Challis's expression that he considered her IQ to be lower than a newt's. The seat groaned under his weight as he leaned forward. Elbows planted on the desktop, he brought his two forefingers together to support his chin. His overt impatience morphed into a forced look of concern.

"I'm the producer and those are my *rules*. Now, your show. Let's talk about the Bradley interview and the incident in the Domain and of course this killer you're so concerned about."

Her hands dropped into a clasp on the table. Barbara felt her colour rising.

"This is just bullshit."

Challis's eyebrows shot heavenwards. A crinkle formed above either nostril as if he'd been subjected to a very bad smell.

"Look. I understand how upsetting this must be for you. I have daughters. So I do have some understanding of how the female mind works. Your tenacity is admirable, but my advice is to relax. Don't fight the system. You can never win. You get what I'm saying here?"

The air of finality couldn't have been plainer. Barbara glanced around the room at the symbols of Challis's achievements hanging in ornate frames on the walls. Some were in the form of photos of him standing next to second-level world celebrities – one a US open golf champion. It was definitely the office of an egotist.

She hoisted herself to her feet.

"We're having staff drinks tonight. If you come along, maybe I can buy you a drink?"

His eyes dropped to ogle her chest. She resisted the urge to fold her arms. Disgusted, she turned and stormed out of the office, slamming the door behind her.

23.

The black Range Rover kept two cars between it and Jeff's BMW. The four occupants sat in silence. There was nothing to be said. They knew what had to be done.

In the BMW, Barbara sat quietly in the passenger seat, still seething after her meeting with Challis. She had spoken to Brian Cunningham and to Amy; Amy would continue with her undercover work but if asked it had been her idea to go it alone. Brian promised Barbara he would appoint detectives to watch over Amy. Challis could go to hell. She was not about to let the biggest story of her career slip from her grasp because her new boss, Hank the Yank, didn't have the balls for it. The page on her notepad remained empty of words; she was too distracted to ask questions. She would give Jeff the third degree on the way back.

An hour and a half later, as Jeff's car ascended the Brynderwyn mountain range, he spotted the Range Rover in his rear-view mirror. He had noticed it earlier but had thought nothing of it at the time. Years of training to spot and slip tails had become second nature. Knowing Akbar was out to kill him had heightened his awareness. Without thought he constantly scanned his rear-view mirror every time he drove. The heavy traffic had made the Rover harder to spot. He slowed and pulled closer to the verge to allow cars to speed past. The Rover kept its distance. He slowed again and again the Rover stayed back. There was no doubt. They were being followed.

"Get Brian Cunningham on the phone, Barbara," he said handing her his mobile phone. "His number is in the contact list."

"Is there a problem?"

"We're being followed by a black Range Rover."

Barbara went to turn but Jeff stopped her.

"Don't look. I don't want them to know we're on to them. Not yet."

Barbara nodded and dialled the number. Cunningham answered. Barbara pressed speaker.

"Brian. Jeff here. I'm at the top of the Brynderwyns and about ten minutes from Waipu. I'm being followed by a black Range Rover. No doubt about it."

"Can you get through to Whangarei?" Brian asked.

"Not without gas."

"Okay, Jeff. Be careful. The driver of the truck we found in Esat Krasniqi's warehouse said he was stopped by four men in a black Range Rover. They were armed."

Jeff said, "Can you do me a favour?"

"Go ahead."

"We're at the top of the Brynderwyns now and I can see the lights of Waipu. Phone the local cop and ask him to meet me in front of the supermarket. Tell him he needs to be armed but dressed in civvies and no police car. I'll drop Barbara off then lead them away. I can't get into a shooting match in a small place like Waipu. Not if these guys have machine guns and there's no time for backup to arrive from Whangarei."

Jeff's eyes were drawn to the petrol gauge. The red light flickered and stayed on. That was all he needed. "I'll be less than ten minutes, Brian."

"Doing it now," Brian said, and rang off.

At the bottom of the Brynderwyns, Jeff slowed. He needed to allow time for the village cop to get to the supermarket ahead of him. It was only a few hundred metres from the police station but shit happened and he could get delayed. Jeff turned off the highway into the Braigh, the road that led into the Waipu village main street: a 500-metre stretch with a smattering of cafés, shops and restaurants. It got busy on market days and in the summer when holiday makers came to enjoy the beaches of Ruakaka, the Cove and Lang's Beach. Jeff had spent much of his youth surfing at the Cove. He checked his mirror. The Range Rover was still behind them. Any suspicions that it had not been following him had now vanished. As he passed the memorial for soldiers lost in past wars Jeff saw a man ahead standing beside a car. Dressed in track-suit bottoms, a T-shirt and running shoes he looked like a holiday maker but Jeff recognised the demeanour of a policeman.

"Well done, my friend," he said out loud, as he pulled over next to the cop.

The Range Rover stopped a hundred metres away and turned off its lights.

He touched Barbara on the arm.

"Whatever you do, do not look at the vehicle," Jeff said. "This needs to look casual and pre-arranged."

"What are you up to?"

"No time to explain. Just trust me. Your safety is what's important. Now get out of the car."

Jeff climbed out before Barbara could protest. He forced a smile as he walked around his vehicle to the police officer. It took great will not to look towards the black vehicle.

"You must be Jeff Bradley. I'm Gareth Wilson," the officer said.

"Gareth," Jeff said, holding out his hand. Gareth shook it but looked confused. "This is Barbara Heywood." He tilted his head toward Barbara now out of the car holding the top of the passenger door. “I’m leaving Barbara with you. I have something in the boot.” Jeff lifted the lid.

“Inspector Cunningham told me I was to do exactly as you asked but I’d still like to know what’s going on,” Gareth said as he leaned forward, now looking even more confused as he watched Jeff fiddle about in the empty space.

“You are to wait a few minutes until I’ve left and then take Barbara back to the station. Do not look but a hundred metres down the road is a black Range Rover. Make sure they follow me before you move. I don’t want them following you. Is that clear?”

“These guys are bad news?” Gareth asked.

“Very bad.”

Jeff took out a bag of tyre-changing tools and passed them to Gareth, then slammed down the boot lid. A worried and bewildered Barbara watched Jeff walk to the driver’s door.

Barbara said, “Where the hell do you think you’re going? I’m coming with you.”

“Just stay here with Gareth. If I have to knock you out and throw you in his car, I will.”

Barbara paled.

“Jeff, I’m the police,” Gareth said. “Tell me what’s going on. If need be I’ll arrest whoever is in the vehicle.”

“Gareth, listen to me. The men in the vehicle are terrorists. They are after me and they don’t care who else they kill to achieve their end. I am going to lead them away and I need you to get Barbara to safety. There is no time to argue.”

“Even so,” Gareth tapped his tracksuit pocket, “I am armed.”

“These guys have machine guns and there are four of them. You wouldn’t stand a chance. It is best I lead them away from the town and along the coast road. My chance will come.”

Jeff held out his hand and smiled. “Make out like we’re brothers. It has to look convincing.”

Gareth reluctantly shook Jeff's hand and then stood back as Jeff climbed into the BMW and drove away. Gareth didn't look up as the black car followed. He caught it passing out of the corner of his eye.

"Okay, Jeff, you're making the sacrifice," Gareth whispered. "I promise I'll get Barbara to safety."

~

Gareth drove the length of Waipu's main street in two minutes. He turned into a driveway beside the pizza restaurant. Barbara observed the eatery was filled with diners, oblivious to the unfolding drama. As with most rural police stations it had a house attached. The lone constable was responsible for all of the surrounding district. Gareth rushed the door to his house and flung it open, Barbara on his heels.

"Miriam," he yelled. "We have company."

"What's up?" A voice called back.

A pretty woman appeared in the hallway, drying her hands on a tea towel. She ran a hand across her hair when she saw Barbara.

"Miriam, this is Barbara. Barbara, meet the wife. We have a problem, Miriam. I'm collecting extra ammunition for my handgun and leaving. I need you to look after Barbara until I get back," Gareth said.

"You can't be serious," Barbara said. "I'm coming with you."

"Like hell you are."

Miriam said, "This must be the reason for the call from Whangarei station. Cars have been dispatched."

"That will be Inspector Cunningham. Good, I'm going to need the help. Right then. Miriam, you man the phones and I'll get my ammo."

Gareth disappeared along the hallway. Miriam turned her attention to Barbara.

"Can I make you a coffee?"

"No thanks, Miriam. I'm going with your husband."

"He won't like it. You'll need to stick to him when he dashes past."

~

The petrol warning light was now permanently on. Jeff assessed he might make it beyond the Cove but not much further. Certainly not as far as Mangawhai, and he'd be lucky to make Lang's Beach. Lights reflected in the rear-view mirror indicated the Range Rover was keeping its distance, its headlights stalking him like the eyes of a mythical beast. Homes along the riverbank to his left and right were dotted across the rolling landscape; the inhabitants settling down to dinner, all unable to help. Another kilometre and he would pass the entrance to the Cove camping ground, and then isolation until Lang's Beach. Nowhere land. That's where they'd make their move. It was what he would do if he were in their shoes. They were not locals and therefore likely to be unfamiliar with the terrain, but Jeff, throughout his military career, had been in many similar situations. They would recognise when the time was right to strike. He always had.

Time to consider his options. The lack of petrol ruled out trying to outrun them. He could abandon the vehicle and run into the darkness. Try and seek refuge in a farmhouse. He dismissed that idea. It would endanger the farmer and his family and secondly, if they had a night scope, he would be an easy target on the barren landscape.

He could now see the glow of lights from the Waipu camping ground. Past it was a winding uphill drive to Lang's Beach. A move needed to be made before then. For what he now had in mind he needed light. The lights from the camping area would be his last chance.

As if reading his mind they closed.

He accelerated. Accelerating meant wasting precious petrol but he needed to stay ahead. As he raced past the camping ground entrance the motor began to stutter. Jesus. Come on old girl, just a little further. He started up the rise then stopped in the middle of the road. The Range Rover slowed and stopped also. The two vehicles were thirty metres apart. Jeff tightened his seat belt. His hand gripped the gear lever.

"Okay, Jeff. This is not a great plan. But a bad plan's better than no plan. Right?" He pulled the gear lever into reverse and crushed the accelerator to the floor. The BMW jumped backwards and sped towards the black Range Rover. He spun the wheel at the last moment and hit it on the driver's door. Both vehicles slid across the loose gravel and over the bank, plummeting three metres into the shallow stream below.

Flickering headlights beamed into the night sky like fairground searchlights.

~

Gareth returned to the lounge with a box of shells. "I'd be happier with a shotgun. Can't be helped. Any news on the cars from Whangarei?" Gareth asked his wife.

"Ten minutes. You be careful. Bullets kill. Keep your silly head down."

He kissed Miriam on the cheek, waved and disappeared through the door.

Barbara noted the worried look on Miriam's face. She had paled. The policeman's wife stood silent in the centre of her lounge; behind her on the wall hung a wedding photo. Barbara recognised a younger Miriam and Gareth. Both smiling. A happy day. Now she saw a different Miriam. The brave face shown her husband erased, now, a worried wife, wringing her hands and her face the colour of chalk dust.

As Gareth opened the driver's door of his police car Barbara slipped into the passenger seat.

He smiled. "No way, Barbara. Police business. You need to stay out of my way."

"Gareth, I'm a journalist. This is what I do. Cover breaking news." She gave her warmest, friendliest smile. "I'm not being left behind. Now let's get out of here. Jeff needs your help."

Gareth eyed his passenger, defeated.

"Just keep out of my way. If Bradley takes a swing at me for your tagging along it's your fault."

"I'll handle Jeff. Let's go."

~

Moana and Cunningham stood against the back wall of the communications room. The dispatcher had logged into the Whangarei police band. They heard Gareth Wilson call in.

"I'm on the Cove road. No sign of vehicles as yet. I have a passenger. Please notify Inspector Cunningham I have Barbara Heywood in the car with me."

Cunningham's mouth dropped open, "Bloody hell, what does she think she's doing?"

"Support isn't far away," the dispatcher said.

"Send one vehicle to the station," Gareth said. "I want home base protected."

"Roger that."

Cunningham said to Moana, "I need to call the Waipu police station. I want to talk to Wilson's wife."

Moana ran her finger down the list of New Zealand police stations on the wall until she found Waipu then dialled the number.

Miriam answered. Cunningham quickly introduced himself.

"What the hell is happening?" Cunningham asked. "And why is Barbara Heywood in the car with your husband?"

"A strong-headed woman that one. She has her mobile with her. She knows more than I do."

Cunningham found his mobile and dialled Barbara's number.

"Barbara? It's Brian. What are you up to, why are you in Wilson's car?"

"I'm a reporter, Brian, I can't go into hiding when the biggest story in decades is breaking, can I?"

Cunningham held his phone in front of him and stared at it, angry and frustrated. There were many words he wanted to say to Barbara right then, most of them unkind.

"I suppose not, but be careful," Cunningham replied, careful to control his tone. "Hopefully Jeff can just keep driving. The Cove road goes through to Lang's Beach and then Mangawhai and then onto the highway back to Auckland. Somewhere along that route we can set up a roadblock."

"That won't happen. He's running out of petrol. The red light went on at the top of the Brynderwyn mountains. He'll be lucky to go twenty kilometres."

"Jesus. I'll get back to you shortly." Cunningham hung up then moved back to stand beside Moana.

"I have a bad feeling that tonight is not going to have a happy ending."

~

Gareth Wilson passed the camping grounds and as he rounded the corner he saw the headlights.

"Bloody hell," Gareth said. "Someone's gone over the bank."

The rear of his car heaved sideways as he skidded to a halt. He flung open the door and made to climb out then stopped. He touched Barbara's arm.

"You need to do what I tell you, Barbara. You do not come anywhere near those crashed vehicles until I have given an all clear. Okay?"

Barbara nodded.

He opened the glove compartment and took out two torches. He passed one to her and a second radio.

"Can you walk back down the road fifty metres and wave at the cars to slow them down? I don't want any crashes. And tell the bloody campers to keep out of it."

The sound of the crash had brought the few campers who lived in the camping ground through winter to gather at the entry gate. The small shop and restaurant were both open and now diners, having heard the crash, cautiously joined the growing crowd of onlookers. "Bang them on the head with the torch if you need to." Gareth ordered.

Barbara frowned.

"Well, okay, don't hit them but make sure they stay back. When the reinforcements arrive show them where to go. And tell them to come armed and not leave their weapons in their vehicles. They already know to do this but a reminder never hurts. Whatever you do, do not follow them. Got it?" His voice softened. "Please don't follow."

"I've got it, Gareth. Get going and be careful."

"You don't have to worry on that score."

Barbara made her way back down the road.

Gareth held his pistol with a thumb on the safety. He moved forward, each tentative step scrunching loose stones and making a sound loud in the silence. Twenty metres from the headlights he edged towards the bank and peered over.

He clicked on his radio. A direct link with the Whangarei police station.

"Gareth Wilson here. I'm at an accident scene. Two vehicles over the bank just past the Waipu Cove camping ground." he said. "One of them is a BMW, the other a black Range Rover. I can confirm these are the two cars I was looking for. Better send an ambulance. Make that two to be on the safe side."

"Roger that, Gareth. Your back up is only a few minutes away. It might be best to wait. Can you see any movement?"

"No movement from either car."

~

Bob Sutton, the senior sergeant from Whangarei, led three of his men to where Gareth knelt on the embankment. He ordered three to take up positions along the bank and keep their weapons trained on the vehicles.

"Okay, Gareth, it's you and me."

Gareth and Bob scrambled down the bank, landing in the small stream that wound its way down through the bush behind them and into the ocean. Waipu Cove was a surf beach. The sound of waves crashing onto the shore could be heard on the other side of the dunes. The black Range Rover lay on its side. The front wheels of Jeff's BMW were still up the bank, the rear rammed into the big four-by-four.

"How are we going to do this?" Bob whispered.

"Take care of the danger first. We need to check the Rover," Gareth replied. "I'll do the check. You cover me." Bob nodded. "Assume a firing position. I'll come in from the right."

Gareth waited until Bob was in position and then moved forward. He would either have to climb up to look into the vehicle or move to the front and look through the windscreen. Either way they would know he was there and if they were armed he would be presenting himself as a target. *Scary shit* was his last thought before he moved forward.

"Okay, cover me," Gareth whispered as he moved forward. He peered in through the shattered front windscreen and shone his torch onto a crumpled shape. Not moving. "I have one person. Either dead or unconscious but not moving." He pressed the barrel of his weapon against the fallen man's foot. Still no movement. Gareth took a deep breath. "Bob take aim. If he lifts a finger, shoot." Gareth reached in and felt the neck for signs of a pulse. It took a minute but he finally found the spot he was looking for. It was weak but the man was alive. With help from Bob, Gareth pulled him from the vehicle and laid him on the ground. A quick check found no serious injuries.

With the terrorist secured Gareth turned his attention to Jeff. He dreaded to think what might have happened to him.

24.

Jeff had underestimated the power of his BMW. The force of the heavy-bodied vehicle had smashed into the Range Rover, buckling the door panels and sliding the black vehicle sideways across the loose metal. His tires screamed as tread burnt into bitumen, shoving the terrorists until they disappeared over the bank.

"Woohoo, take that you assholes," Jeff screamed with delight. "Holy shit."

To his horror, the BMW followed. Jeff gripped the steering wheel. He looked straight ahead, keeping his body firm against his seat and his head against the head rest, and waited for the jolt. He reached out and pressed the button to stop his engine. It revved and then went silent. Then came a sickening thud as the BMW scrunched into the Range Rover and Jeff was flung back into his seat.

He was facing back up the bank like a NASA astronaut waiting for the launch countdown. At least the car hadn't rolled. He looked into the rear-view mirror. It was too dark to see anything.

"Okay, Jeff, relax. Think straight, think quickly," he muttered to himself. "Safety belt." He felt along the strap, found the buckle and pulled the release. It opened. He wriggled his arms free. "Now open the door." He tried the handle. The door wouldn't budge. "Fuck it. Do not panic, Jeff. Use the passenger door." He swung his legs across first and when they found the footwell he manoeuvred the rest of his body into the passenger seat. He pulled on the handle. Nothing. "Bloody hell. Think. Window. Electronic." He found the button and pushed. "Thank you, God." The window opened. He climbed through the gap then let himself fall the last few feet. He bounced off the Range Rover's tires and landed on his back. Water rushed over him. A shallow stream, one he had splashed about in as a child. He shuddered as the icy water seeped through his clothing.

He heard noises. The Range Rover. Were the men inside climbing out, readying themselves to come after him? He scrambled to his feet. A blinding light forced him to shield his eyes. He was standing in the rover's headlights. As he stepped back he saw movement inside the terrorists' vehicle. They would be entangled in seatbelts. It gave him time. The only exits were up through the driver window or passenger window or through the front windscreen or the rear window. He needed a weapon. Anything would do. He spotted a piece of driftwood the length of his arm and as thick as his wrist. He reached for it. The narrow end was slim enough to hold in one hand. He hit it on the ground. At least it wasn't rotten and felt solid enough; light but heavy enough to do damage.

The driver's door window opened. A rifle barrel appeared, then the whole weapon. Jeff recognised it as a Kalashnikov. He looked at his piece of wood and back at the automatic rifle. Outmatched. A head popped up.

He took three strides and swung the piece of drift wood as hard as he could. The sickening thud brought a grunt and then a scream. The connection jarred his arm but he smiled at the terrorist's cry of pain. The head disappeared back inside. The Kalashnikov teetered on the doorframe. He grabbed for it. Too slow; it fell back inside.

The night erupted with gunfire.

The Rover's windscreen shattered. Pieces of glass flung over the light of the headlights, a shower of sparkling diamonds. Jeff had little choice. It was time to run. In a few seconds they would be out of the vehicle and a piece of wood was no match for an automatic rifle. He didn't have time scramble up the bank onto the road. With the vehicle's lights he would be an easy target. He ran across the stream into the brush. After fifty metres he was at the top of the small hill where he followed the well-used track down onto Shelly Beach. Running on ground shell that was not as fine as sand was still as bad as running on sand, if not worse. The spongy bed sucked at his feet, slowing his pace, the effort of movement tightening his calves, and small fragments found their way inside his shoes. After a few minutes it felt like he was wearing sandpaper.

It was a small bay with a cliff face at either end. In the dark it would be too risky climbing rocks. He ran across the sloping shore to the sound of the crashing waves. In the distance he heard sirens and the incoming security of the police but there was no turning back. The terrorists would be chasing him and they were between him and the road.

~

"Gareth Wilson," Gareth said into his radio.

"Go ahead."

"I have one man down from the Range Rover. He's not moving. I've checked his pulse. He's still alive."

"An ambulance is on its way," the radio operator said. "What about Jeff Bradley?"

"Gone, and no sign of any others. There have been shots fired on the beach. I have to assume Bradley is the target. I'll leave men to guard the guy in the vehicle. The Sarge and I will go looking for Jeff."

"Take care."

"Should we be going out there just the two of us?" Bob asked.

"It's nighttime," Gareth replied. "Too many of us and we'll end up shooting each other. It's better this way."

"Yeah, right. Lead the way. I'm right behind you," Bob said.

"Now don't get in front of me. I'm going to shoot at anything that moves and I don't want that to be a cop."

"Don't worry, Gareth, I know how to play tail-end Charlie."

~

Jeff stopped to catch his breath. When he had it under control he listened but heard nothing. The noise from the crashing breakers drowned out any chance he might have of picking up approaching footsteps. The moon, now high in the sky, increased visibility. Jeff could clearly see the rock face in front of him. Too sheer to climb. He had run himself into the seaside equivalent of a blind gully. It suddenly dawned on him that if the moon was silhouetting the rock face then it must be silhouetting him. He dived onto the shells and then spun round and looked back the way he had come. There was only darkness. He could see lights in the distance. Farmhouses and holiday homes.

He couldn't go any further. Back towards the road were the hills and bush, and his pursuers. Behind him was the ocean. He cursed himself for being all kinds of stupid and not sticking with the bush. Too late now. He crawled towards to the sea until the first lapping of sea water splashed cold on his hands. He shivered. Hesitated. Too long in this water and he'd be suffering from hypothermia in no time. He looked back. In his sightline shadowy figures were closing in. He continued his crawl into the water. When he was waist deep he turned his back to the incoming waves. Unsteady on his feet. His shoes, filled with water, were sticking in the now sandy bottom. He should have removed them. He tried to kick them off but the water acted like glue.

The three shadows stopped short of the tideline. Eyes searched the darkness. At any moment they might turn and see him. Jeff crouched down his head barely above water. He saw one of them point in his direction. They must have assessed this as his only escape option. He looked behind him. The ocean was frothing up, the waves growing bigger. At any moment a freak wave might hit and wash him ashore, plonking him at their feet. He shuddered from the chill. They raised their weapons. Aimed in his direction. He had no choice. He turned, and as they fired he dove into the surf.

~

When Gareth and Bob heard the burst of machine gun fire they dropped.

"Sarge, are you okay?" Gareth whispered.

"Yeah. I'm okay."

"So they are either lousy shots or they weren't firing at us."

"I hope you're right. It sounds as though we might be a little out gunned."

The sky again lit up with gunfire. The noise was deafening.

"Holy shit. Sounds like a bloody war. One thing is for sure. Jeff is still alive and is pissing them off," Gareth said. "Let's crawl to the top of the hill. Keep your head down."

"Don't worry, I won't be standing up."

Another burst of gunfire.

"How many bullets do they need to kill someone?" Bob asked.

"I don't care how many shots are fired. As long as they're shooting, Jeff is still alive."

Gareth and Bob paused for a breather. They had crawled fifty metres. There had been no shooting for more than a minute. They crawled up the last few metres to the top. They now had a good view of the beach but saw no one. "HQ are you there?" Gareth whispered into the radio.

"Go ahead, Gareth."

"The shooters seem to have gone. They must have cut back up into the bush. They didn't come past me. We need road blocks and cars patrolling up and down the road."

"Roger that, Gareth."

"Okay. I'm moving forward to the water's edge." Gareth said. "Stay behind me, Sarge. If you see anything then shoot but make sure you don't shoot me."

~

Jeff watched as the two figures split. Where was the other one? They could be setting a trap. He was frozen. He needed to get out of the water. He wondered why they were not clearing off. They must have heard the sirens. He could see the flashing lights of torches from where he was; they must see them as well. Then the two figures were back together, talking. Rather loudly. They were being a little too casual. He heard the unmistakable sound of a radio receiver. Torches were now being shone towards them from the dunes. The two figures stayed still and in fact one of the men was waving. Police?

"Hello," He called out.

"Jeff, is that you?" Gareth yelled back.

"I'm in the water."

Gareth and Bob ran to the water's edge. Jeff waded inshore. Bob and Gareth grabbed an arm each.

"That answers one question," Gareth said. "Smart move running into the water."

Jeff didn't answer. His body shook. He rubbed his hands.

"Come on, let's get you up on the road and warmed up. Keep an eye out, Sarge. Those guys are still out there somewhere."

~

Cunningham had been sitting in Moana's office waiting for news. She appeared in the doorway, smiling.

"Jeff Bradley's okay," she said.

"Thank God."

Moana opened the bottom drawer of her filing cabinet and pulled out a bottle of scotch. She poured two shots into the paper cups.

"To Jeff," Cunningham said. They touched cups and sipped the whisky. "Jesus, what a relief."

"Our Jeff Bradley is certainly an unusual man," Moana said.

Cunningham nodded.

"What now?" she asked.

"Go home. Get some sleep. We're heading north in the morning. We need to talk to the prisoner. He knows where Zahar Akbar is and I intend getting something out of the little shit."

"That's out of my jurisdiction, Inspector, it belongs to Whangarei police."

Brian nodded. "Then come as my guest. How does that sound? It's the weekend. Think of it as an outing."

25.

By the time Cunningham and Moana arrived in Waipu, the village was bustling with activity.

First light brought the police helicopter into action. Roadblocks were in place from Whangarei through to the Auckland side of the Brynderwyns and the back roads through to Mangawhai Heads and Dargaville. Dog teams had joined in the search. All police officers in the region had been called back from leave. A Special Air Service unit was on its way from their base in Papakura.

But the three terrorists remained elusive.

Cunningham pulled up beside a policeman controlling traffic and asked for directions to the police station. The officer, irritated and under pressure, advised Brian in a not-so-conciliatory tone that he was holding up traffic and that he needed to move on. Cunningham flashed his badge. He brushed aside the mumbled apology and drove on, following the given directions.

"Jesus, it looks a bloody carnival."

"There's the station house up ahead on the right," Moana said.

Cunningham turned into the driveway but was again blocked.

He wound down his window.

The policeman stooped. "Sorry, sir, you cannot come in here."

Cunningham again showed his credentials. The officer nodded and waved him through, pointing to a section of freshly mown lawn now turned into a temporary car park.

"Let's go find out who's in charge."

Moana followed Cunningham through the small crowd milling about outside and into the station house.

"Who's running this show?" he asked a constable just inside the door.

"Superintendent Carlyle."

"Jimmy Carlyle?"

"That's him. He's through there in the lounge," the constable said, pointing to a door off the corridor. Cunningham knew Carlyle. They met at conferences and spoke often on the phone. Carlyle was standing in a corner of the room speaking into his mobile. When he saw Cunningham he waved him over. He quickly finished his conversation and put the phone in his jacket pocket.

"Brian Cunningham." He smiled, holding out his hand. "Good to see you again."

The two men shook hands.

"You look like shit, Jimmy. I suppose you've been up all night?"

"You've got it in one. I understand you Aucklanders are to blame for this fiasco?"

"I'm afraid so," Cunningham replied. "What's the latest?"

"Not much more to add to what you probably already know. We have one in hospital. There are three on the run but as yet no sign of them. They have either turned into trees or gone to ground. The army is on its way. The dogs haven't found a trail and the only sighting from the police chopper so far is green fields and cows. But we have the region surrounded and closed off. We'll get them."

Cunningham nodded. He was not about to tell Carlyle the terrorists had probably flown the coop. For most of their lives they had been evading the world's best intelligence agencies. They'd had most of the night to escape. Even in the dark they could easily cover three to four kilometres an hour. Stick to the road and only go cross country to steer clear of a roadblock. Right now they could be fifty kilometres away. In his opinion a vehicle from Auckland would have already collected them. However he could be wrong, and there was no point winding down the search just yet.

"You head up the STG, don't you? Where the hell are they?"

Cunningham said, "The SAS boys are on the way. Tracking down this type of enemy is what they're trained to do. Might as well leave it to the experts."

"Then what brings you here? Not just sightseeing are you?"

"Do you have somewhere private we can talk?"

"Sure."

~

Jeff had a pang of sympathy for Gareth and his wife. Journalists and television news teams had begun to arrive in Waipu en masse. Gareth's home was the centre of activity. Extra police had been brought in from the surrounding towns. Gareth's wife, Miriam, busied herself making coffees and sandwiches. The women from her book group had rallied round to help her.

As news of the violence spread throughout the area, first by word of mouth and now live television news broadcasts, locals from the surrounding valleys and farms poured into the small village. The Post Office, pizza restaurant and the local pub and cafés opened early. Everyone wanted breakfast and coffees and to share stories and pass on exaggerated information. This was the most excitement Waipu had seen in many decades. Like the cafés the owners of other retail outlets recognised the opportunity and also opened early.

Jeff had rented two rooms in the Clansman Motel; the only accommodation on offer in the village. He had slept, then woke hungry and in need of decent coffee. The hot-beverage sachets in the room were not going to do it for him. He tapped on Barbara's door and asked her to join him at the Art Gallery Restaurant. They took a table by the window that overlooked the town's only intersection and less than a hundred metres from the police station. Jeff mindlessly watched cars, farm vehicles and pedestrians criss-cross each others' paths as they hurried to nowhere in search of information no one had. A hawk glided across the skyline then swooped. A field mouse or rabbit foolish enough to leave the safety of their hide had just become a meal. Jeff thought through the events of the night before. He had brought violence to this tranquil piece of New Zealand. He thought through his impulsiveness. Why had he followed Esat Krasniqi the night of Quentin's nightclub opening? He wasn't a policeman. It wasn't his responsibility. He was a wine grower now, not a soldier.

"It's not your fault, Jeff. None of it," Barbara said, breaking into his reverie. She spooned sugar into her coffee.

"A journalist *and* a mind reader."

"I'm a talented woman. How are the aches and pains?"

"Nothing like an hour in freezing salt water to ease the bruising. I hate that I've brought this nightmare to town."

"As I said, Jeff, you're not to blame. You're just as much a victim as the rest of us."

"I'm not so sure."

He saw Brian Cunningham and Moana Te Kanawa crossing the street and walking towards them.

"We're about to have company."

Barbara followed his gaze.

"That was quick. How would they know where we were?"

Jeff smiled. "The motel owner would have told them we walked off to have coffee. There aren't that many places. Besides, you are a celeb, Barbara. Even the village of Waipu has television. Have you not noticed the people staring?"

"I thought they were looking at your nose," Barbara teased.

"Morning, Brian, Sergeant," Jeff said. "I suppose I shouldn't be surprised to see you two here."

"We left Auckland early this morning. Mind if we join you?" Cunningham said as he pulled out a chair.

Moana waited for Jeff's invite before she sat.

"I've spoken with Bob Carlyle. He's heading up the search. He's of the opinion that even though it's still early days the three terrorists will be caught. You and I know that's not likely. We've seen enough of these shits to know they've probably well and truly got away by now, or at least are hiding somewhere where they'll never be found."

Jeff nodded. "Too isolated to get roadblocks in place fast enough, and besides they can always walk round them. Standard evasive training. Waipu is in the middle of nowhere and there are so many roads, plus bush and a million hiding places. And of course there are miles of coastline where they could be picked up by boat. I agree, they've gone. Not to mention these days with handheld GPS navigation systems they don't need to be familiar with the area to know how to get out of it. Every bloody phone has one."

"We need to discuss your safety, Jeff. This was a very clear message. They want you out of the way. I don't suppose you'd consider getting lost somewhere until all this is over?"

"Not an option, Brian."

"I didn't think so. Okay. Fair enough. We'll need to think of something else. My status will probably change tomorrow. Police politics will rear its ugly head. I'll be pushed back to my STG office to wait for deployment phone calls. Someone higher up the ladder will take the lead. What it means is that you and Barbara will be out of the loop. I've stretched the rules already keeping you on the inside." He looked at Barbara. "Sorry. It will become a closed shop."

"I can't operate blind, Brian," Jeff said. "Not now that I know for certain Zahar's men are after me."

"Out of my hands, Jeff."

"Maybe not."

He pulled out his mobile, rescued from his BMW before he was taken to the motel.

"If it was just about you and Moana I probably wouldn't give a shit. But I need to protect myself and to protect those close to me. To do that I need intel."

Jeff found Caldwell's number on his contact list and pressed dial. The phone rang seven times before it was answered.

"It's Jeff Bradley."

"Hi, Jeff. You've done it again. You need a clock that shows US time. I need my sleep."

"There have been developments. When do you arrive?"

"I leave in the morning. It was the earliest flight I could get."

Jeff quickly brought him up to date.

"You have been busy."

"I need you to do something for me."

"Go ahead."

Jeff caught Cunningham's eye.

"Inspector Brian Cunningham. An Auckland cop. Ex SAS. He's one of us. Heads up the Special Tactics Group. Internal politics will see him kicked out of the game. In my opinion that should not be allowed to happen."

"You want me to fix it?" Caldwell asked.

"Yes. I want you to fix it."

"Okay, Jeff. Send me a full report in the next hour to my email address."

"Okay, will do." Jeff closed his phone.

"Who were you talking to?"

"I'm sorry, Brian. At the moment I can't tell you. If he wants you to know he will tell you himself."

Moana stared at Cunningham, mouth open. Incredulous. He shrugged.

"Moana and I are going to have a chat with Akbar's man in Whangarei Hospital. I'll let you know what we find out."

Jeff smiled. "I won't hold my breath."

26.

Jimmy Carlyle was waiting for Cunningham and Moana outside the hospital room. There were two constables stationed by the door.

"Is he talking?" Cunningham asked.

"Not a word."

"Can he be moved?"

"The doctor said he had concussion but apart from a swollen head and a very bad headache they see no reason he can't be moved from tomorrow onwards. They want him to stay overnight for observation purposes," Jimmy replied. "I take it you want him in Auckland?"

"At some stage, yes. Can we see him?"

"Go ahead. I have to make a phone call. I'll join you in a few minutes."

Cunningham and Moana entered the room. Two constables stood either side of the bed, backs against the wall and keeping a good distance between themselves and the prisoner. Cunningham smiled, impressed by the professionalism. He noticed the terrorist's left wrist had been handcuffed to the metal frame holding the mattress. A nurse holding a clipboard stood at the end of the bed. A check of her watch led to scribbling a notation onto a page unseen from where Cunningham stood.

The prisoner was in his late twenties, Cunningham assessed. A stubble of beard growth. His black hair and olive skin suggested he could be from the Mediterranean region; he guessed it was more likely to be the Middle East but he wasn't going to jump to any conclusions. He might easily be Portuguese or Italian. Hostile eyes flitted between Cunningham and Moana. Both officers met his gaze with equal belligerence. Cunningham smiled, the man in the bed was not about to be intimidated. This was going to be hard work.

"How is he?" Cunningham asked the nurse.

"Recovering from concussion, but apart from a giant headache and a lump the size of a football on the side of his head, he'll be fine."

"Cigarette?" Brian asked, pulling a pack from his pocket and offering it to the prisoner.

The nurse frowned. Smoking was banned in hospitals and almost every other public place in New Zealand. She looked to Moana for guidance. Moana shrugged and said nothing. The nurse made to say something but decided against it. She raised her eyebrows at Moana and left the room.

The prisoner took a cigarette. Cunningham lit it up for him. He poured some water into a paper cup to use as an ashtray.

"How is your head?" Cunningham asked.

No answer.

"Do you have a name? Can you give us that? I need to call you something. My name is Brian."

Still no answer.

"Very well. I will give you a name. Stupid asshole. Write that down will you Sergeant Te Kanawa. First name, Stupid. Family name, Asshole."

Moana wrote it down.

"Now, age. Hard to tell. But with a name like Stupid Asshole you would have to have a mental age of thirteen years. What do you think, Moana?"

"Not more than thirteen years," she replied.

"What sex are you, Mr Asshole? Male or female?" Cunningham watched the terrorist's eyes. Looking for a flicker. Nothing. "Okay not male, not female. Write down donkey, closest member of the animal family to the ass in asshole, don't you think?

"What about your father and mother?"

No answer.

"Okay. Moana, write down mother is a whore and father is a loser."

The eyes narrowed. Cunningham threw Moana a wink. He was certain that if the prisoner hadn't been handcuffed he would have swung a fist at him. Cunningham had spent enough time in middle-eastern countries. Family honour was important. Insulting the family was unacceptable.

A light tap on the door and it pushed open. Jimmy Carlyle poked his head through the gap. "Am I intruding?"

"Not at all, Jimmy." Cunningham waved him in. "Jimmy, have we charged Mr Asshole here with anything as yet?"

"Not as yet."

"Okay. How about child molestation?"

"Sounds good to me, Brian."

"Good. Now let's get some cameras in here. I want his face on international television. I want the world to know that Mr Asshole here whose mother is a whore and whose father is a loser is being held by New Zealand police for child molestation and if anyone knows who this sick asshole is please make contact."

Akbar's man spat the cigarette at Cunningham.

"You will die for this, pig," he said in accented English. Then a curse followed in a language Cunningham did not recognise. Cunningham smiled.

Cunningham, Moana and Jimmy Carlyle filed out of the room. "Congratulations," Jimmy said. "You got him talking."

"Did you get it all, Moana?" Cunningham asked.

"Sure did," she replied pulling a small tape recorder from her purse. She played back the conversation and it came through loud and clear.

"Great. Let's get him fingerprinted and get that tape to the Auckland University Language department. See where Mr Asshole comes from. Hopefully the police in that country might be looking for him."

"Have you finished with him, Brian?" Jimmy asked.

"For the moment, yes," Cunningham replied. "Short of torturing him I don't think he is going to talk to us willingly. As soon as the hospital releases him let's get him to Auckland."

"We're stretched to the max with the search as you might expect, but I think if we haven't caught them by tomorrow we will have to accept they got away. I'm sure we can send him down within the next forty-eight hours. That okay for you?"

"Good enough, Jimmy."

"You don't suppose this has to do with the submarine do you? Bit much to think it might just be a coincidence," Carlyle asked.

"We've given that a lot of thought but the enquiries so far say it's not possible. Security will be tight. Those things are pretty much indestructible. No one is ever going to get close enough to put a bomb on board. Rockets need heat to target them. Handheld rockets need to be fired close up. Difficult to make an effective hit because of the sub's shape. Hell, I've fired a handheld and could never hit anything a hundred metres away. These guys would never get that close. Anyway, a handheld might bring down a helicopter or destroy a tank but would do little damage to a sub. Let's face it, 90 percent of the damn thing is under water, and the hull is several feet thick. I'm guessing it will be a bomb in the city or some shit like that. Make a big statement and kill a few civilians."

"A little scary, isn't it," Carlyle said. "I'm glad I'm just a small city cop and all we need worry about is traffic control on market day."

Cunningham raised his eyebrows.

Carlyle smiled. "Well, okay, we do have the odd bit of violence but you know what I mean. Nothing like your metropolis."

~

Jeff turned the hire car into his driveway then slammed his foot on the brake. Barbara had been dozing and the jolt flashed her eyes open.

"Jesus," Jeff whispered. "My front door is open."

"You didn't leave it open by mistake?"

"No. Not a chance."

"Why aren't the police watching your house?" Barbara asked.

Jeff laughed. "Well, firstly they're not a security company and secondly I can look after myself. I could add they don't have the manpower but even if they did Brian wouldn't send anyone. Now let's get out of here."

He backed across the road and stopped in front of his neighbour's garage.

"If anyone is inside hopefully they'll think I was turning round. They won't recognise the car that's for sure. Come on, get out."

"What are we going to do?" Barbara asked, worried.

"I'm going to walk you into the neighbour's backyard."

"You know them well?"

"Only to say the odd hello but they seem nice enough."

"Great. What if they're having dinner?"

"If you're hungry I'm sure they'll feed you."

"That's not what I meant and you know it."

Jeff led Barbara down the side of the house. He recalled that the woman of the house was a fashion designer of some sort and her husband a well-known yachtsman. He hoped they wouldn't be home. As long as he could hide Barbara somewhere safe until he cleared his house. The dining room was a glazed addition to the back of the house. The family sat round the table, easily seen by Jeff and Barbara and the backyard intruders easily seen by the family. No backing away now.

The door opened. The yachtsman eyed him then smiled when he recognised his neighbour. His wife came up behind him.

"Good evening. I'm Jeff Bradley, from across the road. This is Barbara Heywood. I'm sorry to barge in on you like this but I might have intruders in my house. Can Barbara stay with you until I check it out? It won't take long."

"Larry Connors," the man said, holding out his hand. "This is my wife Donna and these two are Daisy and Maisie."

The infant blonde twins clung to their mother's legs, eyes firmly fixed on Jeff and Barbara.

"Please, come in, Barbara," Donna invited. "You're most welcome."

"Thank you, guys. I won't be long."

"Should I come with you?" Larry asked. He followed Jeff to the corner of the house.

"No need for that, I can handle it. But in case a problem does develop better you're here with your family."

Larry nodded. Once Jeff had disappeared he went back inside the house.

"Darling, will you get Barbara a glass of wine?" his wife asked.

"So we finally get to meet our famous neighbour, if only fleetingly," Donna smiled. "Jeff has been in the news but not as much as you, Barbara. Can I say, I enjoy your show. An objective journalist. A rare breed these days." Larry returned with a glass of wine. "I was just telling Barbara we've been following Jeff's exploits."

"Yes. He's certainly an adventurer."

"He is that," Barbara said.

"Well, don't go north at the moment," Donna said. "Have you seen what's been happening in Waipu? Well of course you have, your station will be all over it."

"I'm afraid I've seen it first-hand."

"You were involved in that?" Donna asked incredulously. "How exciting."

"Donna, I assure you it was far from exciting, Jeff was almost killed. Then I was caught up in the media frenzy, mostly dodging interviews then working with a crew to film a segment for this week's show. Thank God the nightly news team sent a journalist otherwise I might still be there."

"You poor thing." (this response from Donna.)

"Sailing is all the excitement I want in my life," Larry said.

"Oh, you're that Larry Connors. I follow your yacht races, Larry. My father was a boatie. I was brought up on sailing."

Larry smiled.

"Cheers."

Barbara lifted her glass then took a sip. She cast a quick glance through the window. Darkness. For just a moment she reflected on the warmth of Larry and Donna's family home. A little enviously if she were honest. Her career filled the gap left by broken relationships, but every so often, occasions like tonight triggered her maternalism. A husband, children, a home, it would be nice.

~

Jeff slipped inside his house. He reached for the light switch then pulled back. The darkness was his security. He stayed in the hallway, eyes glancing sideways until his night vision adjusted to the dim light. His ears strained for the slightest sound. Nothing but the groans of hundred-year-old timber as his bungalow settled after a day of sun. The bathroom tap dripped, a reminder he needed to call a plumber.

He stepped forward using the balls of his feet, his body now loose, prepared to fend off any would-be assailant.

It took fifteen minutes. Satisfied his house was clear he switched on the lights.

Papers strewn across the floor of his office appeared to be the only evidence of home invasion. He re-checked each room. All was in its place. He dialled Cunningham's number.

"Brian Cunningham."

"Brian. It's Jeff. Someone broke into my house. I've cleared it."

"Could it have been burglars?" Cunningham asked.

"Unlikely. Nothing seems to have been taken. There's even a laptop in the office. Someone messed up the office and that's it. I think the mess is a message. 'We know where you live and we can enter at will'. That sort of thing."

"Do you need help?"

"No. But I've still got Barbara here. I'm about to send her on her way. It worries me that Akbar's people saw her with me."

"You're telling me I should look out for her?" Cunningham asked.

"A loose cover. Some new locks on the door."

"All right, Jeff, I'll take care of it. Have a good night. And be careful."

27.

Amy Monroe stepped off the city link bus at the top of Symonds Street and walked down the slope to her new place of work. Her third morning as a professional protestor. The buildings that ran from the intersection of Newton Gully and Symonds Street to the motorway overpass had been preserved by the city council as historic. The facades of the once shiny, glossy, retail stores sat neglected, their paint peeling, corrugated roofs rusting and walls covered with posters promoting band tours, a day at the zoo and Cirque du Soleil.

Word had it that the council had denied the landowners the right to bulldoze the two-storey wood constructions built in the early years of the twentieth century. The owners in turn refused to pour money into upgrading useless retail edifices in the wrong part of town that would only ever offer cheap rental returns. The cheap rentals were ideal office space for the 'Keep New Zealand Nuclear Free' campaigners.

By the end of the first day she had learnt all there was to know about her new boss and protest leader, 66-year-old Charlie Agnew. Sporting a grayish ponytail sliding from a balding head, Agnew regaled anyone in the office interested enough to listen with tales of the halcyon days of street marches and sit-ins and was ecstatic that once again his time had come. He constantly bemoaned, to anyone that would listen, that modern youth had lost their way, and that nowadays the student populations of university campuses were only interested in building careers instead of a better world.

As the protest organiser, he supposedly coordinated the making of banners, printing leaflets and making sure all his people were on the streets at their allotted times. Mostly though, he drank at the student pub and ogled the younger women lured into joining his group. There was always the chance a naïve, idealistic, drunken student might allow themselves to be bedded by an aged mentor. Amy made sure she extricated herself as soon as Agnew's head sagged and a hand crept its way onto her knee.

After two days the initial excitement of nightly parties and waving banners on the wharf had given way to boredom. Sitting in a musty, damp old building all day had brought on sniffles. Amy's bag bulged with tissues. The group in the office had little depth to their discussions. Tired old anti-nuclear clichés, learned from literature handed out by Agnew, fell easily off the end of tongues, but lacked passion. The cold war and nuclear catastrophes were a generation ago and held as much interest as a couch potato holding a remote flicking through channels. In fact none had had any idea a visit from a nuclear submarine was imminent until they joined the group. They were there for the money. Minds focused on studies and maintaining scholarships, and discussion topics centred around careers and potential incomes. Even worse, many of the protesters actually seemed excited by the visit and not in the slightest bit angry. As one put it, "A giant sub in the harbour, how cool is that?" For the students, protesting was more fun than working at McDonalds, better money too, and the general consensus was that life did not get much better than it was at the moment.

Amy discovered Agnew had managed to sleep with two of the girls. There was no accounting for taste, was all she could think. She found him repulsive, and couldn't imagine how anyone her age could climb into bed with a 60-year-old man. She had caught him eyeing her more than once. One of the women warned her he preyed on the new faces. Let him try, Amy thought. However, today was payday and if she uncovered the identity of the money-man she would not be back tomorrow. Word had gone out that the cash was on its way and a crowd had gathered in the office. Amy asked Lucille when the paymaster would come. She had been with Agnew the longest and was a kind of de facto office manager. Not that there was much to manage, but she was experienced enough to know the answer to most of Amy's questions.

"The money man never brings the wages to the office," Lucille said. "Agnew is phoned and then collects it."

"I haven't seen him with a car," Amy said.

"He doesn't drive. Always walks. He's usually gone for about an hour. When he gets back we get paid and it's off to the pub. How cool is that?"

"You don't care where the money comes from?"

"Why should I? It's just a job. When I worked at McDonalds I never met the owners," Lucille offered. "Same thing isn't it? Don't get too serious, Amy."

"I'm not. Really. I'm like you. I love this job but I lost my last job months ago and now I've finally found employment I'm really keen it lasts."

"Me too."

Amy set off in search of a hot drink. Arguing against Lucille's logic would only give her a headache. As she stirred two sugars into her coffee she caught sight of Agnew reaching for his jacket off the deer antlers screwed onto the wall. Amy prepared to follow. She rubbed her right breast. The police microphone in her bra had moved and pinched her skin. Turning her back she made a quick adjustment. Now she worried her fiddling had disrupted the transmission.

She checked her watch. It was 2.30pm. Time to check in with Barbara. Agnew had wrapped a scarf round his neck, and whispered something into Lucille's ear. Amy slid the strap of her bag over her shoulder, her eyes not leaving the aged hippie. As she pulled her phone from her bag Agnew walked through the door. She let the phone drop back. The protestors milling about paid her no attention. Once the boss had left the office, work gave way to coffee and coke and lounging on the tatty sofas. As Amy made her way across the office a conversation on the best suburb in which to buy a house had begun.

Outside pedestrian traffic had increased but Amy quickly picked out the striding figure of Agnew making his way down Symonds Street towards the university campus and a meeting with the man funding the protests. Until he reached the intersection of Karangahape Road and Grafton Bridge there were no side streets. Amy could stay back and still keep him in sight. She gripped the strap of her shoulder bag. As she set off there was a spring to her step and a smile of anticipation lit up her face. This was a great adventure.

Detective Jessica Andrews and Detective Red Dawson sat in the unmarked police car. They had seen Agnew leave and waited for Amy to follow. Her conversation with Lucille had recorded clearly. The wire she wore working as it should. Agnew was off to meet the paymaster. Red started the car and pulled out. Amy was walking quickly to keep up with Agnew but Red let her get well ahead. She had instructions to give a commentary of her movements. If they lost her they would find her again quickly enough.

Sami Hadani watched from the café opposite. After the fiasco in Waipu, he was taking no chances. No more mistakes. He wanted to make certain no one followed his man making payments to the protest group. They might not make the connection between Zahar and the protests, but the protestors had caused chaos and young people talked. If the cops found out someone was paying to create the demonstrations they might come looking and arrest his man dealing with Agnew. That could cause him a headache.

Sami had seen Agnew leave as soon as he received the phone call. He waited and watched, and his caution had paid off. At first he thought the girl might be chasing after him because she had a message. But no, when she kept her distance no doubt lingered in Sami's mind she was tailing Agnew. Amateurs, he thought to himself.

The second tail surprised him though.

He had noticed the car parked in the bus stop opposite but thought nothing of it. There was nowhere else to stop as the bus stop ran the length of the street. He had seen a number of cars drop off or pick up passengers and assumed this to be another instance. When the female passenger got out, the mousy-haired girl following Agnew turned and gave the woman a thumbs-up signal. The car trailed but kept its distance. Police, he surmised. It could only mean they knew about the payments.

Well, it wasn't that much of a secret. These kids were getting drunk every night and bragging about being paid. Sooner or later it was bound to happen. It was improbable they would link the protests to Zahar and his men but if they caught the man making payments he might talk. For Sami the security of the mission came first. This part of the operation had run its course anyway. With the submarine due any day the flashpoints had filled with veteran protesters, with more coming. Paid teams were no longer a necessity.

He found his man's number on his mobile and dialled it. No answer. Lenny must have his phone switched off. There was no need to follow Agnew and the others. Sami hailed a taxi. He knew the meeting place and would get there ahead of everyone.

~

Charlie Agnew knew the man he was to meet as Lenny. He knew it wasn't Lenny's real name and had labelled him Lenny-No-Name. He didn't care why Lenny wanted to remain anonymous as long as he paid the money. He also didn't care why Lenny supported the protest as long as the money allowed him, Charlie Agnew, to make a statement. He hated the idea of anything nuclear coming into New Zealand and prided himself that his past activities had helped bring about the nuclear ban. Over the years, for most of his friends, their youthful idealism waned as life took over and family and mortgages took precedence. Not for him. He had stayed active, joined Greenpeace and the countless other conservation groups that came and went over the decades. But none of these other causes had brought the passion that nuclear weapons and nuclear power evoked. That Lenny had sought him out was flattering. Agnew had promised at the first meeting he would not let him down. That Lenny's money had brought a side benefit of women and booze, Charlie considered a well-deserved reward for long service to the cause.

The meeting place was always different. This time they met in a café off Wakefield Street. Lenny was already seated at a corner table when Agnew entered.

"Hey, Lenny," Agnew said. "Good to see you again."

"Mr Agnew. You are on time as always. This is good," Lenny replied.

Lenny noted the greed in Agnew's eyes. In another few hours, after a bout of heavy drinking, the eyes would be glazed over. He had watched Agnew for the first week to see if he could be relied upon to be inefficient. True to character, Agnew had turned out to be nothing more than a lecherous drunk. He had chosen well.

"Can I get you a coffee?" Agnew asked. "I'm having a cappuccino."

Lenny shook his head. Agnew ordered then sat down. "As you asked I have added more people to the group."

"Yes. This is good. I have been watching. You have done a good job. I am pleased."

Agnew smiled, then his eyes dropped to the upper portion of Lenny's jacket. The money envelope would be lodged in the inside pocket. Lenny noted the shift of focus and it pleased him. Agnew ogled his chest like he would a woman's breasts. The perfect subservient.

Lenny took the envelope from his pocket and slid it across the table. Agnew grasped it with both hands and subconsciously felt the thickness before pushing it into his trouser pocket. Lenny almost laughed, and then his mouth fell open when he saw Sami Hadani enter the café. Something was wrong. Sami would never show himself like this. His boss nodded towards the toilets then walked through the door.

Lenny waited a moment, "Excuse me a moment my friend. I need the toilet."

Sami turned on him as soon as Lenny closed the door.

"Where is your phone?"

"I left it at the warehouse."

"You're an imbecile."

Lenny grew cold. It felt like insects were crawling over his skin. He knew Sami's moods and now the big man's grey eyes revealed he was on dangerous ground.

"Sorry, Sami. But the business is now concluded. No harm done."

"How wrong you are," Sami spat at him. "Do you think I am here for pleasure? Your man Agnew has been followed. By the police. They have found out about you."

"We had discussed that this might happen. I will just disappear."

"It is too late for that, the police are outside."

Lenny wiped his brow. He needed a towel. There was no back way out of the toilet block. He had little option but to re-enter the café and be arrested. Sami smiled and patted him on the shoulder.

"Okay, Lenny. Everyone makes mistakes. But be careful. No more. Understand?"

"No. I will be careful. I promise, Sami."

Sami smiled assurance and Lenny noticeably relaxed. "Get back in there and finish up then walk out with Agnew as if nothing has happened."

"What about the police?"

"They're only watching. They will probably tail you, I'm betting. Trying to find out who else you are working with. Slip them as soon as you can and make your way back to the safe house."

"Sure thing, Sami."

As Lenny turned to re-enter the café Sami shot him in the back of the head with a silenced handgun. He spat on Lenny's body as he stepped over.

~

Amy watched Agnew through the window. Her hippie boss kept looking about him but it wasn't nervousness. The man he had been sitting with had gone to the bathroom and Agnew was probably wondering what was taking him so long. Amy was wondering the same. Finally Agnew stood up and walked to the toilet door. He hesitated a moment. Embarrassment, Amy surmised. Men don't go chasing each other into toilets. She watched as he pushed the door ajar, enough gap to poke his head through. He jumped back and continued the backward steps to the door. Odd, she thought. Then he spun round and ran outside.

As he ran off up the hill Amy spoke into the microphone in her bra. "Something is wrong, I'm going in to have a look."

There was no two-way communication. Red cursed and leapt from the car. Jessica, already chasing after Amy, was right behind her when Amy pushed the toilet door open.

~

Cunningham and Moana were sitting at the table in the crime room drawing up a new duty roster when Moana's phone rang.

"Jesus," Moana whispered under her breath. She nodded as she listened then closed her phone.

"The protestor's paymaster has been murdered."

Cunningham frowned. Rubbed the bridge of his nose. "What the hell happened?"

Moana related the information.

"Jesus bloody Christ." He threw the documents he held across the table. "This is way out of control."

"What makes it worse," Moana said, "is that the killer must have walked out right under our noses. I'm going down there to check it out for myself."

She stopped in the doorway.

"Look, Inspector, I've had a thought. It might lead to nothing but right now we're scratching at dirt and only getting grubby fingernails."

Cunningham nodded. "What are you thinking?"

Moana stepped back into the room. "This Esat Krasniqi must have organised new premises for these guys before they killed him. They're hiding whatever it was in that container somewhere."

"Apart from stating the obvious, Sergeant, do you have a point? We've checked all his documents and found nothing."

"I worked in fraud for a while. I had to find things. People go to great lengths to hide ill-gotten gains. You'd be surprised how many trust funds there are out there hiding money. Trusts are difficult to trace."

"Yes, and you have pretty much answered your own question. Where the hell would we start?"

Moana stiffened, locked eyes with Cunningham.

"I apologise, Moana. This is your investigation. I was a bully at school." He offered a conciliatory smile then stooped and picked up a document from the floor. "Too used to having my own way. An officer and all that."

"I'm thick skinned. Don't worry. You are still the senior officer," Moana said. "My guess is that the new premises must be in the same area as the other one. Not too far anyway. They couldn't risk moving gear and equipment, especially weapons, too great a distance. More chance of discovery. Some dumb-ass cops, like us, might pull them over for a broken tail light. Krasniqi has only been in New Zealand four to five years. There are only so many real estate companies that deal in commercial properties. They might not have Krasniqi's name on an agreement but they might be able to tell us how many properties were bought by trusts. Then it's a matter of elimination."

Cunningham looked interested.

Moana shrugged. "I think it is worth pursuing."

"So do I."

"After I've checked out the café I'll have someone follow up on the warehouses."

Cunningham sat back in his chair and kept his eyes on the sergeant as she left the room. She had impressed him. Smart, capable and not unattractive. If they weren't colleagues and she wasn't married he might be tempted to ask her to dinner. He shrugged and dismissed the thought. It wasn't going to happen.

He phoned Barbara Heywood and outlined the incident at the café, then ordered a car to deliver Amy to the television station. The shock of seeing a dead body for the first time was not a pleasant experience; he still remembered his own first time. Amy would be traumatised and would probably be much better off in a crowd than at home on her own. He would call by later to talk to her but doubted she would have anything further to add to what they already knew.

Agnew would be picked up but other than being able to identify the body he doubted he would have any useful information either. Zahar Akbar was smart. Nothing led to anything. Typical terrorist operation. Work in cells. No connections. Kill off the links when compromised.

But it did lead to an interesting question. Without the paymaster the financing of the protestors was at an end. His gut told him it no longer mattered. And that worried him to hell.

His phone rang.

"Cunningham."

"Inspector, I'm Area Commander Galbraith's secretary. Can you please come up to his office? He apologises for the short notice but wishes me to assure you the matter is urgent."

Cunningham closed his phone. He had known this time was coming. It surprised him it had taken so long. Someone else was about to take over. It irked him but what could he do? The newcomer would not have the experience he had dealing with these types of criminals but his superiors would believe a more experienced and higher-ranking police officer would be more capable of leading the investigation.

The secretary waved him on in to the commander's office. He didn't think he should push his luck and ask for a cup of tea. There were three men seated together on one side of the small meeting table. He recognised Galbraith but not the other two. A lone chair sat opposite for Cunningham. Jesus, he thought, a bloody inquisition.

"Sit down please, Inspector," the commander said quietly, forced politeness. No hint of a smile. Not that the commander ever smiled. Always the same stony-faced exterior, no one ever knew what he was thinking.

"Thank you, sir," Cunningham said.

"Any new developments, Inspector?"

Cunningham nodded. "Yes. Another killing. An hour ago."

"And this is to do with the case Sergeant Te Kanawa is leading or the shootout in the north?"

"Both, really. A suspect was under surveillance. A good lead. Unfortunately they must have twigged we were onto him."

"I see," the Area Commander said. "One might be forgiven for believing we were at war. Are we at war, Inspector?"

"Not yet but we're close."

The commander glared.

"Perhaps you might bring us up to date," said one of the two men sitting next to the police chief.

The commander made no attempt to introduce his guests. Two sets of stranger's eyes studied him like two scientists looking at a microbe in a petri dish. It pissed him off.

"And you people are . . ."

"You'll find out soon enough, Inspector Cunningham. Just answer the question."

"Yes, sir."

Cunningham spent the next twenty minutes going over the details and the chain of events. How seemingly isolated incidents were slowly linking together. The connection Jeff Bradley had made to Kosovo and Barbara Heywood's theory that the idea was to stretch police resources. He did not however mention Barbara by name. He knew his bosses well enough to know that allowing the press to have unrestricted access to the inner workings of a police investigation might not go down well.

"And do you have any theory as to what the real purpose of these people is?"

"Guesses only, I'm afraid. This man Akbar and his brother liked big crowds to plant bombs in."

The commander frowned.

"I see. But for the moment you have no reason to believe this might be about to happen."

Cunningham shook his head, "No, sir. The counter argument is, why come to New Zealand to blow up a bomb?"

The commander looked down at the documents in front of him and then back at Cunningham. Here it comes, Cunningham speculated, I'm about to be replaced. Cop to scapegoat in the time it took to draw a line through his name.

"You realise of course I'm under enormous pressure from almost everyone," the commander said. "Understandable of course. Citizens are being killed. Gun battles in the north. Now you tell me of another murder downtown. To say that chaos reigns might be an exaggeration but you can understand these are the words being bandied about. Not good, is it, Inspector?"

"No, sir," Brian replied.

"I have everyone on my back. The Prime Minister's office, the army, the secret service, civil defence, not to mention the Minister of Police, my superiors and of course the mayor. They want a result. They want it finished. They are screaming at me to put someone in control with the experience to get the job done. I'm sure you will agree a detective inspector with only a few years' behind you, you're not equipped to handle the political manoeuvres needed to coordinate the various branches. You certainly don't have detecting skills, nor the required rank to get the job done."

So there it was. The commander could not have been more clear.

Cunningham sat back in his chair. It was a fait accompli. Life in the public service didn't come with guarantees of fairness. He had given it his best shot and had been deemed inept. Now he was to be replaced and his career was as good as over. There would be no surviving this type of demotion.

"Yes, sir, you are probably right," Cunningham answered. There was no point arguing. He had been in the services long enough to know that once a decision had been reached it was final.

"That I am right, there is no doubt. It is the natural order of things," the chief went on. "So why is it that I am sitting here with a directive from the Police Minister advising me that not only has the Prime Minister himself insisted you are to be in charge of the investigation, but you are also to be given a ranking that will allow you access to any government department? This includes the air force, navy, SAS and anyone else you might see fit to utilise. Within reason they will not turn down any request from you. All the departments have been notified. As of now someone else has assumed your role at the STG. Right now your job is to hunt down whoever these criminals are, stop whatever it is they are doing and bring them to justice."

Cunningham straightened. Eyes wide in disbelief. The commander's two guests watched his reaction with mild amusement.

28.

The two glass doors beneath a large screen displaying New Zealand scenes slid across to allow arriving passengers into the terminal. Jeff waved to Lee Caldwell. Caldwell gave a nod of recognition and walked towards him.

They shook hands.

Caldwell said. "I read your report on the plane. Any further developments?"

"Some. Let's get out of here. We can discuss it in the car. Where are you staying?"

"Nowhere as yet. Take me into the city. I'll find something."

"You can stay with me if you like," Jeff said.

"Thanks for the offer. But, no. I like to be a free agent and I have a good budget. Take me to the best hotel in town and I'll stay there."

"Maybe we should bring Brian Cunningham in on this right away. He's the police officer I told you about."

"Sounds good to me."

"I'll give him a call." Jeff said and pulled out his mobile. "Brian. It's Jeff. What are you up to at the moment?"

A pause.

"If you must know I'm checking up on Barbara Heywood. Brought some Chinese and we were about to have dinner. You're not going to ruin our evening are you?"

"Sorry. Can't be helped." Jeff laughed. "I'll be there in about twenty minutes."

~

Barbara and Cunningham were sitting in the lounge with glasses of wine when the doorbell rang.

"Brian, let me introduce Lee Caldwell," Jeff said.

"Mr Caldwell. Nice to meet you. Seems I owe you a thank you for saving my career," Cunningham said, shaking hands with the American.

"It might not turn out to be the favour you think it is when all this is over."

"Be that as it may, thank you anyway. I might ask how you come to have the influence but I guess you wouldn't tell me. So I won't ask."

Cunningham studied the American. Slightly built and close to forty he guessed. It was hard to tell. He had a friendly demeanour and his overall appearance was unremarkable. He looked more like a businessman than a soldier or law-enforcement officer. He would not stand out in a crowd. But the eyes. There was coldness there. The mouth smiled but the eyes did not.

"Why don't we sit down," Barbara said.

Caldwell gave Barbara a once over. Jeff caught it.

"We can talk freely in front of Barbara. She has been in on it from the start. Was with me in the car the other night when they tried to kill me," Jeff said, answering Caldwell's unspoken query.

"She's a journalist but has agreed to confidentiality until I give the go ahead. For that she gets to be on the inside," Cunningham chipped in.

"Fair enough, but I'm never to be mentioned," Caldwell said, speaking directly to Barbara.

"We've never met," Barbara smiled back. Reassuring.

Caldwell nodded. Cunningham saw a hint of skepticism in Caldwell's manner. Well, screw him – Akbar was in New Zealand because Caldwell and his mob let him go. He was not prepared to give Caldwell an inch when it came to determining who was allowed access to information.

"Reminds me of Kosovo, Jeff. You're gathering a new ragtag team," said Caldwell. "No offence intended."

For the next hour they went over the detail of what had taken place to date. Caldwell only interrupted to clarify a point and to ask where he could find Waipu on the map.

"Now, this prisoner," Caldwell started. "When do you expect him to be brought to Auckland?"

"Day after tomorrow. The police Special Tactics Group will escort him," Cunningham said.

"Not the SAS?"

Caldwell leant forward, making an arch with his fingers, and then leaned his chin on them. Thoughtful.

Cunningham said, "If it was up to me, and thanks to you it is, the Squadron would have the lead. But the police have jurisdiction when it comes to transporting a prisoner from town to town. I have confidence they can cope."

Caldwell nodded.

"So apart from the prisoner you don't have any leads."

"No. Not really."

"And you still have no idea what these guys are planning?"

Jeff said, "We're guessing that whatever is going down has to do with the arrival of the submarine but we've dismissed a direct attack."

"Hmmm, that makes me nervous. The eyes of the world will be on the visit. Let's hope they're not going to set off a bomb. I've already seen Akbar's dirty work first hand."

Barbara looked worried. "They wouldn't, would they?"

No one answered.

Cunningham told Caldwell what he had found in Esat Krasniqi's warehouse.

"I'd like to see the warehouse. As soon as possible."

"We can go in the morning. I'll pick you up from the hotel. Where are you staying?"

"When I know I'll let you know."

After Jeff and Caldwell had departed, Barbara sat on the couch next to Cunningham.

"What do you think of Mr Caldwell?" Barbara asked.

"I think you need to be extra careful keeping his name out of your broadcasts. A slip of the tongue and I could be bringing flowers to your graveside every Sunday."

"He seemed harmless enough."

"Yes. Harmless like a snake," Cunningham responded. "I'd like to know just who he is and who he works for. When Jeff phoned Caldwell in Waipu I thought it was all pie in the sky but after my promotion he has shown himself to be a man of great influence."

Cunningham refilled their glasses. "Brian, what is it between you and Jeff? When I asked him he didn't want to talk about it. In fact he said he couldn't because it was a matter of national security. Is that true?"

Brian tilted his head and gave a tight-lipped smile.

"It does still have a security classification, but really the secrecy is no longer necessary. The knowledge of what took place can no longer affect the people most involved."

Barbara stayed silent. She sensed Brian was about to tell her something and an interruption might break the spell. He cradled his wine glass.

"We were on a mission in Afghanistan. I won't tell you all the particulars but Jeff had a contact named Josef. For some months Josef had fed Jeff a regular supply of intel on regional tribal movements, including the Taliban and Al Qaeda. It had led to a number of captures, and killings when capture was impossible. Apart from the money, Josef had personal reasons for helping us: the Taliban had killed his mother and father. He hated them more than we did.

"Anyway, it was getting dangerous for Josef. Terrorists like the Taliban might not lead lifestyles we would agree with but they weren't stupid and they were beginning to suspect that when raids followed Josef's visits that maybe he might be responsible. And they weren't interested in western legal practices. They didn't need proof of guilt, suspicion was enough to have him killed. Josef received word that a rebel named Banderman was about to arrive in his uncle's village. The allied forces had been after Banderman for a year and to stop him would bring an end to Al Qaeda and Taliban movements throughout the region. Banderman's tribe was strong and could guarantee the terrorists safe passage but without his ruthless leadership his men would fall into disarray.

"Josef, in an attempt to remove suspicion from himself and his uncle, took his wife and children with him when he made the visit. To make it look like an innocent family get-together. Once Banderman arrived, he would inform us and we would go in and take him out. Our section sat on a hill overlooking the village waiting for his signal. A drone passed overhead and fired missiles destroying the house. Banderman was visiting and also Josef's uncle's house. I will never forget the look on Jeff's face. He had promised Josef that he and his family would be safe but the Americans had decided that it was too risky to trust taking out Banderman in a raid by our section. Better to blow the place apart. Josef and his family would be unfortunate collateral damage.

"Of course, I knew of the plan but I hadn't given this information to Jeff. As the sky filled with dust from the explosion Jeff turned on me. The look of naked hatred for that one moment was truly fearful. I thought he was about to open fire on me. But he didn't, instead he slung his fist full into my face."

Cunningham rubbed his jaw as the memory of the day flashed by him.

"Jesus, poor Jeff," Barbara said. "You killed his friend. I know Jeff well enough now to know when he accepts you into his life there is no middle ground."

"You're right, and I rather expected him to react that way."

Barbara leaned forward, confused. Brian gulped a mouthful of wine.

"Josef wasn't just working with Jeff, he worked with the Americans. For them he had established a network of spies across Afghanistan and the Americans had paid out a lot of money to set it up and keep it going. Josef had been smart, he had worked out early on that his personal security was not threatened as long as he kept his list of spies secret. The Americans did not like it but the intel was so good they accepted Josef working for them on his terms. A few hours before Banderman was to enter Josef's uncle's village, the Americans learned that Josef had been betrayed by one of his own spies. The reason for Banderman's visit was in fact to kill Josef and his family. Men working for Banderman had purposely let it slip that the tribal chief was to pay a visit, knowing that Josef would make the trip as well. The Americans could not afford to lose Josef and his contacts."

"What did they do?"

"Josef and his family arrived a day earlier, made a show of walking through the village and chatting to as many people as they could to ensure Banderman's men were aware of their presence, and in the middle of the night the Americans smuggled them out. Josef, his family and the uncle."

Barbara raised her eyebrows. "I don't understand – if Josef and his family weren't killed why is Jeff so pissed off with you?"

Cunningham said, "The Americans knew that Banderman's men had been watching Jeff. When the drone went overhead and Josef's uncle's house was destroyed Jeff had no idea they were not in it. He reacted exactly the way we knew he would. Your character assessment of Jeff was accurate. He would lay his life down for his friends and his worse fault is he always feels so fucking responsible for everyone. So Jeff belted me one. Hitting an officer in the field on active service is a serious offence. A sham court martial took place. Jeff was the only one who thought it was for real. Of course I refused to testify and it was suggested to Jeff he resign. Which he did."

"But why? If Banderman was dead why keep the charade going?"

"Banderman wasn't killed. While the Americans were playing games so was he. He sent someone disguised as himself. So it was important that Banderman be convinced that Josef and his family died in the bombing. That meant sacrificing Jeff's career. There were spies everywhere and we made sure it became common knowledge that Jeff had struck a superior officer because his friend had been killed by the Americans. We were later informed that Banderman accepted this as true."

"Bloody hell, Brian. Poor Jeff. And he continues to live with the guilt. Why the hell haven't you told him? If you can tell me, why not Jeff?"

"Jeff would never believe me and I no longer have proof of the truth."

"Why not?"

"A few months later Josef and his family and his uncle were having dinner in a Kabul café which was destroyed by a suicide bomber."

"Jesus. And you don't think telling Jeff would help him?"

"Jeff is a soldier. He'll get over it."

Barbara gulped some wine. "Fucking men."

Lee Caldwell paced his hotel room, an idea formulating. He had had a shower and was sipping a scotch as he moved about. The unfolding drama was puzzling. What the hell were the terrorists up to? It hadn't surprised him to find that Jeff Bradley was at the epicentre. And, as had happened in Kosovo, a group of loyal friends were gathering round him. Bradley's actions had managed to bring the cockroaches into the sunlight and in his opinion the path to Zahar Akbar was the prisoner in Whangarei, but getting information from him might prove difficult. This was New Zealand. Three small islands, four million people and a bunch of sheep stuck at the bottom of the world. New Zealanders believed everyone was good and everyone had rights. If the prisoner chose not to speak then he wouldn't be forced to.

Caldwell opened his phone and checked for messages. Nothing from the Admiral. That surprised him. When he started a new mission the Admiral liked to keep tabs and he expected regular updates. He was struck by a mental image of his square-jawed boss with the bulldog bearing, pacing his office as he waited for news. He must be at dinner. Even bulldogs had to eat.

Caldwell's business card read that he was a Technical and Management Advisor for Devon Securities. What it didn't show was that Devon Securities was a subsidiary branch of Incubus, the world's second-largest private security company. Caldwell's directive was to ensure the safety of American citizens outside the United States, especially high-level government personnel, and then find those who threatened American security and American lives and get rid of the garbage. The Admiral protected him and others working to the same objectives from crusading politicians. In practice Caldwell and his colleagues had a free hand and access to any government agency they needed but to keep a low profile. With men like Bradley in the mix, it made that particular order difficult. The village of Waipu was now splashed across the front pages of the world's newspapers and the lead story on major television networks.

He dialled a number.

"American Embassy."

"I know it's late," Caldwell said, "But I need to talk to the ambassador urgently. Please contact him and have him call me back." Caldwell gave the number of the hotel. "My code name is Nemesis."

29.

Caldwell was in the Hilton Hotel lobby when Cunningham arrived. "Would you like a coffee before we start?" The policeman asked.

"I've had my fill. If you don't mind I'd like to get this out of the way. I have a busy schedule today."

Cunningham gave Caldwell a sideways glance as he led him to the car, and Caldwell suppressed a smile. Cunningham was probably wondering how a man who'd only just arrived in the country – friendless – could have any schedule at all. He didn't see any point in attempting to explain, not yet anyway. He was waiting on a response from the Admiral and until he had one there was little point discussing his plans with the New Zealand police officer. That he had demonstrated he had influence should be enough for Cunningham. He figured Cunningham was smart enough to know that if he had something to tell him he would, and in their world they did not idly chinwag about state secrets to pass the time. However, New Zealand did have laws and he knew Cunningham was probably worrying whether he should be allowing an American he didn't know to wander Auckland streets uncontrolled.

Caldwell stayed silent as they drove through the city. His appraisal of Cunningham was that as an ex-military man he was making a reasonable fist of policing, but doubted he could ever truly be a cop. Special Forces soldiers were trained to make their own rules. They followed their instincts to survive, which meant sometimes the rule book had to go out the window. From what Jeff Bradley had told him, Cunningham was already operating outside police dogma, which was to obey the law without question.

Cunningham had no future in the force. He was a good man to have on side in a fight. He undoubtedly could handle himself. With the SAS training he could at least make a decision, think outside the box. He guessed Cunningham's ready acceptance of him was because of Cunningham's SAS cloak-and-dagger background and his experience working with men who lived in the shadows. Jeff had been right to insist Cunningham stay in command.

The policeman guarding the entry to the warehouse stood aside to allow Cunningham to drive in.

"This is the way you found it?" Caldwell asked as he climbed out of the car.

"Pretty much. A forensics team has been through it but nothing has been moved from the premises."

The small entranceway had two doors. Cunningham opened the first.

"This is the office. We didn't find much of interest. Seems at least in here legitimate business was conducted in a normal manner. All the documentation and the information found on the computers thus far relates to the export company. In the next few days forensics will move the computers out of here."

"Which is Krasniqi's desk?"

"At the end of the room by the window," Cunningham pointed.

Caldwell nodded and walked towards it. Cunningham followed but kept a distance. He would give Caldwell room to manoeuvre. From where Cunningham stood the view through the window was of a high fence and a line of trees. The trees meant the compound was insecure. Any kid could climb a tree and scramble over the fence in seconds. Other than the security issues his men had not found anything of interest in the outside surrounds.

There were four desks. Maps and a calendar hung on the wall. The desks were covered in files and documents. Nothing unusual at first glance. But for Caldwell this was a terrorist site, and he knew there would be something here. He walked slowly from desk to desk. Caldwell sensed Cunningham was about to say something. He held his hand up for silence. He needed to concentrate. He might miss it.

Cunningham took the hint and moved back to the doorway, watching in silence. For the next hour Caldwell searched each desk. He pulled the drawers out, checked behind them. He emptied the filing cabinet and checked the toilet complex. Next he checked the walls, running his hand over the texture checking for imperfections. Then he turned his attention to the ceiling. There were two long fluorescent lights; double tubes covered by a translucent plastic cover. In Eastern bloc prisons this was where prisoners hid smuggled mobile phones. Caldwell pulled across a chair and, standing on it, removed the cover and handed it to Brian. He undid a knob at one end and the tube housing dropped down. Caldwell put his hand between the gap.

"Bingo."

He removed something that looked like a radio, some rods and a small case like a flat laptop. He climbed down from the chair.

Cunningham recognised it. "A satellite phone." His tone was terse. He made a mental note to blast the forensics team. Caldwell had just made him look like an asshole.

"Yes, it's a satellite phone," Caldwell said, placing the parts on the table. "This will be a direct link to Avni Leka. I'd stake my life on it. We could put a trace on it but the only person who knows which number to dial is dead."

"One of the others might have one. We could get lucky." Cunningham nodded an agreement.

"I'm surprised they left the phone behind," Caldwell said.

Cunningham said, "That's easy. They were in a hurry. The phone is untraceable so why waste time retrieving it."

"Makes sense," Caldwell said. "Akbar and his men have killed off Krasniqi but they will still need assistance. I think we can safely assume there are others out there. Show me the warehouse."

Cunningham led the way back into the foyer and through the second door.

"Everything is pretty much as we found it except there was a hijacked container truck here. We dusted for prints and released it back to the owner. The truck was of no interest to us, only the contents of the container. As you can see, everything has been cleared out except for a few empty crates. I think whatever it was they received was loaded into small vans and not trucks. Otherwise they would have forklifted the crates and taken everything."

Caldwell approached one of the empty crates and plucked out a sheet of wrapping paper. He sniffed it then shook his head.

"Oil. Weapons, probably Kalashnikovs, maybe some handguns," he said holding up the paper. "Too many wrappers for my liking."

"I'd pretty much come to that conclusion myself. What about the bigger boxes?" Cunningham asked.

"I would think these held missiles. The sort you fire from the shoulder. Ground to air."

"Jesus," Cunningham said. "They can't shoot down passenger airliners with shoulder launchers. Self-defence, I would think. Choppers?"

"I agree," Caldwell said. "They didn't come all this way to blow an airliner out of the sky; they could do that anywhere."

"The submarine?"

"No. I doubt it. These things are heat seekers. A sub would give them nothing to target. I think you were right first time. If a police helicopter or military plane comes a-calling they'll blast it out of the sky."

"Okay. So the big question remains. What the hell are they up to?" Cunningham said, more to himself.

Caldwell was bent over one of the two larger crates, ten or twelve feet in length and three feet wide.

"Well, well. Now we know." Caldwell held up a plastic bag. "I might be one of the few people in the world who know what these are. I can't tell you how I know, but these trinkets," Caldwell rattled the bag, "are a master cylinder repair kit for an MK 46 torpedo."

"You're sure?" Brian asked.

"Yes I'm sure, and the crates are the right size."

"Then the crates held torpedoes?"

"There could have been something else in there but I think we assume the worst and if we're wrong, well, who would care. MK's are easy to get hold of and in the eighties were modified for use in shallow water. They can be launched from any type of boat including a recreation launch with the right apparatus attached." He shrugged. "It's easy enough to make a launch chute."

Cunningham kicked at the small table and sent half-filled coffee cups sailing through the air. "Then it is the sub they're after?"

Caldwell nodded. "It's the sub."

To date the idea of the submarine had never been seriously considered as a target because it had seemed impregnable, but now neither man had any doubts.

"I don't suppose we can convince the powers that be to cancel the submarine visit?" Cunningham asked, breaking the silence.

"Not possible," Caldwell replied. "Believe me, if it were that easy I would organise it. But think about it. It has taken thirty years for New Zealand to accept visits from nuclear-powered vessels. The reason for the ban in the first place was because citizens of your country were frightened of an attack on the ships and they'd all die of radiation poisoning. If the US backs down now they will be agreeing and the ban goes back on. We need to be in these waters."

"Okay, I get the point."

Caldwell went on, "I'm afraid this has to be done the hard way. Find them and stop them. We will alert everyone needing to know and I'm assuming the submarine commander will have defensive measures he can put in place. Question is how far are you prepared to go to get the answers we need, Inspector?"

Cunningham looked across at Caldwell. "I take it you have something in mind?"

30.

His name was Jamil Khallid. A 29-year-old Egyptian national. It had not taken the Language Department at Auckland University long to determine that the language on Moana's tape recording was Egyptian Arabic. A visiting student had been able to translate. Cunningham ordered Jamil's fingerprints be sent to police in Cairo. He had telephoned himself to speak with his equivalent rank and explain its urgency. The Egyptian police cooperated and responded quickly. Khallid was known to them. He had been arrested a number of times. Petty crimes mostly. They suspected him of involvement in a car bombing. Now that he was captured they would be very interested in speaking to him. Under no circumstances should the New Zealand police release him. Cunningham had assured the Egyptians that this wasn't going to happen.

All Whangarei police officers had been called into the station, even those on leave. A 200-metre perimeter of armed officers surrounded the station. The search for the other terrorists had been scaled down. Inspector Jimmy Carlyle reluctantly accepted that they were probably back in Auckland by now. The three terrorists might have escaped but if they wanted to try and rescue their comrade it would not be successful on his watch.

Khallid was brought out from the cells, handcuffed and surrounded by six members of the SAS. This move surprised Carlyle. He had been informed that the duty of escorting the prisoner was with the police anti-terrorist team, the STG. The SAS replaced them at the last minute. There were another five squadron members outside. All armed. Carlyle gave a nod of approval. Brian Cunningham was taking no chances.

At first he had been miffed that it was not he and his men escorting the prisoner to Auckland but he had kept the disappointment to himself. When Cunningham phoned he had convinced him that if Khallid's friends made an attempt to rescue him, the SAS was better trained to handle it. They had the military experience. Most had served in Middle East hot spots. Begrudgingly Carlyle saw the wisdom behind the decision and acquiesced. But he was not happy about it and said so. He wanted it on record that he and his men were fully capable of ensuring a prisoner could be delivered to Auckland.

Secretly though, he was pleased to be rid of his unwanted guest. None of his men, including himself, had any experience with these types of offenders. Over the last two nights he had worried that armed terrorists might try to rescue their captured comrade. His men would have had no chance.

There were three vehicles, one to carry the prisoner and two escorts. A helicopter would follow them into Auckland. This had also confused Carlyle. Why didn't they just chopper him to Auckland? When he asked he received no reply. All police stations on route had been notified and officers would be lining the highway at varying intervals to control traffic and ensure the convoy was not held up.

Carlyle led the way outside. Khallid and his escort followed. He was pushed onto the back seat. A soldier sat either side of him. At the end of the street a crowd had gathered. Journalists, press photographers and television news teams were everywhere. One of the cameramen had a CNN insignia. Jesus, Carlyle thought. Now we are international news. He hoped nothing went wrong until they were well out of Whangarei. He admonished a constable standing next to him for not having a button done up. Now was not the time to look sloppy.

~

The main highway back to Auckland passed through the rural township of Wellsford. It had long been the supply centre for local farmers and a stop-off point for motorists. The kilometre-long main street started at the top of the hill just past the Wellsford High School, and ran down to the bend in the road leading to the food hall that included a McDonalds restaurant, and on to the outskirts of town and the continuation of the highway to Auckland. The right-hand side of the road all the way down to the McDonalds was lined with cafés and retail shops, and on the left a service station and a pub – the meeting place for farmers and locals alike to meet and discuss everything from the fortunes of the local rugby team to the unpredictable weather. The stores and side streets offered everything from hamburgers to seeds and tractors. It was an active town and with the many tourists passing through a prosperous one too. Little happened and everybody knew everybody; a trusting community.

Mid-morning in Wellsford was not unlike any other weekday. Traffic was heavy with trucks and buses moving goods and people back and forth from Auckland, and cars carrying locals and tourists. The pavement bustled with early morning shoppers. Patrons sat at outside tables enjoying coffees in the morning sun. The townsfolk, preoccupied, failed to notice the group of men in dark clothing assembling at the bottom of the hill.

There was an air of anticipation in the village; the same excitement that built up each year leading up to the annual Santa parade. All knew of the events that had taken place in Waipu and that today the captured terrorist would be driven through their town.

Television and radio bulletins alerted the locals that the convoy was getting closer, and latecomers dashed from homes to line both sides of the street, housewives escaping the drudgery of their daily routine and farmers decided to leave the hosing of cowpats off the concrete floors of their milking sheds until the drama had passed.

The *whoop whoop* of the police helicopter blades signalled the convoy's approach. All eyes looked skywards and then towards the top of the hill. The police cars rounded the bend at the top of the main street and began their descent with media vehicles in hot pursuit. The CNN crew was rushing back to Auckland to prepare for the arrival of the submarine. They had footage of the terrorist leaving the police station and had settled down in their vehicle to relax and enjoy the drive.

At the bottom of the hill a truck attempting to pull out of a side street and turn onto the main street had been stopped by a police officer. No traffic was permitted until the convoy had passed. The officer offered a friendly smile and informed the driver it would only be a few minutes. The driver nodded and waited patiently.

The convoy passed the service station and neared the bend.

A blaring horn drew attention from bystanders. Something was amiss. The blaring continued. All eyes turned to the intersection. Gasps from the crowd as the truck now accelerated across the road sending the point duty police officer leaping for safety. The truck stopped, blocking both sides of the road forcing the convoy to a complete stop.

"Bloody truckies!" someone yelled.

There were no dissenters to the statement, just a lot of nodding of heads. Everyone had been trapped behind a truck that refused to pull over and let them pass. No one liked truckies. Then finger pointing and yelling turned into screams. Men with black balaclavas pulled over their heads moved out from the crowd. Strange weapons held at arm's length were turned towards the crowd and bullets sprayed over their heads. At first no one moved. Startled rabbits eyes wide open. More shots came and legs pushed overweight and undersized torsos in random directions. People ran in circles, running into each other, the smallest knocked to the ground and the biggest pushing and shoving their way to safety. In seconds locals had disappeared down side streets or into shops or prostrated themselves on the pavement in a mass religious submission to God, praying to be safe.

One of the first to react was the CNN cameraman. He had had experience in the Middle East and knew immediately what the sounds were. Their vehicle had come to a halt just as the others had. He took hold of his camera and leapt from the vehicle, already filming before he managed to stop his forward momentum.

The SAS took up shooting positions but held fire. The crowd ran in all directions. The local officers who had been controlling traffic, like most New Zealand police, were not armed. The SAS pulled them to safety. The firing from the men in balaclavas increased in intensity. The first two SAS soldiers out of their vehicles had fallen to the ground. Not moving. Hysterical bystanders ran across the road between the police cars to escape the black clad invaders, adding to the confusion. Some patrons in the outside cafés had pulled the tables over and were using them as shields.

Heavy fire forced the soldiers back. Masked men surrounded the vehicle that held Jamil Khallid. Out gunned, the soldiers inside put their hands up. To fight back would be suicide. They would have no chance. The other police officers now held their fire. They had lost control and their comrade's safety came first. No one needed to die trying to protect a terrorist.

The CNN team now had live coverage feeding into their satellite link. From behind the safety of his vehicle, a journalist reported on the action as it unfolded, interspersing his commentary with a summation of events over the last few days. Instant news, being the lifeblood of CNN, ensured the feed from the small village of Wellsford was going into living rooms across the globe.

The passenger door opened and the soldier was pulled from the car and was made to stand to one side. Khallid climbed out. He was smiling as he stood, ecstatic that his comrades had made such a daring rescue. No attempt was made to remove his handcuffs. Two men in black took hold of him by the arms and ran to the other side of the truck. Others lined either side of the truck lay down covering fire. The white plume of a missile passed in front of the helicopter hovering above. The pilot turned away and disappeared beyond the horizon.

Then they were gone.

Eye witnesses said they escaped in four white SUVs. The local car dealer from his position under a table confirmed they were Toyota Prado Land Cruisers. Ambulances arrived and the fallen men were loaded into them. The truck that had blocked the road delayed the SAS pursuit, and without the helicopter they had no idea where the fugitives had disappeared to. There were too many country roads that led to too many hiding places.

Locals rose from the pavement. Stunned silence turned to nervous chatter. Women with children in tow made their way home and the men gathered in the pub. The landlord had already phoned the wholesaler for more beer. The most exciting event ever to take place in Wellsford would be discussed late into the night. Later, as drinks disappeared into stomachs sagging over strained belt buckles and the stories became more exaggerated with each glass, the townsfolk would agree how fortunate they had been that with all the shooting no civilians had been injured.

31.

Like everyone else, Barbara Heywood watched the CNN broadcast mesmerised by the shootout in Wellsford. She envied the CNN journalist, who until this moment had been an unknown and now in the space of a few minutes had become an international star. The follow-up would continue and with the arrival of the submarine he would remain in the public arena for at least the next two weeks. The murders, the protests in Auckland, gun battles in the north; to the outside world New Zealand must be taking on the appearance of a country under siege.

Her heart went out to Brian Cunningham. He had been promoted, given absolute control, and had then lost New Zealand's most infamous prisoner. Barbara knew the way of the public service well enough and no doubt jealous underlings would be baying for his blood. She knew he had the inner strength to cope but leadership was a lonely post and political pressure would eventually take its toll. She considered phoning him and offering support but decided against it. He didn't need his space crowded with well-wishers at this moment.

~

Jamil Khallid's smiles had turned into a permanent grin. As he saw the rural landscape change to forest he wanted to laugh out loud and slap his thigh. For the moment he would have to wait before he could animatedly express his joy and thank his rescuers. Ten minutes from the scene of his escape he was still in handcuffs and none of the four men in the car had removed their balaclavas. His attempted communication brought no response. A quick assessment of his situation and the answer was obvious. Zahar was not pleased with him. The price for failure was understood by all. Why then had they not just killed him as he sat in the car? Was this a show of strength? Was Zahar trying to show the New Zealanders that he had the power to do as he wished and for them to be wary of confrontation? He hoped his death would be quick. Would he still go to heaven? Would he still be considered a martyr even if he was killed by his own men?

The vehicle turned off and drove deeper into the forest. Was he to be buried amongst the trees? No marker for his grave. If this was to be his fate then so be it. He would show no fear.

∾

Brian Cunningham looked over the heads of his team as they watched a replay of the shootout in Wellsford. No one spoke. Dispirited was the appropriate mood label in Cunningham's view. Again they had been so close to finding Akbar and again the connection had been taken from them. The loss of fellow officers added to the gloom. When the replay finished Cunningham ordered the television turned off.

There had been no grumbling when he assumed command.

He had taken Moana to one side and told her before he told the others. "Am I pissed off? Yes. No one likes to be moved aside," she had said. "But to be honest, Inspector, this is such a mess; I'm out of my depth. I have a feeling this is becoming more military than it is police work. Besides," she smiled, "I think it's more beneficial to my career to have you carry the responsibility."

"I'll need your office."

"Just make sure you keep my plants watered."

"Thanks Moana. If the plants die I'll buy you new ones."

With morale at a low ebb, he needed to give his team direction. Snap them out of it.

"Okay, people, I know how disappointing this must be but we need to remember our killer and his men are still out there and it's our job to find them. We now know the submarine is the target. It's a start. We also know these guys are hiding out in a warehouse somewhere. Moana, how is the warehouse hunt?"

"So far it's a long list. Ross is out talking to more agents. We should be finished by tomorrow and then it's a matter of knocking on doors."

"Okay, let's hand out the addresses you already have and get checking. No lone cowboy shit. I want everyone in pairs and everyone armed. You know what you have to do, let's get out there and do it."

They filed from the room. Moana stayed back and when they were alone sat down next to Cunningham. He drummed his fingers on the table top.

"Inspector, I just wanted to say how sorry I am Wellsford turned out the way it did," Moana said. "The pressure from above must be unbearable."

"Shit happens, Moana. What can I say?" Cunningham said. He smiled. "Maybe I'll start a security company when they throw me out of here. Supply guards to banks."

"The team asked me to tell you that we're behind you 100 percent. Don't ever forget that, will you?"

"Thanks, Moana. I appreciate the support and I haven't thrown in the towel yet. A break will come our way. We will nail these assholes I'm sure of it and then Wellsford will be forgotten."

Moana nodded but was not convinced. Many years of police work had taught her that sometimes the good guys simply didn't win.

~

The vehicles came to a halt in front of a concrete shed. Two men in the front vehicle climbed out and went into the building. Jamil watched with growing concern. Still no one had spoken. For Jamil, time and the silence had proved a leveller. His initial bravado was dissipating and he no longer wanted to die. When he met with Zahar he would explain it wasn't his fault. He wasn't the team leader, after all. If the mission had failed, could he, Jamil Khallid, be held responsible? No. This was not fair. He was the victim. Zahar was ruthless but he was no fool. Zahar knew he was loyal and capable. He could not afford to lose such men. No, he would see reason.

One of the men who had gone into the building came back out and waved. Jamil was pulled from the car.

"Where is Zahar?" Jamil asked. "Bring Zahar to me. I can explain everything." No one answered. He was pushed into the shed. It was dark and difficult to see. Nowhere to sit. He needed to use the toilet.

"I need to piss," he said but no one answered.

He was forced onto his knees. This is it, he thought. A bullet in the back of the head. At least it would be quick and painless. That was something. A bag was placed over his head and a string pulled it closed. Tight enough to ensure it was secure but not tight enough that he would choke. He felt handcuffs fastened to his ankles and then his hands were secured to them with a third set. He could not maintain his balance and fell on his side. There was no attempt to right him. He waited, eyes closed, for the gunshot but instead heard the sounds of boots leaving the building and then heard the door slammed shut. He relaxed a little. Then he urinated over himself.

32.

Zahar Akbar stood in the centre of Sami Hadani's lounge, hands tightened into fists, and every so often he swung at an imaginary figure. He was not a superstitious man, but as a young boy in the refugee camps an old woman had told him to be careful not to make God angry. If you do he will unravel your destiny. As a small child he had no idea what the old hag was talking about but now from the far reaches of his memory he dragged up her image. He believed in luck, God knows he had experienced enough of it, but was his luck running out? Had God sent Bradley to destroy him? Was God protecting this man? His brother had failed to kill the New Zealander and his own attempt to kill Bradley had failed. Now this. The capture of one of his men he could accept. In war prisoners were taken and soldiers killed, but the events taking place in the small New Zealand town unsettled him. The television journalists were calling it a rescue attempt but he knew better. Who were the men who had taken Jamil?

The presence of CNN had turned the incident in Wellsford into an international story. Members of the intelligence fraternity who might never have given New Zealand a second thought would now look this way. He had little doubt that from now on more resources would be made available to the police. A murderer would have stayed a police matter but terrorism brings in the military.

How much had Jamil told the police while he was in their custody? Not a lot. He didn't know much. This was New Zealand; they would not resort to torture and as long as Jamil had kept his mouth shut there would be no information forthcoming.

Whoever had taken him showed ruthlessness. Not afraid to fire on civilians and police. These men might make Jamil talk. He would assume that after twenty-four hours of interrogation they would know everything. At least Jamil did not know the location of the warehouse and his safe house had been cleared. Zahar was satisfied any link back to him had been cut.

He replayed the recorded CNN coverage of the attack. They were certainly carrying Kalashnikovs, which ruled out the police and the New Zealand military. Whoever they were they moved as a unit, the action disciplined. These guys were professionals. He sat on the coffee table and replayed the tape again. Then paused it.

"Sami!" He called out.

"Yes, Zahar? What is it?"

Sami walked into his sitting room, a steak sandwich in one hand and a glass of cognac in the other.

"Come look at this." Zahar replayed the tape. "Look at the men attacking the police. The way they are moving. What are your first thoughts?"

"Military," Sami replied, breadcrumbs spitting from his mouth. "Show a little more."

Zahar pressed the play button.

"Stop."

Zahar pressed pause.

"Look at that." He pointed to one of the men in black. "The way he is kneeling, elbow on his knee, his rifle at the ready, steady. That is military training. No doubt."

They watched the rest of the tape and then replayed it. The CNN cameraman had shown true professionalism. He managed to get close-ups. During the attack the two lead vehicles had been strafed with machine-gun fire and two policemen killed. Something caught Sami's eye. Zahar saw the indecision.

"There's a problem, Sami?"

"I don't know. Something is not right." Sami placed his steak sandwich and cognac on the coffee table and moved forward. Face inches from the screen. "Play the tape again." Zahar did as he was asked, pleased that Sami agreed that something was amiss. Again the tape came to an end and again Sami turned to Zahar and told him to run it again. Over the past weeks Zahar had concluded that Sami had the same feral instincts for survival as himself. They had both spent a good proportion of their lives as hunted men and survived. If there was something wrong Sami would discover it, of this he was certain.

"Pause it there." The picture stilled. Zahar watched as Sami scanned the screen. "Praise to Allah," he whispered. "That's it," he said rising from his crouching position.

"What is it? What do you see?" Zahar asked.

"Wrong question, Zahar. The question is what you don't see."

"I'm listening."

Zahar had risen from his chair and was staring at the screen but could not see anything out of the ordinary.

Sami pointed at the screen. "These cars have been sprayed with Kalashnikovs. Where are the bullet holes?"

Zahar leaned closer. "There aren't any."

"Exactly. And that is just not possible."

Zahar stepped back and sank into the leather sofa chair, his brain spinning as he attempted to assemble this information into some semblance of reason. "You are right, Sami, and in all the chaos no civilian casualties. Not even minor injuries. And the two policemen, taken away in the ambulance, there has been no report on their injuries." Reality dawned. "Blanks. They were shooting blanks."

"Had to be. You and I have fired enough of these weapons in similar situations. We know what they can do," Sami said.

"Yes. Then all this was theatre. The shot policeman. Bodies on the ground."

"If the shooting was theatre then we must assume all of it was theatre."

Zahar scratched his face, thoughtful. "But for what purpose? The police are bringing Jamil to Auckland for questioning. They stage a very visible mock attack and the whole country believes it was us rescuing our comrade – but of course we know better. In the end the police still have him and all they can do is question him. So why?"

"Maybe they think that we might try to kill him and that if we don't know where he is he will be safe."

"Yes. You might be right but if they were going to place him in a safe house why not just do it?"

"Anyway," Sami started, "this is not the Middle East. They cannot torture him, can they? Not under New Zealand laws. So nothing has changed."

"I agree. The New Zealand police cannot make Jamil talk but I have a feeling that maybe Jamil is no longer in the hands of the police."

Later, Zahar called Avni Leka on the satellite phone. Leka had not been pleased. He did not like failure, and he left Zahar in no doubt that somehow Bradley was connected to the abduction of Jamil.

"Your brother," Leka had said, "paid dearly for underestimating Bradley. Mark my words, the Jeff Bradleys of this world have a habit of falling down black holes and surviving. They destroy all in their path. Like a fucking elephant in a corn field. He needs to be dealt with, Zahar."

Zahar had listened. What else could he do? Avni Leka paid the bills. But he would make his own rules. The money that would secure his future meant the mission came first. He agreed with Avni that Bradley needed to go. But an open confrontation right now was foolish. He would continue with his original plan. Make Bradley suffer. Have him running in circles looking to protect his friends and when all was done he would pay him a visit.

~

For the first time in her career, Barbara Heywood was speechless. She poured herself a scotch and fixed her eyes back on Brian Cunningham seated opposite. He watched her, expressionless.

"I suppose the question that has to be asked is why?"

Barbara knew before she asked she was not going to like the answer.

"There are people in this country killing citizens. There is every reason to believe more will be killed. These terrorists are linked to an organisation that is responsible for bombings and many deaths throughout Europe. I want to catch them before it is too late, as do a number of international organisations. But we are New Zealanders. We have laws. Due process. Jamil Khallid is our only link to Akbar and his men, but Khallid does not want to talk to us and we have no way to make him talk if he stayed in prison. He'll be given a good lawyer. Hell, he might actually be released on bail."

"So you arranged for him to be given over to others who are beyond the law?"

"That's about the strength of it," Cunningham said, feeling uncomfortable under Barbara's accusatory gaze.

"Who has him?"

"I'm afraid I can't tell you that."

Barbara nodded thoughtfully and took another sip of her scotch. “I suppose that man Caldwell is behind it? I guess the next question is why are you telling me?”

“I promised to be up front with you.”

“Cut the crap. This is so not the sort of information you lay on anyone. How many laws have you broken? I guess it doesn’t matter since it will be reclassified under national security and it will never come out. In the meantime the poor sod is being tortured and then what? Executed? I think that can be the only outcome can’t it.”

Brian shrugged. “You’d have preferred I hadn’t told you?”

Barbara looked at her hands. “Of course I’d prefer you hadn’t told me,” she whispered. She looked up. “Why did you Brian?”

“I needed to speak it out loud. There was no one else.”

“Gee thanks. These are crimes, Brian. Now I’m implicated. Did you think of that?” He pursed his lips. “No, of course you didn’t. Now I feel as dirty as I know your hands must be. A boundary has been crossed, Brian. You’ve dragged me across the line with you. It brings up the argument of how far do you go before you’re just like them.”

“It wasn’t an easy decision, Barbara. I’ll resign from the force when this is over.” Cunningham stood up. “I have to get back. Don’t get up. I’ll see myself out.”

Barbara sat quietly and said nothing.

Cunningham left the apartment without looking back and Barbara didn’t call him back. She stayed in her seat cradling her glass, looking out at the city but not really seeing it.

~

Cunningham sat alone in the crime room going through files. In a few days the submarine would arrive. Half the team were sleeping in the cells below, the others in the cafeteria eating before heading back to the streets. He had thought of calling Barbara but dismissed the idea. The look on her face had said it all. When he had walked out of her apartment she had made him feel like a leper. He would leave her be for the moment. What was there to say?

The door opened. Red poked his head in.

"Inspector, you're wanted upstairs," Red said.

Cunningham pulled on his jacket. A quick look in the mirror. He straightened his tie. He had been expecting the call and was surprised it had taken so long. He wasn't quite certain what it was he would say. He was tired and had not prepared a response. How could he explain away the taking of his prisoner in Wellsford?

The Area Commander's secretary was not about when he entered reception. He checked the small kitchen. She was not there either. He knocked on the commander's door and entered. There were three men inside and the commander was not one of them. Two of the three had been in the office the day he had been given his reprieve and promotion. They sat either side of the new face. A lone chair sat in the centre of the room.

The man in the middle said, "Inspector Cunningham, please come in. Close the door and sit down." Cunningham obeyed. "My name is Percy Croydon. I am the Director of the SIS. These other two men are from Foreign Affairs."

Their names were not offered.

"I'll be honest with you, Inspector: when you were kept in charge of what seems to be an escalating problem I was against it. Nothing personal mind, but it concerned me that a policeman might not comprehend what we are up against with terrorists and might not react in the appropriate manner." Percy paused and gave Cunningham a quizzical look. "Then I had you checked out. Surprise, surprise. Your military career was exactly what I would have looked for if I wanted to put my own man in your position. The Americans spoke highly of you."

Cunningham offered a wry smile. "And this is why you have met with me. To tell me how wonderful I am?"

"No. I am meeting with you because I want to know what you have done with Jamil Khallid."

Cunningham raised his eyebrows.

"That façade in Wellsford might fool Joe Public but not us, Inspector. Please don't mistake us for idiots."

Cunningham nodded. Mulled over what to say. There was no point playing games. The SIS would find out sooner or later. He was surprised the Americans had not already informed the New Zealand Secret Service.

"Khallid is with the people he needs to be with to get the information I need," Cunningham replied.

"It is admirable that you're not wasting my time, Inspector. You have overstepped your authority," Croydon continued. "You realise this will ruin your career if it is ever made public. Probably even if it's not."

Cunningham nodded.

"May I ask why you're prepared to jeopardise your future and possible imprisonment?"

That shook Cunningham. He had never really thought through the consequences. His reaction did not go unnoticed by Percy Montgomery.

"The bottom line is I have a city full of killers and my investigations have led me to believe that their mission is going to cost many New Zealand citizens their lives. It is my duty to stop that from happening. I only had the one source for information – Khallid. Normal procedures needed to be put to one side. I had already decided that once all this is over my resignation will be on the table. I might add that this was my decision alone and no one else in my team knows anything about it."

Percy Croydon studied Cunningham for a moment and then smiled.

"It seems I have underestimated you, Inspector." He reached into his pocket and took out a card and passed it to Cunningham.

"This is my private phone number. Please keep me informed. After all, we are the SIS. We do have a right to know. In fact I'm sure the prime minister would expect us to know."

"I'll give a daily update," Cunningham replied.

"Excellent." Croydon stood and Cunningham did likewise. "Catch the bastards, Inspector."

"We will, Mr Croydon."

"One last thing, Inspector. Do we know what they're up to?"

"They're going to try to torpedo the *Ulysses*."

~

"Have you any food? I'm starving," Jeff asked.

Mary Sumner was lounging on the settee, half watching television half reading a magazine.

"Sorry. I haven't had a chance to do any shopping. There are some crackers somewhere."

Jeff glared. "I'm in the mood for a hamburger and fries. There's a fast food takeout only a block away."

"Jeff, it's raining. Why not order pizza?" Mary asked.

"I always eat pizza. I need a change of diet. I've got an umbrella and I need some exercise."

Jeff had been against her moving back into her apartment but Mary was adamant she needed her own space. Jeff insisted he stay with her for the first few nights and Mary had readily agreed. Jeff had arranged for a twenty-four-hour security guard to be parked outside. He wanted to be forewarned if Zahar decided to have another try at Mary. The guard was in a position to see her apartment and

Mary only had to put her head out of the window and help would be on its way.

"Can you get me a burger? I need food as well. No fries, I'll have some of yours."

"Not a chance. You can have your own bag of fries and I'll eat what you can't."

Mary stretched. "Want me to come with you?"

"Not if you don't want to. It's only a block away."

"Good, the couch is my favourite spot at the moment. And I don't want to get drenched."

Jeff stood in front of her, "Will you be okay on your own?" he asked.

Mary nodded, "I think so. I have to get used to it, don't I."

"I tell you what," Jeff said. "I'll call you when I get out on to the street and we can talk to each other all the time I'm away."

Mary smiled, "Thanks Jeff. I'd like that."

33.

The rain fell, heavy and unceasing.

All afternoon Zahar prayed for it to cease but his plea to Allah had gone unheeded. Sami had stolen him a Mitsubishi L300 van that belonged to a carpet-cleaning company. He would wear overalls when he entered the building. He'd even had Sami buy an industrial vacuum cleaner to complete the disguise. He would be going in late at night, but it shouldn't raise any alarm bells. Workmen always went unnoticed.

He parked across the street from the apartment entrance.

He already knew where to go. This would be his third visit to the blonde's apartment. Almost old friends. It astonished him that she had returned. Fortunately he had kept her apartment under surveillance. Now he would stab his knife through Bradley's heart by killing his lover.

He moved to the back seat and pulled on the overalls, then studied his environment. From his vantage point he could easily see the apartment window. The lights were still on. No matter; this time he was not waiting for her to go to bed. The uniformed security guard sitting in a marked vehicle had been easy enough to spot. He guessed the reasoning was that a show of his presence would be enough to deter an intruder. Bad luck for the guard. His man watching the building and had said no one had entered who looked like a police officer. Zahar had ordered him to take care of the security guard. Zahar looked out through the van windows. As far as he could see the cars close to hand were unoccupied. He placed his jacket into his backpack and carefully pushed the pack under the front seat.

൭

Cunningham and Moana Te Kanawa lolled on their chairs in the crime room, exhausted. Weakened eyelids collapsed causing Moana's shoes to stomp the floor as she tried to stop her slide from the chair.

"You could go home for a few hours. See your kids," Cunningham said.

"They're not kids any more. They'll be out on the town. Hopefully not in the back of one of our patrol cars."

Moana yawned.

"What about George? You haven't seen him for a few nights."

"We separated six months ago."

"Really? I'm sorry."

"So am I."

Cunningham fell silent.

Moana settled back in her chair. Cunningham hadn't needed to ask the reason for the breakup. His own marriage had only lasted six months. He had no answers so he was not about to give advice.

Moana said, "Last time I looked my eyes had become blackened circles. I've given up trying to hide the rings behind foundation; in fact as you've probably noticed I don't wear much make up at all these days. No wonder George left."

Cunningham cast an eye over his sergeant. There was nothing wrong with the look of her that a few days' sleep wouldn't fix. She'd opened up to him. Interesting. Moana had always kept her private life private. Tiredness and stress. Maybe they were the same reasons for his opening up to Barbara about Wellsford.

The rest of the team rested in emptied cells in the basement. Cunningham had commandeered the lockup as temporary accommodation. Anyone to be held in custody was transferred to the Mount Eden Detention Centre. New arrests were transported to stations in the outlying suburbs.

His mobile rang.

"Cunningham."

He nodded as he listened.

"Okay we're on our way. Less than ten minutes." To Moana, he said, "The security guard parked outside Mary Sumner's has not reported in. He's not answering his emergency beeper. They're sending someone to check on him but that might take twenty minutes. They have instructions to phone here if anything is out of the ordinary. Just before he went off air he reported a van parked opposite. Belongs to a carpet-cleaning company. The security company checked the registration number. It was stolen this afternoon."

Moana was on her feet. "It's him."

"That's what I think," Brian answered. "Rouse the team and let's go."

~

Zahar pulled on the surgical gloves, opened the side door and climbed out, then reached back and picked up the vacuum cleaner. Doors pulled shut and the van locked, he dashed across the street. The rain was easing but still heavy enough that water dribbled off the end of his nose as he stood in the foyer. He pressed the button for the elevator doors. As they closed behind him he heard the main door open. Whoever had entered missed the chance to ride with him by seconds. He pushed the button for the sixth floor.

As he ascended he opened the top of the cleaner and pulled out the small pack of plastic explosive. Just enough to blow the door. He held it in one hand, the detonator and length of wire in the other. When the door opened he placed the vacuum cleaner between the sliding doors to stop the elevator from closing. No one would be coming up behind him. He checked his watch. From now, two minutes. Zahar set a small knob of the plastic explosive on the door.

~

It took Cunningham and his team less than seven minutes to arrive at the building. Cunningham and Moana ran to the security vehicle.

"Jesus," said Cunningham, pulling open the door. The guard rolled out onto the road, lifeless eyes looking up at the two police officers. The bloodied opening across his throat reached almost to his spine. The front of his grey security shirt was stained crimson.

Police cars now blocked both ends of the street with others closing in to establish a wider perimeter. Cunningham wanted to make certain his man was not going to escape.

"That must be the van," Cunningham said pointing across the street.

Moana dashed across the street and tried the door. "It's locked," she yelled.

Cunningham said, "Okay. I doubt it will be of much help to us for the moment so we'll worry about it later. Come on back. Now, where's Red?"

"Right here."

Cunningham turned. "Have you got through to Mary or Jeff?"

Red shook his head, "Both lines are engaged."

"Moana, I want two men behind the building and two in the doorway right now. Anyone trying to leave I want held until cleared."

Cunningham led the remainder of his team in. The light above the elevator door showed it was on the sixth floor. He pushed the button. The floor light didn't move. "The door has been jammed open. That means he is still here. He might be killing Mary right now."

Without speaking Red smashed his gloved hand through the fire safety glass and onto the protruding fire alarm button. The building immediately resonated with the sound of sirens and bells. It was deafening. Red looked at Brian.

"My decision. I accept full responsibility," Red said.

"Absolutely you do." He pointed to Red and Ross. "You two take the stairs."

~

Zahar pushed in the detonator and took a few paces along the corridor, then flattened himself against the wall. He flicked the switch. The sound of the blast echoed off the walls and the hall filled with the smell of explosives, burning and wisps of smoke. He pulled his pistol from his pocket and stepped through the space where the door had been. He saw the blonde disappear into the bathroom. The door slammed shut.

"Silly girl. That's not going to help," he muttered.

He rushed to the door and smashed his shoulder into it. It gave a little. He tried again. Wood splintered around the lock. She had something against it. A cabinet of some sort he guessed. He reached into his pocket for more explosive then there was a sharp bang and a hole appeared in the door. He jumped to the side. A bullet hole. She had a gun.

"You bitch. That won't help." He fired at the door, from an angle. Then another hole appeared in the door. Smart girl, he thought. She is not going to empty the magazine. He placed a knob of the plastic explosive on the door.

Zahar's head snapped round as he heard a loud clanging sound from the corridor. He ran to the blasted doorway and peered into the hall. An alarm. From within the building, not her apartment. It had to be a fire alarm. The fire brigade would not be far away. Police behind them. He ran to the window and looked down into the street. He stiffened. Stepped back. The police were everywhere. His van surrounded. They knew he was here. How? Had they set off the alarm? They must have.

He paced. Thinking. He went back to the hole. People were moving through the corridor in various stages of undress; dressing gowns, unlaced track shoes or slippers. What to do? Instincts kicked in. He took off the carpet-cleaning overalls and pulled his shirt out of his trousers. He grabbed an umbrella from the stand. It was a woman's. Even better. He tousled his hair and stepped out into the corridor.

He followed the residents in to the stairwell and down another level and then slipped through the safety door. Police would be climbing the stairs. He would hide until he heard the footsteps climbing the stairs had run past him. He waited two minutes then re-entered the stairwell.

At the third floor he peered through the stairwell window. The police were everywhere, checking residents as they left the building. There was no escape. He was trapped.

~

The fire engine forced its way through the police blockade and parked, two wheels on the pavement. The incoming firemen added to the confusion. The fire brigade wanted control.

Cunningham and Moana stood under umbrellas, watching the residents stream outside. The two constables standing either side of the door, shining torches into confused faces, were suddenly overwhelmed, pushed aside by angry residents fleeing an imaginary emergency.

"What do you think?" Moana asked.

"I think we get in there and sort it out."

In the foyer he saw the elevator lights flashing. It was moving again, but a fireman blocked them from entering.

"Can't go in there, mate. It's out of use until we give the all clear," he said firmly.

"Get out of my fucking way, you idiot. We set off the alarm because there is a killer in this fucking building and now we are trying to catch him. Now get outside or I'll have you arrested. Do you understand me?" snapped Brian.

The fireman stepped back, his face contorted with anger. He gestured with his head to tell his men to back off.

Cunningham entered the lift, Moana right behind him. He did not bother to look back at the firemen and offer a conciliatory smile. Right now he couldn't care less about their sensibilities.

Red was waiting inside the apartment. "Mary Sumner is still alive," he said.

"Lucky for you," Cunningham said.

"He left these behind." Red held up a pair of overalls.

"Clever bastard," Brian said. "Trying to make himself look like he just climbed out of bed. He could still be in the stairwell. If he is in the building he is not getting out."

~

The heavy rain had returned. The residents were not happy. More than a hundred were now crammed into the lobby and those allowed to pass had been forced away from the building and the protective cover of the green awning that sheltered the entrance. 'The Towers' in gold lettering was printed along the front overhang.

They became abusive as they became sodden. They pushed through the police cordon and sought shelter across the street. Bystanders from surrounding buildings gathered on the street, curiosity dragging them from cosy apartments.

As Zahar watched from his vantage point he could see that even in the confusion the police were still managing to check anyone leaving the building. The fire engine blocked his van. It was hopeless. A pity.

He took the trigger mechanism from his trouser pocket. His van had been ignored by the police, more interested in catching him. A bad decision. The small street was circled by high rise apartment buildings, forming the perfect canyon. The perfect confined space, and now it had filled with people. The explosives in the backpack would turn the van into a giant grenade, sending shrapnel in all directions cutting through flesh like a scythe through wheat. He stepped back up the stair until he was clear of the window.

He squeezed.

A flash of white. Splinters of glass ricocheted off the cement walls of the stairwell and then the thundering sound of the blast followed. He had held his ears but they still rang when he took his hands away. Now haste was needed. He made his way down the stairs. Glass scrunched under the leather soles of his shoes. An old woman looked up at him, her face bloodied. He ignored the outstretched arm. The sound of wailing heightened as the injured felt pain. Outside, smoke rose from the blast centre and from the cars now on fire. The road and small park were strewn with debris and bodies. The injured lay unmoving and others staggered directionless, blinded by the explosive flash. The fire engine lay on its side; underneath the machine Zahar sighted the sleeve of a firearms jacket and from it an arm protruded, the hand twitching, closing and unclosing.

On the outer rim he saw movement. Police and injured onlookers were moving forward.

Opposite was a driveway that ran down between buildings. At the bottom lay a gate that Zahar already knew led to a back alley. He picked his way across the street. No one stopped him, asked him where he was going. He knelt beside the nearest body and rubbed his hand across the neck wound then smeared the blood over his face. He now limped and managed a bewildered look. The police and helpers would pay him no attention. He was one of the lucky ones. No one cared. Then he froze. He recognised him immediately. Jeff Bradley ran past, brushing against him. Then he reacted. Searched for his pistol. Before he had it pulled from his pocket Bradley had disappeared into the building.

Halfway down the driveway he straightened his clothing and made his way through the back alleys until the screams were lost in the distance and the sounds of sirens engulfing the city. He stepped into the shadows of a doorway, pulled out his mobile and dialled Sami Hadani's number.

34.

Cunningham used the coffee table to lever himself from the floor. Moana had rolled onto her back. Blood ran down her forehead from a cut above her left eye.

Cunningham looked down at her. "Are you okay?" he asked.

She nodded. He took her outstretched hand and pulled her to her feet. "In case you were wondering, that was a bomb."

"Really? Now I know why you can be such an asshole sometimes. Spending half your life in the military putting up with that crap would stuff anyone's brain."

Cunningham smiled. "Good girl. You really are okay."

The explosion shattered the window panes from their frames launching a thousand barbed-glass missiles. They embedded themselves in the plaster board walls and flesh. Red appeared in the doorway, a constable peering over his shoulder.

"What the hell happened?" he asked, banging the side of his head. "I think I've gone deaf."

"You'll live." Cunningham stepped to the window and looked out. "Fucking hell." He turned back to Red. "A bomb has exploded and there are casualties. Take care of things up here and you," Cunningham said, pointing to the constable, "start on this floor and check all the apartments. If there is no response kick the door in and check. I'll send help if and when available. Weapons drawn. Our killer might still be in the building but I'm guessing he just opened himself a doorway and has scarpered."

Mary emerged from the bathroom.

"Mary, are you okay?" Cunningham asked.

She nodded, a little shakily.

"And where the bloody hell is Jeff?"

"Right here." Jeff stood in the doorway. He walked across to Mary and put his arm round her. "I'm taking her to my place. If you need to talk that's where we'll be."

Cunningham nodded. "All right, Jeff, for now it's best you're both out of the way. And Jeff, Mary has a gun. Know anything about that?"

"No, she hasn't, Brian," Jeff said, taking the weapon from Mary and pushing between his belt and shirt. "Can we go now?"

"Yeah, get out of here."

"Moana, we need to get on the street and coordinate emergency services."

"What about Zahar Akbar?" Moana asked.

Cunningham didn't answer. He was already in the corridor. At the bottom of the stairwell Moana paused in front of a body, a hand to her mouth. She shut her eyes. Cunningham touched her shoulder. She shrugged it off. Looked at him then straightened. Cunningham understood. Now was not a time for weakness – they had a job to do.

The walls and door of the bottom floor were now rubble. Looking through the gap Cunningham saw into the kitchen of a ground floor apartment. A woman lay, unmoving, on the breakfast bar top, a man bent over her weeping. He stepped outside. In the small piazza surrounded by apartments the dead and dying were entangled and amongst the debris lay severed limbs from those closest to the blast. The fire chief knelt, beating down on the chest of one of his men. A few metres away a woman sat, hair darkened and matted, moving her head side to side muttering incomprehensibly. Her pyjamas were shredded and her legs bleeding. The bloodied bundle in her arms was a baby.

The acrid smell of the explosives hung heavy in the air, now mixed with smoke from the smouldering buildings and burning cars.

Ambulances, police cars and fire trucks were descending and in the distance were more sirens.

"All right, Moana, you take the top of the street, I'll take the other. We're not equipped to help the injured but we can coordinate the emergency services. Get a flow through going. Reinforcements are on their way."

As Cunningham stepped over bodies his gut wrenched when he recognised a police uniform, but he didn't stop. Jeff was right, he was nothing but a callous asshole. Did he have no feelings? He gnashed his teeth and kept walking.

At least the rain had stopped.

When Cunningham was finally relieved he stepped away and sat on a small wall where the media crews had gathered. He saw Barbara Heywood standing in front of a camera, a mic in her hand. She was giving a report. Then the cameraman swung away to film the carnage. Barbara saw Cunningham. She passed her mic to an assistant and made her way to him.

Cunningham waited, readied himself for the onslaught. Barbara leaned forward. Her face barely inches from Cunningham's.

"You get those fucking assholes, Brian. I don't care what you have to do but you hunt them down. Get them. Kill them. I don't give a shit."

Before he could respond Barbara spun on her heel and strode back to her team.

~

Sami Hadani eased his car along the lane. He accelerated when he saw Zahar step out of the shadows. When he stopped he reached across and pushed down on the passenger door handle.

Zahar climbed in and slammed the door behind him.

"Get me the hell out of here."

"You're soaked. There's a blanket on the back seat."

Zahar reached back and took hold of the blanket. He wrapped it round himself. It would stave off the chill until they made it back to Sami's house.

Red lights flashed past as they turned onto the main road.

"What happened?" Sami asked.

"Somehow the police knew I was there."

"How could they. No one knew where you were, only me."

Sami felt the killer's eyes narrow on him. He quickly spun on him.

"Don't even think that, Zahar. And don't even think of threatening me. I'm not one of your minions."

Zahar smiled.

"The New Zealand police are clever," Sami said. "Not like the shit we have to deal with in our countries. Somehow they found out. Found the van."

More sirens.

"Something's happening. What have you done?" Sami said, worried.

"I was trapped. No way out so I detonated a bomb I'd placed in the van. It worked. Nobody tried to stop me. I just walked away."

Sami pulled over. Turned to face Zahar. Confused.

"Were there any casualties?"

Zahar nodded.

~

Jeff and Quentin sat in the reception area of Quentin Douglas and Associates. The door was locked. An unopened bottle of whisky sat on the small coffee table. They were surrounded by Mary's bits and pieces. Her pot plants, a print, some small ornaments. Her desk was laden with paraphernalia that neither Quentin nor Jeff had noticed before, but now everywhere they looked they saw Mary. In the short time she had been with Quentin she had made this her domain. She now lay on the settee. Jeff's hand rested on her leg. Reassurance that allowed her to sleep.

"We're going to stay here tonight, Quentin. He won't think of coming here."

Quentin poured two whiskies. He was shaking. Jeff reached across and held his friend's hand and extracted the glass of whisky, half of which had splashed onto the table.

"I'd better get home to Jeannie and the kids," Quentin said quietly. "It's not fair to leave them alone."

"Quentin, you are to go home and pack whatever you need and take your family away from here tonight. Stay away until this is over," Jeff said firmly. "Go to Wellington or wherever. The further away the better. But get the hell out of here." Quentin made to open his mouth, but Jeff held up his hand. "No arguments. This is pure vindictiveness. Aimed at me. No one I know will be safe until these guys are caught. I do not want anything to happen to you, Jeannie or the kids. I could never live with that. I'm having enough trouble coping with the fact there are bodies in an Auckland gutter because of me."

"I'm not going to argue with you, Jeff. I had already been thinking along those lines. What about you?"

"I'm going to hunt the bastards down."

Quentin said, "Jeff, you do know you're not to blame for what these people have done, don't you?" But he knew his words had fallen on deaf ears. "I'm leaving. I'll let you know where we are."

"No, Quentin. No contact until this is over."

Quentin nodded.

He threw Jeff a key. "Lock up when you leave. And for God's sake be careful."

35.

How are we doing on the warehouses?" Cunningham asked Moana.

His team was still in shock. He knew the signs. All soldiers in war zones went through it. The first attacks, the first time being bombed and shot at and the first time they had lost comrades. Three of the team had been killed and another seriously injured, but just like in war soldiers needed to keep going. The enemy was still out there and was still determined to kill. Akbar had escaped their trap. But they needed to keep moving. The terrorists weren't resting and neither could they. He was getting more manpower. He had been told every spare cop in the country was on their way to Auckland, but the key word was *spare*. They wouldn't be bringing the expertise he needed. The tactics team was on permanent standby as were units from the SAS but they had been deployed to secure government buildings and key personnel. It made his job that much harder but at least he was still in control. The investigation would be split into specialist teams now. New squads with their own team leaders would be talking to witnesses, gathering information, forensics, media control and so on. He would keep his own team as a roving squad with one objective: to follow the leads and find Akbar and his men.

Moana said, "It's slow work but we are more than halfway through the list. Some of it is access. Locked doors, etc. Especially at night. Then trying to contact owners takes time."

"Okay, I understand. From now on you carry bolt cutters and sledgehammers. Cut the chains and smash the doors down. Do not leave the building until it is cleared. Anyone hassles you, you direct them to me."

"Is that legal?" Red asked. "What about warrants?"

"I will take the heat for it. You may suffer a little but this situation is not normal. More people are going to die and I'm not going to have that happen because I couldn't enter a bloody warehouse. Anyone have a problem with these methods, please say now. I'll allow you to leave the team. No hard feelings." Cunningham scanned the faces but no one replied and no one moved. "Okay, thank you." He sat in his chair. "Now anyone else have any thoughts?"

"I have something that has been bothering me." It was Red.

"The floor is yours, Red." The rest of the team looked up from their doodling.

"There is a group of men, international terrorists, moving about our city and the countryside. We don't know how many but I think we can assume from the mattresses we found in the warehouse not less than six, probably more. Let's make it a round figure and call it ten." Everyone nodded in acceptance. "We can also assume, I believe, that for all these men or at least most of them it is their first time in New Zealand." Again a general nod of agreement. "We now have a city in a complete state of paranoia reporting all suspicious movements of anyone who looks remotely like they might have come from the Middle East yet these guys have remained unnoticed."

"I think we agree with everything you say, Red. Is this going anywhere?"

"Yes. Hear me out." Red was not to be put off so Cunningham sat back. "They must be getting help from locals. Think about it. Ten men. Living in accommodation or a factory somewhere. They have to be fed. They have needs. But they are not being seen coming and going. Someone is doing it for them. Jeff Bradley uncovered Esat Krasniqi because of the link to this Avni Leka. We now know that Leka set him up in New Zealand when he came here as a refugee. We've assumed Esat was the end of it and we've been screening the Kosovan Albanian community for anyone who might know Krasniqi and might be working aiding him to help the criminals. But what if it wasn't like that. What if Krasniqi is not the only businessman? What if Avni had helped others establish businesses? Bradley said he had lots of money."

"Jesus, Red, you just earned yourself a bottle of scotch." Cunningham jumped to his feet. "Get onto immigration. I want a list of all Kosovan refugees that came here around the time of Krasniqi and then give the list of names to the tax department. Look for export businesses. I want current addresses and I want it yesterday."

Red ran from the room.

"As for the rest of you, Moana split up the warehouse list. I want it cleaned up today. Any more questions?" No one answered. "Right then. I have to go upstairs and give a report. You all know what to do. Let's meet back here at 4pm."

36.

Jeff sat, grim faced, while Barbara made coffee. When he had arrived at her apartment she had welcomed the distraction.

"So much violence and death and more to come," she said.

Jeff nodded. He found the brandy on the top shelf of Barbara's kitchen cupboard and poured a splash into the two cups he placed on the coffee table.

"Are you okay?" he asked.

"I'll be fine. My first husband said I had no sensitivity, especially when I chose to ignore his whining. But I can tell you the scenes at the bomb site have left me numb. These people aren't civilised, Jeff."

"No, they aren't."

Barbara wiped her eyes. She gave Jeff a fleeting smile. "So tell me, why are you here?"

"I needed someone to bounce some ideas off," Jeff said. "I don't expect you to get involved but I have to find these murderers and bring it to an end. I will be taking no prisoners, Barbara. I want you to understand that right from the beginning."

Barbara nodded.

"What are you thinking?"

"Well, for a start Brian and I agreed these guys have local help. People like Esat Krasniqi."

"Other Kosovan Albanians?" Barbara said. Jeff nodded. "There must be a few hundred families. Where would you start?"

Jeff said, "I need to get into Esat's office. See if I can find anything in his computer files."

"The police will have already have searched the computers, won't they?"

"No, they haven't. Brian made a point of telling me they had been left in Krasniqi's office. I was slow on the uptake and thought he'd had too many whiskies. But he was giving me a message. They're short staffed and the Brian Cunningham I know will prioritise and he knows I will use my Kosovan connections. These guys are operating in cells. They all work independently of each other and usually are not aware of the other cells until show time. Brian will certainly believe that checking out Esat Krasniqi's computers needs to be done ASAP but he will also know it's a dead end for anyone who doesn't know what to look for. I have the Albanian contacts so he's using me by putting bait on the trail. He can't just hand them over to me. He expects me to go in there and take them. That's how I'd do it. I know it's not good policing but then Brian's not really a cop in spirit, even if he thinks he is. We're both SAS and we do what needs to be done."

"Won't the police be guarding the compound?" Barbara asked.

"Just the gate. But it will be a private security company. They won't expect the terrorists to return. We can get in from behind."

"So what is it exactly I might be agreeing to here?" Barbara asked, already knowing it involved breaking the law.

~

Barbara had persuaded Jeff to use her car and she was driving. She slowed as they passed the entrance to Esat Krasniqi's warehouse; as Jeff had said, a security guard sat in his car parked in front of the gate. She followed the side streets as memorised on her map and parked directly behind the warehouse. It was a no-exit street with a small children's playground backing onto the wall Jeff was to climb over. Approximately fifty metres of grassed area to cross. Opposite were private houses and either side of the park more homes. A strategically placed street lamp ensured the play area was lit. Trees ran down the fence line.

"Not the best place to stay parked without arousing suspicion, is it," Jeff said.

"That's a high fence. We should have brought a ladder."

"I used to scramble over fences that high when I was a kid."

Barbara patted Jeff on the chest. "Yes, well you're not a kid any more."

"Don't worry, I'll get over it. I'd better get moving."

Barbara watched Jeff until he disappeared into the trees. She unscrewed the cap off a bottle of mineral water and took a swig. Then she remembered the neighbourhood she was in and locked the doors.

~

Jeff was gone twenty minutes. She was relieved when she finally saw him scrambling back over the fence. The lights of an oncoming car caught her attention. It was moving slowly. She could just make out it was a police car.

"Shit, shit, shit," Barbara muttered to herself.

The door opened and Jeff climbed in beside her.

"That's a police patrol car. Someone must have reported us."

"Well, we can't just rush off."

"Quickly. Cuddle up to me," Barbara said, moving closer.

"Are you sure?'

"For God's sake, Jeff, you do know what to do with a woman don't you?"

Jeff shook his head, laughed then took her in his arms. As the patrol car drew alongside he kissed her. Barbara responded.

A torch was shone through the window and they pulled apart. Barbara waved and smiled. The policemen talked to each other. Jeff tried to look relaxed. Barbara stroked his hair and nuzzled the top of it. Jeff kissed her again until the light switched off. He ran his lips across her neck. Barbara let out a soft moan. The stayed locked in each other's arms longer than necessary. Long after the patrol car had disappeared into the night.

"Well, there goes my reputation," Barbara whispered as they slowly untangled themselves. "I'm sure they must have recognised me. By tomorrow the whole city is going to know I have a new lover."

37.

Jamil Khallid had no idea what time it was, or what day for that matter. There had been no respite from the discomfort of the cold, hard, damp concrete floor. Every bone poked against his flesh and had gone from a dull ache to agony. Every few hours someone removed his hood and a water bottle was placed on his lips. He gulped water until he coughed. Still spluttering, the hood was replaced and he was left alone. In the dark, images of his childhood merged with the faces of those he had killed. He tried to sleep but whenever he succeeded in escaping into slumber he was woken by his captors.

He heard the door open. Footsteps come towards him. Water-drenching time. He had come to welcome it. The removal of the hood was a moment of pleasure.

This time, a difference. Hands gripped his wrists. The click of a key then his handcuffs fell away. Strong arms pulled him to his feet. He stamped the numbness from his legs and rubbed his wrists. His legs wobbled and his head spun but strong arms held him steady. Joints ached and stiffness remained but the relief was immediate. The hood was still in place and he made no attempt to remove it. A chair was pushed against the back of his knees and he collapsed onto it. When he settled the man behind him lifted the hood. He blinked at the light and covered his eyes with a hand. It took him a few minutes to adjust. Finally his vision cleared. Four men wearing balaclavas surrounded him. One of the men pulled a table and a chair from against the wall until it was in front of him. A man in a suit came and sat in the chair placed opposite. He did not wear a balaclava.

"Good morning, Jamil." The man was an American. "My name is Lee Caldwell; I'm here to talk with you."

So he was not in the hands of Zahar. The Americans had taken him. He relaxed a little. He was not going to be killed. They would only want information.

"You would like some water?" Caldwell asked. Jamil nodded. "Give him some water."

A small bottle of mineral water was placed in his hand. Jamil twisted off the cap and swallowed a few mouthfuls then screwed the cap back on.

"Now, Jamil, I'm sure you must be hungry so as soon as we get this over with you can have something to eat. Do you understand?"

Khallid nodded.

"Good. Now tell me. Why are you here, Jamil? What is your mission?"

Jamil looked at him. Who did this American think he was talking to? Did he really expect an answer to these questions? What could they do if he didn't? This was New Zealand. There were laws. They couldn't torture him. Jamil found his bravado returning. He didn't have to tell this man anything. So what if he went to jail. The prisons were civilised and the prisoners well fed. Besides what did they really have on him? Nothing. He had been driving a vehicle that had been rammed off the road. He was the victim here.

Jamil smiled his non-response back at Caldwell.

"I see," Caldwell said. "You don't want to talk with me." Caldwell sat back in his chair. Jamil watched him, satisfied he had won the first round. They had kept him locked up for days. Made him soil himself and then expected him to have weakened. They had guessed wrong. He was made of sterner stuff than that.

Caldwell pulled out his mobile phone and dialled a number.

"Are you in place?" He listened to the reply all the while looking at Jamil. Then Caldwell held out the phone. "It's for you, Jamil."

Jamil looked confused.

"Go ahead," Caldwell said. "It's your mother, Jamil. Talk to her."

Jamil hesitantly took the phone and placed it to his ear.

"Hello," he whispered into the phone.

The sound of his mother's voice replying shocked him. Caldwell pulled the phone away.

"We have your mother, father and two sisters in a safe house in Cairo, Jamil. Do you believe me?" Jamil nodded, "Good, that is very good." Caldwell spoke into the phone.

"If I have not called back within ten minutes kill the mother in front of the rest of the family. I want them to be able to describe it to Jamil." Caldwell rang off.

"Did you really think I was going to waste time on you, Jamil? I know that inside that sick mind of yours you will find some semblance of bravery and justification for what you do. These things I do not care about. No – either you tell us what we want to know or your family will be killed."

"You cannot do this," Jamil said. "They have nothing to do with this. They are innocent. You are an American, you will not kill innocent people."

"You are right, Jamil. An American would not intentionally kill innocent people but your family is not in the hands of Americans, they are in the hands of people just like you. Cairo criminals. They will do anything for money and the price for killing your family is very cheap, Jamil. Now do we have an understanding?"

Jamil nodded.

"Good, very good."

~

There had been three computers in Esat Krasniqi's office. Jeff had downloaded the contents of two onto one memory stick and the one he had assumed to be Esat's own computer onto a separate memory stick. They opened his file first.

"Jesus, it's in Albanian," Jeff said. "We could spend the rest of our lives here and not find what we're looking for. It's a pity Sulla isn't here."

"Sulla?" Barbara asked.

"He helped me in Kosovo. He now manages Arben Shala's vineyard for the Shala family."

Barbara nodded. "How about transferring the data to him? That's easy enough."

Jeff laughed. "Of course we can do that. My brain has gone dead." Jeff pulled out his mobile. "Okay, I'll call Sulla. Hopefully we'll have something back by morning."

~

Senior Sergeant Moana Te Kanawa decided to check one last warehouse before they called it quits. She was tired, but experienced enough to know that even though the searches might be proving fruitless the elimination process brought them closer to their goal. As she looked at the gates she sensed this one was different. They were in a heavy industrialised area of East Tamaki. The long lane that ran down between two two-storey buildings was an ideal entrance to a secluded location. Certainly the warehouse was not visible from the road. Both sides of the lane were lined with trees.

Moana ordered the driver to proceed with caution. Slow and steady. Now, at the end of the lane, she and her team stayed sitting in the car scrutinising the chained gates and the two-metre high wall that surrounded the complex. Two black Range Rovers were parked outside the office block.

"What do you think, Red?"

"Same as you do. If I was looking for somewhere to hide this would be it. I smell spices. Someone inside has been cooking."

"Campers? Then the question to be asked is, are we going to be silly or sensible?"

"I think," he began, "that we back out and park in another driveway and call in backup. It might be nothing but better to be safe than dead. If it's a false alarm then you can buy everyone a few beers and we'll laugh it off."

Moana smiled. "Good call. You might make sergeant one day."

"Maybe, but I won't get there if I let my current sergeant get shot up."

"Why do I get the bullet? Why not you?" she laughed. Moana reached to pick up the handset. "I'll call it in."

Red reached across and touched her arm.

"I think it might be best if you call Inspector Cunningham on your mobile. We should assume they have equipment tuned into the police band."

"Yes, you're right. You really might make sergeant. I'm impressed."

~

Caldwell felt he had everything he was going to get from Jamil. As with most of the modern terrorist operations they operated in cells and the men were on a need to know basis. If they were captured the final mission would not be compromised. They were operating in groups of four and would only come together when Zahar the leader called them in to do so. Each cell had a team leader and only he would be in contact with Zahar. His team's job had been to hijack a container truck and deliver it to the warehouse. Another group had then taken over. They then returned to an apartment to await further orders. No, he hadn't known what was in the container.

The trip to Waipu had been ordered by Zahar. The man they had been chasing was to be eliminated. Their apartment was in the city but they moved every few days. Sometimes they stayed in a warehouse and then another apartment. Once a house in the suburbs. Someone would come daily with food and newspapers and whatever bits and pieces they wanted. He gave the location of the warehouse and of the apartment. Caldwell shook his head. They already knew about the warehouse and the apartment would have been cleaned and abandoned by now.

The terrorists had flown in from various locations in the Middle East. He did not know of the others but he flew in from Syria on a Syrian passport. The visa was arranged by a New Zealand export company.

He flashed Jamil a reassuring smile. The terrorist looked tired but relaxed. Caldwell was convinced that he had told the truth. They had all that Jamil was going to give them. That was unfortunate for Jamil. But lucky for his family.

It took thirty minutes for Cunningham and his team to arrive at the warehouse. Cunningham crept down the lane. The top of the two-metre-high wall was covered in broken glass. He scrambled up the tree closest to the wall. The warehouse was an oblong shape with a two-storey office complex on the far end. It was surrounded by a sealed parking area and security lights had been mounted on each corner of the building. Sensors picking up movement would turn night into day. With fifty metres of ground to cover to the warehouse it would be difficult to approach without being seen.

A lone figure walked out to the first vehicle and started the motor. Then he started the motor of the second vehicle. A second man crossed the courtyard to the gate and unlocked the chain. He let it drop to the ground and pulled the gates open. He walked back across the courtyard and both men went back inside the warehouse.

Cunningham climbed back down and hurried back down the lane and joined the others.

"Okay, guys, there are two black Range Rovers inside and a light on in the upstairs office. They have just started the engines and opened the gate. They're about to leave. Red, call the Tactics Group and tell them to get their asses here right now."

Red pulled out his phone.

Eyebrows arched. Heads turned, checking the reactions of the others. Feet shuffled. Tension mounted as each team member contemplated the reality of what was about to take place. They were all armed but none of them had ever been in an armed confrontation.

"Now the plan. Not a great one I'm afraid." Cunningham smiled trying to make light of the situation. "We have to hold them until the STG get here. Jessica and Red, you will stay here and use the car to block off the lane." Speaking directly to them both, he said, "Make sure no one gets past. If you hear gunfire take up a defensive position. Behind the vehicle would be best. Got that?"

They both nodded, but Cunningham picked up the puzzled looks.

"Lie on the ground or take cover so if they shoot your way they won't hit anything. Now, once we're in Ross and Jim will take up positions either side of the gate and cover our approach. Keep an eye on the second-floor window. They will have a lookout. Communicate our movements to Red and Jessica. Under no circumstances are any of you four to leave your posts. Okay, everyone check your weapons."

They were all wearing bullet-proof vests. Cunningham waited a few moments for each of them to mentally prepare.

"You are joking aren't you, Inspector," Moana said, dumbfounded. "This is a job for your lot. The STG are on their way. We should wait. They're trained for this, we aren't."

"By the time they get here these guys will have flown the coop."

"The bad guys get away sometimes. That's the lot of a police officer. We live with it."

"Point taken, Sergeant, but this is not a normal situation. These assholes exploded a bomb and killed some friends of ours. We all know what these guys are. If they get away there is every chance it will lead to a gunfight on the street and people will die. You know that. It's our job to protect the public whether they want us to or not. Now I'm going in. Are you with me or not?"

Moana glared then she pulled her gun.

"All right let's do it," Moana spat out. "But I think you can lead. I'll be right behind you."

The others nodded in agreement with their sergeant.

Cunningham smiled.

Red and Jessica watched Cunningham lead his group down the lane until they disappeared from sight, then they parked the police car in the lane and took up firing positions behind it.

~

Jamil stood and waited as his hands were again handcuffed behind his back. It hadn't been so bad, he thought. He had told them everything he knew which, really, in the end wasn't much. He had saved his family as was his duty and now he would be taken to prison. How long, he wondered. He was young. He would get through it. His knowledge of New Zealand prisons was favourable. They would be humane. The food would be good and there would be television.

He wanted to shower. He smelt and it was disgusting. Yes, a hot shower right now would be welcome.

He was led outside. It was dark. He did not know whether it was early evening or early morning but then what did it matter. It was over and that was all that counted. It was good to breathe in the fresh air. The smell of pine needles a welcome aroma compared to the stench he had been forced to endure over the last few days. The bag was again placed over his head. Security. He understood the procedure. He allowed himself to be led. He counted off thirty metres. He waited for the sound of the car door to be opened. To his surprise, he felt himself falling. Confused and disorientated, he grunted as his shoulder hit the soft earth. What was happening? He tried to move his legs, his body, but it seemed to be confined by his surroundings. Horror replaced confusion as reality dawned. He was in a pit. He began to scream.

Caldwell stood above the freshly dug grave and looked down at the screaming, struggling Jamil. He felt no sense of remorse. He had lost those emotions long ago. Jamil was a merciless killer. He had killed many innocent people and he was in New Zealand to kill hundreds more. He should just shoot him and be done with it. But now Jamil had experienced how it felt to have death come calling, he might be more willing to talk on other matters. The CIA would be interested in how he was recruited and any other connections.

He turned to the three men behind him. “Drag him out of there and take him back to your base. Put him in a body bag so he doesn’t soil the vehicle.”

Everyone was in place.

"Okay, Moana, let's do it." Brian whispered.

They sprinted across the open area. Half way across the security lights flashed on. "Move it," Cunningham yelled.

Shots rang out.

38.

More shots followed the first.

Red and Jessica, feet glued to the pavement, stretched to look down the alley then turned to each other then back down the alley. Neither had heard gunfire except on the police training range. Confused minds struggled to accept a real live gun battle had erupted within metres of where they stood. A staccato burst.

"Jesus, bloody hell," Red blurted. "That sounded like a machine gun. This is it."

Jessica dived into the driver's seat and picked up the microphone. Red pressed a button on the handheld radio.

"Inspector, come in. Inspector, are you there?" No answer. "Shit. Shit. Shit."

Jessica returned to Red's side. "The STG are on their way." Her face was pale but she had her sidearm in her hand, knuckles white on the grip. Red noted her finger across the guard not on the trigger. As frightened as she was she wasn't about to fall to pieces. And she wasn't about to shoot him accidentally. Safety first and by the book.

"The Inspector isn't answering." They both looked down the lane. The shooting was heavier.

~

"Keep moving! Run to the wall!" Cunningham yelled.

The shots came from one of the upstairs windows. Cunningham raced ahead, giving a lead to the others. They ran like him, weaving from side to side. Instinctively ducking but keeping running.

"Now drop to the ground!" he ordered as they made it to the safety of the warehouse roof overhangs. Now no one above could see them.

Cunningham did a quick head count. All accounted for. They were not in a good position and a squad of inexperienced amateurs fighting automatic weapons with handguns was a fight they were never going to win. His people had limited ammunition and who knew what other armaments the terrorists had. Rockets, and maybe hand grenades. Their only advantage was time. The terrorists would know that from the time they opened fire, reinforcements would be on the way.

Cunningham could hear Red screaming into his headset.

"Red. All is okay. No injuries, just lots of shooting."

"You're not kidding. The whole city must be able to hear it."

"How about backup?"

"On the way, sir. Do you want us down there?"

"Stay where you are."

Cunningham yelled to Moana, "Reinforcements are on the way but don't expect anything for at least twenty minutes."

"Too long," Moana said, her voice cool and controlled.

Her demeanour impressed Cunningham. The sergeant was tougher than he'd given her credit for. Most soldiers experiencing combat for the first time were scared shitless.

"Just stay where you are, Red, and keep that bloody escape route blocked."

"Roger that."

"We're sitting ducks out here," Moana whispered over Cunningham's shoulder. She had crawled up beside him.

"We can't retreat, not just yet," Cunningham said. "Crossing the open ground is not an option. Now they know we're here they will be expecting it. We'd be dead before we made the gate. Those two vehicles are their only escape and they need to cross open ground to get to them. Bit of a stalemate I think."

"Unless there is an exit out the back. They could be running through it right now," Moana said.

"You're right, and if that happens so be it." The lane that ran down the back of the warehouse had a two-metre-high fence running parallel and no cover. "If I send anyone down that alley it would be like sending them into a tunnel. Even a blind man couldn't miss with an automatic weapon."

"I wouldn't worry about that decision, Brian. We aren't soldiers, just cops. You won't be getting any volunteers for a suicide mission. Best if we wait for the backup."

Cunningham smiled at his sergeant's sarcasm.

"Unfortunately the bad guys will know there is no time. They have to make a break for it. I want everyone to stay flat on their stomachs. Weapons held out in front. Make as small a target as possible. If they do make a break for it they'll be firing on the run. Unlikely they'll hit a grounded target."

He checked everyone was obeying his orders. He mentally kicked his own ass. What an idiot he was. He had reacted emotionally and not professionally. He had not wanted to bring in the police anti-terrorist squad on a hunch. There had been no evidence of the terrorists being in the building and even so with his team he had felt they would be more than a match. Now he was forced to face reality. Zahar Akbar had more men than they had estimated and they were well armed. He had made a terrible mistake. He needed to make sure no one paid the ultimate price for his stupidity.

Two men burst from the building and took up positions behind the first Range Rover. The speed of their movement and the unexpectedness of it meant no shots were fired by Cunningham or his team.

"Everyone, stay down. This is it. Don't move until I give the order."

One of the gunmen fired in Cunningham's direction. The other at Jim and Warren behind the gate posts. There was no possibility of returning fire. Two more men burst out and climbed into the second vehicle. As the Range Rover moved forward the two who had been giving covering fire jumped into the back. The vehicle sped forward, the terrorists firing through the open windows. Cunningham watched helplessly as it sped past and through the now open gate. He leapt to his feet and chased after it. He was already halfway across the compound before the others responded.

"Red and Jessica," he shouted over his shoulder to Moana.

Warren and Jim fell in behind Brian. They were eighty metres from the end of the lane. They would be far too late.

~

After the shooting had started Red and Jessica stood beside the blocking vehicle debating what it was they should do next.

"I'm not certain standing where we are is such a good idea," Red said. "Let's say for argument's sake they manage to get clear in a vehicle and it comes speeding down the lane towards us. We've blocked the lane. They will have no choice but to ram us."

"Agreed," Jessica answered nervously.

"If we stand behind the vehicle we're dog meat. The car could flip back over us. At worst we will be forced to get out of the way and that means we become sitting ducks."

"What do you suggest?"

"I think we position ourselves behind that wall. That's twenty metres away. We are secure and have good cover and we also have a good view of what's happening and have time to react."

"I agree, Red. Let's do it."

Once they were in position Red touched Jessica on the arm.

"Everything will be okay. We take no risks."

Jessica nodded. "I'm shit scared, Red, but I won't let you down."

"I know you won't, Jessica, I know you won't. Now remember we do not stand up and say, 'Police drop your weapons'. These guys have machine guns. We shoot and shoot to kill. Got it?"

Jessica nodded. Uncertain.

The dull roar grew in volume as a vehicle raced down lane.

Red touched Jessica's shoulder.

"This is it." He held his gun out in front and rested his arm on the wall. Jessica mimicked his action. She couldn't stop her hand shaking.

Out of the corner of his eye Red saw a flash of black as the Range Rover careered towards the police Holden Commodore. Metal impacted metal groaning and wrenching and windows exploded, spraying shattered glass through the air like a park fountain. Airbags filled in an instant trapping the occupants in their seats, but only for seconds. The bags deflated quickly and then the doors were flung open. Armed men looked to escape their mangled vehicle. The two closest to Red and Jessica saw the crouching figures of the young police officers and aimed their hand guns.

"Fucking hell," Red cried. "Just fire at the vehicle, Jessica. You the front seats, I'll shoot at the back seats."

They pulled their triggers.

~

Cunningham fired his police issue glock as he ran. A terrorist leapt from the car. Disorientated for a moment, maybe concussed from the car smash, he swung his head in different directions like a chicken looking for seed. Cunningham pumped two slugs into his chest. The man crumpled to the ground. Cunningham fired twice more then switched his focus. He didn't need to check to know his target was dead.

He turned and yelled at the team members behind to get down. He continued moving forward firing his pistol as fast as he could pull the trigger. When the magazine emptied he stopped. He pushed the release lever and the empty magazine dropped to the ground. He reloaded. Sporadic shots came from the left. Jessica and Red.

He yelled, "Red. Jessica. Hold your fire." Cunningham waited. The shooting stopped. "Are you okay?"

"We're good," Red yelled back.

"Okay, I'm moving forward. Hold your fire."

"Come ahead," Red yelled back.

"Moana, with me," Cunningham ordered. "The rest of you stay down until I call you forward. Moana, stand over there and cover me. Anyone moves, shoot them. Got it?"

Moana nodded. "I've got it."

She held her weapon at arm's length. Hand steady.

Cunningham smiled. Sergeant Moana Te Kanawa would not have been out of place in Afghanistan. He walked cautiously forward until he reached the rear of the Range Rover. He placed his hand on the rear guard then slid it forward, his body following. Reaching the open rear door he relaxed. A thumb flicked the safety and his gun went back into its holster. The three men inside were dead.

"All clear."

He looked skyward and whispered a thank you.

The sound of sirens. Cunningham couldn't help but think that sirens were becoming an unwelcome but regular addition to the sounds of Auckland city. He walked across to check on Red and Jessica. The two young police officers sat on the ground with their backs against the wall.

"I guess we did okay," Jessica whispered to Red.

"I guess we did."

"My hands won't stop shaking, Red. Fuck it." She dropped her pistol on the ground. "I killed a man, Red."

She was crying. Red put his arm around her and she didn't resist as he pulled her to him.

Cunningham peered over the wall. Red caught his eye. They needed a few moments. Cunningham nodded and walked back to the others.

Moana said, "I've checked the bodies. No documents. Nothing to identify these guys. We'll take prints and send them to Interpol but for the moment it's another dead end."

"There are four less to concern ourselves with, that's a plus."

Flashing lights raced towards them.

39.

Jeff had walked to the top of Mount Victoria. The township of Devonport had been built on the mountain's slopes in the 1900's and its southern reaches ran along the shoreline from the naval base past the ferry terminal to North Head and round to Cheltenham and Narrowneck, then back towards Takapuna and the harbour bridge. From where he stood he looked down on the sprawling naval base and across the inner harbour to the Auckland CBD. Using binoculars he followed the line on the city side across the ports to Mechanics Bay and then the waterfront drive that ended at St Heliers Bay. A mist had drifted in from the Hauraki Gulf and settled over the Eastern Suburbs. The waterfront traffic was heavier than usual. Motorists driving through fog from the suburb of St Heliers to the city were forced to observe cautious driving habits. Jeff guessed the usual half-hour drive was now taking an hour.

All along the waterfront drive not covered by mist, he could see excited crowds thronging every vantage point. Thousands lined the walkways and beaches and more spectators on the hill that was Bastion Point. Protest boats sped back and forth across the inner harbour. The bombing that had partially destroyed Mary's apartment building had not deterred the masses gathering. Closer to the city the crowds, building up on the pavements, had now spilled over onto the road, bringing traffic to a standstill and adding to the chaos.

The atmosphere of anticipation that shrouded the city was electric. Thousands of pairs of eyes were fixed on the harbour entrance hidden behind the wall of cloud. Eyes squinted as the masses searched the misty wall seeking signs of movement, shadows. The New Zealand frigate the *HMNZS Te Hana* appeared first, its greyness matching the gunmetal sky. It slowly forged a path through the armada of dissident boats.

And then there it was, emerging from the mist, the black shape of the conning tower of the Virginia-class fast attack submarine the *USS Ulysses*. The 7800-tonne, 377-foot-long nuclear-powered submarine slid through the water as easily as a killer whale, its sleekness as deadly as its magnificence. A cacophony of marine horns announced the arrival of the long-awaited visitor. The crowds surged forward, captivated by the sinister boat, but stayed silent as they experienced mixed emotions of awe and fear.

Protest boats crisscrossed the submarine's path, police and naval launches in pursuit.

Motorised rubber dinghies were now leaving the shores from both sides of the harbour, manned by protestors in wetsuits whose sole purpose was to bring the submarine to a halt. The protest leaders knew they could never prevent the submarine getting to anchor, but stopping it would be a success in their eyes. Some got close enough to hurl flour bombs.

Two tugs emerged from the naval yards, water cannons mounted on their bows. They quickly took up position in front of the *Ulysses* and began drenching the protest boats, forcing them back. Some of the smaller boats overturned. New Zealand navy inflatables moved in quickly to rescue the crews and dump them ashore.

Crowds on both sides of the harbour now cheered at the chaotic scene. Although the protest vessels slowed the progress of the *Ulysses* the convoy continued on its course, but not to the naval base but across to the city side, Bledisloe Wharf.

After thirty minutes the tugs manoeuvred the submarine into its final position and ropes secured the vessel to the docks. Navy boats formed a protective curtain to block the protest runabouts and it was all over. The mass of protestors on both sides of the harbour were confused. Uncertain. No one had expected Bledisloe Wharf as a final destination. On the city side it was blocked from view and the side roads leading to the port already blocked off. The vigil at the naval base grew quiet as protest leaders met to decide the next course of action.

Grim faced, Jeff pushed his way through the crowd on Mount Victoria and made his way down to his car. He needed to get to the city side. Whatever the terrorists were up to would happen in the next three days.

~

Cunningham and his team re-assembled in the crime room. Restless sleep had left everyone tired but still hyped. Coffee and adrenaline had not succumbed to the shots of whisky Cunningham had ordered them to drink. In the military alcohol had been a prime pacifier after ops and a shootout in an Auckland suburb more than qualified. However he noticed a spring in their step. They'd had a win. Red and Jessica sat together, listening to the banter but not joining in. He made a mental note to keep an eye on them.

"Good job last night, people. That's one group of bad guys that won't be killing any more of our citizens. The bad news is, after a thorough going over there was nothing in the warehouse. We have to assume it was a safe house only. This means for those of you who aren't rocket scientists there are more of these assholes out there, maybe a lot more."

A nod of heads acknowledged the statement.

"Unfortunately, because they are organised, killing off one cell takes us back to where we started. No leads."

Cunningham thought of Khallid. Caldwell had been in touch and informed him that Jamil was no longer able to supply information. He hadn't elaborated and Cunningham didn't ask. He had misgivings about Lee Caldwell's lone wolf status but it was too late now. He had made the decision to allow him to roam the prairie unhindered and would now have to see it through to the end. The danger to the nation overrode Queensbury rules.

"The submarine is here. I don't have to tell any of you what that means. Whatever shit is going down will happen over the next couple of days. Red, you and Jessica follow up on the immigration list."

Red nodded. Jessica sat, wide eyed, looking in his direction but through him. Blank. He wondered if he should stand Jessica down. She needed counselling. He was certain of it, but he was so short staffed.

"The rest of you get out to the warehouse. See if you can't find something. Right, let's do it. Moana, stay back a moment, will you."

When they were alone, he said, "I'm concerned about Jessica. She could be in shock. Happens to first-time-combat soldiers."

"Should I have a doctor look at her?"

"Keep an eye on her. Soldiers get over it. You be the judge. We're too bloody short staffed and can't afford to lose expert personnel."

"What about the other cities?"

"You know the answer to that. The police manning levels were already low. Most of the regions are operating on skeleton staff as it is. The personnel they're sending are not the trained investigators we need."

"I have a thought," Moana said. "How big is your budget?"

"I don't think money is a problem anymore. What did you have in mind?"

"Well, I know it might not be desirable," she said, "but most of the private investigators in the city are ex-coppers. How about hiring a few to do some of the donkey work? Like the immigration lists for example."

"Good idea. I'll put it to the chief and twist his arm until he writes the cheque."

~

Caldwell sat in his hotel room. He had watched the arrival of the *Ulysses* and taken in the news reports of the incident in East Tamaki. Four killed. Just how many more terrorists were there? It worried him, and he didn't for one moment believe that the loss of a few men would have any effect on their overall mission. They would have calculated losses into the planning and ensured they had more than enough manpower.

It surprised him that Cunningham and his team hadn't suffered casualties. He had put that down to sheer luck. Next time they might not be so fortunate. He had a lot of respect for the New Zealand policeman. He liked that he was prepared to operate outside the boundaries, but this was now an American problem. They were going to attack the *Ulysses* and he had Pentagon approval to do whatever it took to stop it. He also needed to meet with the submarine commander to inform him of what was about to take place. He hadn't any ideas on how Akbar was going to fire his torpedoes but they were fanatics and when the time came the torpedoes would be fired.

~

Cunningham and Caldwell met in the café in the foyer of the Hilton. Caldwell didn't want to meet at the police station and Cunningham did not want him there anyway. He didn't have time to waste dodging questions about the American.

"Tell me about last night," Caldwell asked.

Cunningham quickly went over their reasons for being there and his reasons for proceeding without backup.

"You've checked the premises?"

"My team is out there now. Nothing to report so far. I think it's going to be a repeat of the last warehouse. Signs all over the place showing that they've been there but nothing to tell us where they might have been going. Another dead end. But we now know Akbar has a mini army."

"And, knowing what awaits them if they're caught makes them even more dangerous. Remember that."

"I do know the type of men we're dealing with, Caldwell."

"Yes, of course you do," Caldwell said. "I need to meet with the commander of the *Ulysses*. He's already received a briefing from my boss but there's nothing like a face-to-face to get all the facts."

Cunningham said, "The submarine is here for three days. I think it unlikely they'll leave it for the last day. They won't strike in daylight, I shouldn't think, so that leaves any one of the next two nights."

"I think not tonight," Caldwell replied. "They would expect security to be tight on the first night until the crew has settled. Now, if they're going to fire the torpedo they'll need a delivery system. A plane or a boat."

"Rule the plane out," Cunningham said. "The sub is between two mountains. They could never get a low enough run to make a drop. Well, at least I assume that to be correct. Besides, they'd have to commandeer an aircraft, of the right size, and then fit it out with whatever would be required to launch a torpedo. Doesn't sound like a realistic option to me."

"I agree. So it's a boat. However the sub commander might give us another option. Would you like to come with me? You know the area. Once we have an idea of how they might do it, it might help with where to look."

"When are you meeting?" Cunningham asked.

"Hopefully, in the next few hours. As soon as I can make contact I'll have a time."

"Let me know."

~

Barbara had put in a half day in the office then made her way home via the supermarket. She bought mince, pasta and fresh herbs. In her larder cans of tomatoes and tomato concentrate clogged the shelves. Italian was her comfort food. A glass of wine and bolognese at her balcony table was a treat she rarely indulged. Today was to be one of those days.

The door buzzer went off. Barbara, wooden spoon in one hand and a teaspoon of pasta halfway to her lips in the other, turned her head to the door and fought the urge to answer it. She blew on the spoon to cool it and nibbled a sample.

The buzzer went off again. This time the finger pushing the button held it down.

"Damn it."

She let the spoon slide back into the sauce.

Jeff Bradley, expecting her to look through the peep hole, waved back.

"I was in the city," he said. "Called in on the off chance you might like lunch. And here you are. So what do you say? Want to come to lunch? That promised meal? Hmmm, something smells yummy."

Barbara smiled. "I was making Italian, and you're just in time. I hope you like spaghetti?"

"I sure do and it will make a change from having to cook for myself." He sat on one of the stools at the buffet. Barbara poured him a glass of wine.

She asked, "Any news from your friend in Kosovo?"

"I haven't checked. Can I use your computer?"

She turned the knob on the oven to low. "Let's do it."

Barbara followed Jeff to the computer. She leaned on his shoulder and watched as he logged onto his email address. Barbara leaned closer, her cheek almost touching his. A whiff of her perfume attacked his senses, made him want to spin round and pull her onto his knee. Jeff clicked on the icon and his mail page opened. The name Sulla Bogdani was fourth on the list of emails in the inbox. Jeff clicked on the line and Sulla's email opened. Jeff quickly scanned the message. Sulla said he had read through the Albanian language documents and all that caught his attention were a few email communications. It wasn't that they said anything in particular, Sulla added, but that the messages had been so vague. They appeared to say nothing at all. Not even hello. In his opinion, within the sentences was a coded message. It was all he could think of that would make sense of it. Either that, or these are two very boring men and you would not wish to invite them to dinner. Jeff smiled as he remembered Sulla's sense of humour. Sulla wrote that the communications were from one man. He had written a name across the page in twenty-four font size and in bold black lettering.

Ibrahim Mustafa.

40.

Cunningham and Caldwell caught the noon ferry across the harbour to Devonport. Cunningham had decided against driving. Traffic on the harbour bridge was down to a crawl, and once across, driving the length of the peninsula to Devonport would be impossible. The ferry was the best option. From the Devonport ferry terminal to the Naval Base entrance was a pleasant walk along the foreshore. Protestors crowded the entrance and although the two men had worn casual clothes to avoid standing out, the crowd had no difficulty in recognising outsiders. Smiling eyes turned hostile as Cunningham nudged bodies aside as he made his way to the base entrance. Caldwell followed in his footsteps.

In front of the entry gate, a barrier of traffic cones and concrete blocks placed thirty metres out marked no man's land. A 'No Entry' sign sat on a pole looking every bit like a traffic stop sign. From Cunningham's observation the crowd had kept its distance. He had little doubt from the officious, stiff-backed stance of the military police charged with enforcing the directive that there would have been arrests if the protestors had not kept their distance.

As Cunningham moved past the stop sign, two burly military policemen moved forward to meet them. Caldwell produced his invitation from the submarine commander and one of the MPs took it and their IDs to the small glassed office. The second MP remained standing in front of them blocking their path. Arms folded. Silent. The protestors, now having someone other than sailors to hurl abuse at, turned their venom on Cunningham and Caldwell. Ignoring them brought on a tirade of obscenities.

"Don't you just love an affectionate public?" Cunningham said.

The MP returned and gave them back their ID cards, but kept the invitation. Cunningham was about to ask for it but thought better of it. Caldwell didn't seem too concerned. Their officiousness reassured him.

"Follow me, gentlemen." They were led through the gates to a waiting Jeep. The MP instructed the driver to take his passengers to the officer's mess. Outside the mess an orderly waited on the steps to greet the guests then ushered them through to the restaurant. Two American naval officers in white dress uniform sat at a table by a window.

"Commander Robert Mann and my executive officer Sean Flynn," Mann said, not bothering to stand. "Sit down, gents."

Mann asked the orderly to bring some coffee. They exchanged small talk until the drinks arrived.

"Now, Mr Caldwell, what is this all about? You have very nervous friends in high places who insist I speak to you. What can be so urgent?"

"How aware are you of events taking place in New Zealand over the last couple of weeks?" Caldwell asked.

"If you're referring to the protestors, we'd expected that. We of course know about the so-called terrorists shooting up the countryside and then of course the bombing. We have received intel that all this might be because of us, but nothing confirmed. There has been talk of a torpedo. But again nothing confirmed. It's all speculation as far as I can tell." Mann leaned forward and picked up his coffee. He rested it on a napkin in his left hand and peered at Caldwell over the top of it. "Is that why you're here? To tell me otherwise?"

"More than a month ago,' Caldwell started, "we're not certain of the date, a man named Zahar Akbar entered New Zealand. Akbar is part of a terrorist group that was previously led by his brother, a man named Halam Akbar. Halam was recently killed in Kosovo. It appears Zahar has taken over from his brother. When he came to New Zealand he brought a bunch of friends with him. We don't know how many but enough. Inspector Cunningham's people have been responsible for killing four of them and capturing one. There have been a couple of others killed by Akbar himself. They're reduced in number but of course we have no idea how many there were in the first place. In any case I doubt the losses have decreased their effectiveness. My best guess is there are plenty more of them out there."

Caldwell continued, "In a warehouse they used as a hideout we found empty weapons crates. They had shipped them in by container then hijacked the truck on its way to a bonded warehouse to be cleared through customs. We now know the crates held hand guns and automatic weapons and plastic explosive. I also think a couple of missile launchers, maybe stingers, and my gut tells me two torpedoes."

Mann leaned forward. "There is no doubt they are torpedoes?"

"There is always doubt, Commander. We did not physically see the torpedoes and they may well have used the packaging for something else, but I think it is safer to assume that these guys have come to town to do your submarine some damage. The timing is just too coincidental for it to be anything else."

"We aren't sitting ducks." Mann turned to his executive officer. "Sean has nets in place supplied by the New Zealanders. As we speak, ships are being anchored between the *Ulysses* and the outer harbour."

"No chance of just leaving?" Brian Cunningham asked.

"None at all," Mann replied. "It's taken a long time for New Zealand to accept a nuclear vessel into their country. We have assured them it is safe to have us here. Can't turn and run now, can we? No we will leave as scheduled. I will expect you two to stop these guys."

Both Cunningham and Caldwell smiled. They liked Mann's attitude.

"There is something you can help us with," Cunningham said. "We've spoken to our military leaders but would really like your opinion. If someone wanted to fire a torpedo at your sub, how would they do it?"

"In this anchorage it would have to be a boat. No other way. The boat would need to be a reasonable length. At least forty to fifty feet. It would need to have launch chutes attached and of course the electronics to fire it. Unfortunately all too easily done."

"Could they have had time to convert a pleasure boat in the last month?"

"Plenty of time. Someone who knew what they were doing could do it in a night. Maybe two."

Cunningham nodded and turned to Caldwell. He had all the information he needed. If they were to convert a boat it could not be done in the open. It would attract too much attention. They couldn't truck it to the water later for the same reason. They would need a boat shed that was on the water. He had something to look for but this was Auckland and it wasn't called the city of sails for nothing. There were boat sheds spread all along the fifty kilometres of coastline that made up the Auckland harbour.

"I need to get choppers in the air," Cunningham said. "We have a large area to search. I'll ask the air force for help. Anything that big we should be able to spot easy enough."

"You do that, Mr Cunningham. I'll make sure our defensive shield is effective."

He passed Caldwell a card. "Here is my cellphone number. Please keep me informed."

~

Jeff looked through the phonebook but there was no listing for Ibrahim Mustafa. That didn't really mean anything though – it could be that he was living with somebody else, using another name or just plain unlisted.

"We need to talk to someone in the Kosovan community," Jeff said.

"What about Brian?" Barbara asked. "Shouldn't we be giving him this information?"

"Yes, we should."

"But we aren't going to?"

"No, we are not. Not yet," Jeff said. "Let's find the guy first. Then we can go to Brian. Back out if you want."

She gave him her best pissed off look.

"Okay. I won't ask you again."

"Where do we start?"

Jeff opened the phone book again. This time the business section, "No matter what, new immigrants from the same country usually gather together and try to create a little bit of home. Like the expat bars in Third World countries. If you want to find a lost soul, that's where to go. The Kosovans and Albanians will be no different. The men love to sit in cafés and drink coffee and cognac. Aha, here we are, four Albanian restaurants. Let's see if we get lucky."

Jeff phoned the first name. No answer. "An answer phone," he said. "They don't open until 5pm."

The second number rang twice. "Tirana restaurant, how can I help you?"

"Good morning. I was supposed to meet a friend for lunch and he said he had booked a table at this restaurant, but I can't remember which time and I can't make contact with him."

"Do you have a name, sir?"

"Ibrahim Mustafa."

"One moment," a pause, "I'm sorry, there is no reservation under that name."

"I'm sorry, my mistake. Do you know Mr Mustafa? Maybe I have the wrong day?"

"No, sir, the name is not familiar."

Jeff hung up and phoned the third number.

"Skenderberg restaurant."

"Hi, I just want to check a booking time, it is under the name Ibrahim Mustafa."

"Just one moment. I cannot see anything but then Mr Mustafa wouldn't normally book. He is a regular."

"He said to come for lunch but did not say a time."

"Usually he will come in at one o'clock."

"Then I will come at one o'clock. Thank you. The Skenderberg Restaurant on Ponsonby Road," Jeff said, hanging up the phone. "One o'clock. I say we go there for lunch. Ask some questions and see what happens."

"Okay," Barbara agreed. "Are we sure this is the right thing to do? Brian was angry last time we ran off on our own."

She could see Jeff was in a determined mood and knew what that meant.

"I'm not comfortable he would make the right decision. Not the one that works best for me, anyway. If I'm looking out for my own skin and probably yours for that matter then I'm going to do whatever it takes. This is about self defence. I'm not prepared to sit back and leave my fate and those close to me, as Akbar's note in Mary's kitchen stated, in someone else's hands. Especially Brian's."

"Right then. Let's go find Ibrahim Mustafa."

~

Jeff dismissed Barbara's SAS escort and drove her car himself to the Skenderberg Restaurant. The restaurant was named after the legendary Albanian hero who fought off the Ottoman hordes trying to invade Albania in the fourteenth century. Jeff had seen a statue of Skenderberg on a horse, sword drawn, in the city of Prishtina.

"Take any spare table you wish," the waitress told Jeff. "There are no bookings. Not for lunch." A corner table afforded the best view of the door and the rest of the interior. He pulled a chair out for Barbara.

"What a gentleman. Thank you."

There were twenty other diners but it was the table near the door into the kitchen that caught Jeff's interest. Five men sat round it, in front of them espresso coffees and cognacs. It reminded him of Kosovo. A scene he had seen many times.

"We at least know who the Albanians are," Jeff smiled.

"Where?" Barbara asked, looking around the room. Jeff grinned.

The waitress brought menus. She was in her early twenties, a pretty girl with a friendly manner and noticeable accent.

"Is this restaurant owned by Albanian Albanians or Kosovan Albanians?" Jeff asked.

"We're all Albanians," the girl replied.

"Sorry," Jeff said. "I wasn't trying to be smart. It's just that my wife and I were in Prishtina not so long ago."

"Really?" the girl said excitedly. "That's where my family comes from. What were you doing in Prishtina?"

"Looking at business opportunities. Did some sightseeing."

"I haven't been there for so long. I miss my friends. We write each other over the internet but it's not the same."

"Maybe you will go back one day."

"Not if my father has his way. He will never return. He loves New Zealand." She put the menus on the table. "Can I get you drinks?"

"Two orange juices," Jeff said. "One more thing." She paused. "I phoned earlier and was told I might find Mr Ibrahim Mustafa here?"

"You're a friend of Mr Mustafa's?"

"Business acquaintance."

"He will be in any time now. Those are his friends over there." She indicated the group of men at the table by the kitchen.

"Good. I'll look out for him."

She turned away.

"Very smooth, Mr Bradley." Barbara said when the waitress had gone. "I think it helped a little that she was pretty. I think she was upset to find out you were married."

"I hadn't noticed."

"No, of course you hadn't," Barbara said playfully.

Jeff was about to reply when a man walked through the door, early forties, an olive complexion, thickset and around 5' 10". He wore a black leather jacket. He gave the waitress a smile as she approached him. Jeff kept his eyes on the man. This was Mustafa, he was certain of it. The waitress spoke to him and he glanced their way. He looked confused when he stared at Jeff. Trying to place me, Jeff thought. Then Jeff saw the look of realisation. Mustafa turned and ran out the door.

"Shit!" Jeff yelled and leapt from his chair. "Now you can ring Brian!"

Barbara was slow to react and by the time she realised what had taken place Jeff had disappeared through the door. When she made it outside she caught a glimpse of Jeff as he reached the end of the

Ponsonby shopping centre and rounded the corner that would take him down College Hill.

~

The police helicopter had taken Caldwell and Cunningham along the coastal waters from Bucklands Beach through to Waiwera then back across the Western Viaduct. Cunningham had a map and was marking off the boat sheds they could see and which would need to be investigated. He was already deflated by the enormity of the task that lay ahead and wondered how they could get the searches carried out in the timeframe left with limited manpower. The flight path now took them back across the inner harbour and over the Westhaven moorings. More than a thousand craft in the marina had already been dismissed. The boat they were looking for would not be out in the open. Cunningham had seen enough and tapped the pilot to head back to the helipad at Mechanics Bay.

The pilot turned in his seat.

"Inspector, there is a call for you."

He passed across the headset.

"Cunningham."

"Inspector, it's Moana. Barbara Heywood just called through. She said they found someone called Ibrahim Mustafa who they think has links to Esat Krasniqi. Jeff is chasing him down Ponsonby Road towards College Hill."

"Are you kidding me? Okay we're not far from there." He tapped the pilot on the shoulder. "Take us over Ponsonby Road, College Hill."

He received a thumbs-up.

As they crossed Herne Bay they were low enough to easily see the pedestrians crossing the intersection of College Hill and Ponsonby Road. Both Caldwell and Cunningham saw the running figure of Jeff Bradley at the same time. They watched as he ran into the passing traffic. Cars swerved. Others stopped. No crashes.

Cunningham tapped the pilot again and pointed to the running figure.

"Follow him," he yelled.

~

The little bastard was quick, Jeff thought, but he was gaining. Running blindly into two lanes of traffic was foolish and both of them had been lucky not have been swiped by a car.

A driver holding his hand on his horn leaned out the window and shouted abuse. "Bloody idiots, what the hell do you think you're doing? I'll call the cops."

"Go ahead," Jeff yelled back. "Get them here pronto."

The angry motorist, puzzled by the answer, gripped his steering wheel and drove off.

Jeff ran faster downhill, his stride lengthening. Ibrahim Mustafa was now only twenty metres in front. Then Mustafa ran into school grounds. At the end of the sports field, a slope covered by thick bush offered an escape. Mustafa was running straight towards it. If he made it he might evade capture.

"That ain't going to happen, Mustafa," Jeff yelled.

It was lunchtime at the school and the sports field was full of children. Some were kicking footballs, others throwing balls and others in groups talking. As Mustafa rushed between them the first child flung aside screamed. The cries alerted the duty teacher and he hesitantly moved forward. Jeff reached down deep for the reserves he knew were stored somewhere in his energy banks and gave a supercharged spurt. Half way across the field he dived and tackled Mustafa around the legs. Both men hit the ground hard. The impact broke Jeff's hold and they scrambled to their feet.

Neither heard the helicopter overhead. Neither noticed the duty teacher gathering the children together and leading them to a safe distance.

As they eyed each other Jeff could sense the discussion going on inside Ibrahim Mustafa's head. To escape he would need to get rid of Jeff. Jeff could outrun him. The only option left was to fight. Mustafa adopted a karate stance. Jesus. Jeff remembered from his Kosovo trip that Bruce Lee was a hero in the Balkans. All the men watched his movies and martial arts was a favoured sport. It appeared Mustafa was a student. Jeff hoped he wasn't a master. Then again he didn't really care; he had already decided Mustafa wasn't going anywhere.

As Jeff stepped forward he took a blow to the head. It came from nowhere. Painful barbs shot through his brain from his sore nose, still tender. He needed to watch the little shit's legs as well as his fists. A blow to his chest. The wind knocked out of him, Jeff sank to his knees as he sucked in air. He sensed rather than saw Mustafa moving in for the kill. Jeff could hear his boxing coach somewhere in the recesses of his mind; when in trouble, clinch. He needed to get Mustafa on the ground.

Jeff flung himself forwards, arms outstretched, and collided with the advancing Mustafa. He wrapped his arms around the Kosovan's waist then pushed forward like a prop in a rugby scrum. The force propelled Mustafa backwards. He lost his balance, then Jeff had him on the ground. Mustafa writhed about like a snared hyena and kicked out, but Jeff managed to hold his grip. A fist smashed into the side of Jeff's skull. Flashes of light followed. He shook his head. A few more blows like that and he knew it might be over. And then he had had enough of Ibrahim Mustafa. He released his hold on Mustafa's waist and grasped two fistfuls of jacket front. Mustering his last reserves of strength, knuckles whitened as he pulled the Kosovan towards him and then smashed his forehead across the bridge of Mustafa's nose. Mustafa screamed like a castrated pig.

Jeff rolled away and climbed to his feet. Mustafa holding his face, looked up at the big man towering over him. Eyes wide open. Uncertain now. Jeff reached down and yanked the shorter man from the ground. He tightened his fist and swung. Mustafa reeled back as the force of the punch buried into his chest, then another under his rib cage and one more into the side of his head. Jeff swung again but this time hit air. Mustafa lay on the ground. Unmoving. Then Jeff felt arms holding him. He twisted his body to break free. The arms held strong.

"Jeff, it's okay. It's me, Brian. Relax. It's over."

Jeff let his arms fall to his side. "Where the hell did you guys come from?"

Then he saw the helicopter. The school children were watching from a distance. The teachers gathered behind them having given up trying to shoo them inside to the classrooms. School had never been this exciting. The sound of approaching sirens meant more fun was about to begin. Jeff looked down at the unconscious form.

"Ibrahim Mustafa," he said. "He's one of Avni Leka's men."

When Barbara arrived Cunningham gave her a look that would turn most mortals to stone. He walked off toward the arriving police cars. Barbara bit her lip.

~

Zahar Akbar stood silently and listened. When he closed his phone he fought to control the urge to throw it against the wall. When this mission was over he was going to cut Jeff Bradley's throat.

41.

I think we're in a great deal of trouble," Barbara said, stating the obvious, still smarting from the look Cunningham had given her. "How is your head, Jeff?"

"Like I've just stubbed my big toe, throbbing like hell."

"Maybe you should consider hiring yourself out to a gym, as one of those punch bags they hang from the ceiling."

"Not funny, Barbara," Jeff scolded, then smiled, and then rubbed his jaw. "Ouch."

Cunningham had sent them to the station in a police car and ordered them to wait until he returned. A constable had brought two tablets and a glass of water. The pain killers had helped but not a great deal. Two untouched coffees sat on the table, going cold.

The door opened.

Cunningham and Caldwell walked in. Jeff noted Caldwell must have decided that protecting his identity from Auckland Police Department personnel needed to be put to one side. Cunningham sat, fiddled with some papers then looked up. Glared. Barbara wilted; Jeff locked eyes and remained unmoved.

"I really don't know what to do with you two. Maybe I should lock you both in a cell until this is over." He paused for a moment. "I thought we had an agreement. You find anything, you tell me. Wasn't that the agreement?"

Barbara nodded.

"So tell me, Jeff, why were you chasing this man?"

"We thought he might lead us somewhere."

"And what made you think that?"

"We had information."

"And where or how did you come by this information?" Jeff looked quickly across to Barbara. Cunningham noted the conspiratorial glance. "Come on, out with it. You might as well tell me everything."

"We got the information from Esat Krasniqi's computer files," Barbara said, coming to Jeff's defence.

"How the hell did you get access to those?"

"We sort of broke into his warehouse and took them," Barbara replied timidly.

Caldwell burst out laughing. Cunningham jumped to his feet and threw his pen against the wall.

Jeff watched the performance. He knew Cunningham was tired, frustrated. Losing men can do that to a leader. Maybe he had forgotten about the computers. But no, Jeff quickly dismissed the thought. Cunningham never forgot anything. The anger was play acting for anyone who might be eavesdropping. Jeff knew what was really pissing Cunningham off was that he expected the information, once found, to be handed over. Cunningham wanted to play lead.

"Look, Brian. These people are after me and anyone who is close to me. I am going to do everything I can to get close to them. I'm not going to apologise for that. Yes we should have come to you first, but we weren't certain our information was right. I just acted on a hunch. Like a bull in a china shop. Make some noise and see what happens. What happened was totally unexpected."

Cunningham sat down again.

"Unfortunately, Jeff, this is exactly what happens. The unexpected. This is not a movie. These people are real." He was calming down.

"Do you want to stop these guys or not? You know I have the skills to fuck these guys. So let me be out there and do what I was trained to do. There could be another bomb."

"How were you able to get this name from Krasniqi's files?"

"Many of the files were in Albanian. I sent them to a friend in Kosovo. This was the name he came back with. We checked the phonebook and found no listings. Then we decided to go to an Albanian restaurant."

Cunningham nodded.

"I saved you a shit load of leg work," Jeff said. "How about a pat on the back?"

Cunningham shook his head. "That's not going to happen." He turned to Caldwell who nodded back to him. Tell them everything see what happens, was the silent message.

"When we raided Krasniqi's warehouse we found crates. Mr Caldwell has identified them as packaging for torpedoes. We have every reason to believe they are going to try and torpedo the *Ulysses*."

"Jesus," Jeff blurted out. "Has the *Ulysses* been warned?"

"We were at the naval base this morning."

"They'll leave immediately, won't they?" Barbara asked.

"No. That's not possible. Too many political implications. They are putting together a defensive shield at the moment. It still comes back to finding the terrorists before they can act."

"Ibrahim Mustafa might help there," Jeff said.

"Yes. But his capture might also force their hand."

"How can they launch a torpedo? Won't they need a boat or plane or something?"

"We discussed this with the submarine commander. He dismissed the plane idea. Too difficult. He felt a converted forty-foot launch or bigger would be more likely. But to convert it they would need to keep it hidden. That was why Caldwell and I were in the helicopter. Flying along the coastline looking at boat sheds. Know how many boat sheds there are in the Auckland Harbour? Lots. But I figured they needed to be inner harbour so we identified sheds and teams are checking them right now."

Cunningham walked to the window. "It will be dark in a few hours. If they try tonight . . . we aren't ready." He turned back to the table. "Barbara, I'll organise a car to take you home. Jeff wherever you're going you can walk."

Cunningham's mobile rang. He turned to Caldwell as he hung up. "They've found the boat shed. Beaumont Street." Then back to Jeff and Barbara. "Go home. Both of you. This is a job for the Special Tactics Group. They can handle it, Jeff. Even without your help."

"Come on, Jeff." Barbara said. "I'll buy you a whisky."

"My sore mouth will thank you if you do."

~

This time Cunningham was taking no chances. He called in the STG. They would lead the raid. This was what they were trained for and Cunningham was happy for them to do it.

"This is a good find, Inspector. How did we get on to it?" asked Moana.

"From the phone around. Seems there's a real estate company specialising in renting boat sheds and moorings. The agent said that a month ago someone paid six months up front. The tenant said he needed the space to upgrade his launch, a forty footer. The agent didn't think much of it but from his shop in Westhaven he can see the waterside of the shed. The tenant had hung tarpaulins so it couldn't be seen into. He thought it strange at the time and couldn't work out why anyone would want to do that. Anyway, he dismissed it until this morning. When asked if he'd rented a shed to anyone unusual this shed came to mind. A few neighbours were questioned. Four or five men had been coming and going. Olive skinned, a witness said, could have been from the Mediterranean. Then an hour or so ago ten to twelve men were seen entering. They have not come out. The tarpaulins are still in place."

Moana nodded. "I heard you caught one of the guys looking after the terrorists?"

"We have someone in custody, yes."

"Another piece of good police work."

"Nothing to do with me, Moana. Jeff Bradley and Barbara Heywood decided to play detective. They found him. I'll tell you all about it later."

Lee Caldwell moved up behind Cunningham.

"I've spoken to Commander Mann. There are boats and barges lined up in front of them but he can't close all the gaps," he said. "The sea is the sea, tides and waves move boats about and that is one big area of water we are trying to cover."

Cunningham saw the curious look on Moana's face. An American in their midst. He would leave her wondering. He turned his attention back to the anti-terrorist squad.

~

Jeff bought a bottle of Glen Fiddich on the way back to Barbara's apartment. She brought two glasses into the lounge and they crashed on the leather chairs. Jeff spun the cap off the bottle and poured. He passed Barbara her drink then went to the computer to check his emails.

"There's a letter from Sulla."

Barbara forced herself to her feet. She took two paces and leant on Jeff's shoulder.

Jeff
I have been approached by a man in Kosovo on behalf of a Kosovan living in Auckland. His name is Demi Myftari ph 695 4320. The man in Auckland knew we knew each other from the newspapers and asked his friend to contact me. I have spoken to him. Demi knows a lot of what is going down. He is too frightened to go to the police but says he will talk to you. Be careful.

Sulla

Jeff reread the letter. He walked over to the telephone on the counter and dialled the number.

"Mr Myftari. My name is Jeff Bradley."

"You are Sulla's friend."

"When can we meet?" Jeff asked.

"Meet me at O'Hagans Irish Bar in the Viaduct. You know it?"

Jeff turned to Barbara and covered the mouthpiece, "Do you know O'Hagans Irish Bar in the Viaduct?" he whispered.

Barbara nodded.

"Yes, I know it," Jeff said into the phone.

"I will meet you there at 6.30pm."

"How will I recognise you?"

"Do not worry. I have seen you on the television. I will come to you. Just be there." He rang off. Jeff put down the phone and turned to Barbara. "I'm meeting him at 6.30pm."

"*We're* meeting him at 6.30pm," Barbara said. "What about Brian?"

"Sulla said no police, and besides, Brian has enough on his plate. He found the boat."

"All the same he was pretty mad at us earlier," Barbara said.

"All that earlier was play acting. For your benefit and anyone else who might be listening. He left those computers there deliberately knowing I'd go there and hoping I'd find something, which I did."

Barbara stared at Jeff, wide eyed. Not convinced.

Jeff walked to the window and looked down into the city.

"I'm getting closer, Zahar. I hope you're sweating."

~

The Special Tactics Leader, Peter Colville, said to Moana, "The good news is it's an industrial area so there's no concern for residents, but there are marine and factory workers within the danger zone. Most of these buildings round here are dilapidated and many back into the water. There are entrances and sheds all over the place; a regular rabbit warren. Anyone could walk out from anywhere at any time. Can I use your people to spread yourselves outside the frontages? Anyone who pops a head out send them back inside."

Moana gave the street a quick scan. She had enough people to cope.

"All of this side of Beaumont backs on to St Mary's Bay," Colville went on. "The police launch *Deodar* is on its way to block the marina entrance. If the terrorists get out into the harbour in the dark we'll never find them. You know what it's like out there, the size of a small country. Well, maybe an exaggeration but big enough to make searching difficult. With the hundreds of craft already on the water it's bordering on impossible."

He turned to Cunningham, "I take it you want to stop them here if you can?"

"You got it in one, Peter," Cunningham replied. "Good luck."

Moana waved to her team and gave orders for Beaumont Street to be cordoned off from Gaunt Street through to Silo Park. Vehicles to be rerouted down Dalby Street.

"Into formation everyone. Let's move it," Colville ordered.

There were thirty of them, all dressed in black fatigues, wearing protective vests and assault weapons held at the ready. As they moved off it occurred to Cunningham how futile and misguided the attack on the warehouse had been. They had been so very, very lucky. Emotion ruled his head. Lately he had begun to question his ability to lead a police unit and had decided he wasn't cut out for it. He had no future in the police force.

Colville assembled his men in front of the compound that had become the graveyard for redundant America's Cup yachts. Their target, the boat shed opposite, had once existed as a fish-processing plant but the two-storey building now covered in rusting sheets of corrugated iron had recently received a coat of gunmetal grey paint. The attempt to spruce it up had failed to lift it above derelict. The number forty-nine had been painted on the roller door. To the left of the roller door was a small wooden door.

"What do you think?" Colville said to his second in command.

"I think I would like to be walking in behind a tank. No sign of any movement."

"Confirm that," Colville replied, looking through his binoculars.

His second in command said, "The only way to enter is through that door. It's also a potential death trap. I've spoken with Rogers. He has a telescope on the Westhaven side and can't see inside. No sign of movement, but the bottom of the tarpaulin is flapping in the wind. Access through that would be easy enough."

Colville nodded. "Tell number one team to go through that sand quarry and make their way along to the rear. We go in through the wooden door. Flash grenades first and then let's gauge the reaction. If these guys have automatic weapons we pull back and lay siege. They won't be going anywhere."

Team one dashed across the open ground and into the sand and on to the water's edge. They split into two sections. Four stayed in position and the others moved across the front of the shed opening to the farthest corner. He radioed he was in position. Colville nodded at the message. So far so good.

The team leader led his team across the street. There was a small window above the door. A camera was raised. Colville and the section leader watched the monitor. The camera was rotated a number of times but no sign of occupants were detected. They could see through to the tarpaulin but only the upper section. A wall fifteen metres in hid the main floor area. The light was fading. No lights had been switched on.

"Worst case scenario," Colville said. "They may have been alerted and in hiding. Assume the shed occupied until cleared."

He spoke to number one leader. In 30 seconds they would smash down the door and lob in the smoke and flash canisters. Then he would lead his team inside. Team one on the waterside would wait and ambush any terrorists trying to escape. Under no circumstances were they to enter until ordered.

"Roger that," team one leader whispered. They synchronised watches.

Colville held up his hand and counted off with his fingers: 5, 4, 3, 2, 1. A steel ram smashed the door open and the canisters were tossed in; the familiar whoosh of the cylinders emptying followed. Smoke began to pour through the open end. His hand held high once more, fingers counting down 5, 4, 3, 2, 1 then team leader two rushed forward, his men at his heels. As they rounded the wall into the shed proper they dived to the floor, weapons raised. Eyes scanned the area looking for a target.

42.

It was a ten-minute walk from Barbara's apartment in Quay West Towers to the Viaduct. Known to the locals as the Viaduct Basin, now renamed Viaduct Harbour, it was built on the site of the old fish processing factories and the city's fruit and vegetable markets. Prime real estate in the heart of Auckland's Central business district and offering water views was never going to remain the home of rotten fish and fruit. The developers moved in and built offices, apartments and restaurants. The inner harbour water ways now featured marinas and moorings for the yachts and motor launches of the wealthy. In the year 2000 the Viaduct had buzzed with the excitement of an America's Cup defence campaign. Jeff remembered it well. He also shared the pain with his fellow countrymen when New Zealand lost it. But life went on, and the restaurants became popular dining and drinking spots.

At the end of the long line of restaurants was O'Hagans Irish Bar; a popular watering hole for not only locals but tourists and backpackers from round the world. Seating was a mix of high tables and bar stools and four- and six-seater tables. Large screen televisions hung from the ceilings, all tuned into live cricket from Australia. The walls were covered in sports paraphernalia, football outfits, photos of football teams and above the bar a set of golf clubs, old bottles, an old typewriter and a Guinness Stout sign added to the variety.

Barbara chose to sit at one of the outside tables under tent-shaped canopies protecting patrons from adverse weather. A waitress in a red T-shirt and black slacks appeared and Jeff ordered two small beers. He surveyed the environment out of habit. Conversations at other tables were in a mix of English and unrecognisable foreign languages.

Jeff only noticed the slightly built man just beyond the restaurant's outside seating area because he paced and looked nervous. Dressed in an open-necked cream shirt, dark blue jacket and grey trousers he looked every bit a used-car salesman. The trim beard and neatly cropped hair completed the image. He did not look like the Kosovans Jeff had met, and definitely did not have a terrorist look about him. However, Avni Leka had a single criterion when he chose the men who worked for him and Jeff had little doubt that if this was Myftari then just beneath the surface lay a ruthless killer streak. Jeff stepped out from the table so he could be easily seen from Myftari's vantage point. It worked – the car salesman nodded and sidled along a row of potted hedging plants which bordered the seating area to the entry point then crossed the slate floor to Jeff's table.

"Mr Bradley? I am Demi Myftari."

"Jeff nodded. They shook hands. "I've brought an associate, Barbara Heywood."

Demi eyed Barbara, suspicious, but did little else to acknowledge her presence. Barbara chose to ignore him back.

"Can I get you a beer, Demi?" Jeff asked.

Demi said, "No. Thank you. I only have an interest in speaking with you and leaving as quickly as is possible. Sulla said you were a friend. This is good. He said if I help you then you will help me. That I should trust you."

Jeff replied, "Whatever you tell us will be held in confidence. If I need to use some of the information no one will ever know it came from you. If I can help you," Jeff shrugged, "then I will."

"Please remember, I am not only putting my life in your hands but also the life of my wife and family."

"What is it you have to tell me?"

"It started in Kosovo. I lived with my family in a village just outside the city of Gjakova. An hour and a half drive from the capital, Prishtina. The name of the village doesn't matter; it doesn't exist anymore. I was away on business the day it happened. Every Thursday in Gjakova was market day. I had taken vegetables there to sell. The Serbs, they moved into the village. Everyone, my wife, my father and mother, my cousins were taken out into the field and shot. One hundred and twenty people. The Serbs had had bulldozers and dug a trench and the bodies were thrown in and they buried them. Then they covered the dirt with scrub, trees and ready-made lawn. You know ready-made lawn?"

Jeff nodded.

"Then the houses were destroyed and the rubble loaded on trucks and dumped at a local quarry. Every piece of timber and brick was cleared away and again covered as before with the lawn."

Demi paused a moment, wiped his eyes. Jeff sipped his beer. Barbara, appalled but engrossed, leaned forward.

"When I returned from Gjakova later that night," Demi continued, "for a time I was confused. I knew I was in the right place but there was nothing to see. I stood on the side of the road that ran into the village. Had I gone mad? This was all I could think. Then I walked down the road and found the scars in the dirt. I had heard stories of other villages disappearing. We had all thought they were rumours but now I knew it to be true. I caught a bus to Prishtina and stayed with my cousin."

"Word filtered through the community that certain countries were accepting refugees. My cousin convinced me this was the right course of action for me. To go somewhere else and begin again. Kosovo would remain a place of sadness and my life still had many years to go. I wasn't opposed to the idea but had no idea how to begin such a process. I had no money. How could I afford it anyway? Nothing is for free. Then my cousin came home one night and told me he had arranged for me to meet with a man who might be able to help. Money was not a problem.

"This man's name was Avni Leka," Jeff stated.

Demi nodded.

"I met with him in his office. He said he would arrange for me to go to New Zealand. He would give me money and help me to start a business but I would be working for him. I would always be working for him and must do whatever I was asked to. The consequences for not obeying him were not discussed but I am Albanian and I knew what the hidden message meant. I was philosophical. I had no choices and there were others he had made the offer to so I would not be alone. So I came to New Zealand and built my business, met a woman and remarried. We have children."

"How many others?" Jeff asked.

"Six."

"Were all seven of you set up in business?" Jeff asked.

"Yes."

"All export businesses?"

"Not all export. I have a manufacturing company but all my produce goes overseas. Only a little into the local market."

"That's unusual," Jeff said. "Very few companies can be totally export focused. What countries did you export to?"

"Mostly to the Middle East but there were some African and Asian countries as well."

"Countries in political turmoil, I would guess," Jeff mused.

"It seemed to be that way, yes. Even the New Zealand Export Institute warned me against such countries. They said there might be payment problems but neither I nor any of the others ever had a payment problem."

"That is interesting."

"Not only that. Some of the prices paid for the goods were high. I know the customers could have bought cheaper."

Jeff thought about this for a moment. He said, "Seven men come to New Zealand and establish businesses, all export orientated, and sell goods at higher than normal prices and payment is never a problem."

Barbara sat quietly as Jeff digested the information. As a journalist she knew when to stay quiet. She had an idea where Jeff's line of thinking might be taking him. The idea of it horrified her.

"In all this time the seven of you were running your businesses did Avni Leka ever ask you to do anything for him?"

"No, never."

"What was in it for him them? The money you made? What happened to that?"

"Avni had a holding company and it held a 49-percent share in each business. He was paid a dividend profit share. After tax."

"And that's all you were asked to do?"

"Yes. Until two months ago."

"What happened two months ago?"

"One of our group, our boss, is a man called Sami Hadani. He was one of the last men Avni Leka helped to start a new life in New Zealand. But Sami made it very clear within a few days of his arriving that Leka had sent him to be in charge. To look after Avni's interests in our companies. None of us protested. When you live in countries such as Kosovo and Albania you quickly learn to recognise the men to be afraid of and steer clear of and Sami Hadani was such a man. Anyway as I said, two months ago he called us to a meeting. He told us some men were arriving and we had to look after them. Provide accommodation and look after all their personal needs. Food, that sort of thing. Warehousing would be needed to store goods. They were coming in groups of four and each of us was assigned a team."

"Jesus," Jeff said. "Twenty-eight? And you had no idea why these men were coming to New Zealand?"

"At first, no I did not know and I did not question. When Sami said to do something you obeyed. He is a very dangerous man. But over the last couple of weeks with all that has happened I started to put the pieces together."

"You didn't contact the authorities?"

"No."

"Why not?"

"This is when we found out what Avni had led us into. He informed us that he had kept a dossier of all our transactions and these documents showed that the profits we had made for him were funding terrorist operations round the world. If he released these documents to the authorities we would spend the rest of our lives in jail and we would lose all we had built. We had no choice."

"You always have a choice, Demi."

Jeff was thoughtful.

"And where are the men you are looking after now? Can you give me the address?"

"It would be no use. I went to the apartment this morning as per the arrangement and they had gone. Their belongings and the vehicle I'd provided also gone. I called the others and for them it was the same. I never rang Sami."

Jeff nodded.

"I need the names of the other Kosovan exporters, Demi."

"This I cannot do. They are my friends. They, like me had no idea what was happening and now like me are very scared. Don't ask me to do this."

"There is no choice, Demi."

"Sulla said I could trust you. I want protection for myself but not to betray others."

"People are dying in the streets of Auckland. Good decent people blown up by bombs set off by the men you and your colleagues are protecting. I want Zahar Akbar, the leader of this little group of killers, and someone in your group knows where he is. Give me the names of the others and I will let you walk away. Barbara, do you have a pad and pen?" Barbara opened her bag. "The names, Demi."

"I cannot betray my friends. It is a matter of honour."

Jeff cringed. "I don't know how many times I heard that term when I was in Kosovo while men like the ones you protect were murdering my friends."

Jeff moved closer to Demi, his eyes cold. "I have no patience for your fucked up sense of honour. Tell me what I want to know, Demi."

Demi paled and shook his head.

Jeff shot out his left arm and grabbed a fistful of the front of Demi's shirt, then swung his right fist up under the Kosovan's jaw. The loud crack when bone crunched on bone caused heads close by to snap round. Jeff released his grip of Demi's shirt and the Kosovan crumpled to the ground, unconscious. He threw Barbara a sheepish grin then shook his hand and blew on it.

"Did you have to do that?"

"Yes. Now call the police."

"Do I have to? I don't know if I'm up to another lecture from Brian."

Jeff glared.

Barbara pulled out her mobile phone and found Cunningham's number on the contact list. She gave Jeff a glare of her own before she hit the number. As she waited for the phone to be answered she looked down at the floor. Demi Myftari had not moved.

43.

There was disappointment all round as Cunningham and Caldwell entered the boat shed. No boat and no terrorists.

"Looks as if we got it wrong," Cunningham said.

"No, I don't think so," Caldwell replied as he moved to the back of the shed. I think we were just too late."

Small paper cups still sat on the table. He touched the coffee pot. It was still warm. "Acetylene torches against the wall. Tools of every description. Sleeping bags. Someone has been very busy," Caldwell said as he cast an eye round the boat shed.

Cunningham looked through the shed to the waters of the inner harbor, the tarpaulin now removed. Night had come.

"What do you think?" Cunningham asked.

"Same as you. I think they're out there and I think it's going down tonight."

Cunningham nodded, already fearing the answer and knowing it to be true.

He turned to his sergeant. "Moana, contact the police launch. I want it out on the harbour checking boats."

"There are lots of protest boats out there, Brian."

"We're looking for a motorboat around forty feet long. It will have some sort of racking that will have a torpedo sitting in it. That should narrow it down."

Moana showed no sign she had picked up on the sarcasm. She walked away a few metres to make the call. However, Cunningham knew she was right. The nightly vigil of protest craft had increased the day the *Ulysses* came into harbour. There were seven wharves from Princes Wharf through to Fergusson. Freighters were anchored in the sea-lane waiting to berth. Tugs were working overtime. Ferries were crossing the harbour at regular intervals from various points of the city to the outer islands of the gulf. It would be like looking for a needle in haystack. His mobile rang. He recognised the caller number.

"Yes, Barbara." He listened as she explained what had taken place. He caught Caldwell's eye. Caldwell moved toward him. "All right, thanks, Barbara. A car is on its way."

~

Patrons of O'Hagans gathered round the unconscious form of Demi Myftari. A man dressed in the same red T-shirt and black trousers combination as the waitress came forward. He had an air of authority. The manager, Jeff guessed.

"What's going on here?" he asked, his tone aggressive.

"Keep out of it," Jeff replied, equally belligerent.

"I'll call the police."

"We are with the police."

The barman looked them over and then down at Demi. Uncertain of what to do, he decided discretion was best and went back to tending the bar. The crowd stayed where they were. Jeff said to Barbara, "I have a feeling that whatever is going to happen is going to happen tonight. If the terrorists have left the safety of their apartments they need to act and get the hell out of New Zealand."

Barbara nodded in agreement.

"I need to get on the water."

He pulled out his mobile. Luckily he had entered his neighbour Larry Connor's number into his address book the night of the barbecue. He pushed the button.

"Larry Connors."

"Hi, Larry. Jeff Bradley here. Your neighbour from across the road."

"Hi, Jeff. What can I do for you?"

"I need access to a motor boat. Something quick. And I need it now. I was hoping you might be able to help me."

"I have one. I use it to hop across to the city from time to time. But right now is impossible, Jeff. I'm about to sit down to dinner. We have guests. Can't it wait until tomorrow?"

"I need it now, Larry, and I'm on the Auckland City side. I hate to do this to you, but Larry, your family is in danger."

"What the hell are you talking about?"

"The terrorists I fought with in Waipu are now on the water and they are going to try and blow up the submarine. It's nuclear. Do I really need to explain the consequences if that happens?"

"No, of course not. Jesus. So why do you need a boat? Aren't the navy and police out there?"

"Everyone is out there, Larry, but when my life is threatened then I'd prefer taking matters into my own hands and not rely on someone else. I'm good at this shit, Larry. I can stop them."

"Christ, Jeff, I don't know. I'm no bloody hero."

"Of course you are and really Larry there is no choice. I need the boat and you need to bring it to me."

"What I should do is drive my family and friends out of here. Right now."

"Yes you should, and if I was in your shoes that's exactly what I would do."

Jeff waited.

"You are an absolute asshole neighbour. All right, I'll bring the boat just as soon as I load the family into the car. Where do I come?"

"There are three small jetties between the ferry buildings and the Hilton. You know where I mean?" Jeff said.

"I know it. Old Admiralty steps. I'll be there in twenty minutes."

Jeff thanked God his neighbour was a natural adventurer.

"Barbara, you need to wait here with our friend and get him back to the station. Tell Brian and Caldwell everything this little shit has told us."

"What if he wakes up before the police get here?" Barbara asked.

"Good point." Jeff surveyed the crowd and his eyes fell upon two bulky blonde men. Not New Zealanders. He waved them forward. They each had a beer in hand but passed them to the girls they were with.

"You guys speak English?" Jeff asked.

They nodded. "Yah. We are from Sweden," the taller of the two offered.

"Good. This is Barbara Heywood, a famous New Zealand television news woman. I have to leave but the police are on their way. If this guy wakes before they arrive, hold him down." He took some money from his pocket and put it on the table. "Free drinks for the rest of the night." Two Swedish faces broke into broad grins. Friends behind cheered.

Two young women approached with table napkins.

"May we have an autograph, Ms Heywood?"

Jeff turned to leave and Barbara held his arm.

"Be careful."

He kissed her on the cheek and left. Barbara smiled at the two girls and reached out for the pen and napkin.

~

The three jetties were seven minutes away. Jeff did it in five. He stepped out onto the middle one and walked to its end. He turned back and took in the scene behind him. The pavement that ran along in front of the Ferry building entrance was a popular promenade and walkway to the Viaduct restaurants and the Hilton Hotel. It was crowded with citizens enjoying an evening constitutional, none of whom had any idea of the drama unfolding on the water. It occurred to Jeff to stop and shout a warning to get out of the city, but dismissed the thought as quickly as it came. He would be viewed as a crazy man and it would be wasting precious time trying to convince them otherwise.

He spotted Larry Connor and waved. Larry turned the stern of his outboard-engine boat towards the steps. When it was close enough Jeff jumped aboard.

"Okay, Jeff, tell me again why I had to give up a relaxing night of wine and friends?"

"The terrorists have converted a launch into a torpedo boat. The submarine is the target, Larry. It's a nuclear sub. Think Chernobyl. Think of the recent Japanese reactor meltdown. Not only the food chain in the inner harbour but much of the gulf will be destroyed and contaminated for a bloody long time. Radiation leakage will mean much of the city will become uninhabitable, not to mention the deaths from radiation poisoning. I could go on but you have an imagination."

Larry gripped the steering wheel. His head dropped. Jeff waited as his neighbour took a moment. Soft words came from his mouth. A prayer, Jeff surmised. He had never considered Larry as religious, but then he was an ocean racing sailor and mariners were never far from God. Just as very few soldiers were atheists.

Larry lifted his head and caught Jeff's eye. "Our home will turn to shit."

"You've got it. Did you send the family away?"

"Yes."

"I'll take you back to the other side and drop you off. Just show me how the boat works. Does it have gears?"

Larry offered a wry smile.

"No need for that. For one thing it would take too long to teach you and secondly I can't have you wrecking the family boat. I'm coming too. No arguments."

"Larry, these guys are armed and there's a good chance we won't come out of this alive."

"I've sailed the Southern Ocean, Jeff. It can't be worse than that."

"Okay." Jeff slapped Larry on the back. "I was hoping you'd say that. Let's go."

Larry pushed the throttle lever and the boat moved forward.

"How fast can this go?" Jeff asked.

"What size boat are we chasing?"

"A forty-foot launch."

"It's powerful enough to run down a forty-foot launch."

Larry pushed to full throttle and Jeff clung to the railing as they sped past an incoming ferry and out into the harbour proper.

~

Barbara was sitting in the public waiting area of the police station, Demi on a seat opposite, watched over by two policemen. The two constables remained unmoved by Demi's protestations that Barbara and a man she was with had assaulted him. Barbara avoided eye contact as best she could but now and then they connected just long enough for Demi to hurl the type of accusatory stare given a traitor. 'Screw you', Barbara thought. She folded her arms and sat stiff backed and locked eyes. She was not about to be intimidated by a man who had helped kill her countrymen. Demi looked away first and Barbara nodded in satisfaction.

"This is the man, Barbara?" Cunningham asked.

Barbara looked up. She hadn't seen Cunningham enter, Caldwell behind him.

"Brian, this is Demi Myftari. He has unwittingly been working with the terrorists. Accommodation mainly, but he knows what has been going on. He also knows the names of the others who have been helping. But he did come forward of his own volition to help expose them. To do the right thing for his new country. I think if you cut him a little slack and make him a deal you'll get all you want."

"Okay." He turned to the constables. "Take him down to a cell and watch him. I want someone in the cell at all times. I don't want any suicides." The two constables marched the complaining Demi away. "Now, tell me everything. Quickly. I'm in a hurry."

"Jeff's friend in Kosovo came back with another name. Demi Myftari. Jeff phoned him and he said he would meet with us right away, at O'Hagans in the Viaduct." Barbara ignored Cunningham's incredulous look. "To cut a long story short, it seems Myftari and six others, including Ibrahim Mustafa, came to New Zealand as refugees and were funded into business by this Avni Leka. Two months ago they were told twenty-eight men were coming to New Zealand and Myftari and his friends had to look after four each. Demi said he had no idea why they were here, but lately he started putting two and two together."

"Well at least we now know how many there are," Cunningham said. "So this Myftari wanted to approach Jeff to hand himself in?"

"Kind of. He wanted to tell Jeff his story. Ease his conscience. Get help to keep him out of it. Maybe ask for immunity. Jeff said if he wanted to leave the bar he wanted all the names of the other businessmen. Demi refused so Jeff knocked him out. That's when I rang you."

This time it was Cunningham's turn to laugh.

"Jesus. Well, okay. Jeff did the right thing. Where is he now? Why isn't he with you?"

Barbara shrugged.

"What the hell is he up to now?"

"Jeff reasoned that if the terrorists had left their burrows then the attack on the sub was underway."

"Okay. I don't disagree. Caldwell and I have come to the same conclusion. So where is he?"

"He's on a boat on the harbour. He rang an acquaintance with a speedboat. They were meeting down by the ferry buildings. He's gone looking for them."

"Bloody hell." Cunningham looked across to Caldwell. "Who does he think he is? Rambo or something?"

"Maybe he is." Caldwell laughed.

44.

After five minutes, spray thrown back by the speedboat smashing through waves had left Jeff saturated. Larry wore the yellow jacket of his wet-weather gear.

"There's only one on the boat," Larry had said when he pulled it on. "Sorry, seafarers' regulations. The captain must be comfy at all times. A clear head makes for competent decisions."

"Yeah sure," Jeff said, not believing a word.

After a few minutes of watching Larry manoeuvre the boat Jeff was thankful the international sailor had volunteered. He would never have been able to drive it as it needed to be. Now, out on the harbour, the realisation of the enormity of the task ahead hit home. Standing on the Auckland city side and looking across the harbour at the northern banks, lit up by thousands of homes, made it appear close enough to throw a stone at. But now, out on the vast expanse that was the harbour, which took a ferry twelve minutes to cross, how would he ever find the launch? The protest and recreation craft and the darkness made the mission impossible. Even with the illumination from the city and harbour bridge the dark patches existed. And there was a danger of being rammed by the smaller vessels. Most did not have radar.

He needed a start point to begin the search. The terrorist boat was coming from the inner harbour. He yelled to Larry to get as close to the no go zone near Bledisloe Wharf as he could and then track back toward the harbour bridge. Larry gave a thumbs-up and spun the boat. The manoeuvre threw Jeff sideways. He clung to the aluminium railing. When they were close to Bledisloe, Larry turned the boat and cruised back toward the harbour bridge. After five minutes he stopped.

"We can't zip about all night. We'll run out of gas," Larry said.

Jeff nodded. After ten minutes the bobbing of the boat was making him queasy.

"Hell, Larry, on land this looks such a small area but out here . . . we'll never see them coming."

"That is why sea rescue is so difficult," called Larry. "There's a hunting light under the seat in the cabin."

Jeff found what looked like a car headlight on a small handle. "Found it."

"Okay, there is a switch on the side. Turn it on for a test but make sure it's pointed away from me."

Jeff did as instructed.

The area in front lit up like day.

"Jesus. It's like a bloody searchlight," Jeff said.

"Okay, switch it off and keep it ready. Now hold on tight. I'm going across current to get out more into the middle of the harbour."

Jeff, thankful to be moving again, rubbed his stomach and dry retched.

~

Cunningham waved to a constable.

"I want the police launch to come into the ferry buildings. I'll be there in fifteen minutes. And I want a car at the door waiting in two."

As he prepared to leave he sensed two sets of eyes on him. He turned to Caldwell and Barbara.

"Okay. It's a big boat. Come on."

Caldwell and Barbara were on his heels as he walked through the door.

"We don't know for certain they're out there yet," Caldwell said when he reached Cunningham's side.

"What do you think, Caldwell? What does your gut tell you?"

"That they are out there."

"What about questioning Demi Myftari?" Barbara asked.

"Not now," Cunningham replied. "He has nothing to tell us. Not about where the boat might be and that's all that counts right now."

~

Larry slowed a few hundred metres short of the tank farm, so named because of the proliferation of empty silos and petroleum tanks, no longer in use. Redevelopment of the area had begun and apartments, restaurants and cafés had turned the farm into a new exclusive suburb. Jeff wished he was in one of the cafés right now. Unable to hold back he leant over the side and vomited. Larry held onto his shirt.

"Are you okay?" Larry asked.

"No, I'm not. I hate boats. Now I remember why I joined the army and not the navy. Next time I ask you to take me out on a boat tell me to get lost."

Larry said, "I've seen many a seasick sailor and there's no answer to it. I tell my crews either take tablets before sailing or get over it."

"Good advice, Larry. I'll try to remember."

"So tell me, Jeff. I know it's not a lifestyle choice, or maybe it is, but how is it you got caught up in all this? I understand you were in the military and then there was Kosovo and now this. You have money don't you? You can afford an easy life. Why aren't you playing golf?"

"Believe me, Larry. After this is over all I will ever do is play golf." His stomach began rumbling again.

"You're like some sailors I know. When ocean racing most of us choose to go round the storms. The madmen who want to win at all costs go through them."

"Believe me I am not doing this by choice." As soon as he said it he knew it wasn't true. Larry was right. He was one of those sailors. "Maybe you're right. But hell, Larry, you've raced in the Antarctic. Icy waters, high seas and icebergs. How sane is that?"

"It's as crazy as hell, that's why I know what I am talking about."

Jeff half laughed then dropped his head over the side again. More dry retching. It was a hopeless situation. As he lifted his head he saw a boat silhouetted against the lights of Stanley Point. If he hadn't been leaning over he would have missed it. The launch's lights were off. But the shadowy shape was distinctive and there was no mistaking the racking on the side. A torpedo chute. It was too dark to make out the torpedo but he supposed it was loaded. The launch disappeared again.

"I think I've seen them," he said as Larry pulled him upright.

"Really? Where?"

Jeff pointed. "In that direction. In a direct line with Stanley Point, they have no lights, but they're way ahead of us."

"Hang on, we're moving."

Larry pushed the throttle to full. Jeff fell backwards onto the fibreglass bottom of the speedboat. As he crawled back to his feet Larry was racing to where he had pointed.

"The tide is coming in. I'll aim the bow higher to allow for drift. Have you actually thought about what you are going to do when we find them?"

"Not really."

"So we have no plan?" Larry said.

"This is the plan. Step one, find them."

"Great."

"Only way I can think," Jeff said. He rubbed his stomach. Fought against throwing up.

"Okay. Grab the light and don't drop it," Larry yelled. Jeff picked it up again. "When I say, flick the switch. As soon as you spot them turn it off again. If they're armed we don't want them shooting at us. But I want to know how much more distance I need to cover."

~

Cunningham instructed the captain of the twin-hulled police launch *Deodar III* to take them in the general direction of Bledisloe Wharf. They would put themselves between the terrorists and the target.

"There are hundreds of boats out here. It's like the Anniversary Day regatta. How will you identify them? It's like looking for a needle in a haystack only this haystack is water," the captain said.

"If we do find it we may have to ram them," Cunningham said. "Can your vessel handle that?"

"The hulls are aluminium plated with a 6mm Sealium alloy. Built for speed not ramming."

"Could you ram a forty-foot launch and do damage?"

"Is that authorised?"

Cunningham said, "No it's not. If our air force had a fighter jet I'd have them blown out of the water or if they had an attack helicopter I'd have them fire a few missiles. But we don't have those options. So it's us. If the navy sees them maybe they'll get off a salvo. But with all the spectator craft they might hold off, who the hell knows. Right now if we find them and we're close enough, we ram."

"They may never give me another boat."

"No, they may not."

"Good. At least that's clear." The captain smiled. "Are you going to enlighten me as to what is happening? Just so I know why I'm throwing away a perfectly good career."

"The boat we're looking for has been converted to launch torpedoes. They are going to try and blow up the *Ulysses*."

"Okay, I can see that would be a problem."

"So if it comes to it, we either wreck your launch or they blow up the city."

"I'll do what has to be done. You can count on me. But what about the *Te Hana*? The bloody frigate is right there. They have a chopper and it has missiles."

"Are you kidding me?"

"No I'm not. I'll get onto them and get it in the air."

Cunningham joined Barbara and Caldwell at the stern. Barbara was rubbing her hands. Caldwell was leaning on the railing looking out to sea.

"The captain has assured me he will ram them if that is the only option," Cunningham said.

"Let's hope it doesn't come to that," Caldwell said. "This craft looks fragile; it might come off second best."

Cunningham nodded in agreement. "However he tells me the *Te Hana* has an attack chopper. We're getting it in the air."

"Have you heard from Jeff?" Barbara asked.

"Not as yet. I just hope he doesn't get himself killed this time."

~

Larry had them in a position where he thought the terrorists' launch should be.

"I can't see anything – Jeff what about you?"

"Not a thing. Should I use the searchlight?"

"Not yet. Not until I'm certain where they are. They must be hugging the shore. I'll get in closer too. Try to silhouette them against the ferry terminal lights."

It took another few minutes until they were in position.

"There they are. Shit, they've got well ahead."

"I see them," Jeff yelled. "They're getting away."

Larry yelled back. "Don't worry we have some muscle in our motors."

As Larry opened the throttle Jeff gripped the railing. This time he didn't end up on his ass. He still managed to hold fast to the handle of the hunting light and tightened his grip as the small speedboat bounced off the waves. He could see they were gaining on the terrorists. The launch passed the top end of the ferry terminal and pointed towards Bledisloe Wharf only a few hundred metres ahead.

"They're lining up the *Ulysses*. Jesus, Larry they're about to launch the torpedo."

"Get ready to light them up."

"Remember," Jeff said, "they have automatic weapons."

"That's a reminder I didn't need."

"Keep your head down."

"Okay, Jeff. Light them up."

Jeff flicked the switch and the beam hit the stern of the launch. It was as if it was the middle of the day. One of Zahar Akbar's men was standing on the stern, a Kalashnikov in his hands aimed straight at them.

~

On the police launch Barbara saw the light first and pointed. They were less than three hundred metres away. Then they heard the burst of gunfire.

"Well at least we know where Bradley is," Caldwell said dryly. "The terrorists look like they're lining up the *Ulysses*. Look, the tide has swung the protection boats apart. There is an opening."

The police launch increased speed but it was never going to make it in time. The *Te Hana* stood between the terrorist launch and the sub, a sentinel towering above the *Ulysses*. Although Cunningham had been on board the frigate he had not been aware it had an attack helicopter. At least it was in the air. That was something. He did know that on the deck below the bridge, a competent naval rating sat at the desk that controlled the Phalanx weapons system, and he hoped a hand on the control handle was lining up the gatling gun or whatever they called the damn thing. The wall of lead it was capable of spitting forth would rip the launch's fibreglass hull to shreds.

"We're going to be too fucking late. Where is that bloody chopper off the *Te Hana*?" Cunningham screamed.

"They're searching but haven't sighted it yet," the captain responded.

"Are you kidding me? With Jeff lighting it up, a Russian cosmonaut on the space station could see it. Get that thing blown out of the water. Right now."

Larry swung the boat to the right as a terrorist opened fire. At the same time Jeff tried to keep the light aimed directly at his eyes. As Larry closed and sped past Jeff made sure he kept the launch lit up. The defensive naval vessels must be able to see it.

"We have to slow them down," Jeff yelled.

"Under the seat are fishing nets. Put the light off and down." Jeff did as he was told and scrambled back into the cabin.

"Found them!" he yelled.

"Okay, we have to tangle the propellers with it."

"Great idea. Do you think they'll let us get close enough if I ask politely?"

"That looks like an old launch. New boats are fitted with a disc around the shaft designed to chop up anything that gets wrapped round it. Let's hope this doesn't have one. I'm going to speed across the bow. You throw one of the nets in the water in front of them. Hopefully when they run over it the propellers will get caught."

"That was my next idea," Jeff laughed.

"Sure it was. That's the trouble with you soldier boys. On dry land you don't have to learn to think."

Larry was turning. Jeff held up the net in both hands. He gave no thought to spreading it. The water would do that. As they turned he could see the dark shape of the submarine.

"Why don't they fire the torpedoes?"

"Probably the incoming tide. They have to get past it a little. Another hundred metres or so."

"I'm ready."

"Okay, here we go. Splay it out when I say."

Larry hit the throttle and the boat surged forward. They were crossing in front.

"There's a gunman on the bow. So keep your head down."

Jeff instinctively ducked at flashes of light emitting from the launch. He was reminded of dancing fireflies.

"How do I do that and toss the net?" Jeff responded.

"If you get shot, make sure the net gets thrown. Okay here we go, ready, ready, now!"

Jeff splayed the net out as they passed in front. Two holes appeared in the fibreglass a few centimetres beneath the railing he clung to.

"It's done. Get us the hell out of here."

Larry swung the boat away. On the terrorists' launch shadowy figures took up positions along the starboard deck. Gun barrels were following the path of Larry's runabout.

"Get your head down," Jeff yelled.

Around them sharp cracks followed flashes of light as metal projectiles from Kalashnikovs rocketed towards them. None had hit the boat. This didn't surprise Jeff. Hitting a moving target while standing on a rolling base would be almost impossible.

"Get the light back on," Larry yelled. "Let's see if we've held them up."

Jeff brought the lamp back onto the launch.

"They're shooting at the light," Jeff called out. "Hold it away from me." Larry swung his boat into another manoeuvre.

"The launch, it's not slowing," Jeff yelled.

"Give it another few seconds."

~

The police boat was closing but was still 150 metres away from the terrorists' launch.

"They're going to fire at any moment," Cunningham said. "Where the hell is that navy chopper?" He searched the sky. There was too much noise to hear whirling blades.

Caldwell watched, frustrated. He checked the line of barges. The gaps had closed again. The torpedo would never get through. The terrorists had got close and failed. But the night was not over and there was always the chance that they might have other tricks up their sleeves.

The crazy New Zealander was lighting them up and deliberately making himself a target. The navy boys must have it in their sights. Why haven't they blown it out of the water? Then he saw protest craft nearby. He shook his head in despair.

"Look," Cunningham yelled. "It's stopped moving."

Cunningham ran to the cabin. The captain turned to him.

"Ram the fucking thing," Cunningham yelled at him.

The captain smiled and shook his head. "No need." He pointed towards the sky over the stricken boat. Hovering above Mechanics Bay was a Kaman SH-2G Seasprite helicopter. It was swinging round and lining up to fire its missiles.

"What the hell is it waiting for?" Cunningham.

Caldwell said, "Look, the launch is turning. Whatever it is Jeff did, it's turning away from the target."

They both saw the torpedo fly through the air a few seconds before it hit the water.

"Oh God, they've launched," Caldwell yelled.

There was a flash of light and the launch disappeared as a wall of water erupted into the air. A deafening roar followed and in all directions shock waves fountained forth from the blast centre. As waves hit the *Deodar III*, the multi-hull vessel rocked back and forth. When the water settled there was no sign of the terrorists' launch. Caldwell and Cunningham's attention switched from the destructive force of the navy chopper's missiles to the direction of the launched torpedo. It was an old weapon with no homing device. It went where it was targeted.

The small rushing wave of water, like a porpoise skimming the surface, was speeding towards Marsden Wharf and directly at the multi-level vehicle carrier *Star of the East*. Its ramp was down and only half its load of second-hand Japanese cars sat across the dockyard. When the torpedo hit the explosion lifted the huge steel hull before it collapsed back onto the water, sending a massive wave back across the harbour. Protest boats were flung from side to side and some smaller vessels capsized. The *Star of the East* listed as it filled with seawater and slowly sank onto the muddy bottom. A mooring rope groaned, then snapped, unable to restrain the thousands of tons of ship from sinking. The rope flicked across the dock surface like a giant whip, catching two port workers who disappeared from sight.

~

Larry stopped fifty metres astern of where they had last seen the terrorist launch.

When the missiles had struck, his boat had been flung sideways. Jeff had managed to hold onto the rail and grab Larry as the sailor slid across the bottom. He held him under his feet until the rocking stopped. Then he saw the exploding vehicle carrier and the wall of water sweeping towards them. Jeff sat down his back against the hull and helped Larry do the same. The speedboat lifted into the air. It stayed aloft. Then the wave disappeared and the boat crashed down onto water now seemingly as hard as concrete. Both men became weightless as they and the boat parted company, then crashed back onto the fibreglass bottom and lay still, winded.

"What the fuck just happened?" Larry groaned as he untangled himself from Jeff. He bashed the side of his head with the flat of his hand then tilted his head side to side. The ringing in his ears stayed.

"My best guess is a missile blew up the terrorist launch and the terrorists' torpedo blew up the Japanese car carrier," Jeff said. Then he managed a laugh. "Won't worry you, Larry. You only buy expensive European cars."

"Is this a time for humour?" Larry asked. "Okay, I get it. You soldier boys change the subject instead of telling everyone you're scared shitless. Good stuff. Did I ever tell you about sailing the Southern Ocean?"

"Not yet, but I guess I'm going to hear it over and over from here on."

Larry nodded. "You got it." He scrambled back behind the wheel. "What now?"

"There's the police launch. Let's get over there."

Jeff held up the hunter's lamp and searched the area for survivors as they cruised up beside the police boat.

Jeff was surprised to see Cunningham, Barbara and Lee Caldwell leaning over the railing.

"Are you okay?" Cunningham yelled.

"Yes. Look, Brian, I was close enough to make out the shapes of those on board, and I don't think Zahar was on the boat. He's not the type to hide in the cabin. He's still out there in the city somewhere. I'd stake my life on it."

Cunningham nodded.

"You and your mate did a good job, Jeff. I owe you one. I need to get back to the city and find Zahar. Maybe we'll get lucky. Someone else can look for survivors. How many do you think were on the boat?" Brian yelled.

"Seven, maybe eight. No more. I'm coming with you," Jeff said then leapt onto the police boat. "Thanks, Larry, get home to your family. We'll talk later."

Larry gave Jeff a thumbs-up then pushed on the throttle. After a few seconds he had disappeared from sight.

45.

Demi Myftari lay on the cot and stared at the ceiling. He contemplated his uncertain future. When he thought it through it wasn't so bad. What did they have on him? Nothing. He had talked to Bradley and the woman but nothing was written down, there had been no tape recording. Then Bradley had beaten him in the restaurant. He had plenty of witnesses. He would bring assault charges against Bradley. If he stuck to his story they would have nothing. Esat Krasniqi was dead so there was no one to link him to Zahar Akbar and his men. His lawyer would easily deal with this and he had the money to hire the best.

His eyes flicked to the door at the sound of a key in the lock. The cell door was pulled open and two police officers entered.

"Mr Myftari. I am Senior Sergeant Moana Te Kanawa, and my colleague is Detective Red Dawson. We want to have a chat."

Myftari swung his legs to the floor and sat up.

"I want to see my lawyer. I'm not talking to you without a lawyer present."

"Sorry, Mr Myftari, that's not possible for now. If you tell us what we need to know then maybe it will be considered."

"You can't do that. I have rights."

Moana opened the file she held.

"Mr Demi Myftari, immigrated to New Zealand in September 2002. Started your own business registered October 2004. You have a factory in Mount Wellington producing a variety of food products, most of which are exported. You have a house in St Heliers. Nice neighbourhood, Mr Myftari. You remarried after the death of your first wife. Your new wife is also a Kosovan refugee and you have two children, both born in New Zealand. Overall life has been very good for you since you arrived in this country. Wouldn't you agree?"

Silence.

"You don't need a lawyer to answer a question like that, Mr Myftari, surely. Wouldn't you agree that New Zealand, our country, has been very good to you?"

Myftari nodded.

"Is that a yes, Mr Myftari?"

"Yes. All right," Myftari replied. "New Zealand has been good to me."

"Good. Your wife and children are happy here."

"Yes they are happy."

"And what about you, Mr Myftari? Do you like it here? Are you a happy new immigrant?"

"Yes. Until now that is. What is it you want from me?"

"You know what we want, Mr Myftari."

"I want my lawyer."

"This is not an interview, Mr Myftari. This is not the interview room. There are no tape recorders. No notebooks. Nothing you say will be used as evidence. You have not been cautioned. Everything you say is off the record."

"What is it you want? I can't help you if I don't know what you want."

"Mr Myftari, we know you were working with Esat Krasniqi helping to house terrorists who came to New Zealand. We know there were seven of you. We know you were being used and that you would be killed if you didn't cooperate. Who wouldn't do what you did under those circumstances?" Moana said, turning to Red.

Red nodded. "I would do what you did. I don't want to die. Perfectly understandable."

"I want the names of the others, Mr Myftari," Moana said.

"I don't know what you're talking about."

Moana looked across at Red.

"It seems Mr Myftari has decided not to cooperate, Red. That's too bad."

"What is it you're afraid of, Mr Myftari?" Red asked. "We will protect you."

"I'm not afraid of anyone. I don't know what you are talking about."

Moana said, "The men you want to protect have committed murders. You have helped them, protected them and now you are lying for them. That makes you complicit in the act. You are just as guilty as they are."

Myftari rubbed his hands on his thighs. They were bluffing. He licked his lips. Uncertain. If he kept his mouth shut then everything would hold together. This was what he must do.

Moana went on. "As Mr Krasniqi is dead, killed by Zahar Akbar, there are now only six of you. If one of you testifies against the others then we might be able to grant that person immunity from prosecution. That person could be you. You would be free to carry on with your good and happy life. You don't want that?"

Myftari said nothing.

"Very well, Mr Myftari. We won't bother you any more," Moana said. "We will now make the same offer to Mr Ibrahim Mustafa in the cell next door. I'm certain he'll be more receptive."

Myftari looked up, uncertain. The two officers stood in the corridor. In a few seconds the cell door would slam shut. They had Ibrahim Mustafa. He was not a strong man but he was loyal. He was to be trusted. But the situation was serious. Under these circumstances maybe Ibrahim might grasp at the offer of immunity. Could he really turn his back on a chance at a good life? And his family? Did he not have a duty to protect them? His shoulders slumped. His head dropped as he nodded. "What is it you want to know?" He focused on the shoes of the two police officers as they walked back toward him.

~

Demi Myftari told them everything. He repeated the information they already had of how the groups had come and how it had been organised. Red and Moana sat patiently and let him speak.

"None of the terrorists we found had passports or identification of any sort," Red said. "We assume they have been kept in a safe place."

"Yes, this is the job of Sami Hadani. He is on the list I gave you. They are to meet with him when it is all over."

"Where are they to meet?"

"This I do not know. It was never discussed with me."

"This Sami Hadani. He has a warehouse." Demi wrote the address on a piece of paper and passed it to Moana.

She stood. "I need to talk to Detective Dawson outside." When they had left the room another officer entered and stood in the doorway.

"We need to talk to Inspector Cunningham," Moana said, taking out her phone and dialling Cunningham's mobile. "Inspector, where are you?"

"Coming into the ferry terminal. Why?"

"I need to talk to you."

"Okay, I'm dropping Barbara Heywood at Channel Nine then I'll swing by. Be there in ten minutes."

46.

And Myftari told you this Sami Hadani has everyone's travel documents and he is passing them out tonight?" Cunningham asked Moana, who had been waiting for him with Red at the public counter.

"That's what he said," she replied.

Cunningham turned to Jeff. "You've spoken with Myftari, do we believe him? We don't have time or resources to go chasing red herrings."

Jeff shrugged. "Who the hell knows? But he has nothing to gain by lying and everything to gain by telling the truth."

Cunningham gave Caldwell a 'what-do-you-think?' look.

"What Jeff says has some logic to it," Caldwell said. "It sounds like good intel to me. If I was in your shoes I'd act on it."

"Okay, we go after Hadani, but he's unlikely to keep the passports at his house, I would think."

Moana said, "It's only an exchange of documents. It could be done at the airport. A public place."

"Too much security at an airport," Cunningham replied. "One guy sitting on a bench in front of God knows how many security cameras; a dozen or more strangers coming up to him and leaving with a package. No, I don't think so. Too risky. Especially now, when all border controls are on a heightened state of alert. Let's phone his home. Moana, you do it. If his wife answers tell her you have a delivery problem and cannot get in touch with Sami."

Moana gave Cunningham a look as if to say, 'why can't you phone, I'm not a bloody slave'.

"I'm hoping a woman phoning will make her comfortable enough to tell us what we want to know. Open up. Not be suspicious."

Moana nodded, took up the phone and dialled the number.

"Hello, Mrs Hadani. I am trying to get in touch with Mr Hadani. He is not at the warehouse. I have a delivery to process and need his authority."

Cunningham gave Moana a thumbs-up.

"My husband has not lived in this house for more than two years now."

"Oh, I see. I am so sorry. Nevertheless it is important I find him."

"Have you tried his mobile?"

"Yes, but I'm not getting through. I have documents for him to sign. I can have a car take them to him but I don't know where he is."

"Oh, that's easy. He's probably at the Kebab. It's a Turkish restaurant on Ponsonby Road."

"I know it. Good food. Thank you, Mrs Hadani. I'll have someone go there immediately."

"She thinks he's at the Kebab," Moana said. "About half a mile from the Skenderberg. But, hang on, won't he go on the run? I mean, after all that has happened."

Cunningham shook his head. "No not yet. Anyone connecting him to Akbar is dead. He won't know we have two of his men. And once the terrorists left the safe houses earlier today he and the others would have had no contact. No, I'm guessing Hadani has no idea what has taken place and will follow through with his task and wait in the appointed spot to hand out the documents. Now for the million-dollar question, is the Kebab that spot?"

47.

The Ponsonby fire station was set back off the road. The perfect spot as far as Cunningham was concerned. He banged his fist on the station house door a full minute before it opened. The fire chief filled the doorway, eyes half open. A stifled yawn exposed he had been dozing.

Cunningham held up his badge. "I need to park a couple of cars on your front courtyard," he stated in a belligerent tone. He wasn't about to make a request. The man was sleeping while the city is turning to shit, screw him.

"What the hell are you on about? You can't block the entry way," the chief responded, suddenly awake.

"Yes, well, if you stayed awake long enough you'd know there are fucking terrorists out there and some are across the road, or likely to be. We need a surveillance spot and your courtyard is the best position."

The chief leaned forward in Cunningham's face. Jeff looked at Caldwell. He was certain the fireman was about to throw a punch.

"Just for the record, you asshole," the chief said through clenched teeth, "I know all about your frigging terrorists. My men were killed in the bomb blast the other night. What is left of my team and I have been on duty round the clock since. So excuse me for taking a fucking nap."

Cunningham held up his hands and stepped back.

"I need to park in the courtyard."

The chief stared daggers. "Park where you fucking like, but don't block the entrance. If I'm called out I'll drive over the top of you pricks."

He slammed the door.

Cunningham turned to the others. "I'm not certain I handled that as well as I could have."

"Jesus, Brian, you need to get some people skills."

"Okay. You heard the chief. A car either side of the entrance. Don't block it."

Cunningham and Lee Caldwell sat in the front seat with Moana and Jeff in the back. In the dim light the cars did not stand out. Cunningham drummed his fingers across the top of the steering wheel. Jeff watched, frustrated by the inactivity. Across the road and fifty metres to the right they had a good view of the Kebab restaurant squeezed between a women's fashion store and a working-men's club. He would love nothing more than to charge in and drag this Sami Hadani into the street and kick the shit out of him.

"Looks as if the restaurant is full. How do we work out who Hadani is?" Cunningham said, more to himself.

"Myftari said he was a big man. Fat pig, as he put it," Moana said.

"One of us has to go in there and scout it out. As much as I'd like that to be me, I'd say the whole gang has my photo with orders to shoot on sight," Jeff said.

"And we're not going to achieve anything blasting the place apart," Caldwell said.

"You called it right there, Lee. A restaurant full of dead, innocent diners and no terrorists would not look good on my CV."

"I need a weapon. Got a spare?" Caldwell asked.

Cunningham raised his eyebrows, Arming an American tourist might not go down well with his superiors. He walked Caldwell to the boot of his car and held up a Glock 17 pistol.

"I assume you know how to use one of these."

Caldwell nodded. He took hold of the handgun and weighed it in his hand. Cunningham passed him a loaded clip. "And if I shoot someone with this, are there any legal ramifications?"

"I don't think so, do you?" Cunningham allowed himself a smirk. "You had the power to keep me in my job; I think you could get a blind eye turned to killing a terrorist who just attacked an American nuclear submarine. Anyway, you have diplomatic immunity and a mandate to protect your own. Now let's catch us some bad guys. Any bright ideas?"

Caldwell said, "We need to start screening everyone who leaves. Not going in. We can concentrate on males only. Either in a group or singles. Couples we let go. To begin with however I would put two people round the back. Maybe the restaurateur knows what is going on and maybe he doesn't, but let's assume he does for the moment. Two people either side of the entrance but fifty metres back, and two more waiting here who will follow up behind depending on which direction they decide to take."

Cunningham nodded.

"Remember, these guys are going to be as jumpy as hell so make sure your people have their weapons at the ready and are not frightened to use them," Caldwell said.

"What about me, do I get a weapon?" Jeff asked.

"Not a chance in hell. You're going to have to duck if the shooting starts. Besides, you have one."

A shake of the head from Jeff. "I left it with Mary. She is still in danger."

"As I said, keep your head down."

"As soon as your people are in place I'm going in. An American tourist looking for something to eat," Caldwell said.

"Moana, I want a couple of men down Anglesea Street to block the rear. Two straight across here by Zambesi Fashions. Another couple further down the street by the Glengarry Wines store. A couple along the road here on the corner of Norfolk. And the wagon to hold prisoners down Lincoln Street. They should find a spot to park. If not tell them to use a driveway. And don't take no for an answer. With us here that pretty much surrounds the place. Everyone else tell them to keep out of sight."

Moana gave a mock salute. "Will do."

Moana's salute brought a smile from Jeff.

Cunningham said to Caldwell, "What about a microphone?"

"No. If I'm sitting there talking to myself it might look a little weird. I will call you on my cellphone and let you know if there is anything worthwhile."

"What if it's a no show?"

"Then you need to grab this guy Sami Hadani, but I think if he is in there then they're coming. They can't go anywhere without documentation. And after tonight they need to run."

Caldwell waited until everyone was in place. He wasn't overly concerned if some of the terrorists got away; as long as they had Hadani the rest would be on the run without a means to escape. But with restaurants busy with diners and pedestrians window shopping there could be casualties.

As Caldwell entered the Kebab his nose was assailed by the aromas of Turkish spices. They triggered memories of nights in Istanbul. A sniff revealed the smell of roasting lamb and a quick search found the rotating spit behind the service counter. The haunting sounds of Turkish folk music playing softly in the background completed his imagery.

He made a quick count of the diners. Thirty, maybe thirty-five, but it was the ten men in the furthest corner that caught his interest. Hadani would be one of them, Caldwell was certain of it.

The men, sitting around two tables pulled together, were engrossed in their conversation and ignored the other diners. They talked louder and louder as each sought to emphasise a point. Then laughter would break out and they would become silent until the next discussion started up. Empty plates sat on the table; the men had finished their meals and were now concentrating on cognac and coffee. He quickly dismissed any of them as being Zahar's men. They were too relaxed. All except for the fat man sitting with his back to the kitchen, his head slightly tilted towards the door. He fitted the description given by Myftari. His eyes flitted round the room every few minutes. He was nervous, his coffee untouched.

Hadani. Caldwell would bet his life on it.

The waitress came and Caldwell ordered a beer and asked for a menu. He wouldn't normally have an alcoholic drink but if someone in this crowd was checking out strangers then a drinker was less suspicious.

As prearranged, Cunningham called him on his mobile. Caldwell did not bother to lower his voice. His actions needed to look as casual as possible. He told Cunningham he was fine and for the moment he could find his own way home. He would phone if he needed a car. The waitress wrote down his order of smoked chicken and a fresh leaf and choban salad and placed a jug of cold water in the centre of the table. Caldwell figured that as he had to wait and he was hungry he might as well eat.

As the waitress returned with his order, two men, undoubtedly Middle Eastern, walked in. They stood just inside the door. Eyes scanned the tables and settled on the man Caldwell had picked to be Hadani. Bingo, Caldwell thought to himself.

They sat at the only spare table. One of the men spoke quietly to the waitress, and as he did so she gave a quick glance at the table where Hadani sat. She tapped Hadani on the shoulder. When he looked up the waitress thumbed at the two men and then carried on into the kitchen. In Caldwell's opinion she was passing on a message and had no idea what was going on, which confirmed his earlier suspicion that it was only a meeting spot and that the owner of the restaurant had no idea.

Hadani picked up his briefcase and walked through to the toilet block. After a few minutes the two men followed.

Caldwell's mobile rang. He answered it quickly.

"Anything yet?" Cunningham asked.

"I think we have two ready to go. Maybe five minutes. Both dark-haired. Late twenties. One white shirt and red jacket. The other a red shirt and black leather jacket.

"Okay we'll be waiting."

"There is something else. Can you send Sergeant Te Kanawa in? She is to be my girlfriend. I want a kiss. Make it look real."

"Okay, will do."

After a few minutes the two men emerged from the toilet block. They passed Moana as she walked through the door. Moana didn't blink. She walked straight up to Caldwell.

"Darling. I am so sorry I'm late. Couldn't be helped."

"That's okay. I started without you. Sorry, but I was hungry."

Moana gave Caldwell a hug and a kiss on the cheek. The men at the two tables had glanced their way when Moana had entered but quickly dismissed them. Hadani didn't give them a second glance.

The waitress came over and Caldwell ordered the same meal for Moana.

"Brian said we are not meant to know that you exist," Moana said smilingly. "Does this mean you will have to kill me?"

"I'm afraid so, Sergeant. No choice."

"Why the urgency?"

"The man with the grayish hair wearing the olive hound's-tooth sports jacket. He is sitting with the group of men in the corner."

Moana placed her handbag on the floor to enable her to have a quick look.

"Got him."

"That is Sami Hadani. Two men just left after collecting documents from him." Moana nodded. "All the documents are in the briefcase on the floor beside him. Your job if something goes wrong is to follow the briefcase. Don't lose it. If you're shot and dying, too bad. Do not die until you have taken possession of that case. If he won't hand it over, shoot him."

"Are you serious? Shoot him."

"Yes. You don't think you can do that? Shoot a man in cold blood?"

"It's against the law."

"Yes it is," Caldwell said. "You are absolutely right."

"Now you're being condescending."

"This is not a game, Sergeant. And yes you do live in a civilised society and if we don't play by the rules then we are no better than they are. I know all the arguments. But these men do not play by the rules. Remember, they just tried to nuke your city. That man is one of them. In his case are the names of all the others. If they get away they will kill again, maybe not here in New Zealand, but somewhere. These are not even men of war prepared to sacrifice their lives for a higher ideal, they are just killers and they do it for money. No other reason. This is one of those times, Sergeant, when the good guys, that's us, have to make the ultimate sacrifice, whether it be our ethics or our lives, the sacrifice must be made."

Moana nodded. "I assure you the case will not be lost. What I do to not lose it will be my decision."

"Fair enough. Now eat your salad."

48.

An hour later, six men had been arrested after leaving the restaurant. Moana and Caldwell had had dessert and were on their second cup of coffee. The Kebab was emptying and they were struggling to keep up their subterfuge as the happy couple.

"What now?" Moana asked. "We can't stay here forever."

"No, we can't. As much as I'm enjoying your company I don't think I can eat any more and I certainly can't drink any more coffee. I think two people in love with each other as much as we are should be home in bed."

Moana laughed. "I'm certain that's what the waitress must be thinking. She looks like she wants to clear the table."

Four men entered.

"We have more company," Caldwell said. "I'm going to ask for the bill."

He waved to the waitress and when he told her he wanted the bill she went to the front desk to make it up. One of the men said something to her as she passed them and she nodded toward Hadani. One of the men glanced Caldwell's way. He whispered something to the others. The other three looked across at Caldwell. The waitress brought back the bill in a leather folder and placed it on the table then went back to Hadani's table.

Caldwell reached across and took Moana's hand. She smiled at him but did not pull away.

"I think we have a problem."

"A big problem or a little problem?"

"I think one of them has a problem with me."

"Why would he?" Moana asked.

"These are men on the run. They have a gut instinct for anything out of place. Potential danger. It saves their lives. If they feel something is not right they assume it isn't. Reach down and pick up your purse. Apply some lipstick or something but make sure your weapon is close at hand."

Moana did as instructed.

"Remember, whatever happens, do not lose Sami and the suitcase."

"We need backup."

"Cunningham will phone again in a few minutes but I do not think it is a good idea for these four to leave the restaurant."

Caldwell could feel the piercing stares but resisted looking in the direction of the four men. Now they would be questioning Sami. Asking about him about the man and the woman sitting at the table by the window. Caldwell took out some money and pretended to be checking the bill, then he placed some money in the folder and waved to the waitress. He knew something was wrong instantly. The excited chatter first and then the sound of a chair crashing to the floor.

Moana looked perplexed as Caldwell rose, pulling the Glock from his belt and thrusting it out in front of him in one fluid motion. Moana, with her back to the terrorists, had no forewarning of the violence about to erupt. As the first shot was fired she dived to the floor with her purse. As she rolled onto her back her gun was in her hand but any targets were obscured by the tables. Caldwell fired and then dived onto the floor beside her. The terrorists were scrambling for the door.

Caldwell turned to Moana.

"Don't forget the case," he yelled, then he was on his feet and after the men running from the restaurant.

~

Cunningham, Jeff and two detectives saw four men approach the restaurant. Their vigilant manner signalled to Cunningham they were another group of terrorists. It had been easy dealing with them in twos. They had simply been outnumbered and had no time to draw weapons or to escape. But four, this was different. This shifted the odds in the terrorists' favour.

Cunningham watched them enter and climbed out of the car in anticipation. The shots instigated instant activity. The restaurant door flew open. Two men rushed out. A third fell in the doorway. Cunningham and the two detectives, guns in hand, dodged traffic as they ran across the street.

Caldwell leapt over the body in the doorway and gave chase. The two terrorists fired behind them as they ran. Caldwell ignored the danger and continued to chase. Fearless, Cunningham noted.

At the corner Caldwell slowed and began to walk. Cunningham was quickly at his shoulder, Red and Ross came out of the side street to join the pursuit. The officers positioned further down moved onto the pavement to block the terrorists. They both assumed a kneeling position with their weapons aimed at the approaching men. The terrorists were flinging pedestrians out of their way in their desperate bid for freedom. Then they saw the danger and stopped, looking about them. Caldwell, Cunningham, and Red had spread out across the footpath. Two detectives walked down the centre of the road. There was nowhere for them to go. They were going to die but not today. The two men lowered their weapons and dropped them on the ground. It was over. Cunningham's men moved forward and forced the remnants of Akbar's army onto the ground. Guns stayed trained on them until they had been handcuffed.

Cunningham saw Red and Ross. "What the hell are you two doing here? Why aren't you at the back of the restaurant?"

"We heard shooting," Red said.

"Moana," Caldwell yelled.

He and Cunningham turned together and raced back to the restaurant.

⁂

Moana lay on the floor, disorientated. The shooting continued but she had no sight of the shooters. When Caldwell leapt over her she assumed it was safe and made to rise. Caldwell jumped over a body in the doorway and she was alone. She made it to her knees and peered over the top of the upturned table. Someone jumped from the floor and ran towards her. She recognised him as one of the four men. This one had not escaped with the others. Moana raised her gun. Hand steady, calm she fired into his right shoulder. The impact of the bullet spun the terrorist round. She scrambled to her feet. The terrorist managed to pull himself upright. Moana shot him in the leg.

She turned her attention to Sami Hadani. He was running into the kitchen making for the rear entrance. Moana flung aside the upturned table blocking her way and pointed her gun at him.

"Sami Hadani, you are under arrest. Stop where you are." The other men who had shared his table stood. Uncertain. Moana swung her gun in their direction. "Sit down."

They dropped back into their seats.

Hadani stopped. Moana moved forward. She recalled Caldwell's words. Shoot him in cold blood. But she couldn't. She was a New Zealand police officer, not a killer. Hadani saw the hesitation and turned, crashing through the rear exit. Moana chased after him.

She caught him on the steps.

He swung his case and it connected with the side of her head, sending Moana reeling. She fell backwards off the step and crashed to the ground. The impact caused her gun to fly from her hand. Sami swung his case again. She turned and took the brunt of it on her shoulder. Moana's head spun but she forced herself to her feet. During her kick-boxing training and the amateur bouts she had fought she had learnt to take a punch. But Hadani was a big man and although the weight training had strengthened her upper body she would be no match for him if the fight continued too long. As she scrambled to her feet she looked for her pistol but couldn't see it. Sami turned to run. Moana dived at him, landing on his shoulders. Two thumbs jabbed into his eyes. Then she dropped her arms into a lock round his throat. He cursed. He let go of the case to pull her hands loose then flung her away from him. Moana slid across the dirt. Sami rubbed at his eyes. Face red and teeth grinding, Moana climbed to her feet and rushed forward, smashing her knee into Sami's groin.

"You bitch." He pushed her away. They both took a moment to catch their breath. Sami Hadani was not tall, he was thickset and much stronger but Moana didn't care any more. She positioned herself between Sami and the lane that led to freedom. His only escape route.

"Put down the case, Mr Hadani. Lie on the ground. You are under arrest," Moana managed to gasp out. She looked around. Where the hell were the two officers guarding the rear entrance? "Put down the case, Mr Hadani. Do not do anything silly."

As soon as the words had left her mouth he ran at her, swinging his fist. She fended off the blow. It jarred her arm. Then he rammed her with his shoulder catching her under her breasts. She was propelled backward into a wall. It stopped her from falling. He punched her in the face. Lights exploded in her head, blinding her. She reached out and managed to grab his jacket. He punched her in the stomach. She retched vomit into his face but held her grip. He turned to break free. She swung her right arm round his neck. Her left arm followed. She locked them in place then lifted her legs pulling all her weight back against his throat. Sami tried to shake her free, but Moana squeezed tighter. Sami stepped backward and crashed her into the wall. Moana grunted. But hung on. He threw his head back onto the bridge of her nose. She screamed with the pain but kept squeezing. Anger replaced the pain and a surge of adrenaline gave her added strength. Sami began to stagger. She squeezed tighter. He was on his knees. Choking. She gritted her teeth and squeezed harder. She was now on her backside, Sami sitting across her lap. He had gone limp. No movement as she squeezed harder and harder.

Then arms pulled at her. Not Sami Hadani's

"Fuck off he's mine!" she screamed.

He was hers.

But hands prized her arms apart. Hadani was taken from her hold. She couldn't see through eyes swollen shut. Then arms held her. Cunningham's voice was in her ear, offering comforting words, soft, gentle. Her head fell against his chest and then she wept.

~

Jeff stood in front of Sami Hadani. The big man sat up, his back against the wall, his grey eyes fixed on Bradley. Bruised lips broke into a grin and displayed a row of bloodied teeth. An attempt at laughter brought a grimace of pain.

Jeff wanted to kick him. His mobile phone rang.

"Jeff Bradley."

"Mr Bradley. I have your woman and I have your Kosovan family. Very touching to have them all so close. I think I will take them home with me."

Zahar rang off.

"Zahar, Zahar . . . Fuck it."

"You think you are so clever but Zahar will have the last laugh," Hadani said then spat blood at Jeff.

Jeff leaned closer. His fist was closed and raised, ready to strike.

"Jeff!" said Cunningham. "What the hell was that?"

Jeff opened his phone. He tapped in Mary's number. "That was Zahar. He says he has Mary and Kimie and the kids." No answer. He dialled the number of Mary's SAS escort. No answer. He dialled the house.

"Where the hell is she, Jeff?" Cunningham asked.

"I took her out to the vineyard. There's no answer from her guard. No answer from the house. Jesus, I need a car right now."

"We can do better than that. I'll bring in the police helicopter." He pulled out his mobile and moved away a few metres to make the call. "Damn it. It will be at least half an hour. It's refuelling." Cunningham tossed him the keys. "Take my car. I'll follow in the chopper with reinforcements. I have to clean up here but we won't be far behind you. And don't do anything stupid."

As Jeff climbed into Cunningham's car Caldwell jumped into the passenger seat. Jeff threw him a quizzical look.

Caldwell held up the Glock Cunningham had given him. "Just drive, I have a gun."

49.

Jeff parked beside the Boundary Fence four-wheeler. The lights in Kimie's house were on and the front door wide open.

"What do you think, Caldwell?"

"I think we leave the car here and move to the house via that shed and stay in the shadows."

"You have the gun. You lead," Jeff said.

"Why don't I give you the gun and you can play point?"

Jeff grinned. "Get moving, I'm right behind you."

The SAS soldier assigned to protect Kimie and Mary lay face down in the hallway, two bullet holes in the centre of his back. Jeff knelt beside the body. He placed two fingers on the guard's neck. Then the wrist, "No pulse," he said turning to Caldwell.

He didn't know the young soldier, but the kid was SAS and that made him family. Another name on the reckoning list he would shove down Zahar's throat when the time came. Jeff got to his feet and smashed his fist into the wall. The plasterboard crumbled under the impact, a puff of white powder sprinkled onto the carpet. Jeff shook his wrist and blew onto his knuckles.

"Okay, so he has taken them," Caldwell said. "But I think it's safe to say Kimie and her kids and Mary are hostages, not dead. If Zahar's purpose was to kill them he would have done that here."

"You're probably right, but who knows what the hell is going on in that asshole's head?" Jeff said. "What do we do now?"

Caldwell shrugged. "Tonight they were escaping, leaving New Zealand. It's all turned bad and now there's been a change of plans."

"When Barbara and I spoke to Demi Myftari, I asked him how Zahar and his men had planned to escape. Demi said everyone would have their documents returned, lay low and over the next days or weeks they would fly out on various international airlines and return to wherever it was they came from, except for Zahar. Demi said he had other plans. Even with a new passport he would never get through immigration. Too easy to recognise."

"How about a boat?"

Jeff shrugged. "Maybe, but I doubt it. A launch wouldn't get them far and I think we can rule out a yacht. Sailing into the deep blue sea takes experience and I doubt Zahar has ever sailed in his life. However he would never have come to an island without alternative escape routes. And now we have Hadani and the rest of Avni Leka's business associates there are no hiding places for him. How about a small plane? Big enough to take four or five?"

"It has to take off and land," Caldwell said. "We might be out in the countryside but they can't just take off and land in a paddock. Not a small jet."

"No, they can't, but this is New Zealand. We have crop dusters and there will be a number of small airfields that could handle a small plane with a good pilot."

"And how do we find out where this airfield might be?"

Jeff held up his mobile phone, "I'll ask Brian to find out."

"One thing though, a small plane isn't going far, is it? Could it reach South America? He can't head to Australia. We can alert their air force. They'd shoot him out of the sky as soon as he came into range."

Jeff's mobile phone rang. "Jeff Bradley,"

"Bradley, I have allowed enough time for you to get to the vineyard. I trust I now have your full attention."

"You have my attention, Zahar. What do you want?"

"I want a helicopter, capable of carrying eight passengers and can cover a distance of two hundred kilometres. You have one hour to organise this. When I call again I will give directions. Any delay and I will kill a hostage. I think the little girl will be first."

The phone went dead.

Jeff stared at the phone and then at Caldwell.

"We have one hour to find him a helicopter. Whenuapai air force base is close, let's get there right now. While I'm driving, you phone Brian and tell him to set up the helicopter. The police chopper is no good. Too small."

~

Jeff stood next to Brian Cunningham, watching the Iroquois helicopter's blades build to their familiar *whoosh, whoosh, whoosh.* The sounds reminded him of his military days and the memories came flooding back. It always surprised him how a smell or sound could trigger such reactions. A military psychologist had explained that war was trauma, and like all traumatic experiences it stayed in the psyche until it was exorcised out. However for Jeff, the sounds and smells never brought on a sense of dread, only regret. The truth was, he missed the Special Forces and times like this were a reminder of how much.

Cunningham said, "A relic from the past, I know, but they wouldn't let us have one of the new NH90's. They cost seventy million dollars each so I was told. This was a take it or leave it."

"The Iroquois will do," Jeff said.

"Jeff, there is something we need to discuss," Cunningham said. "Whatever it is Zahar intends to do, he is not going to let anyone walk away from this. Mary, Kimie and her children will be killed."

"I know it," Jeff said.

"They cannot get on the helicopter. You know that, don't you."

Jeff stepped closer to Cunningham, bringing his face to within inches, eyes wide, jaw set firm. "Don't tell me, Brian, let me guess. You've brought in D Company to take everyone out. Is that what you're trying to tell me?"

"I'm not a murderer, Jeff, and neither is the squadron. No, this time I have no plan. Do you?"

"As a matter of fact I do," Jeff said, with one last aggressive stare before he turned away. He checked his watch. An hour had passed. "Why the hell hasn't Zahar rung." He paced.

Then the call came.

"Yes, Zahar, tell me."

"Bradley, you are not playing games, this is good. The young girl will be very grateful. You have ten minutes. The Huapai Golf Club. Come in slow. One of my men will guide you in with a torch. Any tricks and your loved ones will die. And be reminded I have missiles, I can blast your aircraft into shredded metal."

The phone went dead.

Jeff ran to the helicopter, Cunningham and Caldwell close behind. The three climbed in.

"Huapai Golf Club," Jeff yelled to the pilot. "And get up to 1000 feet." He received a thumbs-up. Jeff had little doubt the pilot would know where it was. The airbase was close and they would have flown over it daily. Jeff knew it as well. He had become a member when he inherited Boundary Fence and had played there many times.

As the helicopter lifted off the ground, Jeff took hold of the parachute he had requested be made available.

"What are you up to?" Cunningham asked.

"I need to get on the ground before you do. The chopper pilot will pass over once looking for the torchlight. I'll jump and be on the ground before you land. Zahar and his men have made a smart move. He has any number of landing spots to choose from. Knowing the course gives me an advantage. Once I've jumped, make sure the pilot circles slowly, and when you get Zahar's signal move slowly toward it. Hopefully I will get to Zahar before you land."

Cunningham nodded. "Not bad. A good plan."

"Whatever happens, Brian, protect my friends."

"Count on it, Jeff."

Jeff knelt and pulled the chute pack straps over his shoulders and secured the chest straps, then bent forward and secured the leg straps. Cunningham came close and checked all the fittings were locked down. The pilot had slung a static line near the door. The doors of the Iroquois had been left open. Jeff slung his legs over the sill. Cunningham secured the static line to the rip cord.

He leaned close to Jeff's ear. "Now don't forget when jumping from a chopper the blades stop the chute developing. You'll have a short drop before it catches," Cunningham said.

"Great, you just reminded me why I hate parachuting."

"Don't worry, you'll be on the ground before you can blink. Don't forget to roll."

Jeff nodded that he was ready, then moved down to stand on the Iroquois' landing rail. He looked down. The golf course was located in the rural lands that skirted Auckland City. There were lights along the highway and the odd lonely lamppost down country lanes but not in the centre of the golf course. It was going to be like jumping down the shaft of a coal mine. Calculations buzzed in his head. He recalled his training. Freefalling would max out at 120 mph and then the fall speed would be 1000 feet every five seconds. On a normal jump he would count to ten and pull the cord. That wasn't about to happen here. Jumping from 1000 feet if he started counting to ten he would be a hole in the ground before he got to six.

Cunningham watched the pilot. He received a thumbs-up.

Brian tapped Jeff on the shoulder. "One thousand feet," he yelled into his ear.

Jeff pushed off and disappeared into the black.

~

Jeff plummeted. He counted to two and then felt the jolt. His chute had deployed and the harness pulled at his shoulders. In a few seconds he would hit the ground or a tree or worse power cables. Even though he had some control over the canopy it was no use. If he couldn't see he couldn't avoid obstacles. Now he remembered why he hated night jumps. There were always injuries in training. And now the ground was racing towards him and he had no bloody idea where it was.

There was no horizon to focus on to keep his head positioned.

Now he could hear his instructor screaming in his ear, "Bradley, bring your knees and feet together. Turn into the wind. Reach up and grasp the risers." Jeff followed the remembered instructions. "Now with your legs reach for the ground."

Jeff looked down at his legs stretched out in front of him. Where was the ground, where was the ground. Then his legs collapsed under him. Training and instinct kicked in. He rolled sideways, moved his head to one side and tucked in his chin and elbows. When he pushed down to raise himself up, his hand sunk into sand. A bunker. Lucky me, he thought, a soft landing. He unsnapped the straps. The chute could stay where it was. One of the club's green keepers could gather it in the morning. He'd buy him a beer next time he played.

Once free, Jeff moved stealthily into the middle of the fairway. He could hear the chopper but not see it. Trees blocked his vision. He ran through the tree line to the next fairway. He searched the darkness and the flashing lights came into view. The Iroquois swung round to begin another sweep, then he perceived a change in rotor sound and looked up. The helicopter hovered. Its nose swung north, then moved forward and at the same time descended. This was it. Through squinting eyes Jeff searched for the torchlight. He spotted a glow underneath the treeline on the first fairway. A torch waved back and forth. Four hundred metres he guessed. He ran towards it.

The Glock Cunningham had given him appeared in his hand. He had few ideas on what to do but as he sped across the expanse of mown grass he tossed ideas about in his head. Zahar and his men had no idea he was on the ground. They had no idea he was running toward them. They'd be looking skyward. The noise of the chopper would cover his boots crunching on dead leaves and fallen branches. He had the element of surprise.

He was still three hundred metres away but the chopper was closer. The chopper's lights silhouetted figures on the ground. Jeff could see four men standing, spread out. Not offering a single target, clever, professional even under stress, impressive. Bayonet training came to mind as Jeff closed. Charging bags of straw dressed as enemy soldiers. Rifle thrust forward and then the scream as the front foot pushed forward and the steel rammed into the bag. Another foot stamped onto the bag next to the blade and then the blade pulled clear. He had already decided this was a bayonet charge. Attack without fear, gain the upper hand and unnerve the enemy. Eighty metres; and the chopper was starting to swing back and forth as it prepared to drop the last few feet.

Then he saw them: Mary, Kimie, Drita and Marko on their knees and huddled together in the centre of the terrorists. Again clever, Jeff thought. Any mistakes and a burst of gunfire would kill the four of them in a fraction of a second. Zahar stood at the front. The man next to him was waving the chopper to the ground.

Thirty metres. Jeff held the Glock at arms' length. He aimed at the man behind the hostages and fired off two shots. He didn't to need to know if they had struck home, he was a crack shot and at this distance, even in the dark, he never missed. The Glock barrel swung to the man on the left of Zahar. Two more shots. Then the man to the right of Zahar fell before Jeff took aim. Flashes caught his eye. Shots fired from the Iroquois. Cunningham. He switched focus back to Zahar but the terrorist leader had vanished from sight.

"Get down," Jeff yelled as he rushed past the group. "Which way?" he yelled to Mary. She pointed toward the first fairway. Jeff dropped to his knee and swung his weapon along the tree line, firing until his magazine had emptied. He turned as Cunningham and Caldwell ran to him.

"I'm going after him. Look after Mary and Kimie. Get them and the kids on the chopper and get them the hell out of here."

Jeff didn't wait for an answer.

At least now it didn't matter what happened between him and Zahar, Zahar wasn't going anywhere. He stopped and waited for the Iroquois to leave. "Come on, you guys, get out of here," he yelled in its direction. After a few more seconds he heard the sound of the rotors increasing in speed, and then the noise was lost in the distance.

Jeff stayed still, silent, listening. A twig broke to his right. And another. It had to be Zahar. He moved slowly towards the sound. It crossed his mind it could be a trap and Zahar was deliberately making noises to lure him like a trout fisherman with a fly. He didn't care. Zahar was probably used to night fighting, but so was he, but the dark protected them both and as long as Zahar stayed hidden he would never find him. He needed to draw Zahar into the light.

But how?

Zahar must hate his guts, Jeff reasoned. Isn't that why he tried to kill Mary? Zahar must want to kill him as much as he wanted to kill Zahar. He held up the Glock and then realised he only had an empty gun. "Damn you, Jeff. You dumb asshole," he whispered, cursing himself. "What are you going to do now? If Cunningham was here he would bawl me out for incompetence, and rightly so."

Jeff pulled a marker stake used for under-sized trees from the ground. It was solid wood, three to four feet long with a pointed end. It would kill Zahar if he hit him on the head with it. That would do. As he followed the noises and closed on the tree line, a plan formed in his mind.

~

Zahar watched, disbelieving, as Jeff Bradley approached. The breaking of the twigs had worked. Foolish amateur. The New Zealander carried a piece of wood as a weapon. What foolishness. He would shoot Bradley in the legs and when he was lying on the ground screaming in pain he would beat him with his piece of wood before he strangled him. He wanted that pleasure. It was his right. Then he would leave New Zealand forever and go to his new life in Iran.

Bradley had closed to within thirty metres. Zahar raised his Kalashnikov and aimed at his legs. His finger pulled on the trigger, but then Bradley did the unexpected and dived to the right, rolling and then zig-zagging into the tree line. Zahar flicked the catch onto automatic and sprayed the bullets in the New Zealander's direction. He moved forward. Bradley must be dead. But he could not be certain. When firing a Kalashnikov on automatic the barrel lifted high and pulled to the right. One metre into the trees Bradley leapt to his feet and ran past him. Zahar brought up his weapon and squeezed. Nothing happened. Empty. He flung it aside and gave chase. The coward was afraid of him.

Bradley ran across the first tee and onto the practice putting green just below the clubhouse windows. The lights from the club house lit up the area. Bradley stood hands on hips panting. He was now on a spot lit up like day. This was good Zahar reasoned. He would be able to enjoy the look of terror in Bradley's face and the fear in his eyes when he cut his throat. Slowly, Bradley turned to face the advancing Zahar. He did not look afraid. Zahar slowed. Uncertain. They were now only ten metres apart.

"Zahar Akbar," Jeff said. "We finally meet."

Zahar watched Jeff. He smiled.

"Do you really believe you can do this? Defeat me? You are a very foolish man."

They began to circle each other, oblivious to the gathering gallery of onlookers at the windows above.

Jeff now had the light he sought. He flexed his fingers. It worried him that the clubhouse was full of people. The club often hired out its restaurant for wedding receptions. Now Zahar had any number of potential hostages if he wasn't stopped. The terrorist was smiling. Confident. Well, let him smile. It would be wiped off him soon enough.

A figure cast a shadow across the edge of the green. Jeff risked a quick look. It was Dennis, the club secretary.

"Jeff. What are you doing on the putting green? It's out of bounds to members at night. You must know that."

"Dennis. Go back inside and don't let anyone come out. Lock the door."

"You're damaging the green. I can't allow that."

"Get out of here, Dennis. Now. Go back inside and lock the door. Do it."

Something in Jeff's manner made Dennis take a backward step.

"Whatever is going on here, Jeff, it will be on the agenda at the next committee meeting. Can't have members on the putting green at night."

Ignored, Dennis turned and went back inside as Jeff told him to do.

Jeff was physically bigger than Zahar but he knew that meant nothing. Zahar was stocky, strong and had learnt the skills of unarmed combat in the Hezbollah camps. He would have killed men with his bare hands. Jeff had not. Jeff had his SAS training but nothing beat the real thing. Zahar had probably crushed windpipes; all he had ever crushed were grapes.

Jeff rushed at Zahar.

Zahar reacted instinctively and with a deft movement Jeff was sent sailing through the air, but instead of crashing onto his back he rolled onto one knee in a smooth movement that would make any martial arts master proud. Jeff could see in Zahar's face that he was quickly reassessing his opponent. That brought an inner smile. He now understood. Zahar had no idea of his military background. A bad miscalculation when confronting an enemy.

Zahar charged the still rising Jeff, but instead of rising to meet him Jeff dived forward and tackled Zahar around the ankles. Zahar crashed to the ground with Jeff clinging to his legs. Zahar writhed about, attempting to kick himself free. Jeff manoeuvred his body and brought his knee crashing hard into the side of Zahar's head. Zahar yelped. Disorientated, he still managed to strike his fist into Jeff's groin. Jeff grunted and relaxed his hold. Zahar kicked free.

Both men rolled away and scrambled to their feet. Zahar, still dazed, shook his head. Jeff rubbed his groin. Their eyes locked. Circling. Two wild animals in a fight to the death. Naked hatred driving both men.

"Why do you waste your time fighting, Bradley? The end of your life is written. I know what you must think of me. A man without a heart. Maybe this is true, but today I will make a special offer. Your end is inevitable. If you stop now I promise I will end it quickly. You will not suffer as you should."

Jeff swung, burying his fist into Zahar's chest.

The force of it caught the Palestinian by surprise. He backed away.

"What's the problem, Zahar? As always with lowlifes like yourself you're all talk."

The haziness caused by Bradley's knee connecting with his head had started to clear. Hatred turned to rage. Strength returned. He stood taller. Eyeing the man in front of him, Zahar reached into his pocket and pulled out a knife. He opened the blade and held it up. Now he would avenge his brother. Cut the throat of his brother's murderer. It was his duty.

He unleashed a guttural scream and charged.

Jeff recognised the routine. All soldiers were trained to scream when attacking. It unnerved the enemy. Instead of backing away as Zahar would expect, Jeff stood firm. He raised his elbow, knocking away the blade thrust at him, then gripped Zahar's wrist with both hands and spun, Zahar's arm now straightened across his shoulder he dropped to one knee, pulling down on Zahar's arm as he did so. Zahar flew through the air. Jeff moved quickly and as Zahar hit the ground he smashed his fist into the terrorist's throat. Gasping for air, Zahar managed to roll away and onto his hands and knees. He still held the knife, holding it out in front of him as he rose to his feet.

Jeff stepped back. He caught his foot in one of the practice putting holes and lost his balance. Zahar saw him falling and reacted quickly. He stepped forward and swung his knife. The blade buried into Jeff's chest.

Jeff dropped to his knees. He looked down. Blood seeped across the front of his T-shirt. Out of the corner of his eye he saw Zahar swing the knife again. He flung himself back. The blade cut through his jeans and sliced into his thigh. Jeff fastened his grip onto Zahar's wrist and held fast. As the terrorist tried to back away he reluctantly pulled Jeff to his feet. Jeff kicked out with his boots, catching Zahar's kneecap. Zahar staggered but could not free himself from Jeff's grip. Jeff grabbed a handful of Zahar's shirt front. Then his legs wobbled and a drum beat inside his head. He recognised the symptom. His blood pressure was dropping. The beat of his heart was becoming irregular. His grip was weakening and he could no longer hold on. Zahar pulled free.

Zahar smiled when he saw the blood. Jeff's eyes flickered. Zahar charged again. The final assault. This time there was no scream. Jeff could see the supreme confidence in the terrorist's eyes, glazed over white with madness as he threw caution aside. Jeff fended off the assault but Zahar stabbed the knife into Jeff's left arm. With his right arm Jeff swung an uppercut with all the force he could muster and all the accuracy of months of training in the boxing gym. He caught Zahar under the chin. The terrorist crumpled to the ground like a sack of wet rags. Jeff pulled the knife from his arm and sat astride the moaning Zahar. Jeff was losing consciousness. One last effort. He raised the knife and plunged it into the killer's chest. The terrorist leader screamed and then went still.

Jeff felt a hand on his shoulder. Fingers unbound his grip on the knife.

"It's over, Jeff," Caldwell said. "Come on, let me help you. Brian, call an ambulance."

Barely conscious, Jeff reached out and ripped away the chain hanging round Zahar's neck. Then he allowed Caldwell to pull him away. On his back he saw the putting green was now surrounded by golf club patrons. Horrified faces looked down through the clubhouse windows.

Jeff rolled his head and looked across at Zahar. "Give my regards to your brother," he whispered.

~

Nine terrorists had been arrested, including Sami Hadani. Two had been killed by Lee Caldwell. The first he had shot through the head inside the Kebab restaurant and the second as he tried to run through the door. The envelopes in the suitcase had confirmed that twenty-eight men had arrived in New Zealand. The ones who had escaped capture and had not died on the boat would now be hunted. Airports would be alerted but Caldwell had a feeling they would go to ground and wait. New passports would be sent. He doubted they would get them all.

Moana had been sent to hospital as a precaution. Jeff Bradley would remain in hospital a number of days.

Cunningham had collected his car from the air base and driven himself and Caldwell back to the station. Caldwell passed the Glock over and Cunningham locked it in the trunk.

"What now for you, Lee?"

"Back to the hotel and a good night's sleep."

"You'll be leaving New Zealand immediately?"

"Yes. There is nothing more for me here and unfortunately there are more Zahars out there."

Cunningham saw the look of resignation on Lee Caldwell's face. There was no regret, no sadness, just an acceptance of who he was and what he had to do.

"Can I drive you?"

"No, I think I'll walk. Clear the head. That sort of thing."

Cunningham held out his hand.

"Good to meet you, Lee. New Zealand is as indebted to you as I am."

"Likewise," Caldwell said, shaking the offered hand before turning and disappearing into the crowd.

Tomorrow, Aucklanders would wake up to the stories of the men who tried to sink the submarine, the killing of the terrorist leader and the shootout on Ponsonby Road. The inside story would be Barbara Heywood's, as had been promised. The chief of police had arrived and had taken control of the media and the clean-up process. His team could take a well-deserved three days leave. Another team of detectives would take over hunting down the remaining terrorists and writing the reports.

His mobile rang.

"Percy Croydon, Inspector. I understand there have been developments in the city tonight."

"Yes, there have, Mr Croydon."

"Can we expect more?"

"The attack on the submarine was averted and most of the terrorists are either dead or in custody. The threat is over."

"Excellent work, Inspector. We will talk further."

50.

Jeff sat in his lounge, warmed by the morning sun.

For the past week, the newspapers and radio and television news programmes had focused their stories on the night of the attack on the *Ulysses* and the events leading up to it. Unbelieving citizens read and listened with wonder at the intentions of the terrorists and the part played by Jeff Bradley, among others, and the police to stop it. He had taken his phone off the hook. He knew eventually the press would find their way to his door, but for the moment he wanted to be alone. His face hurt and the bruises on top of older bruises and the stab wounds were still tender and painful.

He found the energy to move and walked to his window and looked out into the street. He waved to the twins playing on their front lawn. They immediately ran to the back of the house. Jeff smiled, thankful that Larry and his family were safe.

Barbara Heywood and Amy were sitting round the board table with Hank Challis. The meeting had been called to discuss the series that would be the station's prime time viewing winner for the next few weeks. Hank had already promised extra people for camera work and research. The editing suites would be hers whenever required.

Hank, however, needed a better understanding of the story and the shape it would take.

Barbara related the story from the beginning. Albeit an edited version. She left out much of her involvement and the heroics in Kosovo of Jeff Bradley. She omitted the staged abduction in Wellsford. This would remain confidential. It took more than an hour and both Hank and Amy sat disbelievingly. When she had finished she sat back in her chair.

"So that's most of it, Hank. I've probably forgotten a few points."

"Well, little lady, you have certainly been busy," Hank started. "International networks will want the story. I spoke to our bosses before this meeting and they agreed that because of my connections with CNN and other US networks, I should oversee final touches and negotiate world rights. We are going to spend a lot of time together, little lady. Prepare for some late nights," he smiled.

Barbara couldn't decide if it was a leer or an ogle, then decided that if Hank was as multi-talented as he declared himself to be he had probably managed to achieve both.

Hank turned to Amy. "We need to keep as much as we can under wraps, not a word."

Amy nodded. "No sir," she said, then turned to Barbara. The look she gave her boss was unmistakable hero worship. Barbara mused that if she were to stay on at the station Amy would keep her supplied with cakes and coffees whenever she snapped her fingers. But it was over. The thought of working with Hank would be as painful as stabbing herself in the liver.

She left the building carrying a carton filled with her personal effects. Cunningham was waiting on the steps. It was an awkward moment for both of them. So much had happened and there was so much to be said but they both knew now was not the time for talking.

"Just wanted to check up on you. Make sure you're okay, that sort of thing. I phoned ahead and was told you were on your way down," he said.

Did they have a future together? Barbara wasn't certain Cunningham even still had a job. When it all settled down the enquiries would start. Politics was politics. They had cut many corners throughout the investigation and when the euphoria died the heroics would be forgotten and heads would roll.

"You've been busy, Brian?"

"Yes I have, but I dare say not as busy as you're going to be."

Barbara smiled. "I've resigned from the channel. I'm going to write the book. I have a healthy advance from a publisher. Enough to keep me in wine and pasta for a while."

"Good for you," Cunningham said. "Look, I might be overstepping the mark here, but how would you feel if I phoned you sometime. Took you to dinner?"

"Like on a date you mean?"

"I guess that's what I mean. Yes, a date."

Barbara smiled. "Why don't you phone me sometime and find out."

Cunningham nodded and shifted from foot to foot.

"Great. Good. That's fine then. Well, okay, I might just do that sometime."

~

In New Zealand's capital city, Wellington, the expected parliamentary debate had gone on long into the night. The opposition was supporting a private members' bill to reintroduce the country's anti-nuclear stance, and members of the government were crossing the floor to support them. After the incident in Auckland public opinion was firmly against any further visits from nuclear-powered vessels. The government was arguing the point but not vigorously. With an election coming up no one was prepared to be seen to be pro-nuclear. By morning it had been agreed and passed. New Zealand had again declared itself nuclear free. No more US ship visits.

In the next cabinet meeting the mood was gloomy. The Australian prime minister had already been on the phone informing the New Zealand prime minister that as New Zealand was not prepared to accept its share of security responsibilities it was on its own. The message from the United States was blunter. Friend or foe. Make your choice. Parliament, by appeasing the population at large, had to now face an uncertain future as a defenseless nation.

The prime minister was not totally at a loss. She was convinced that when the time came the United Nations would deal with any threat. And as New Zealand was not a threat then it would not become threatened. The older and wiser heads shook their heads in despair, knowing full well the UN was not to be relied upon.

Five kilometres from the outskirts of Rome, Avni Leka stood on the balcony of his villa. It was a warm, clear day and he could see to the end of the valley stretched out before him. He had checked his bank account and the thirty million euros had been deposited. His clients had been very happy with the events in Auckland. Nuclear ships were now banned. New Zealand was defenseless, and phase two of their operation could begin.

Avni turned his thoughts to the men he had lost. It was a pity to lose Sami Hadani and especially Zahar. Reliable killers were hard to replace, but not impossible. And then there was Jeff Bradley. Once again he had interfered and once again he had proved to be troublesome and once again he had survived. But his time would come. Sooner or later luck runs out, and the day it ran out for Jeff Bradley would be a truly happy day for Avni Leka.

~

Jeff, his arm in a sling and his chest heavily bandaged, stood in the park outside Mary's apartment. The small grassed area was now a memorial site covered with crosses, flowers and teddy bears and cards and letters. Mary clung to Jeff's good arm.

"So many innocent lives lost," Jeff whispered.

They moved forward and placed their bouquets next to a cross, then said silent prayers before stepping back. Jeff dipped his hand into his jacket pocket and ran fingers across the chain he had ripped from Zahar Akbar's neck. He made a silent promise to the dead that he would find Avni Leka and shove the chain down his throat.

Mary removed a tissue from her bag and dabbed at her eyes. Jeff put his arm around her shoulders and gave a comforting squeeze. As the wind whistled through the leaves of the oak that stood at the park entrance, he cast an eye one last time over the crosses and flowers. He would carry the image with him until Leka was dead.

"What now, Jeff?" Mary asked.

"I have an auction to worry about, but first, I'm taking you to lunch."

ACKNOWLEDGEMENTS

Many have helped with the writing of this novel and apologies to those of you I have forgotten. Thank you to Conan and Renay Brown, Emma Skelton, Shawn Rutene and to Bernard and Gaynor Brown for their continued support. To Capt. Martin Knight-Willis MC Rtd. and Capt. K.E. McKee-Wright MBE Rtd. for advice on military tactics. To Adrian Blackburn for invaluable assistance in identifying so much I didn't know. Assessor Cate Hogan (www.catehogan.com) for her invaluable wisdom and insights. As always a big thank you to Emilie Marneur and Katie Green and the rest of the very talented Thomas & Mercer team.

ABOUT THE AUTHOR

Photo: © Sharlene Ferguson, 2013

Thomas Ryan has been a soldier in a theatre of war, traded in Eastern Europe, trampled the jungles of Asia and struggled through the trials of love and loss: ideal life experiences for a would-be author. Schooled by professionals who have helped him hone his literary style, Ryan is quickly establishing himself as a skilled writer of riveting thrillers and short stories. He considers himself foremost a storyteller, a creator who has plunged his psyche into the world of imagination and fantasy. Taking readers on a thrilling journey is what motivates Ryan as a writer.